# BULLETPROOF CHRISTMAS

BARB HAN

# DELTA FORCE DADDY

CAROL ERICSON

MILLS & BOON

First Published in Great Britain 2018
by Mills & Boon, an imprint of HarperCollins*Publishers*
1 London Bridge Street, London, SE1 9GF



ISBN: 978-0-263-26607-8

1218

MIX
Paper from responsible sources
FSC™ C007454

This book is produced from independently certified FSC™ paper to ensure responsible forest management.

For more information visit: www.harpercollins.co.uk/green

Printed and bound in Spain
by CPI, Barcelona

*USA TODAY* bestselling author **Barb Han** lives in north Texas with her very own hero-worthy husband, three beautiful children, a spunky golden retriever/ standard poodle mix and too many books in her to-read pile. In her downtime, she plays video games and spends much of her time on or around a basketball court. She loves interacting with readers and is grateful for their support. You can reach her at barbhan.com.

**Carol Ericson** is a bestselling, award-winning author of more than forty books. She has an eerie fascination for true-crime stories, a love of film noir and a weakness for reality TV, all of which fuel her imagination to create her own tales of murder, mayhem and mystery. To find out more about Carol and her current projects, please visit her website at www.carolericson.com, "where romance flirts with danger."

## Also by Barb Han

*Sudden Setup*
*Endangered Heiress*
*Texas Grit*
*Kidnapped at Christmas*
*Murder and Mistletoe*
*Stockyard Snatching*
*Delivering Justice*
*One Tough Texan*
*Texas-Sized Trouble*
*Texas Witness*

## Also by Carol Ericson

*Delta Force Defender*
*Locked, Loaded and SEALed*
*Alpha Bravo SEAL*
*Bullseye: SEAL*
*Point Blank SEAL*
*Secured by the SEAL*
*Bulletproof SEAL*
*Single Father Sheriff*
*Sudden Second Chance*
*Army Ranger Redemption*

# BULLETPROOF CHRISTMAS

BARB HAN

All my love to Brandon, Jacob and Tori. And to all the grand adventures that lay ahead.

To Babe, my bulletproof hero, for being my great love, my place to call home. This life is everything.

# *Chapter One*

*Patience. Silence. Purpose.* The mantra had kept Rory Scott alive while tracking some of the most ruthless poachers in the country. Belly crawling toward a makeshift campsite on the Hereford Ranch in Cattle Barge, Texas, he adjusted his night-vision goggles to gain a better view and evaluate the situation.

A two-person tent was set up twenty-five feet ahead and slightly to his left. It looked expensive, like it was from one of those stores in the city that overcharged for basic camping supplies, promising to guard people from the elements or turn desk jockeys into outdoorsmen with the right backpack.

A campfire was spitting blue-and-yellow embers into the frigid night air not ten feet away from a brown-and-beige pop-up tent. The light coming from the blaze would be a beacon to anyone who might be traveling in the area. Of course, this was private property so there shouldn't have been anyone around. The Hereford Ranch was one of the rare few in Texas that was successful enough selling cattle that the owners weren't forced to lease parts of the land for hunting. The land and mineral rights were owned by one of the wealthiest families in the state, the Butlers. Rory had personal knowledge that no one had been given permission to be there. This campsite was a trespassing violation at the very least, possibly more.

A law meant to crack down on illegal hunting made it a felony offense to poach on someone's land. And that sifted out the less-experienced thrill-seekers. The pros upped the ante, which also made them more dangerous than ever. Rory didn't mind putting his life on the line for a good cause since he didn't doubt his skills and could net a bigger paycheck because of the increased risk. Besides, he had no one at home waiting for him to return and that was the way he liked living life.

This campsite looked set up for a romantic rendezvous but Rory had too much experience to take anything at face value. He wouldn't put anything past a skilled poacher. This whole scenario could be cover for a scout, someone who fed information to poachers.

Surveying the perimeter, Rory located a small bag of trash tied to a tree roughly ten yards away from the campsite. Every experienced outdoorsman knew to hang his trash far away from his campsite or risk attracting dangerous wildlife searching for an easy meal. By contrast, most didn't shop at those overpriced stores.

Rory took a breath of fresh Texas air in his lungs. He'd been working on a ranch in Wyoming for the past five months while trying to keep his thoughts away from the woman he'd walked away from. Time was supposed to give perspective. He sighed sharply. Clearly, it would take more than five months to rid his mind of Cadence Butler.

When her brother Dade had called to say he needed the best tracker, Rory wasted no time getting on the road.

Of course, the Butlers didn't know he was coming. He'd refused the job with his friends because it was best that no one—and that included the Butler family—knew he'd be on-site. Not just because of his past relationship with Cadence. *Relationship?* That was probably a strong word. More like *history.* It was their history that had caused him to momentarily lose his grip on reality by spending one too many nights with the off-limits heiress. Keeping the family, and everyone else, in the dark would give him the element of surprise. If one of the Butlers knew he was coming, word could get out.

Dade wouldn't have called if he'd known about the fling. Rory and Cadence had kept their relationship on the quiet side, or so he had thought until her father confronted him. The charismatic Maverick Mike Butler had been right about one thing: Rory had no business seeing the man's daughter. She was out of his league and Cadence would never survive his lifestyle of living on the range, being constantly on the go.

The thought of settling into one spot made Rory's collar shrink. He had a cabin built for one in Texas near Cattle Barge that he called home. One was his lucky number.

No matter what else, it was best that the Butlers had no idea he'd be around. One slip would cause word to get out, since a small family-oriented place like Cattle Barge wasn't known for being able to keep a secret. Hell, the town's business had been plastered across every newspaper for months ever since Maverick Mike Butler's murder last summer, which Rory was truly sorry for when he'd found out about it. Mr. Butler had given Rory a job when he was lost and alone at fifteen years old. Rory had kept his life on the straight and narrow because of the opportunity he'd been given and he would go to his own grave grateful for the hand up when he'd been down on his luck and searching for a steady place to land. Rory had never minded hard work, and Mr. Butler's only caveat for keeping his job had been that Rory finish high school.

He had, and his boss had attended his graduation. He'd patted Rory on the back and told him he was proud of him.

Granted, the man didn't like Rory having anything to do with Cadence. But Rory couldn't blame a father for wanting to protect his daughter. Maverick Mike seemed to know on instinct the same fact Rory had surmised early on—that he'd only cause Cadence heartache.

Even though her father had had harsh words for him, Rory respected the man who'd grown up a sharecropper's son but made good on his life.

His heart went out to the family for their loss and his thoughts often wound to Cadence in the months since, wondering how she was handling the news.

Being in Cattle Barge and thinking about the past caused memories of his parents' volatile marriage to resurface. Heavy weights bore down on his shoulders and it was doing nothing to improve his sour mood.

To make matters worse, Christmas was around the corner. He'd lost touch with his sister, Renee, who was the only other sane person in the family. She'd split at seventeen years old, and then he took off shortly after.

The holidays made him think about her, wonder where she was now and if she was happy.

Rory shook off the emotions wrapping a heavy blanket around him. No good ever came of thinking about his family or the empty holiday he faced being alone. He reminded himself that it was his choice to be by himself. He had no use for distractions.

He performed a mental headshake in hopes of clearing his mind. Surveying the campsite again, he skimmed the area for signs of people. It was cold tonight and he doubted the warmth from the fire would be enough. A piece of material meant to secure the tent flapped with the wind. Inside, it was empty.

Rory rolled a few times on the cold earth. His movement stealth-like and with purpose. This vantage point allowed him a better view inside the small tent. There were two sleeping bags that had been placed next to each other inside.

Being back on Butler land made him think about the time he and Cadence had stayed up all night talking in her father's barn. It was the first time he realized his feelings were careening out of control. Because staying up all night with a woman *to talk* had never held a lot of appeal before her. Cadence was the perfect mix of intelligence, sass and sense of humor. She was always on the go and sometimes acted before she thought something through, but her heart was always in the right place. His chest clutched while he thought about her. He needed to stop himself right there. That was the past. *She* was the past. The best way to end up thrown from his horse was to keep looking backward.

Besides, nothing could be changed and he'd only end up with a crick in his neck.

A log crackled, sending another round of burning embers into the air. Rory hoped like hell the couple who'd lit it didn't have plans to go to sleep with the blaze still going, *if* there was a couple. There was no accounting for lack of skill and knowledge. If this was a situation with inexperienced campers they might not even realize they'd set up on private property. A place as massive as Hereford was impossible to cordon off completely from the outside world, even though security would be tighter following Mr. Butler's murder.

Rory changed position again, moving stealthily along the tree line near the lake. He crouched behind the trunk of a mesquite tree, watching, waiting. A blast of frigid air penetrated straight through his winter jacket. It was twelve in the morning, which could be considered early or late, depending on point of view. Tomorrow was supposed to be even colder. The mornings were already crisp and the forecast said a cold front was moving in for Christmas Eve in five days.

He shouldn't complain. This was nothing compared to December weather in Wyoming. Forty degrees was practically a heat wave.

The twenty-hours-straight drive had tied Rory's muscles into knots. They were screaming to be stretched. Exhaustion and cold slowed his reflexes. He'd have to take that into account if he confronted the campers.

Protecting the Butler property took top priority for reasons he didn't want to examine. He'd known the family since he was a kid. His father had worked in the barn for part of Rory's childhood before blowing up at his boss and getting fired. Rory had plenty of fond memories of spending time with the twins, Dalton and Dade. The Butler boys had treated him like one of them from the very beginning. That was most likely the reason he felt compelled to take this job and why he felt so damn guilty for having the fling with Cadence.

Rory could rest later when he turned over the bad guys and collected his paycheck.

At this time of night, the campers should have been in their tent. The wind had picked up and Rory was certain the temperature had dropped ten degrees in the last hour.

Moving silently along the perimeter of their camp, he repositioned away from the water, noting that this location was a little too close to the Butler home for comfort.

A noise on the opposite side, the place where he'd first set up, caught his attention. Rory flattened his body against the cold hard earth. Wind whipped the fire around as he flexed and released his fingers to keep blood flowing.

A man came into view of the firelight. He had to be roughly five feet ten inches, if Rory had to guess, a good four inches shorter than him. The guy had on jogging pants, tennis shoes and a dark hoodie. A smallish dog—on closer inspection, it looked like a beagle mix—trotted behind City Guy's heels. That was bad news for Rory because the dog would pick up his scent and give away his location. Even with the fierce winds, it was only a matter of time before the beagle found him.

To avoid that fiasco, he would make himself known. He hopped to his feet and moved about fifteen feet closer before making a loud grunting noise to call attention to his presence. He needed a good reason to be out there alone this time of night…

"Dammit," he said loudly as he stalked out of the shadows, making as much noise as one man could without a herd of elephants behind him. "I seem to have lost my hunting knife. It was a present from my girlfriend and things haven't been so great between us lately. I really don't want to have to go home and explain that. There's no chance you've seen it, is there?"

From this distance, Rory could see the man's face had a day's worth of stubble and he was wearing one of those expensive compass watches. No way was this an outdoorsman.

City Guy seemed thrown by Rory's presence, making him believe the man was either up to no good or scared out of his wits. Poachers were generally harder to detect and it usually took days, sometimes weeks, to track them. They rarely ever set up camp unless they were armed to the nines or stupid, and the latter were easily caught.

The man quickly recovered a casual disposition, bending down to grab his dog by the collar. He took a knee next to the beagle. "Sorry, what did you say you're looking for?"

"A knife about so-big." Rory made a show of holding his hands out, palms facing each other, to indicate a roughly nine-inch blade and subtly lead the man to believe that he wasn't carrying another weapon. In this position, it would take Rory approximately three seconds to drop, roll and come up with the handgun in his ankle holster. Everyone in this part of Texas carried for protection against wild animals, so he assumed City Guy was armed, too.

"What makes you think it's around here?" City Guy said, keeping a cautious-looking eye on Rory while covering most of his face with the brim of his ball cap.

"According to my GPS, I was somewhere around this area hunting this morning." He glanced at his watch. "Technically, yesterday morning. Guess it was pretty early, around daybreak." Rory was fishing to see when the guy set up camp.

"We didn't get here until noon. I checked the area as I set up and didn't see anything." The guy shrugged.

"I'm Rory, by the way."

"My name is—" there was a hesitation so brief that Rory almost wrote it off as his imagination but then City Guy finished "—Dexter but everyone calls me Dex. And this is Boots."

He made a show of scratching the dog behind his ears.

Even though Dex was considerably smaller than Rory, it was obvious the guy hit the gym. And Rory would put his life savings on the fact that the guy's name wasn't Dexter.

"Nice to meet you both." Rory picked up his earlier ruse by pretending to search the ground using his phone's flashlight app. Maybe he could needle the guy for a little information or see if he could get him talking and trip him up. "I'm such an idiot. How does someone lose a nine-inch knife?" He shook his head and threw his hands in the air.

"It most likely slipped out of your pack," Dex said. "Could happen to anyone."

"You're probably right." Rory scanned the ground. "And I'm starting to think I was crazy to think I could find anything in the dark."

"Your flashlight might catch the metal," Dex said, keeping one eye on Rory.

"That was my thought, too." If he could get the guy to think he was an amateur, he might be able to lower his defenses even more. In this case, it was hard to know who was playing whom. "You come out here a lot with Boots?"

"No. My girlfriend, Lainey, is here. We're doing a romantic thing for the night. I thought it would be a good idea. You know, the whole under-the-stars thing, but I'm not so sure she agrees. She might've ditched me and headed to a roadside motel." He laughed and it sounded a little too forced. "You didn't bump into her, did you? She'd die of embarrassment because she asked for privacy to take care of business. She's a red-head and she's wearing a white down coat, full length, with snow boots."

Dex was giving too many details as he described her. Was he nervous? Lying? There was no reason to describe his girlfriend out here. If Rory saw a woman at this hour, it would have to be her.

"Maybe I'll stick around until she gets back so I don't catch her off guard," Rory said, pretending to keep busy while waiting for a reaction.

Dex wore a red ball cap and kept his face angled toward the dog, making it difficult to make out his features, even though he was near the fire. "As long as you return the way you came, there shouldn't be a problem."

"Good point." Rory figured the more Dex believed

he agreed the better. "How long are you two planning to stick around?"

Again, he listened for a slipup.

"Just the night," Dex said.

"Ah, here it is," Rory bent down and picked up something from the ground. He bit out a curse. "Never mind. It's a flattened soda can."

"Bad luck," Dex said.

"Always," Rory quipped, trying to make the guy think he was being buddy-buddy. Comradery could go a long way toward lowering Dex's defenses and getting to the truth. Why was he camping on Butler land? Rory didn't believe for one second that it was for love. This guy was here for a reason… But what?

"I better head out before your girlfriend gets back. Wouldn't want to ruin the mood." Although, if she was really on a bathroom break, Rory couldn't imagine that was possible. But stick around much longer and Dex would become suspicious. As it was, the guy was being cautious. The campsite. The nonexistent girlfriend. The innocent camper act.

Everything was off about this situation.

"Catch you around." Rory turned and caught sight of the glint of metal in Dex's hand against the glow of the fire.

A weapon?

He decided to stick around another minute.

CADENCE BUTLER CLOSED the door to her bedroom. She was home, only it didn't feel like it since her father's murder. The place would never be the same without him. She put a hand on her growing belly as a wave of sadness crashed down around her, threatening to chew her up, toss her around and then spit her out into the surf.

Other than one quick stop over the summer, which netted an unfortunate incident with the law, she hadn't been home for good reason. Trying to scare her half sister, Madelyn, out of town had been a childish lapse in judgment. Those were racking up.

How she'd concealed her pregnancy for so long was a mystery. At six months pregnant, she was surprisingly big. Or at least she'd thought so. Her doctor had reassured her that it was perfectly normal for a woman carrying twins to show as early as she had.

Another wave of melancholy hit as she thought about the babies who would never get the chance to know their grandfather.

"I can't wait to see you running around on this land someday. Just like I used to when I was a little girl," she whispered, resting her hand on her growing baby bump.

It was late and she was grateful to have slipped inside the house without seeing anyone, without any drama. Come morning, there'd be a million questions and she still didn't know what to say about the pregnancy. Her fling with Rory had been kept secret. He'd wanted to tell her brothers but she'd convinced him not to say anything.

There was a practical reason for her coming home that didn't include the big reveal of a pregnancy with twins. She thought about the poachers encroaching on the land, taking advantage of the distractions following her father's murder. Her blood heated thinking about the kind of person who would try to capitalize on a tragedy.

Running Hereford Ranch had its challenges. Ones her father had made look so easy. But then people had known better than to mess with the ranch while her father was alive. Poachers must see the new regime, including her, as weak or they wouldn't be encroaching. They were about to be taught a valuable lesson, she thought. Her thoughts shifted to the best tracker in the country, Rory Scott. Rory was in Wyoming tracking other poachers. He'd broken her heart when he ended their fling and walked out five months ago. Thinking about it, about *him*, stressed her out.

A warm bath would do wonders toward relaxing her tension knots. Strain wasn't good for the babies. Neither was sadness and that was part of the reason she'd stayed away from the ranch. Being here without her father…

Cadence couldn't go there.

She slipped inside her room, grateful there hadn't been a big deal made over her return. No one would bother her until morning and that would give her time to think up an excuse as to why she was coming home six-months pregnant with Rory Scott's twins.

Thankfully, her bathroom was adjacent to her room. Access was restricted. She didn't want to deal with her brothers and sister tonight. She wanted to get her bearings first. Being home, facing the ranch, brought back so many memories. Good memories that made her wish she'd had more time with her father. She gulped for air.

The father she rarely understood but always loved was never coming back.

Her heart clutched. Moving past her window, a chill

raced up her spine and she got a creepy feeling. It was most likely her imagination. Or…

Was someone out there watching?

# *Chapter Two*

"I'll be on my way before your lady friend returns. Wouldn't want to ruin the moment." Rory could see the tension building in Dex—or whatever his name was—and it was time to make his exit before this situation escalated. The glint he'd seen was most definitely from a weapon and that shot all kinds of warning flares.

Watching the campsite would be tricky with the beagle, but Rory figured he could put enough distance between them to keep off the dog's radar.

When Rory really thought about it, using a dog was smart. Dex's cover was perfect. Not many people would notice the subtle things, like the fact that the guy might be playing dumb when it came to nature, but he seemed to know enough to tie up his trash away from the site. Or that after spending a good fifteen minutes snooping around, the guy's so-called girlfriend hadn't returned. There was no alcohol on the site, either. Wouldn't that be part of a romantic camping trip for two people of drinking age? There didn't look to be any food supplies, either, which struck him as odd for someone planning to spend the night.

Was he a poacher?

Rory didn't see any of the usual supplies, consisting of water and weapons. This guy could be a scout, sending information back. This campsite was close enough to the Butler ranch that Dex might be there to watch out for ranch hands.

"Much appreciated. Camille is already skittish out here," Dex said with a wink, seemingly unaware of his mistake. Rory immediately noticed the name change. He'd called his girlfriend Lainey five minutes ago. Suddenly, her name was Camille.

Rory concealed the fact that he was scrutinizing Dex's features. The man would be fantastic at poker. For the most part, Dex kept his cards close to his chest.

"Thanks for letting me take a look around your camp." Rory offered a handshake, needing to wrap this up. He'd seen enough to know that Dex required watching. He was involved in something illegal, but there was nothing to go on besides trespassing at present. Keeping an eye on the man might lead Rory to the real source, which could be poachers. Another thought struck and that was Dex could be a reporter. Although the headlines involving the Butlers had died down a bit recently, with the will reading coming up, there'd been renewed interest in everything Butler.

"No problem." Dex stood and took the offering. The minute their palms grazed, Rory realized how nervous the guy had been. His hand had just enough moisture to reveal his emotions. Rory had to hand it to Dex, he came off as cool as a cucumber and that fact sent a few more warning flares up.

Rory walked away, careful to make sure he disappeared in the same direction he'd arrived. He could almost feel the set of eyes on his back as he walked farther from the campsite and listened carefully for any sounds that Dex might be following. He'd probably stuck around a little too long. The handshake could have been overkill. Damn.

His mistakes could lead to suspicion.

Forty-five minutes had passed since Rory recovered his previous spot, watching the campsite from afar. There'd been no movement. No Lainey, or Camille… or whatever her name was.

Rory had known that for the lie it was.

Dex tied Boots to a tree trunk. With the fire still blazing, he grabbed a walking-type stick and headed north, the opposite direction of the Butler estate.

What was he up to now?

Rory watched intently, using his night-vision goggles. He checked the time. Where did Dex think he was going at this hour?

The only evidence Rory had against the man so far was trespassing. Not exactly a strong case to entice the sheriff's office to send a deputy out immediately. The office would most likely take the complaint and promise to investigate. Sheriff Sawmill and his deputies were still too overrun to follow up on every lead unless Rory could present compelling evidence that this was more. It was hard to believe the sheriff still hadn't arrested Maverick Mike Butler's murderer.

A pang of guilt hit him like stray voltage. He'd wanted to stick around after learning that Mr. Butler had been murdered. He could only imagine the devastation the family felt and especially Cadence.

There were a few too many times in the past five

months that he'd wanted to return and be her comfort. The news coverage on Cattle Barge had almost been 24/7. He'd seen the story of her arrest and then release after she tried to run off someone claiming to be her half sister. He could only imagine what Cadence had been going through to cause a lapse in judgment like that.

Walking out five months ago had been his attempt to protect her. A relationship with Rory was the worst of bad ideas. He needed to be outside somewhere. Anywhere. And she needed a comfortable bed with soft sheets. Soft like her skin had been when he grazed his finger along the inside of her thigh.

Damn.

Thinking about Cadence brought on a surge of hormones and a wave of inappropriate desire. Hell, at least he wasn't dead. Since walking away from her, not many women could stack up to the memory of her silky skin and sweet laugh. She was beautiful and sexy, but that wasn't the best part. She was smart, and funny, and outgoing, and…

His heart clutched, squeezing a little harder this time, reminding him what a bad idea it was to think about Cadence Butler.

Being on her family's land would bring back a certain amount of memories, he reasoned, but the onslaught of reasons why he missed her caught him off guard.

Chalk it up to weakness. Being with her had made him weak and almost forget about their differences—differences that would drive them to squabble and make each other miserable given enough time. He thought about his parents' marriage and how toxic their love had been.

Rory checked his watch again. Twenty minutes had passed while he'd been distracted by his reverie. He couldn't let that happen again.

Besides, there was no sign of Dex. He waited another full thirty minutes before making a decision on his next move. It was still too early to call the sheriff.

Patience won battles.

So, he'd hold off.

Rory waited a full hour before deciding to move closer. The dog was still secured. None of the obvious supplies had been taken. The guy's expensive-looking backpack was still leaning against his compact fold-out chair. Every sign pointed to Dex coming back.

Was he out scouting so he could relay information to his boss?

Or had he abandoned the site?

Another ten minutes wired Rory's nervous system for the unexpected. An adrenaline spike got his pulse racing and blood speeding through his veins. All his internal systems spiked to critical mass. And, like always in these situations, he felt his senses alighting, awakening. He felt alive.

He listened for any sounds that Dex was circling him, coming up from behind for a sneak attack or studying him in order to make a move. It was possible. Hell, anything was possible out here. But Dex wouldn't get the best of Rory. Rory was damn good at his job, considered the best tracker in the country.

If Dex tried to pull something, Rory would be ready and waiting.

Reaching down to his ankle holster, he pulled his

Walther 9 mm and palmed it. He rested his thumb on the safety mechanism, just in case he needed to fire.

Normally, all this action and adrenaline would have boosted his mood, made him happy. Instead, a sense of dread overwhelmed him along with the energy burst. *What was that all about, Scott?*

*Cadence*, an irritating little voice said. Being here on her father's land. It would belong to her and her siblings now. Plus, the two surprise family members who'd shown up after Maverick Mike's death. Rory wasn't sure how either of them played into the equation but all looked to have been smoothed out based on media reports.

*It's none of your business*, that same little voice reminded, even though a little piece of his heart protested that everything about Cadence was.

Again, it proved nothing more than the fact that he was alive. And it was good to know that he still had a beating heart in his chest. He knew because it fisted every time he thought about her. *Having a working heart might come in handy someday*, he mused.

Although, all it had done so far was make him feel weak and angry. He thought about his family and about leaving them to run away from home at fifteen years old because he couldn't watch his parents participate in their mutual misery anymore. He'd begged his mother to leave the abuse behind, to go with him, and still couldn't understand why she'd told him to mind his own business before willingly staying with his father. The man's bouts of jealousy and anger became almost daily shows by Rory's teenage years. She'd scream and cry in the moment, threaten to leave him. Everything always escalated from there.

By the next day, always, she'd defend the man, saying that he got angry because he loved her.

A sudden burst of cold air brought his focus back to the camp twenty-five yards in front of him.

There were other possibilities for why Dex was in this part of the county, possibilities that heeded consideration. Thinking of his parents always reminded him of domestic violence. Dex could be a hothead or a common criminal in the wrong spot at the wrong time. He might've brought a girlfriend here, killed her and dug her grave. She might've already been dead and he dragged her limp body into a shallow grave.

Icy tendrils wrapped around Rory's spine at the same time that anger spiked through him.

Facing the unexpected usually kept him on his toes, reminded him he was alive. This time was surprisingly different. It lacked the excitement that normally accompanied an adrenaline rush of this scale.

Since there hadn't been activity at Dex's camp, Rory decided to go in and see if he could gather more intel. Boots was asleep and there was a chance he wouldn't bark since he'd already met Rory. The winds had picked up and the howling would mask any noise the little dog made.

What else could he use to distract the dog? Considering he didn't own a pet, nor had he ever, he didn't exactly carry around dog biscuits. Rory would have to have been willing to commit to one spot for a while in order to have his own dog. But he did have something.

He could break off a small piece of a peanut-butter power bar and give it to Boots.

Dex not returning was starting to weigh on Rory. Why would the man leave the camp without taking his backpack and his pet?

Investigating could be tricky and could compromise Rory's position. What if Dex returned? What if the animal barked? Rory could be caught or shot.

Did he have another cover story? There was no good sell for being out there alone and checking out the campsite for the second time.

What if the dog didn't bark? Could Rory slip in and out without leaving a trace while Boots slept? All he'd need would be a few minutes and he was confident he could get answers.

He had to consider all possibilities.

Rory crouched low and eased across ten yards of terrain without making a sound. The howling wind played to his benefit because he could come in at an angle so the dog wouldn't easily pick up his scent. Of course, the wind chill was cutting right through his hunting jacket, which he wore in order to give off the impression he was passing through on a hunting trip. It was prime deer hunting season and that would play to his advantage. Of course, most recreational deer hunters were already locked down in a bunk on their deer lease.

Stealthily, he moved along the perimeter of the campsite.

This time, he looked for any signs that a heavy object, such as a body, had been dragged out. But then, if Dex was a murderer—and that was a big *if*—he might've already done away with the remains. The campsite could be part of his cover—girlfriend stormed off just before midnight after an intense fight. She doesn't return. Body is never found. With all the animals out searching for a meal, her remains could be scattered across the land.

It wouldn't be the first time such a tragedy had occurred. Rory had come up against similar situations and worse in his ten years as a tracker. And even though his work brought him face-to-face with everything from hardened criminals looking to hide—and willing to kill whomever stood in the way of freedom—to profiteers seeking to make a quick buck on the black market, a trade that was unfortunately thriving, to traffickers—human and animal—he'd always brought them to justice.

In his life, no two days were the same and the variety kept his blood pumping. Most of his meals were cooked and eaten out in the open. There was something about food heated over an open fire that made it taste so much better than anything he'd ever tasted from an oven.

He could admit that life on the fringe had lost some of its appeal recently and that probably had to do with the beating heart in his chest, making him think about things he knew better than to want or expect, like a real home.

This life was uncomplicated. He didn't spend his time glued to an electronic device like people in town. He didn't answer to anyone or have to spend time with anyone he didn't want to see, which also sounded lonely when he put it like that.

Taking in a slow breath, he inched forward.

Out on the range, a person's mind could wander into

dangerous territory if he wasn't careful. Being alone with his thoughts for long periods used to clear his mind but not lately.

Inevitably, his thoughts would wander to Cadence. Conversations with her had always been enjoyable and especially with her spunk. Her smile was quick and genuine.

His heart acknowledged that she was dangerous and he knew deep down she could do a whole lot better in life than be dragged down by the likes of a man like him. He might've walked away first but she would've eventually. She would've figured out they were no good for each other. And his heart might not have recovered. For the hundredth time in the past five months, he reminded himself this was the only choice and that he'd done her a favor.

He'd catch the poacher who was running the show—if that man wasn't Dex—which would shut down the heart of the operation. And then get back to Wyoming, where he'd taken personal leave. He was needed on the SJ Ranch as soon as he tied up this loose end. If he was going to show his hand, he'd admit that the possibility of seeing Cadence again caused all kinds of uncomfortable feelings to surface.

For now, he'd deal with what was right in front of him, the camp. He'd managed to inch close enough to see that there was no cooler. Was Dex gone?

Rory palmed the makeshift dog treat. Improvising was the name of the game out in the wild, where he'd learned to make do with what was on hand.

Boots opened his eyes and lifted his head as Rory dropped down next to him. Rory was no dog whisperer but he knew his way around animals. Another survival tactic. One he enjoyed.

"Shhhh, it's okay, Boots." He held out the broken pieces of power bar on his flat palm as he surveyed the area. Dex could show up any minute.

And then his gaze landed on the object that Dex had been hiding…a rifle with a scope pointing south, the direction of the Butler home.

Hold on. From this vantage point on the land, could he see as far as the estate? It would depend on the power of the scope.

Rory emptied his hand of the treats, dropping them next to the dog's mouth. Boots wagged his tail as he happily went to town on the bits.

Rory pulled his night goggles down from his forehead and secured them over his eyes. Another quick scan of the area and everything looked copacetic. Of course, the goggles only allowed him to see fifteen feet around. Pitch-blackness circled the camp like a heavy fog.

He gave another pass to the area in order to make sure he and Boots were alone.

Dropping down to check the angle of the scope, he removed his goggles.

A curse rolled up and out.

Dex had a perfect angle.

The rifle was aimed at the Butler estate all right.

Rory would recognize that bedroom window anywhere.

It belonged to Cadence Butler.

## *Chapter Three*

Rory backed away, making sure he didn't damage any of the fingerprints on the rifle or scope, and then he called the sheriff.

"There's a situation on the Butler property you need to be aware of," he said to Sheriff Sawmill. Rory could almost see the frustration that accompanied the heavy sigh coming through the line. "I can give you my GPS coordinates."

"Mind sending a few photos of the site?" Sawmill asked.

"Not if it'll help," Rory said. He didn't mind taking a few risks if it meant helping Sawmill figure out who Dex really was.

"I don't have anyone near your location. I'll get a deputy out before morning," he promised.

"Thanks, Sheriff." There was no use pressuring him. Rory could tell by the man's tone that he wished he could do more but didn't have the resources. He also knew how overstretched the sheriff's office had been since the murder. Pressure mounted to find Mr. Butler's killer as time went on and that had to be weighing on the sheriff's mind.

After snapping pictures from multiple angles and then watching over the site for another half hour, Rory assumed Dex wasn't coming back. The most likely scenario was that Rory had scared Dex away and he wouldn't return. The man had taken off in a hurry after Rory had invaded the camp and the probability there'd be fingerprints on the weapon were slim to none.

The fire had burned out. Since Rory couldn't rightly leave the little dog to freeze, he took the shivering beagle into his arms and placed him inside his jacket so he would stop shaking.

Dex would know someone had been there if he returned before the sheriff's deputy arrived. Rory highly doubted the guy was coming back, though, based on experience.

*Game on*, Rory thought as he tracked east. He'd circle around to his conversion vehicle and take the beagle, which couldn't be more than a year old, with no tags, with him to the Butler ranch. If Dex thought he could outsmart him, he needed to think again. No one was better out on the range than Rory and he had no doubt that he could track Dex and see to it that the guy spent the rest of his life behind bars.

Cadence was home. Rory wasn't supposed to know that. No one was. However, he couldn't help himself and had tracked her whereabouts. She'd left Colorado that evening and would've arrived an hour or two ago. He needed to warn her and her family that she could be in danger.

A dark thought hit. Had Dex already made his way to the main house?

That thought had Rory picking up the pace. In a

full-out run, Rory made it back to his vehicle in record time. He secured the beagle in the front seat and took the driver's seat before heading southwest toward the main house. From his current location, it would take an hour to wind around on the country roads to get to the place. He knew a shortcut that involved going off road but could possibly get a lot of attention from security.

Rory spun the wheel left. He needed to get to the house as fast as possible. It was possible that Dex had moved closer to get a good shot. Damn. The man might've left his rifle behind but he was still carrying a handgun.

It was also worth considering that he was an amateur and had abandoned his plan altogether.

Rory managed to locate his phone while driving and used Bluetooth technology to make the call to Cadence.

The recording said the number was no longer in service.

When did she change her number? She'd had the same one since high school.

Then he thought about everything that had happened to the family in the past few months after Maverick Mike Butler's death. With all the media scrutiny, it made sense that she would make it more difficult to reach her. He hoped it had to do with the media and not their breakup. It shouldn't bother him that she'd changed her number. It wasn't really his business anymore no matter how much his heart argued.

*Okay. Plan B.*

He pulled over and checked his call log. Dade had been the one to reach out, so his new number must be on the log. Rory called that number. He didn't realize he'd been holding his breath until the call rolled into a generic-sounding voice mail and frustration nipped at him.

Instead, he tapped the gas pedal harder and raced toward the house, hoping like hell that he wasn't too late.

Someone in the Butler household knew there'd been a security breach because Terrell Landry stood with his rifle shouldered and aimed at the conversion vehicle speeding toward the back side of the estate. Based on his disposition, his finger hovered over the trigger mechanism. A team of six formed a semicircle around Terrell twenty yards in front of where Rory stopped the conversion vehicle and put his hands where everyone could see them as he exited his vehicle. He'd be no use to Cadence or anyone else if he got himself shot on the property and he wouldn't risk one of the men he didn't know getting too excited with his trigger finger.

"Rory Scott?" Terrell said, more statement than question.

"In the flesh," Rory answered. "Permission to approach?"

Terrell's next words allowed Rory to exhale.

"Of course. Stand down," Terrell told his men, lowering his own weapon. "But what are you doing here? I was told that you refused the job."

"Misunderstanding," Rory said as he walked to the head of security, planning to meet him halfway. He'd known Terrell for half of his life.

"Good to see you," Terrell said, sticking out his hand between them.

Rory shook it as the others flanked them. And then a few seconds later he found himself flipped on his backside, heaving for air after being slammed into the cold hard pavement with the wind knocked out of him.

"What the hell, Landry?" he managed to get out through gulps of air. His lungs burned.

"I'm sorry, Rory. I have orders," Terrell said. "I've been instructed to contain you and call the sheriff in order to file a trespassing complaint."

"The Butlers offered me a job. Who would give you orders to have me arrested?" Rory ground out.

"I got the order directly from Cadence Butler." He shot another apologetic look. "She called it in yesterday."

She had to know that Rory would have been asked to help. Yes, he'd walked out on a relationship with her but this was over the top. Even for Cadence.

Twenty minutes later, Rory stood in the foyer of the Butler home with his hands in zip cuffs and Boots at his side.

Dade came rushing toward him as Boots sat next to Rory's shoes. "I'm sorry, Rory. I don't know how this order slipped past the rest of us and ended up being issued. It should never have happened." He glanced toward his head of security and then the zip cuffs. "Take those ridiculous things off."

Rory's anger almost overshadowed the real reason he'd shown up to begin with as Terrell removed the bindings. He rubbed sore wrists. "I caught a guy on your property with a scope on Cadence's room."

Dalton entered the foyer, stress cracks around his eyes and mouth. He looked exhausted and Rory didn't like being the one to deliver more bad news. "Where?"

"Due north from the main house," Rory supplied. "Is she here?"

"Haven't seen her yet but she was due in last night," Dade supplied after shaking his friend's hand. Dade was wearing jeans without a shirt or shoes. He'd obviously been roused from sleep. "I'm sorry again for the misunderstanding." He motioned toward Rory's wrists.

This was no miscommunication, but he wasn't angry at Dade or Dalton for it.

"You want me to take care of this guy?" Landry asked, motioning toward Boots.

"He belong to you?" Dade asked.

"Does now."

"All right if Landry takes care of him while we talk?" Dade nodded toward the beagle.

"Fine by me. Cadence needs to know how much danger she's in." She wasn't stupid and if she realized how close she was to being shot, she'd take the right precautions. Rory didn't even want to think about what might've happened if he hadn't been there. Was he still frustrated with her for the stunt? Hell, yes.

But he didn't want anything to happen to her.

It was probably guilt for walking out on her that had him wanting to protect her and not residual feelings. Rory didn't *do* those with anyone no matter how much his heart wanted to argue at thinking about seeing her again.

"I need to talk to Cadence," Rory said as Landry picked up Boots and then disappeared.

Dade stepped aside, allowing access to her hallway in the massive rustic-chic, log-cabin-style home.

It looked more like a resort than private residence and he knew the layout well.

"She doesn't want to talk to you." Ella Butler stepped into the hallway in front of Cadence's room.

"Too bad," Rory said. "She needs to."

Ella was shaking her head and she looked rattled by the ordeal. "We understand what happened and will take it seriously. My sister has nothing else to say to you."

"Like hell she doesn't." He started toward her room.

Ella stood there, arms folded over her chest. He would never do anything to hurt a woman so he flexed and released his fingers to keep them from reaching out to pick her up and move her.

"What's going on?" Dade's brow was hiked.

"Good question," Rory added, focusing on Ella. "Your sister can have me arrested if I set foot on the property when I've been summoned, but I don't get to warn of her the danger she's in or ask why she's so intent on not seeing me?"

"No, you don't. Now, leave," Cadence said from her room.

"This is none of our business, Ella," Dade warned and Rory wondered if his friend knew about the fling. He doubted it, considering how determined Cadence had been to keep it under wraps.

Just when Rory thought Ella was going to dig her heels in and fight, her expression softened and she said, "You're right. We should stay out of it. I'm sorry, Cadence. But he deserves to know."

Cadence didn't respond.

"I'm sorry, Rory," Ella said with a look as she, Dalton and Dade wished him good luck before disappearing down the hall.

*Deserved to know what exactly?* Rory questioned.

Rory tapped on Cadence's door with his bare knuckles. He was the one who'd said there was no future for the two of them and then taken a job in Wyoming. When he really thought about it, she had every right to be upset with him. Not to trust him. Having him detained for being on Butler land was going too far but Cadence had a flair for the dramatic and she was probably still acting out of hurt—hurt that had been his fault.

"It's important or I wouldn't be here, Cadence. Open up," he said.

"Go away."

CADENCE STOOD ON the opposite side of the door, her heart thundering in her chest. This wasn't how she'd envisioned telling Rory that he was going to be a father. She'd had every intention of telling him when the time was right but that time never came and she'd eventually decided to wait until after the babies were born.

There'd been so many times she'd wanted him to know but to what end? What did she want from him? Child support? Marriage? She almost laughed out loud at the thought of tying Rory down with commitment. He'd been all too clear that he wasn't the type to stick around.

When he'd first walked out of her life, she thought that if she gave him enough time, he'd come back on his own. He'd realize that the two of them should be together.

As far as drinking the Kool-Aid went, she'd gone all-in with that fantasy.

He'd seemed content to stay away and her heart was still trying to heal from the snub.

So far, Ella was the only one who knew about the pregnancy and her sister had literally found out five minutes ago when she'd come in to check on Cadence.

"Stay away from your windows, Cadence. Someone was camping on your property and you're being targeted." Rory wasn't trying to scare her. His voice was steady steel.

"Okay. Now I know," she retorted, chiding herself for being so quick to dismiss him.

Several more taps came.

"I'm sorry about what happened between us." His voice was low and gravelly. It was the same voice that had been so good at seducing her.

*And the same that had told her the two of you didn't have a future*, a little voice reminded.

"Fine. I'll take this seriously. Consider me warned. Now, you can leave." He deserved to know he was a father but not like this. A cramp nearly doubled her over. She made it to her bed and sat down, gripping the mattress, trying not to make a noise.

She'd sent for a doctor four times in her first trimester, thinking the cramps were a bad sign that something was going terribly wrong. Turned out they were normal and especially common in a first pregnancy.

Before she could stop it, the doorknob twisted.

"No, Rory! Go!"

"I just wanted to tell you face-to-face—" His jaw fell slack the minute his gaze landed on her stomach.

Defensively, she brought her hands around her large belly to cover it.

Rory stood there, frozen, as though unable to speak. A few seconds ticked by before he seemed to gather his thoughts well enough to say something.

"Do you mind telling me when you intended to share the news that you're pregnant?" he finally asked, and there was so much betrayal in his voice.

She was pretty sure he was decent at math but also certain he had no idea how far along she was or the timing of a pregnancy. And part of her realized he had every right to be angry.

"I'd say it's none of your business but that's not exactly true since you're the father," she said, watching intently for his response.

A look of complete shock darkened his features as his gaze practically bore through her. His jaw clenched and released a few times, and it looked like he was grinding his molars. His stare became a dare when he said, "Then marry me."

# *Chapter Four*

"For what reason, Rory Scott?" There was a time when Cadence would've said yes in a heartbeat to a marriage proposal from Rory. But this one had the stench of obligation attached to it and from the sounds of it, anger. Just how well would that work out for her or the babies?

She'd seen firsthand the problems with that logic. Her father had married her mother because she'd been pregnant with Cadence's older sister. Her mother had apparently been so miserable that she'd taken off when Cadence was still in diapers.

"You're pregnant for one. It's what a man does," he stated, squaring his shoulders.

"We're done with this conversation," Cadence said, covering the hurt. His words were knife jabs to her chest. Because a part of her she didn't want to acknowledge still had feelings for him. A whole lot of good that did. Of course, she cared about Rory. He was the father of her growing babies.

"No, we're not anything, Cadence. You can't run away from this." His words had the effect of bullets from a machine gun, slamming into the target wildly and with inaccuracy.

"Why don't you just leave again? Take off. You know you want to," she shot back. The two of them were just as opposite as they had been when he'd broken off their fling and taken off five months ago. Nothing had changed. Neither one of them was different. Okay, that part wasn't exactly true or fair. Cadence was different. She put her hands protectively around her belly. "It must feel awfully hot in here to you."

"You're trying to make it that way." He had a lot of nerve blaming her.

"I'm sorry that you're finding out this way. This is not what I had planned. None of this was on my agenda, actually. But the only thing a pregnancy does is make us parents, Rory." She blew out a breath. This wasn't the way she'd intended for him to find out and emotions were already running too high. Someone needed to have some common sense, and they both needed to cool it for a minute before her blood pressure careened out of control. "I need a drink."

He shot her a look that dared her to have a glass of wine.

"Of water." She stormed past him, needing to break the bad energy in the room. She stomped down the hallway, into the kitchen, and stopped in front of the fridge after grabbing a glass from the counter. She filled it while he made himself at home with the coffeepot. And then she whirled around on him. "What are you really doing here, Rory? I know you didn't come to see me."

"You're in danger," he said.

"That's not answering my question," she shot back. "You couldn't have known that until you arrived."

"Your brother called and offered me a job. I need the money," he said.

Dalton and Dade walked into the kitchen, both stopped and stared at Cadence.

"I'm pregnant," she said to her twin brothers, watching as their jaws fell slack.

"Hold on a second," Dade said, looking like he was trying to absorb the news. It also seemed to dawn on him that this was the reason she'd objected to their calling in Rory for the job.

"You two?" Dade looked from Cadence to Rory and she was pretty sure she saw a look pass between her brother and Rory. Shock? Anger? Betrayal?

This was exactly the reason she'd wanted to keep their fling quiet. She hadn't needed her brothers weighing in on her love life and they'd been close with Rory growing up. He'd wanted to tell them but she'd known better than to clue them in. Seeing the look of guilt on Rory's face now had her questioning her judgment.

"I didn't know anything about the pregnancy until ten minutes ago but I take full responsibility," Rory said with a look of apology toward her brothers. He was trying to do the right thing by her and she could appreciate the act of honor. She was also realistic enough to know that a forced marriage wouldn't make either one of them happy; she'd seen what could happen when two people had children who didn't love each other. "I asked her to marry me but she turned me down."

"Why would you do that?" Dalton asked Cadence.

"My personal life is off-limits to you and you." She pointed her finger at each brother individually in case they didn't get it that she was talking about both of them.

Dade started to argue but Dalton stopped him with a hand up.

"We have a bigger issue to deal with right now," Dalton said.

Ella joined them with an awkward look at Cadence's bump. What was that all about? She knew her sister wasn't making a moral judgment. Dalton was right. There was another pressing problem to address.

"My family filled me in on what's happening on the land with poachers. I get that someone's on the land that we need to get rid of but I thought you didn't want the job," she said to Rory.

"Not *you* as in the family. I mean *you* as in," he motioned toward her with his hands. "*You* personally."

"What happened?" Dalton said as her brothers closed ranks around her. "And she's right. You refused the job. So what are you doing here?" There was more than a hint of aggravation in his voice. Again, Cadence would deal with her family later. This was exactly the reason she didn't want to be in Cattle Barge in the first place. Her siblings had always acted more like parents to her and she was a grown woman.

"I thought it would be best if no one knew I was working or in the area. That's the reason I refused the job. I had every intention of helping, paid or not. I hope you know I'd do whatever it took if any one of you needed me." He had a long history with the family and was the same age as the twins. As their little sister, she'd trailed behind on their adventures, wanting to be included, but she had been so young. She had known Rory and vice versa for ages and that was exactly the reason Cadence knew a real relationship with Rory would never work. He craved independence a little too much to be tethered by a family of his own. She'd known it from the beginning and that was probably half the fun of spending time with him. He was untamed and untamable much like the land. There was a certain beauty to that freedom, which she admired.

Just like a too-wild horse, putting a saddle on it broke its spirit. She didn't have the heart to do that to Rory.

Cadence had always been drawn to a challenge. She couldn't regret the pregnancy, not since she felt her children's first movements, but that didn't mean the situation wasn't complicated. But losing her father and the subsequent attacks on her siblings had given her a new respect for how quickly everything could be taken away from her. She was learning to appreciate every day and embrace the adventures life brought.

Rory stood there in the family kitchen and she couldn't deny that he still looked good—damn good. It was probably hormones making her weak, making her notice the sexy dark stubble on his chin. He'd always had rugged good looks and she'd tried to forget how handsome he was. Dark hair, dark eyes. He was intense. About everything. Including making love. Especially making love.

A trill of awareness skittered across her skin at the memories.

Lot of good thinking about that would do.

She tuned back in as he was explaining the campsite he'd come upon. There was an animal, a beagle, which he'd brought with him and was now in the sleeping quarters with the ranch hands.

"Why is he out there and not in here?" Cadence asked a little too forcefully.

"I have no idea if Boots is housebroken and I couldn't leave the poor thing alone on the land with all the coyotes," Rory said.

"I wasn't suggesting you should leave him out there." She swept her hand toward the backyard.

Rory started to speak but cocked his head to the side and compressed his lips.

"The rifle was trained on the house and when I checked the scope it was aimed at Cadence's window," he said, glancing at the open shutter. He moved to the double doors that led to the patio and started closing blinds.

Dalton smacked his flat palm against the counter and grunted a swear word before joining Rory.

"It would be a tough shot but it's possible with a high-powered rifle," Dade said after a thoughtful silence. He muttered a few choice words under his breath as he worked to close the blinds in the great room.

Ella stared at the granite countertop. "We need to let security know what's going on. They'll want to take action against the threat."

"Good idea. But keep in mind a trained shooter can hit a target from quite a distance and Landry didn't find the guy. I did," Rory supplied. "A professional would know to account for wind and velocity as well as other variables, even with a difficult shot."

"We need to call the sheriff," Ella said.

"Already did."

"How about the guy? Did you get a good look at

him?" Cadence asked. The horror of what was going on started sinking in.

"Yes." He provided a description. "Do you know who he is?"

"Not off the top of my head." Cadence searched her brain. Surely, she'd seen the guy before.

"Which means Cadence doesn't go anywhere," Dalton said with a look toward her. "Agreed?"

"Are we sure someone is after *me*?" She couldn't fathom the thought, even though, to be fair, several of her siblings had been targeted since their father's death. With the reading of the will coming up, everything could be stirring up again.

"I can't think of who would want to hurt you but I'm giving Terrell the description of him so he can alert the others and keep watch for the guy," Ella said. She was already texting.

"I'm guessing that you're limiting access to the ranch based on recent events," Rory said.

"That's right," Ella supplied.

It was probably just because she needed to eat but Cadence was dizzy and felt a bout of nausea coming on. This couldn't be right. She'd been in Colorado for months now and had hoped to return the minute the will was read. This definitely wasn't the time to tell her family that she had plans to move to Colorado on a permanent basis but Cattle Barge was proving to be unsafe for a Butler. She realized she'd been touching her stomach without noticing it. The move was becoming habit. She was already attached to the little people inside. "I'm not saying that we shouldn't take every precaution but the wind could've moved the gun. I mean, it's cold and windy outside and I don't even think anyone knows I'm home."

"Good. Let's keep it that way. Maybe this guy was aiming at a random room and it had nothing to do with you personally," Rory offered. There was enough hope in his voice to make Cadence believe he still cared about her. At least in general terms, and he probably cared even more now that he knew she was pregnant with his child. This didn't seem like the time to tell him she was having twins.

He might've made it clear that he wasn't the settling-down or parenting type when she'd thrown caution to the wind and had the fling she'd craved—or was it excitement? Who could tell anymore? Point being, he didn't want the responsibility of a family and she hadn't planned on any of this happening, either. There they were. Stuck in a situation and now it seemed that her life was on the line.

"WHAT KIND OF rifle did you say he had?" Dalton asked.

"M40." One look at Cadence—at the hurt Rory had caused her—was all it took for him to know Maverick Mike Butler had been right. Rory was bad for Cadence. The senior Butler had given Rory a job on the ranch when he was destitute with the condition that Rory stayed away from his daughter. He must've seen the way Rory had looked at Cadence then. He'd given his word—and that was all he had to give at the time because he was poor—that he'd leave her alone. As soon as he came to his senses during their fling, realizing that Cadence would always be a Butler and he would never be the man she needed him to be, he'd done what he should've long ago and cut her loose.

At the time, she'd told him it was fine with her. She'd been convincing and he'd believed her. Until now. Until he saw the hurt deep in her eyes that she was trying to cover with anger. Until he realized she was hurting because of his rejection.

She could literally have any man she wanted. If Rory lived to be a hundred and ten years old he wouldn't understand her. Her express rejection of his marriage proposal had him scratching his head and more than a little offended. He knew he was broken, but did she have to rebuke his offer so fast? Did she have to cut him down so quickly? He also couldn't understand why she didn't seem to want protection and especially while she was in such a fragile state. He almost laughed out loud. Cadence fragile? Pregnant or not, she'd always been a firecracker. Although, judging from the looks of her determination and everything he already knew about her, she didn't seem at a disadvantage in any way shape or form, no matter the obstacle.

In fact, she seemed like even more of a force to be reckoned with now that she was carrying a child. *His child.* The fact that he was going to have a baby hadn't really absorbed yet. Maybe when this whole scenario was over and the Butlers were out of danger, he could consider what was going on. Laser focus and the ability to shut everything else out had kept him alive so far.

Besides, how could he feel good about bringing a little person into the world with his messed-up background? His parents were the epitome of explosives and an agitator. Those two fought like cats and dogs, if cats and dogs were venomous creatures. The only person he'd been close to growing up had been his sister and he hadn't seen her since he was fifteen. She'd taken off the minute she'd turned seventeen and never looked back. Back then, there was very little social media and Rory wasn't the type to be online anyway. Hell, he still wasn't. His smartphone didn't even have email loaded. It had the capability but he'd never felt like he needed to be reached that badly.

Dade and Dalton had been like brothers. Rory had been friends with the Butler twins, Cadence's brothers, since they were all knee-high, and being close to a tight-knit family—at least from the perimeter—had been one of the best experiences. It had almost given him hope that he could have that someday, too. And that thinking was what had gotten him into bed with Cadence in the first place. It was also the line of thinking that had had him imagining everything would magically work out.

Wishing was for kids with quarters standing in front of fountains.

The look of betrayal in Dade's and Dalton's eyes was a knife to the chest. Rory deserved it.

He clued back into the conversation going on around him when he heard the words *it could be the same.*

"I mean, the guy, or person, who shot our father had the same kind of rifle," Ella said.

"It's one of the most popular rifles around." Rory didn't say that it was popular with criminals.

"But we can't rule it out," Ella continued.

"Not without a ballistics report," Dalton interjected.

Ella locked eyes with her sister. “Don’t take this the wrong way, but have you pulled any of your stunts lately?”

Cadence folded her arms across her chest. “Do I look capable of doing anything besides eating and sleeping?”

Ella turned to Rory after another quick glance at her sister. “I’m sorry about what happened to you earlier with our security.”

His hands were already up to stop her before she could say anything else. “You have to be careful and no one expected me.”

“We didn’t suspect you of anything. You know that, right?” she continued.

“Of course not.”

“Then will you stay on?” Ella asked. Cadence grunted.

“And where will I go?” she asked.

“Right here.” Ella must’ve caught on to the fight she was about to get from her younger sister because she threw her hands up. “I realize the plan is not without complications. But now that security has seen Rory and presumably the man who wants one or all of us dead has, too, we need all the extra help we can get around here.”

Cadence started to speak but Ella shot her a severe look.

“Our dad’s will is going to be read in five days and the town is already starting to work itself into a frenzy about a big revelation in the will. Maybe the guy who aimed a gun at this house has something to lose,” Ella continued. She moved toward the coffee machine. “I doubt I’ll sleep tonight and work is good for feeling anxious. I'll throw on a fresh pot. Is anyone hungry? I could cook something—"

"I appreciate the offer but I'm better off sleeping out there." Rory motioned toward the ranch hands' bunkhouse. He didn't feel right sleeping in Maverick Mike's house, knowing that the man wouldn't want him there. It seemed wrong and that might be twisted logic considering Cadence was pregnant. But Maverick Mike was gone and Rory wanted to respect the man's wishes as if he were still alive.

"No way," Ella protested.

Cadence issued another grunt and her frustration shouldn't have made him want to chuckle. He suppressed the urge, figuring he'd only make matters worse.

"At least stick around long enough to help us come up with a plan," Ella said.

Rory noticed that Dade and Dalton had been mostly quiet so far. They had to realize he'd had no idea about the pregnancy. But he'd betrayed their friendship by not telling them about his relationship with their sister.

When they were young, Cadence had been the annoying little sister. Dade and Dalton had refused to let her hang around. If they had, Rory might've viewed her like a younger sister, too. He'd felt a brotherhood with the twins that hadn't extended to Ella and Cadence since he hadn't been close with the girls. Mr. Butler had made damn sure his daughters hadn't had anything to do with the hired hands. But the boys had been like brothers. More guilt nipped at him thinking about it.

And then there was Cadence.

She sure as hell didn't seem to want him underfoot based on the way she stood there alternating between touching the growing bump and fisting her hands at her sides when she looked at him. Did she realize how much danger she was in? Did she know he had no plans to leave until she was safe?

The idea of becoming a father crashed down on him while looking at her.

Dammit, she looked even more beautiful.

"If I'm the target and it's only me this person is after, doesn't it make more sense for me to leave the ranch so everyone else will be safe?" Cadence asked after a thoughtful pause. "What if he confuses me for Ella and she accidentally gets shot in my place. I'd never be able to forgive myself if a bullet meant for me hit her."

Ella swiped at a tear, clearly getting emotional over her sister's revelation. "That's not going to happen."

Even so, Cadence had a point. Plus, security had been compromised on the ranch. The place wasn't set up for attacks on the Butlers. Poachers, yes. And there was general security at the main house. The guard shack in front and foot patrols kept away the kinds of threats they normally faced. But there'd been several attempts on Butlers in recent months and although thankfully everything had worked out, that didn't mean their luck would hold. Mr. Butler had been murdered on the ranch and the killer had been crafty enough to get away with it so far.

Looking at Cadence, it was clear to Rory that she had an idea of just how much danger she was in. Although, she looked to be taking everything in and considering possibilities.

"Where would you go?" he asked her.

"I'd be safer anywhere but here in Cattle Barge,

where everyone knows our business and every move we make." It was clear that she was building up to something.

"What did you have in mind? Europe?" Getting her as far away from the ranch as possible didn't sound like the worst possible idea. Especially if it meant he could keep her out of the line of fire until he figured this out.

"I was thinking more like Colorado," she said.

"Why would that be safe?"

"Correct me if I'm wrong but I've already been there for months, ever since Dad…" Her voice broke. "And no one has tried to do anything to me so far. It's clearly safer for me there, which also raises the question, if this person was after me in the first place, why come here?"

More good points.

"I'll give you that the person might not've known you'd be coming home. Maybe he was watching until you did," Rory argued. "There's something to be said about going back to Colorado and possibly being safer, except that it would be easy to follow you now that he's found you. I don't think it's worth it to travel all the way there. But believe me, this is a win in his mind even if I threw off his immediate plans. He knows where you are. Could he have known when to expect you?"

"I doubt it," Cadence said.

"Have there been any new hires on the ranch recently? Anyone who could've tipped this guy off?" Rory continued.

"No one knew I was coming home except for my family, our lawyer and May," Cadence supplied. "I trust every one of those people with my life."

"Agreed," Rory said. The family lawyer, Ed Staples,

was like an uncle to the Butler siblings and May, the housekeeper, had been a surrogate mother.

Rory needed to think. He paced around the kitchen.

"We could let this guy know where you'd be," he said.

"Why would we do that?" Ella quipped.

"Let him finish," Dalton said. It was the first sign of support since the news of his relationship with Cadence had been revealed earlier.

"Maybe there's a way to make a big deal out of pretending you've come home. Set up a time and place the guy thinks you'll be somewhere while I sneak you away from the ranch."

"We could throw a baby shower," Ella interjected. "Pretend that you're here and it's happening tomorrow."

"That's a solid possibility," Dalton offered. "Word travels fast in Cattle Barge."

"How soon can I leave?" Cadence asked.

"Out of an abundance of caution, you should go soon," Ella said. "If someone's trying to get to you, I don't want to risk your life or add strain to the pregnancy."

Dade, who had been quiet up until now, stepped forward. "The only way I'll agree to this is if Rory goes with her."

"Hold on a minute," Cadence defended. "I'm old enough to make my own decisions and I don't need the family to—"

"I know you won't put you or your child's life in danger by rejecting help," Dade said sternly. And Rory could almost see the hairs on Cadence's neck stand on end.

She was gearing up for battle and the stress couldn't be good for her or the baby she was carrying. He needed to have a serious sit down with her once this storm blew over and figure a few things out, but for now, he needed to find a way to keep her calm.

"If she's good with me helping, I'm all in. I'm more than willing to offer assistance but not without her agreement," Rory said, although he fully believed that he had every right to make sure his child and its mother were safe. "The last thing she needs is more stress and I've already caused enough by showing up."

She stared him down like a prizefighter from across the ring. Her arched brow gave away that she was trying to figure out his game. He didn't have one. All he wanted was for Cadence to be safe and he was the best man for the job.

"I'm leaving," Cadence stated. "I'm perfectly capable of taking care of myself and the last thing I need is a babysitter."

Surely, there was some way to change her mind. Looking at her right then with her determined gaze and jutted chin, Rory feared there wasn't.

"Forget it. She's too stubborn," he said.

# Chapter Five

To Cadence, this situation was no different than the time Dade and Dalton had stepped in between her and Granger Peabody on the playground. Standing up for her was fine, appreciated even, but they'd steamrollered right over Granger when the two of them were only playing and hadn't listened to her when she'd tried to reason with them to let them know he wasn't hurting her. The two had been playing Damsel in Distress and he was the villain.

Granger had been a friend until her brothers warned him to stay away or else. The ten-year-old boy wouldn't have anything to do with her after that and it had been a lonely rest of the year. Fifth grade had spiraled into sixth when the twins had knocked the tooth out of the first boy who'd kissed her.

Granted, he hadn't had permission but she'd been prepared to stand up for herself and not look like someone who couldn't take care of herself.

Instead of being her saviors, they'd turned into her worst nightmares. Because of them she'd been teased her entire life for not being able to fight her own battles. That was one of the many reasons she wanted to live in Colorado and not Texas. Her heart would always be with the land and her family roots but no one felt the need to stand up for her in Colorado. She was free to live without the burden of the family name. And, yes, Maverick Mike Butler's name—and reputation—certainly traveled with her, but he was too big for life in Texas, making it impossible to step out of his shadow.

Her brothers were too overbearing here and she could only imagine how much more protective they'd be of her babies. Especially since she'd be bringing them up on her own.

When she was on her first date, both of her brothers had shown up at the movies and sat on either side of her and Rickie Hampton. Exactly what did they think she was going to be doing in public at the theater on Main Street? Kiss? It had been bad enough that Rickie had had to go through a security gate in order to pick her up. Talk about the death of a social life. Everyone believed the Butlers thought they had their noses in the air anyway and she guessed their sticking together hadn't helped much. No amount of Ella's volunteering had made a hill of beans difference. People thought what they wanted despite all evidence to the contrary.

Cadence had learned that lesson the hard way. The few friends she'd made had been using her, believing there'd be some kind of benefit to being a Butler friend. School had been lonely. Dade and Dalton had had each other. She knew the twins and Ella loved her, but smothering her wasn't the same as being close.

To Cadence, having her family following her every move—well intentioned as it might've been—had been suffocating. Madelyn and Wyatt were welcomed additions now that Madelyn had forgiven Cadence for her childish behavior when her newfound sister had first come to town after being summoned by the family lawyer.

"There's just one problem with our plan," she finally said.

"And that is?" Ella asked.

"No one is going to believe a baby shower being set up in a few hours," Cadence said.

Rory nodded. "He'll see right through that."

"There's something else we could use, though," Cadence said. "The will." She referred to the stipulation that it be read on Christmas Eve with the entire family present.

"If all of you are in the same place at the same time it'll be easy to strike and take down more than just Cadence," Rory said.

Ella paced as the twins nodded in agreement.

"How about this?" Ella finally broke through the quiet of the last few minutes. "What if we send out word that the will is going to be read tomorrow night instead?" She checked the clock on the wall. "Make that tonight."

"Is there time to set that up?" Cadence asked.

"We'll let it leak online and then it'll get picked up as gospel. We all already know everything we say and do gets reported," she said, looking to her brothers and then Ella. "Even when it's wrong."

Dade's eyes perked up. "It could work. Tell the right source. Set up a fake meet up and see what happens."

"Cadence would be far away," Rory interjected.

"But no one has to know that," Ella said.

Cadence had to admit the idea might just work. The faster the sheriff caught the man targeting someone in the family—her?—the quicker she could come clean about her future plans to her siblings. She might have a temper and make decisions she sometimes regretted after acting in the moment, but she wasn't a liar. Keeping secrets from the family didn't feel right. Everything they'd been through since losing their father had made them even closer. *Father.* She couldn't even think about him without a lump forming in her throat. What would he have thought about twin baby girls for grandchildren? She rubbed her belly again without thinking about it.

Although Maverick Mike Butler had a wild streak a mile long, he'd become more even keeled as he aged. Getting older had been nice on him. He'd worn his years well and seemed to settle into his personality more. Like there was more softness about him and less to prove. He'd confided in her that he had an announcement to make to the family. She'd suspected he was going to tell everyone that he wasn't going to be a bachelor much longer.

Her idea to move to Colorado permanently had hit her after talking to her father. Give him and the rest of the gang at Cattle Barge up and make a life for herself in Colorado. She wished she'd told her father about her plans. Was it weird that she still wished for his approval?

"If this is going to work we need to get Ed Staples involved," Ella said, pacing around the kitchen island.

"True," she said.

Dade stood at the island while Dalton put on another pot of coffee.

"Let's start planning." Dade pulled his phone from his pocket and set it on the counter. "Now, who should we tell in order to spread the word fastest?"

"That's easy," Ella said. "We'll start with the *News-Now!* reporter, Cameron-something, who's been hiding inside almost every bush I've walked past for months on end."

"Won't he question suddenly having a real story fall in his lap?" Dade asked.

"I doubt it," Ella said on a sharp sigh. "He's hungry for any piece of information he can get on us. He won't question the source, especially when the information will come from a Butler."

Dalton rocked his head in agreement, a look of disdain darkening his features.

"We haven't talked about this yet, but is there anyone you can think of who would want to scare you, Cadence?" Dalton poured a cup of coffee for himself and offered one to Rory.

"No," she admitted as Rory took the cup from her brother. She really was clueless as to who would want to hurt her. "I haven't even been in Cattle Barge since Dad's murder and I kept a low profile in Colorado. I doubt anyone could've tracked me there."

Rory issued a grunt noise.

"What's that supposed to mean?" She whirled around on him.

"I knew where you were and when you left," he said, and then it seemed to dawn on him that he'd revealed he'd been watching her.

"How good can you be at your job, Rory? You didn't even know I was carrying your child." She regretted the insult as soon as she hurled it. "Look, I didn't mean that. I'm just saying—"

It was too late. Rory had already stalked out back and slammed the door behind him.

"I WASN'T TRYING to upset you," Cadence called after Rory, stopping him in his tracks.

He immediately backpedaled as he glanced around. It was pitch-black outside save for the light above the barn door and another at the back porch. "Are you crazy or just trying to put yourself in harm's way?"

"What?" A look of confusion knitted her brows.

"Anyone could be hiding in the tree line. Get back inside, Cadence."

She looked like she was about to mount an argument but then her gaze darted around toward the darkened areas of the yard. Much to his surprise, she turned tail and headed back inside. He followed her.

The kitchen had cleared out, which was good. He didn't want to say what he had to in front of her siblings no matter how close he was to her brothers.

"A lot has happened and you should probably think about getting some rest," he started and before she could become indignant, he held up his hands in surrender and said, "I'm not telling you what to do. Do what you want. It's a suggestion."

Her heart-shaped lips bowed. "I didn't take it the wrong way." She stopped short of saying *this time*. But he'd take it. At least she didn't look ready to hurl a coffee cup at him. He'd call that progress.

He'd also seize on the good will.

"I don't want you anywhere around the fake reading of the will," he admitted.

Did she realize how much she cradled her stomach?

Rory battled against the strong urge to protect her. He'd only push her away. Cadence's independent streak had always been longer than the Rio Grande. She might be stubborn but she wasn't stupid.

"You're right."

He almost performed a double take. Was she agreeing with him? Did she have another agenda that she was about to lay down?

"I know you want to go back to Colorado. Promise you won't make that decision without at least letting me know before you leave?" he asked.

She blew out a breath. "Believe it or not, I'm not trying to make any of this harder than it already is, Rory."

Somehow, he doubted that. But he didn't want to send her blood pressure up again, so he didn't comment. "Does that mean you'll discuss your plans with me before you act?"

She cocked an eyebrow. She looked good standing there in the kitchen. Even better than he remembered and that was saying a lot. Was it the pregnancy making her skin glow? He'd heard horrible things about what pregnancy did to a woman's body and yet it sure as hell looked good on Cadence.

His fool heart squeezed at the thought of her having his child. First, he had to get them both out of danger.

"You have a right to know where I am."

He bit back the argument that said he'd had a right to know about the baby from day one but she hadn't exactly shared that information until she was forced to. In fact, if he hadn't shown up, he would still be in the dark. But all he cared about right now was finding the guy who'd called himself Dex.

"Dalton asked about anyone you can think of who might be upset with you," he continued. "Have you thought of anyone? This guy said his name was Dex but he'd be an idiot to use his real name and he didn't strike me as naive." The whole camping scene had been set up to look like Dex was a less-experienced outdoorsman. The guy was better than Rory had initially given him credit for because he'd slipped out of Rory's reach.

"Seems like having Butler for a last name is enough to put me on the wrong side of a rifle scope," she said with a frown. "But no one comes to mind."

"Fair enough," he said, feeling her frustration peel off her in waves. "Until we figure it out, you'll need to keep a low profile."

"Understood." She pinned him with her stare. "What's going to happen to Boots?"

He gave a noncommittal shrug.

"Dex was obviously using him as a decoy, so there won't be anybody looking for him. I'd like to keep him here at the ranch if you don't want him," she said, and he couldn't figure what she'd want with the little dog.

Rory had only briefly considered keeping the puppy for himself. Taking the dog on the range while tracking poachers wasn't the best-case scenario for the dog or Rory. A wrongly timed bark could put Rory in grave danger. He'd be no good to the dog dead. Rory's life was smoother if he traveled alone.

Plus, a home with Cadence would offer far more stability than anything Rory could propose. This was the first thing they'd agreed on since the baby bomb had been dropped just hours ago. Rory still hadn't wrapped his mind around being a father. Figuring out the rest that came along with it was going to be a slow climb. As far as the dog went, he could give her that. "Okay."

What was up with the empty feeling that overcame him at the thought of giving up Boots? It wasn't like he had enough time to train a dog or the lifestyle to support one. Sure, Boots was cute but Rory couldn't have truly bonded with the animal in such a short time. A voice reminded him that he'd always wanted a dog and that was most likely the reason for the melancholy that wrapped around him at the thought of giving up Boots.

He looked at Cadence, who was staring him down, and he could tell that she was trying to figure out what he was thinking.

Ella broke the moment when she entered the kitchen. She froze as though she realized she might've been walking in on something.

His talk with Cadence was progress and Rory would take any ground he could gain with her. Another pang of guilt took a swipe at him for leaving her to deal with the pregnancy on her own this long. If he'd stuck around, he would've known.

"I had to wake a few people up, but everything's been set up for—" she glanced at the wall clock "—noon today."

Rory glanced at the same clock. That didn't give him much time. He locked on to Cadence's gaze, trying not to think about the way her silky skin goose bumped when he skimmed his lips across that spot on her hip, the one on her right side. Or the sexy mewl she made when he slid his tongue over her stomach and then across her bare breasts. *Good job, Scott. Way to be strong.* He cleared the frog in his throat before meeting Cadence's gaze again. Her face was flush, which almost made him wonder if she was thinking about the same things. No. Definitely not. She was probably just having a hot flash, or whatever pregnant women had when they wanted to strangle the man standing across the kitchen island from them. "I know I said you'd better rest but now I'm thinking you should pack a few things instead."

"You're right." Again, he was caught off guard when she didn't argue. "I'll be back in a few minutes."

Rory turned to Ella. "You might want to get a few hours of sleep, too, before everything goes down."

"I doubt if I could," she said. "I'm not feeling well from all this stress and I don't want to wake up Holden."

He'd heard about her husband. Holden seemed like a good guy. Rory could see himself going fishing or having a beer with him. Of course, now that news about his and Cadence's so-called quiet fling was out, no Butler or Crawford would ever trust him again.

Ella moved to the fridge and pulled out a ginger ale.

"Congratulations, by the way," he said. "I hear you and Holden got married over Thanksgiving."

She smiled. "Holden's leaving for Virginia tomorrow. He has a few things to take care of back home."

"I was hoping to meet him and shake his hand." It seemed like everyone was coupling, finding happiness.

"He'd like that," Ella said.

Rory figured family life was in the cards for some.

Not him.

His collar tightened just thinking about settling down. He tugged at it but it didn't loosen. He glanced around, wondering if someone had turned the heat up.

"You okay, Rory?" Ella asked. She walked over to him and zeroed in.

No. He felt like he was going to pass out. But he wasn't about to admit to her the idea of becoming a father made the air whoosh out of his lungs and the room shrink. Or maybe it was just the thought of marriage doing that to him.

"Fine."

"TELL ME WHAT you need and I'll get it for you," Rory offered, and it immediately occurred to Cadence why he would say that. The feeling of being hit by a bus slammed into her. The rifle had been trained on *her* window. There was a shooter out there who wanted to put a bullet in *her*. The depth of those statements was starting to sink in. She wasn't as concerned about herself as she would've been six months ago, which seemed strange. Times had changed. She had other lives depending on her. The thought that anything could happen to her babies almost knocked her back a step.

Anger shot through her and she could only imagine how much stronger her protective instincts would become once the twins were born and she held them in her arms. For a half second she thought about telling him there were two babies. Deep down, she feared it would be too much for him. That he would get spooked and take off again.

Rory would be protective of them, too.

Would he fight her for custody? She'd been immature before. Made big-time mistakes. Would Rory use them against her in court?

"Cadence." Rory snapped a finger near her ear.

"What?"

"I asked about your things. What should I pack for you?" he asked with a concerned look.

"Oh. Right." She shook her head as if that could get rid of the bad feeling. "I'll go with you."

He seemed reluctant to agree.

"I'll stand at the door far away from the window," she said.

His lips compressed into a thin line, which was a sign of anger for most people but it meant she was making progress with Rory.

"All right," he finally said, turning on his heel.

It didn't take long to pack, considering Cadence hadn't completely unpacked yet. Still, she only wanted to take a change of clothes and a few bath products. Rory placed them in her old backpack from high school that was in her closet, saying it would be easier to carry them around this way. He added that it would also be easier to slip out unnoticed.

"So, what's the plan exactly?" she asked.

"Mr. Staples is coming through the front gate at around eleven forty-five. There'll be a slew of activity out there as his car arrives. Ella plans to be in the front, looking like she's finishing decorating. We'll slip out the back. There'll be a four-by-four waiting for us."

"Sounds easy enough," she admitted.

"But then we're going off road toward the east side

of the property," he said. "Think you'll be okay going over a few bumps?"

She rubbed her belly. "I guess so."

"Don't worry. I'll take it as easy as I can," he said. "The four-by-four vehicle will get us to farm road 12 where a vehicle is parked."

"What about Dex? Think he found it?" she asked.

"We'll see when we get there." He zipped her pack and threw the strap over his shoulder. "Ready?"

She was so ready to get out of there. Being at the ranch without her father was hard. The events of this morning had distracted her but nothing felt the same without Maverick Mike Butler around.

Waiting for the right moment to slip out the back door seemed like it took an eternity. She'd eaten and thrown a few protein bars in her backpack to tide her over just in case. It seemed like she was always hungry these days since she was eating for three.

A small group of ranch hands went out every day on four-by-fours to check fences and keep an eye on the herd, so she and Rory joined the caravan that split in opposite directions once they cleared the barn.

Her nerves were frayed thinking that Dex or someone might be out there, waiting for them. An ambush could easily be set up even with all the precautions they were taking.

And then there was Rory. Being in close contact wasn't a good idea. Her body seemed to remember all the nights they'd spent together and ignored her brain that was telling it to cool its jets. There was something about pregnancy hormones that made her crave sex even more once she'd gotten over the initial hump of wanting to vomit on everyone. Hormones were strange.

Wrapping her arms around Rory reminded her how easy it was to be with him and how built he was. Then there was the excitement of keeping their fling to themselves, telling no one about their relationship. It seemed so much purer that way without her family's interference.

Plus, she doubted her father would've approved. He didn't like her seeing hired help socially.

Those endless nights with Rory came rushing back into her thoughts, showering her with memories. Memories of lying there tangled in the sheets, gasping for air, completely happy. Memories of staying up half the night talking. Memories of waking up in his arms the next morning.

Was it the happiest she'd ever been? Yes. She could admit that part to herself. She'd been happy with Rory, which had made his ultimate rejection sting all that much more.

SNEAKING OFF THE ranch as the family lawyer arrived had worked as planned.

"Where to now?" Cadence asked as Rory navigated onto the two-lane highway.

"I have a place on the outskirts of town." Rory's place had always been viewed as his personal haven so he never brought people there. Cadence Butler wasn't exactly "people," considering she was the mother of his child, an annoying voice reminded.

She got quiet and he could only guess his revelation had hit her in a bad place. This was her first visit.

The rest of the ride was spent in heavy silence, like a storm brewing.

The fact that he cared about Cadence's opinion of the small cabin tightened the coil that was already overly wound up in his gut. It was one of the reasons, okay the main reason, he'd insisted they meet up somewhere else when they were together.

She moved from the living room to the dining room, the kitchen and back. He couldn't read her expression. Was she disappointed?

"One bedroom?" she asked and for the first time in probably her life, she sounded nervous.

"All I need," he said a little too quickly. He glanced at her bump and decided the first thing on his to-do list once she was safe was find a bigger cabin or start plans to add a room to this one.

He studied her expression as she took in the place. Frustration nipped at him that he couldn't tell what she was thinking and he sure as hell didn't have any plans to ask. His small cabin wasn't big enough or good enough for someone used to living in a place that looked like some high-end resort. She had people who cooked for her. She'd most likely never cleaned up after herself a day in her life. To say his place was modest would be putting it lightly.

She quirked a smile before taking a seat on the leather sofa.

"What?" he bit out a little harsher than he'd intended. He was frustrated that her approval meant so much to him.

"Nothing." She shrugged, looking offended at his sharp response. "I just didn't expect you to have any furniture."

"That's fair." He smiled. He couldn't help it. "There are dishes, too."

"How about a pillow and a blanket?" She bit back a yawn and when he really looked at her, she had dark circles under her eyes.

"In the other room where I want you to sleep." He motioned toward the door off the living area.

"I'm fine right here. This couch is actually comfortable," she suggested.

"It'll work for me." He walked over to her and offered a hand up.

She didn't take it. Instead, she pushed up to standing and then walked past him.

# Chapter Six

If Rory thought Cadence was incapable of finding a glass by herself he needed to think again.

Even so, she was surprised that his place was so cozy. A corner fireplace made of tumbled stone anchored the living room. A simple mantel consisted of a long darkly stained wood plank. Instead of the obligatory massive flat-screen TV every bachelor seemed to have, Rory had a wall of shelving with keepsakes and a few books.

The place felt so much like him. She didn't want to feel this comfortable at his place. She could also clearly see that his cabin was meant for one—a number Rory liked. She'd been sucked into believing he had real feelings for her once. And for Rory, he probably had. But he could only go so far before he cut himself off from emotions that could make him want to stick around. Now it was her turn to laugh. Rory Scott staying in one place for more than a few days? Now, that was funny.

"Let me know if you need anything," he said from the door.

"Okay." She peeled off her ballet flats, thinking how much water weight her ankles held now. Let her eat one potato chip and they'd swell.

It was nice to climb under the covers. Even though it was early afternoon by now, she was tired. Lack of sleep and pregnancy weren't friends. She immediately drifted off and felt like she'd barely closed her eyes when an urgent-sounding voice shocked her awake.

She tried to mentally shake off the fog and force her eyes open. It didn't work. She had the feeling that came with being in a deep sleep and something jerking her awake. It was like moving in slow motion. She forced her eyes open to confirm what she already knew. It was Rory. He was standing over her, gently shaking her with a serious expression on his face.

"Wake up, Cadence," he said again with more urgency this time. His voice was laced with anger, too.

"What's wrong?"

"Someone followed us." She heard him mutter a string of curse words before glancing at her and apologizing. "Someone's here."

"Where?" she asked, pushing up to a sitting position. And then she heard a noise outside. "Never mind. What do we need to do?"

He set her ballet flats on the bed next to her before locating a fold-up chair from the closet and positioning it against the closed bedroom door.

"Be as quiet as we can," he said in a whisper.

She rubbed blurry eyes in time to see that he was clutching a rifle with his left hand as he checked and then opened the window.

The urgency of the situation hit full force when Cadence heard the wood floor creak in the next room. Her pulse raced and her hands started shaking as she slipped into her flats.

Rory was beside her in the next instant, taking her hand and leading her to the now-open window.

Panic roared through her at what they might find outside. In broad daylight, it would be harder to hide.

Rory helped her out the window before following her in the next heartbeat. It was clear by the stealth and quickness of his movements that she'd wind up holding him back.

He broke into a run toward the thickest part of the trees surrounding the cabin, which happened to be around back. She thought about the angry lines etched in his forehead when he'd spoken to her. Did he resent the fact that she would slow him down?

"Can you run a little faster?" he asked as she heard the back door of his cabin smack against the wall.

"There," a strong male voice said and she didn't dare risk a glance back. She was already having a hard time keeping up.

She struggled for purchase in the slick-bottomed shoes she wore.

Another voice cut through the air and ripped down her spine. The men had seen them and were coming. She pushed harder, ignoring the burn in her thighs.

Throwing everything she had into moving faster, she caught the side of a large rock at an odd angle and rolled her ankle. She tumbled and her first thought was the babies. She prayed they'd be okay as Rory helped her up.

He looked like he had to make a quick decision, help her or keep the shotgun.

With no time to evaluate her injury, he chucked the weapon and they took off running again, this time without her right shoe because there was also no time to hunt for it. Rory was the only thing keeping her upright.

Adrenaline couldn't completely mask the pain pulsing from her right foot as she felt every sharp rock and branch against the pad of her foot.

Whoever was behind them would gain ground if she so much as glanced down to see how bad it was. She could feel a cool liquid running down her ankle and it made her foot slick. She had no idea what she was stepping on…a mix of rocks, branches—creepy bugs?—or who knew what else. Cadence involuntarily shivered at the thought of crunching a cockroach with her bare foot.

A grunt escaped and she felt Rory's hand tighten around hers.

"I'm okay, keep going," she quietly urged, knowing full well he'd stop if he thought this was too much for her. She couldn't afford to be the reason they were caught and especially since someone wanted to put a bullet in her head.

In the thickest part of the trees, she couldn't see twenty feet ahead. She knew that Rory had done that on purpose and yet it slowed them down, too, as they winded through underbrush and weaved through mesquite trees. He started zigzagging and she was pretty sure he'd circled back to where they'd started—it all looked the same to her out there—when a pair of men jumped them from behind a bush.

Instincts from having brothers who loved to wrestle with her when she was growing up caused Cadence to throw up her elbow instead of panic. She connected with the face of a thin but wiry man. Wiry grimaced and then threw his arms around her in a viselike grip. She dropped down and twisted, breaking his hold on her.

Rory was nearby and he lunged at Wiry, knocking him off balance. He looked at Cadence and shouted, "Run."

She hesitated for a second because she didn't want to leave him alone. Plus, her ankle was screaming with pain.

Rory was strong. There was no doubt about his fighting ability. But two against one?

Rory made eyes at her as he pinned Wiry down between his thighs.

She pushed to her feet, almost lost it and fell when a branch jabbed her heel, but powered through enough to run.

A football-player-looking man dove at Rory. He twisted out of the guy's way but he was in for a fight. If she weren't pregnant, she would've stayed to help but she had to put the babies first and that's what Rory wanted.

The voices behind her grew faint until they disappeared. Cadence pushed as hard as she could, considering her right foot felt like it had been shredded.

By the time she located a water source, a creek, she was barely able to make progress on that foot. Pain screamed at her and she was hobbling, grabbing on to anything that would keep her upright.

Cadence plopped onto the earth beside the rushing water. She eased her foot into the stream before flipping off her left shoe and doing the same with it. The cool water soothed her aching feet and gave some relief to her swollen ankle. Both of her feet were filthy and in pain but all she could think about was Rory and keeping her babies safe. She wished she knew what had happened back there after she'd taken off.

Another thought struck. She was alone in unfamiliar territory. She had no idea how to get out of the woods and Rory might not be able to find her.

The creek pooled ten feet downstream and she glanced at the surface for water moccasins. Also called cottonmouths, these snakes were venomous and aggressive, and they seemed to be in every creek or lake in the state of Texas.

She glanced around, scanning the area, aware of being vulnerable to an animal attack unless Wiry and/or Athlete found her first. Was there anything she could use to stand and maybe help her walk? Better yet, was there anything around that she could use as a weapon?

Sticks? Branches?

Those things had done serious damage to her foot already. In fact, she'd have to figure out something because walking with her ankle swollen might not get her very far. Then again, sticking around could put her and her babies in worse danger. Cadence wiped away a tear that sprang at the thought that her babies weren't even born yet and she was already having trouble protecting them. Would she be a good mother? Could she be a good mother when she'd had no examples of one from her own parents?

She might not live long enough to find out.

As she swept her hand over the ground, she made contact with a sizable branch. She pulled it over to her, aware that her muscles were already screaming at her from all the movement and running.

Seemingly out of nowhere, a male figure appeared from behind her. She gasped and spun around to get a better look.

"Rory." Tears sprang to her eyes.

"We have to go," he urged, as he moved next to her and helped her to her feet.

Cadence dug deep to stand and his gaze flew to her bad ankle.

"Did you lose your shoes?" She remembered him being intense before but not so angry. What had happened?

"One is all I have left." She motioned toward the left shoe.

He immediately slipped off his tennis shoes and offered them to her, muttering a curse.

"These are too big." About three sizes in her estimation.

The sound of branches crunching caused her to gasp again. And then there were voices.

"We've got to go." Rory glanced around, and there was a desperate quality to his features that she'd never seen before. *Her fault?*

Feeling responsible for someone else when he had always been such a loner seemed to create a whole new hell for him and his emotions were playing out on his features so clearly.

He slipped her left shoe on before standing and taking her arm to pull it over his shoulder.

"Lean on me." He put an arm around her hip and she ignored the fission of heat that pulsed through her at the contact. This wasn't the time to think about how well their bodies fit together or how intense and satisfying their sex had been. “Will you be okay?”

“Yes. Let’s go.” It wasn’t okay, because angry pulses shot up her leg with every movement, but what was the alternative? Stick around and be killed?

Leaning on Rory, she was able to deal with the pain. She ignored all the electricity vibrating from where they touched, chalking it up to her body remembering how incredible they’d been together in bed. Sizzle and passion may have made for the best sex of her life—and created the two biggest gifts—but it didn’t make two people compatible outside the bedroom. And when she really faced the situation honestly, most of life happened in the other rooms. What good was the hottest sex if it didn’t translate into an amazing relationship?

The fact that he’d been able to sneak up on her without making a sound earlier made her realize just how good he was at his job—a job that was as necessary as breathing to Rory.

She didn’t know how long they’d been running but everything hurt and there was no sign of the men who’d been chasing them.

“Can we stop?” she finally asked, gasping for air.

“Not yet,” he responded with no such sounds of struggle. She’d always known Rory was in tip-top shape; remembering the ripples in his muscled chest wasn’t helping matters in the attraction department. But he wasn’t making any noise breathing. No panting. No gulping air. *Seriously?*

After what felt like an eternity, he finally slowed the pace before stopping. He put his other hand up to make sure she knew to be quiet. She was doing the best job she could under the circumstances, because she hadn't run like that since high school track and she'd been a sprinter, not a pregnant woman who had fallen off her strict exercise routine a couple of years ago. She'd worked the ranch and that had made her strong, but it wasn't the same kind of cardio she needed for this.

Rory crouched low and listened. There was so much intensity to his actions.

She did the same but couldn't hear much over the sound of her own breathing.

Glancing at her feet, pain registered. Her right ankle looked like Shrek's. Her foot had been jabbed by sharp tree limbs and looked angry. She wiped at the blood to reveal fresh cuts oozing more of the red liquid. She had no idea where she and Rory were and no idea how to get out of the woods.

Pain throbbed from her ankle to her hip as adrenaline faltered and she started to shake.

And there was Rory, looking at her like she'd just punched him in the face.

What was his deal?

RORY CURSED UNDER his breath. What good did it do him to have skills if he couldn't keep Cadence and her baby safe?

He dropped down and examined her ankle and then her foot, ignoring the frissons of heat that came with touching her. This wasn't the time to think about those long silky legs wrapped around him as he drove himself home.

A mental headshake loosened the inappropriate image. He missed more than great sex with Cadence.

She was intelligent, fiery and had a sense of humor that had calmed him down even when he was wound tight after a tracking job. To be honest, that had happened more than he cared to admit. A voice reminded him that it was easy for her to be carefree. She had her father's fortune to back her up and hadn't suffered a day in her life. Deep down, he knew that wasn't completely true or fair but he wasn't in the mood to argue with himself.

Getting her and his child to safety was priority number one. *His child. Damn.* That was going to take some getting used to.

"You can lean on me the rest of the way," he offered.

"Okay." She winced as she stood and a fire bolt shot straight through him. None of this should be happening and now he was damn certain the rifle being pointed at her bedroom window was no coincidence. He thought about having to ditch his own shotgun because he hadn't accounted for enough variables. Hell, it was his fault that she was in this position to begin with. His mistakes were racking up.

Leaning her weight against him sent a lot of other feelings he couldn't afford swirling through his body. He gripped her waist a little tighter, noticing how much fuller her hips had gotten because of the pregnancy. It was sexy on her, he thought, even though he shouldn't have allowed himself to notice.

He glanced down at her right foot, noticing the amount of blood. He did the best he could by making a field bandage with his undershirt. Cursing himself again for not having supplies out here might not be productive, but he did it anyway.

At least she didn't have to walk on the foot. She could

lean on him for support and hop on her left. He'd made a critical error in underestimating the enemy. Rory hadn't seen anyone follow them to his place but those two guys must've done just that. It was the only explanation for why they'd shown. But who was after Cadence and why? There were more questions looping through his thoughts. None he had answers to.

After walking for a half hour, she doubled over and took in a sharp breath.

"What happened?" Panic tore through him like a tornado strike.

"Cramp," she said and there was desperation in her voice.

"Has this happened before?" he asked.

She nodded as he supported her weight.

"What do you need me to do?" Rory had never felt so helpless in his life.

Another sharp breath and this time he had to ease her to her knees. She grabbed her stomach as her face turned red. "Do you have cell reception out here?"

He palmed his phone and checked the screen for bars. "No. There's no cell tower out here to pick up a signal on."

Watching her bent over, wincing in pain because of his mistakes, shredded everything inside him.

"I need to get to the ER," she said.

No bars on his cell. She couldn't move with those cramps. Her foot was torn up.

An owl hooted and Rory tried not to put too much stock into the omen. Many local Native American tribes believed it to be a sign of death.

Anger ripped through him. No one was dying on

his watch. He also knew that determination to live was often the dividing line between life and death in a survival situation. He knew Cadence. She would put up one hell of a fight. That spark was part of the reason he had fallen for her. The operative words being *had fallen.* When it came to emotion, he could only get so far before his warning system flared and he pulled back. Of course, his job made sticking around long enough to have a real relationship next to impossible. His feelings for Cadence had caught him off guard five months ago, causing him to retreat. It was most likely familiarity—he had known her since childhood—that had had him falling down the slippery slope of love. Love? Had he loved her?

No. He couldn't have. Rory didn't do that particular emotion.

The owl hooted again, bringing his focus back to Cadence. With her in this state, they'd be traveling even slower than they already were.

"How'd you get away from them?" she asked. "You were outnumbered."

"I know this area better. It gave me an advantage." The guys who'd caught up to them a little while ago were most likely still in the woods searching. It could only be a matter of time before the pair showed up again. These guys were new to the picture.

"Was it the guy from the campsite?"

"Nope." Neither one was Dex and that really threw Rory for a loop. He didn't have time to examine the implications right now, but he'd need to get this new evidence over to the sheriff as soon as possible. Any new information or lead could break this case and possibly Mr. Butler's murder open for Sawmill.

Rory had learned a long time ago that it was best to work with law enforcement rather than against it.

"Hold on," he said to Cadence, easing her to a sitting position.

He scouted the area and located the best tree to climb. Height could give him an idea of what was around and also if the pair of men on their tails were catching up.

Rory didn't doubt his tracking skills but a pregnant woman was not something he'd had to factor in before.

This was one in a long list of signs that reminded him he was in no way prepared for fatherhood.

But he was surprised at how deeply the thought of losing this baby cut into him and the bottomless well of anger that sprang up when he made mistakes that put Cadence and her—*their*—child in jeopardy.

# *Chapter Seven*

"The coast is clear for now," Rory said through gritted teeth. He climbed down from the tree and helped her up. "A few more steps and we'll be near a clearing."

Cadence knew that he was frustrated with the situation and not at her. Although, she wouldn't have blamed him if he were considering how much she was slowing them down.

She was worried about the breath-stealing cramps, about her cut-up foot catching some kind of jungle disease—never mind that she wasn't actually in the jungle—and about never finding their way out of these cursed woods.

Thankfully, Rory seemed to know exactly where they were at every turn and she could see why he excelled at his job.

While she believed they were walking in circles—everything looked the same!—he cut a steady course toward freedom. Her injuries were slowing them down, though. She prayed the men stalking them were lost and far away because if they caught up, there could be more trouble than Rory could handle. In her condition, she was no help whatsoever.

"I don't want to leave you alone but I can hide you in a small cave not too far off the road and go get my vehicle. It'll give you a break from walking and speed up getting you to the hospital."

Just the thought of being tucked into a cave in her state was enough to cause icy fingers to grip her. What would be in there? Spiders? Snakes?

An involuntary shiver rocked her body. Her mouth went dry thinking about it. Then there was poison ivy. She'd learned a long time ago how allergic she was to it and remembered her childhood saying: *leaves of three, let 'em be.*

But what choice did she have?

The cramps were almost nonstop and there'd been no break in the pain pulsing up from that ankle. The worst part was that she couldn't feel the babies move and that scared her more than anything else. She'd had cramps before and her doctor had reassured her that everything was normal. But these felt different. More intense. Or maybe it was just the situation causing them to feel that way.

Cadence was tired, thirsty and she wanted to go home, take a warm bath and go to bed. A good night of sleep always did wonders to help erase a bad day. But this was more than that. Her life was on the line. Her babies' lives were threatened. And no amount of sleep could stop the people stalking her or erase this nightmare.

Since curling up in a ball and throwing her own version of a temper tantrum wasn't an option, she decided to suck it up and not complain.

"There won't be any creepy crawlies in there, right?"

she asked, trying to sound as brave as she could under the circumstances.

"Shouldn't be. I'll double check if it makes you feel better." His steady voice was surprisingly reassuring and kept her nerves at a notch below panic.

"I can't believe I lost my shoe. Sorry to be such a hopeless case in an emergency," she said.

"You're not. You can't help what happened back there and you kept yourself and the child safe. Sometimes things get lost in the shuffle. You should be proud of the way you handled the situation," he said, and there was a hint of admiration in his voice. Or was that something she wanted to hear but didn't exist?

A wave of guilt hit her at not telling him earlier that she was carrying twins. This was definitely not the right time to distract him with the news. It had come as a complete shock to her and she could only imagine what hearing it would do to him.

Rory squeezed into an opening at the base of a small hill that looked like a lump of leaves. The trees in this area were thick enough to make it impossible to see in a straight line. There was a lot of underbrush to cover the opening, which most likely had been created by coyotes. Wolves? Or some other den animal. Okay, Cadence could admit that she was letting her imagination run a little wild.

Nothing inside her wanted to crawl inside the unknown.

Growing up on a ranch had taught her everything she needed to know about scorpions and snakes. With twin brothers, she'd had her fair share of spiders being tossed at her. The boys had grown out of those antics early on, but she still remembered the times when they'd come running at her with some creature in hand. She got the willies just thinking about it and it felt like a hundred fire ants were creepy crawling across her skin, ready to attack at a moment's notice.

But she was determined to do whatever it took in order to protect her babies, even if that meant facing some of her worst fears. Getting from where she was to the den was another issue. Okay, she could do this. Maybe not walk the entire distance with these mind-bending cramps, but she could get to the next tree. It felt like all the blood rushed from her as she sucked in a burst of air and planted her right hand on the tree trunk next to her. She could take one step. She did, pausing after in order to breathe and regain her balance.

Rory emerged from the opening. "Nothing scary in there."

"Great." She took in the distance between them. She could make it to the small boulder two feet in front of her…take another step or two.

"What are you doing? Hold on there," Rory said but it was too late. She made it to her next goal.

"I can do this," she said. So much of her life in the past year had been about taking one step at a time, not looking too far ahead because her head might explode.

The next thing she knew, Rory was beside her. She took in a breath meant to fortify her before taking hold of his outstretched arm.

One more step. She could make it to the mesquite tree near the opening.

Getting inside the small opening was the easy part.

Not letting her imagination run wild was going to take some effort.

"A few more steps and you're there," he said in that low timbre that was so reassuring.

She knew on some level that Rory wouldn't put her in jeopardy. At least not on purpose.

"I'll be back as fast as I can," he promised before his face disappeared. She'd known that he was good at his job before but seeing him in action brought her awareness to a whole new level. She didn't hear one single tree branch break or a hint of Rory's footsteps. He was like a ghost and it was even more apparent to her how much she must've been slowing him down and how much attention she had been drawing with her heavier footsteps. Her right foot felt every scrape, rock and branch.

Rather than focus on the amount of pain she was in, and it was staggering, she decided to recap what she already knew.

There were at least two men after her, three counting Dex.

Why?

Cadence searched her memory to find anything she'd done that could make someone want to take her life. But then, like she'd said before, being a Butler was dangerous and especially while her father's killer was still on the loose. Her siblings had had brushes with criminals and the law. Thankfully, they'd come out on top.

Other than her half sister, Madelyn, Cadence hadn't had a disagreement with anyone recently. Heck, she'd spent the past few months in Colorado, so she really drew a blank as to why she'd be targeted the second she came back to Cattle Barge. It made sense to focus on everyone she knew locally.

She heard footsteps outside the den and immediately knew that it couldn't be Rory. He'd been stealthy before.

Cadence listened.

"Any sign of her over there?" one of the male voices asked in a hushed voice.

"Nope." She recognized the voices as belonging to Wiry and Athlete.

A mind-numbing cramp hit and she bit her bottom lip to stop from screaming. Blowing out a breath was too risky. Fear seized her. What if Wiry and Athlete had gotten to Rory?

She heard the two men stomping around, making so much noise that animals and birds scattered.

Rory must've covered her tracks. Of course he would think of doing that and probably several other things a less experienced survivalist wouldn't. She'd never been more grateful for his skill set because that was most likely the only reason the men weren't walking right over to her and dragging her out of the small den. If hiding had been up to her, she would never have been so clever.

She just prayed she could keep quiet until they moved on.

"Hey, come over here and look at this," one of the men said. She thought it was Wiry but everything had happened so fast earlier she couldn't be certain.

Her heart clutched. Had they found her?

Oh, no. She felt around for a stick or something she could use as a weapon. Even though it was light outside, she couldn't see a thing. It was dark inside the little den and that made it a good hiding spot. Not so great for her nerves as she felt something crawl over her left wrist. *Please don't scream. Please don't scream.* The thought of anything happening to her babies clamped her mouth shut. There was no pain so great that she'd put her little girls in jeopardy.

Slowly, quietly, she focused on taking longer breaths. She breathed in through her nose and out through her mouth like she'd learned in yoga class last year in order to calm her racing pulse.

A few minutes passed and she realized the voices were gone. She listened a little longer, breathing as quietly as she could. More minutes ticked by and she had no idea how long she'd been in there or if it was starting to get dark outside. What time was it anyway? Ever since she'd started carrying a cell phone, she stopped wearing a watch. Not having her electronic devices set her nerves on edge.

Suddenly there was activity at the mouth of the den.

"It's me." There'd never been a better sound than Rory's voice.

Relief flooded her.

"They were here. They almost found me." She grabbed on to his hand and used it to shimmy out of the den. As soon as she was free, she threw her arms around his neck and leaned into him. His body felt so good and warm against hers after lying on the cold ground.

He muttered a curse low and the sound of his voice calmed her racing heart.

"It'll be dark soon. We should move," he finally said. "How are the cramps?"

"They aren't better and they aren't worse. There's

hope in that, right?" The question was rhetorical and when she got a good look at his face, she could see how dark his features had become. Dark with frustration? Regret? Or worry? It was probably just wishful thinking, but she hoped for the latter.

She wanted to know that he cared and told herself it was reduced to primal survival. Offspring of most species had a better chance of survival if the father was involved in their care. But then she thought about lions and bears and how males would kill a cub. She'd seen that on a nature show once while she was nursing a sick stomach early on in the pregnancy.

Rory wasn't like that, her mind reasoned. He'd do whatever it took to protect his own. He'd already demonstrated that. It was her fool heart wishing that he'd done it out of his feelings for her. That he could love her and really be there for her.

She leaned her weight on him as he helped her to the conversion vehicle on the side of the road.

Once inside, she finally felt like she could exhale.

"I have a few emergency supplies, water and ibuprofen," Rory offered.

"Water would be nice," she said.

He rounded the back of the vehicle, popped open the back door and then returned a minute later with a bottled water in hand.

She took the offering before he climbed into the driver's seat and pulled up the nearest hospital on his GPS.

"I hope we're far enough away that no one will recognize me," Cadence said. Getting away from a place had never felt so good as leaving those woods. Emotions filled her and released in the form of hot tears.

She turned her face toward the passenger window, away from Rory and did her best to conceal the tears.

"That'll be tricky. Nurses and doctors have to maintain confidentiality, so even if they realize who you are, they won't be able to tell anyone," he said.

"True." She hoped her name wouldn't leak. "Hitting an out-of-the-way location should keep us out of the paparazzi nightmare. I think they have someone stationed at the hospital, the funeral parlor and every restaurant in the town."

"Since you've been out of town, there aren't a lot of recent pictures of you being posted and hardly anyone knows about the pregnancy," he said.

"Right again. If I see one more picture of me from my high school yearbook, I might scream."

"It's cute." Rory laughed and so did she. Another cramp cut the moment short, but levity felt good and she liked putting a smile on Rory's face.

Puppies were cute. She wanted to be a gorgeous woman in Rory's eyes. He'd made her feel every bit of that and more during their fling.

"First to the ER and then to the sheriff," he said.

"Agreed." Another thought dawned on her. "If the check-in nurse doesn't recognize me, I'd like to give a fake name."

"That's a good point. We can check you in as my cousin, Hailey, from Oklahoma," he said.

"You have a cousin?" She spoke before reason kicked in.

"Of course I have a cousin," he countered and there was a hint of defensiveness in his voice.

"I guess I knew that." She knew it was possible, but Rory had never spoken about his family.

"She's on my mom's side and it wasn't like she came to visit before I took off," he added. "I met her a couple of times when we saw my mom's family around the holidays."

"You never told me what happened with your family. Why did you leave them when you were so young?" she asked.

Rory's gaze intensified on the stretch of road in front of them and he clenched his jaw. "Isn't much to tell."

With that, he put his blinker on and changed lanes.

"Okay then. I'm Hailey from Oklahoma," she said, trying it on to see if it felt natural. Even though she'd known the man next to her for more than a decade, he'd never shared anything about his childhood or his parents with her. It struck her as odd after they'd been intimate that she knew so little about his background. She could tell by his change in posture that the subject was a sore one, so she didn't press. But was it possible to really know a person without knowing where they came from?

Another thought struck. "But what about insurance?"

"I can figure out a payment plan. I'll put the bill in my name and we'll tell the truth. We don't have insurance," he said.

"There's no need to do that." She had a sizable trust and would be inheriting one-sixth of the Butler fortune. There was no reason that Rory should have to struggle to make payments. She wiped away her tears and looked at him when he didn't respond.

Anger practically radiated off him. Was it about the money?

When she really thought about it, her brothers would want to pay if one of them were in this situation. Had she just insulted Rory by not wanting to put him in a financial bind?

"Hospital fees can be really expensive for the silliest things," she continued, and another look at Rory said she was digging a deeper hole.

Why was he so hard to talk to?

ONCE CADENCE WAS checked in to a hospital room and settled Rory needed to get some air. The fact that he had no medical insurance to cover a baby let alone her visit to the ER sat in his stomach as though he'd eaten nails. He'd worked and saved his money, so he had a small stash of cash. From everything he'd heard, babies were expensive and he wouldn't be able to take the risks he took now. The thought of how much his life was about to change almost paralyzed him.

He was in no way ready to bring a child into the world. He'd forgotten to ask Cadence about the due date with everything else going on but it couldn't be too far off. Wasn't pregnancy nine months? She looked to be at least halfway there. Maybe more. Although, he was the last person to be able to calculate a due date.

And how the hell had this happened?

Rory had always been careful. There'd always been a condom because he'd never wanted to be in this position.

Now that he was picking the situation apart, he realized that it wasn't even the unplanned pregnancy that had him twitchy. It was Cadence. She'd been hiding this news from him for months. Sure, he'd ended the fling but didn't she trust him at all?

Granted, he'd been on the range in Wyoming, where he didn't exactly get cell coverage most of the time, but Cadence was resourceful. If she'd wanted to reach him, she could've.

That annoying voice in the back of his head piped up again, reminding him how clear he'd been about wanting space from her. The high truth was that he'd needed her to move on before he did something stupid, like ask her to marry him and force her into a life well below what she was accustomed to. A life that would make her miserable.

The stubborn look in her eyes when she'd told him to go ahead and leave that day five months ago had faltered. Hell, his parents had spent a lifetime making each other miserable in the name of love.

As strange as it might sound, Rory cared too much about Cadence to ever let it come down to that.

Rory wondered if his folks were still together. He hadn't spoken to either of them since taking off at fifteen after one of their world-class brawls. His mother had broken the lamp over his father's forehead, swinging it like a baseball bat after he knocked her into the wall. Drywall had broken her momentum, which had been so intense the wall had given. Picture frames had flown off. The glass in them had shattered long ago. His mother hadn't bothered to replace it. Even she knew it was only a matter of time before the next all-out fight with her husband.

The worst part wasn't witnessing the fight. That was

bad, don't get him wrong. Horrible. And he tensed up thinking about the abuse. But his mother making excuses for her husband after made Rory sick to his stomach. She'd roll up her sleeve to reveal several bruises and tell him that's how she knew his father loved her. She'd said a man wouldn't fight with a woman he didn't have passion for.

Rory had known at a young age how twisted that logic was. He'd tried to convince her, too. But she'd smile at him and tell him that he had a lot to learn about relationships. If that was love, Rory wanted no part.

His sister, Renee, who was two years older than him, had kept him sane during all the screaming matches. When she'd taken off at seventeen years old to follow her musician boyfriend across the country, Rory had seen no reason to stick around at home.

A job on the Butler ranch and a room in the bunkhouse had saved his life and kept him out of serious trouble. Mr. Butler had covered the legal arrangements. Rory's friendship with Dade and Dalton had been a lifeline during his teenage years. And how had he repaid the family? By having a secret fling with Cadence, getting her pregnant and then walking away. Granted, he hadn't known about the pregnancy but he wasn't ready to let himself off the hook.

*Way to go, Scott.*

Sarcasm couldn't make a dent in his frustration with himself. He clenched and released his fists a few times, allowing a blast of frigid air to strike as he walked into the parking lot.

There was no question that he'd do the right thing

by his child. Part of that was going to be getting along with the baby's mother.

Rory made a couple of rounds in the parking lot to burn off his excess energy and focus. Exercise always had a way of clearing the clutter in his mind and helping him find his center.

By the fourth lap, he realized that if he and Cadence were going to get along, the first thing they'd have to do was establish trust.

The fact that she didn't trust him was his fault. He could own that. Because he'd walked out on her and she probably assumed he'd do it again. On the drive over, she'd asked about his background and family. He'd gone quiet on her. The odd thing was that he wanted to tell her. Maybe it was to release some of the frustration and shame that he couldn't fix his home life.

Either way, she needed to know that he planned to be in his child's life and that meant being part of her life.

Damn, it wasn't like he didn't have feelings for her. He could use those to develop a friendship, right? Anything more was too risky with his blueprint for relationships. There was no doubt in his mind that he would never put a hand on a woman. That was without question. Hurting someone in the name of love—as his mother had always tried to make him believe—made even less sense to him.

But every time he tried to talk to Cadence, he ended up frustrating her and the last thing he wanted to do was argue. They'd made a little progress in his vehicle when she'd cracked a joke. But that had barely made a dent in the distance between them.

As it was, she stood on one side of the river and he

stood on the opposite. There had to be a way to build a bridge so they could meet somewhere in the middle and especially for the child's sake. He could admit that being near her brought up old feelings—feelings he'd shoved down so deep that he hadn't thought they existed anymore. Dwelling on them was as productive as putting a Band-Aid over a bullet hole.

Speaking of which, his finances had been on the right track. He'd been taking some risks in order to amass more money. Stupidly, he thought he could find a magic sum in his bank account that would allow him to take care of Cadence in the right way. Taking care of the ER visit might put a healthy dent in his savings account but he'd do whatever was necessary to step up as a father.

A few deep breaths followed by repeating his favorite mantra—*patience, silence, purpose*—to psych himself up and put him in the right state of mind to check on Cadence.

Rory walked back inside the hospital and located her room. He stopped when he heard voices inside. There was a male voice that he recognized as the doctor's from earlier. He didn't feel right intruding, so he stood outside the door and listened, hoping to hear good news. The look on Cadence's face when she was cramping earlier had him worried that something might be wrong with the pregnancy. He couldn't even think about something going wrong with her health.

"I know you said you were worried about the lack of movement in the past few hours but both babies look good..."

*Both?* Did that mean what he thought? *Twins?*

Anger roared through him at the thought that he'd been deceived twice.

First, she'd hidden the pregnancy and then she'd lied to him?

Rory didn't realize he'd started pacing until a concerned-looking nurse stared at him. He cut right and took a few steps down a different hallway so he'd be out of the line of sight of the nurses' station.

Several trips up and down the stairs got his blood pumping and helped stem some of his frustration. Besides, Cadence was already in enough distress. He didn't want to make the situation worse.

He located Cadence's floor and pushed the door open, ramming the metal edge right into a janitor's back.

"Sorry about that," Rory said.

The guy didn't turn and look at Rory. He waved a hand and then took off in the opposite direction in a hurry.

There was something about the interaction that caused Rory's warning bells to sound off.

*Cadence.*

# *Chapter Eight*

Cadence's door was closed and that sent another warning flare soaring high into the sky. The fact that he'd left her alone when he should've stayed put and kept vigil over her punched him. His temper had put her in danger.

Rory muttered a few choice words as he beat feet, wasting no time in getting to her room. His instincts were finely tuned because of his work on the range and those predispositions were screaming at him to get to Cadence.

He blasted through the door in time to see a nurse inserting something into Cadence's IV.

"Stop," he commanded severely. "Step away from her and drop that thing in your hand."

A flash of fear followed by determination darkened the medium height, medium built, brown-haired nurse. "I'm sorry, sir. But you can't be in here."

"Like hell I can't." He darted to the nurse as she tried to sidestep him. He shot a glance at Cadence. "Get that thing out of you."

She sat up with a panicked look on her face as she jerked the IV out of the vein on her right arm.

Rory tackled the nurse and the two of them flew into the side chair.

"Call for help," he shouted to Cadence.

"I hit the panic button as soon as I got a look at your face," she said, and he registered the sound of an alarm coming from the nurses' station. "What should I do?"

He was on top of the brown-haired nurse, pinning her arms to her sides with his thighs. "Can you get dressed?"

"Yes." She immediately moved to get her clothes, walking tenderly on her bad ankle. He saw that she had on some kind of compression boot that was giving her structure and support and he was glad for that at least.

But damn. He'd put her in jeopardy again. She was injured and needed him to be solid for her and all he could think about before was his anger. It was the curse of his parents to put himself first over others in his life and let anger override rational thought.

"Who are you?" he asked Brown-haired.

Before she could respond, a blond-haired nurse popped her head inside the door. "What do you need, sweetie—"

Panic rippled across her features as her gaze swept the room.

"Annalise, are you okay?" The stress in her voice was meant for the nurse on the floor.

"Your friend here just tried to drug my friend," he bit out.

"Help," Annalise said, and he almost wished he had knocked her out so she couldn't talk.

The door closed, the nurse disappeared and Cadence

looked at him with a helpless expression. It was only a matter of time before security showed.

"What do we do now?" Cadence asked.

He'd tell her to run but there was no use. She couldn't get far and Brown-haired would most likely scream. She already was, in fact.

He reared his fist back and looked her dead in the eyes. "Keep it up and I won't hesitate to shut you up myself." The threat was idle but she didn't know that.

Based on the fact that she clamped her mouth shut, she believed him. And that was a relief because nothing inside him could ever allow him to strike a woman.

"What did you put in her IV?" he barked.

Tears sprang from Annalise's eyes. Her lips compressed into a thin line and she shook her head.

Footsteps fired off in the hallway. He was running out of time.

"Annalise, you have one chance to get this right. Tell me why you did this and I won't press charges." She'd have hell to pay for her actions as soon as Administration figured out what she'd put in the IV. "At the very least, you're looking at losing your job and a lawsuit. At the worst, jail."

Annalise's brown eyes widened.

"I'm dressed," Cadence said. "Let's get out of here before everyone comes back."

"We're safe. It's this one who should be worried." He held Annalise's gaze. "That's right. They'll lock you up and throw away the key, Annalise." He could see that he was gaining ground with her. "And I'll testify to exactly what I saw. The evidence supports my story, by the way."

She faltered, her chin quivered, and it looked like it was taking great strength to keep her emotions in check. There was so much fear in her eyes and something else, too. Helplessness?

"I'm sorry." Her gaze bounced from Cadence and Rory. "What have I done?"

"Nothing, because I stopped you," Rory ground out.

"I'm a single mom and he said he'd kill my kids if I didn't put that in her IV." Her desperation caused her chin to quiver again as tears streamed down her cheeks. "It's no excuse but I was so scared."

"Did he say what the substance is?" Rory shouldn't have been shocked when tears streamed down her face but she'd caught him off guard. Her tortured expression punched him.

"No and I didn't ask. How was I supposed to make a choice?" Annalise shook her head. The thought of having to choose between a pregnant stranger in her care and her children twisted her face with guilt. "I didn't want to know."

He could relate to her conflict because he had a similar one going on inside. Hurt a single mother's career when it sounded like she was the only parent to a pair of kids or throw justice to the wind. She wouldn't have done this if not for extreme circumstances.

The door burst open and a man wearing a security uniform barreled into the room. He was middle-aged, his hair a solid white, and Rory could take the man down in a heartbeat if he wanted. Instead, he put his hands in the air. "We don't want any trouble."

"This is a huge misunderstanding, Robert," Annalise said with a glance toward Rory. "I'm okay."

Rory hopped to his feet and held out a hand. She took it in a show of trust. "We don't have a problem here."

"I made a mistake, which caused a problem. None of this is their fault," Annalise admitted as she sat up. She was trying to force even breaths. "I'm one hundred percent to blame for this. I take full responsibility."

Cadence stood in between the security guard and Rory as she mouthed, "It's time to go."

"Hold on, ma'am. That's not advisable." The nurse who'd been standing behind Robert took a step beside him.

"I'm leaving and there's nothing you can do to stop me, so save your energy." Cadence folded her arms and glared at the nurse standing next to the security guard.

As far as security went, Rory couldn't imagine what an overweight fiftysomething man could accomplish. He'd be no match for Rory. But he had no intention of getting into a fight or pushing to see how far the guy would take that stun gun resting in his palm. Robert had come in hot, geared up for a fight. And like a cornered animal, he'd come out fighting.

"It's fine, Meredith," Annalise soothed. "Like I said, totally my fault. I tripped on his shoe and we both fell over. This guy was checking to make sure I was okay before he let me get up. That's all. I'm sorry I yelled earlier. It's under control." Annalise said it like it was nothing, like she was brushing lint off her scrubs.

Based on her scowl, Meredith wasn't buying the excuse. She wore her skepticism like a billboard, front and center with a spotlight trained on it. One eyebrow cocked, she asked, "Are you sure you're okay, Annalise?" She made eyes at her coworker.

"Yes." Annalise wiped her hands down her scrubs again. "I'm a little shaken up from taking a tumble. I knocked my head on the tray stand and took a pretty good fall. But I'm good." She lifted her arms up and made a show of giving herself a once-over. "See."

"Where do we sign out?" Rory asked Annalise.

"I'm afraid I can't advise you to do that," Meredith interrupted.

"Either way, we're walking out that door," Cadence insisted.

Meredith stood there for a minute, staring into Cadence's eyes. "Are you sure you want to risk your babies?"

Cadence's chin jutted out at the suggestion she'd do anything purposely to hurt her children. "You need to do a better job of keeping people safe in here. A stranger walked in and started tampering with my IV and where were you? I think my babies and me will be safer on our own."

It was Cadence's turn to shoot a furtive glance at Rory and he saw a flicker of emotion behind her eyes. Guilt?

She'd lied to him. Again. Building a bridge between shores seemed insurmountable but none of that mattered right now. He needed to get her out of the ER.

"She wouldn't hurt her children," he snapped at Meredith, who drew back as though he'd physically punched her.

The woman could think what she wanted. Cadence might be a handful and she wasn't being honest with Rory, and he was presently upset about that fact. But no one could say she wouldn't be a good mother.

He moved to her side and urged her to lean her weight on him before walking her out the door and to the elevator.

Once inside, he pushed the *L* for lobby.

"Thank you for what you said back there about me being a good mother," she said once the doors closed and they were alone again. "Did you mean it or was it your way of telling them to back off?"

"Both." He took her hand and stormed out of the hospital. He led her to the passenger side of his vehicle and then took the driver's seat. He gripped the steering wheel and bit back his anger. "When did you plan on telling me there was more than one baby?"

"LATER. WHEN I THOUGHT you could handle it." Cadence should've come clean with Rory from the beginning. There was no good answer for her actions, so she leaned back against the headrest and pinched the bridge of her nose in an attempt to stem the raging headache forming between her eyes. The cold had ripped right through her while walking to the vehicle and the frigid air caused her brain to hurt. At least she had a compression boot on her right ankle now and that was giving her relief. She'd refused pain medication, even though the doctor had reassured her she could take a low dose.

"What the hell is that supposed to mean?" Rory's voice was low and steady, angry.

"I still can't figure out how I'm going to take care of one baby, let alone two," she admitted. "I'm sorry I didn't tell you but—"

"No excuses, Cadence. If we're not honest with each

other there's no point in trying to candy coat this. The babies will suffer and I don't want that." He was right.

Cadence took a minute to let those words sink in. "We're not off to the best start, are we?"

"No, but it doesn't have to be that way." Again, Rory made sense.

"I can do better. I want to do better. The babies deserve it." Maybe she and Rory could establish some common ground from which they could build some trust. She shelved her fears that he'd ultimately take off, leaving her to hold the bag for the time being.

"What about the sex of the babies?" He paused a beat. "Do you know?"

"We're having daughters," she supplied.

"When?" His voice gave away nothing of his thoughts. But that was Rory. He needed time to digest.

"I'm due in March but my doctor warned me they could come early." An odd feeling of relief washed over her at spilling the details. She'd kept the news about the girls to herself so long. Talking about them, about the pregnancy made it feel less daunting.

"That's soon," he said and she could tell the news was sinking in.

It didn't feel all that soon for her. But then she'd had more time to reconcile the pregnancy.

"Girls," he said low and almost under his breath. There was a reverence in his tone that warmed her.

"That's right."

"Have you thought about names?" he asked and then held up a hand. "We can discuss the babies later. Right now, we need to find a place to hide out for a few days."

His statement closed the subject for now. She could

almost hear the questions swirling in his thoughts, questions he must have. Talking to him about their daughters felt better than she knew to allow.

"I'd like to make contact with Ella or one of the twins to make sure everything is okay on the ranch," she responded.

"We can do that before we stop off to rest." Rory pulled off the highway. He bought one of those prepaid phones that didn't require any identification or a credit card. "No one can track this phone back to us."

Did she want to know why he was so adept at hiding in the shadows? Or why that life was so appealing to him? What did that say about him? Did this have anything to do with his upbringing? All she knew for sure was that he sure seemed comfortable with all this. Whereas she was so far out of her element it wasn't funny. At least the nurse was able to put some magic salve on her foot to soothe the cuts and insect bites.

Rory handed the phone to her once they were back inside his truck.

She called Ella's number. The line rang but her sister didn't pick up. "She won't answer because she doesn't recognize the number."

"Too many reporters calling?" he asked.

"Yes, among other unscrupulous people." The call rolled into voice mail so she left a message. "I know she'll listen to it, so we should wait a few minutes to give her a chance to call us back."

"While we wait, can I ask you a question?" His

tone was deep, serious, and that sent a warning ripple through her body.

She sat straight up.

"You can ask me anything, Rory."

## Chapter Nine

"Why didn't you contact me when you found out you were pregnant?" Cadence couldn't read Rory's emotions based on his steady tone but her heart dropped anyway. Should she admit just how brokenhearted she'd been when he walked out and slammed the door behind him? How devastated she'd been when days turned into weeks and weeks turned into months without hearing from him?

What good would it do to admit it to him now? An annoying voice in the back of her mind reminded her that nothing would change between them no matter how many heat-of-the-moment revelations there were.

She'd had a crush on him from the day she'd seen him in the barn on that cold October morning when he'd come to live and work on the ranch. They'd grown up around each other but not together. She'd spent the first summer doing the most ridiculous things trying to get him to notice her. Fifteen seemed so grown up compared to a twelve-year-old. She'd picked up a cigarette butt and had pretended to be smoking to seem older to him. And when he'd told her those things will make you sick, she'd dropped it faster than a hot iron skillet handle.

When she'd embarrassed herself in the barn trying to kiss him, she'd given up. He hadn't noticed her much anyway except for being kind to her like the other ranch hands were. She'd lost interest when he'd given her no sign of sharing her affection.

She'd gone away to college and he'd started tracking poachers. He rarely ever came back to Hereford but the few times he did when she was home on break caused her stomach to flip. Old times, she'd told herself. Unrequited love and all that.

And then late last spring had happened—a wild fling with the best sex of her life—and he'd regretted it so fast that he'd broken up with her, walked away and never looked back. He was only in Cattle Barge and on the ranch because of a job, because of work offered by her brothers.

"By the time I found out I was pregnant I had no idea where you'd gone," she admitted. That part was true. Could she have found him? Probably. Her brothers didn't seem to have trouble locating him in order to offer a job.

He shot her a look that said he was thinking the same thing she was.

"Be honest. If I'd asked you to come back without telling you the real reason, would you have?" she asked.

He stared out the front windshield for a long moment. "Guess we'll never know."

He didn't speak it out loud but he was right. Being forced back together wasn't the same thing as coming together voluntarily. The pregnancy clouded everything.

Plus, he'd shown up at the ranch for a job. When it came to their relationship, he'd walked out once. And since history was the best predictor of the future, he'd do it again. If she weren't in danger, would he have stuck around this long? She doubted it.

But then she didn't figure Rory would desert his own children.

The throwaway cell phone buzzed and that could only mean one thing. Ella's call was perfectly timed to break the awkward tension filling the cab.

"Are you okay?" Ella's voice was frantic.

"Yes. Had a close call," she admitted, owning up to one of them. "But Rory is here and we're safe for now."

"Where are you?" Ella asked and then immediately said, "Never mind. Don't answer that. I'm just happy that you're not hurt. I've been worried sick about you and the baby."

Rory grunted.

She ignored him. This didn't feel like the right time to share the news she was having twins.

Cadence understood why her sister would be in a panicked mode. Each of the Butlers had been targeted or involved with someone who'd been targeted for murder since their father's death over the summer and the bad news didn't stop there. They'd found out about dozens of lawsuits trying to lay claim to their land and their father's fortune. It seemed the whole world had spun out of control following their father's death and Cadence felt like she hadn't gotten a chance to mourn his loss. Colorado had been more of an escape. Being pregnant and so very sick that first trimester had distracted her.

Or maybe she just couldn't face the fact that her father was gone and never coming back.

"I'm fine and the babies are good." Because of Rory, but she didn't explicitly say that. Ella would know. "What about at the ranch? What's going on there?"

"Not a thing. It's been quiet and that's why I was worried about you. That, and you haven't answered any of my calls or texts," Ella admitted.

"I lost my purse a while ago. Phone was inside. So no one bought the will being read early?" Cadence asked, remembering that Christmas Eve was Near. Wow, the first Christmas without their father. How sad was that? His presence would be missed so much. And her babies? She rubbed her belly. They would never know their grandfather. A tear escaped and she swallowed a sob. The sudden burst of emotions caught her completely off guard, but she was beginning to realize that pregnancy hormones had a way of bringing on the internal drama.

"Nope," Ella admitted.

"I don't like that," Rory said under his breath but loud enough for Cadence to hear.

She nodded because she was thinking the same thing. It meant someone on the ranch could be involved. There was no way anyone from security would allow themselves to be compromised or turn against the family, at least she hoped. Although, that could explain a lot.

"What about Ed? I thought he was out of town. Is that true?"

"Ed's in Amarillo. He headed there right after he left the ranch this afternoon," Ella supplied.

"If someone's tracking his movements, he should be warned," Rory said.

Ella gasped. "That's a good point. I'll call him to let him know as soon as we get off the phone."

A horn honked somewhere behind them, causing Cadence to jump. She glanced around, noting that someone was getting impatient for a car to relinquish its parking spot. Relief flooded her. Of course, the people trying to get to her wouldn't be making any noise to give her and Rory a heads-up that they were coming. Instead, there'd be a bullet flying toward her most likely aimed at her chest.

Again, Cadence couldn't think of one person who would want to hurt her or her babies.

"We better go," she said to her sister, needing to keep moving.

"Rory," Ella started. He acknowledged her. "Take care of my sister."

For once, it didn't sound like an insult. Cadence didn't mind having someone else watch her back and especially since the person was Rory. He might be angry with her and maybe even a little hurt—and she could give him that after hiding her pregnancy from him this long—but he would take a bullet for her if need be. She didn't question his loyalty to her and, even though he might not admit it yet, the babies.

After ending the call, a thought struck.

"Is there any way the person after me is trying to get to you?" she asked.

Rory's jaw fell slack for a split second, indicating that he hadn't thought of the possibility. He straightened in his seat and started the engine. "The guy with the rifle on your land had the business end pointed at your bedroom window."

"That still strikes me as odd when I think about it. How did anyone know that I was home?" she asked.

"The will reading was big news. There's no telling how long he'd been there. He could've been camped out on your property for days." Rory navigated onto the highway, put on his blinker and steered into traffic. "I know how to find out, but we need to find a place to camp for a few days to let your ankle heal."

"Christmas Eve is in four days. We don't have time," she said, noticing it was after midnight.

"I'm doing a lousy job of keeping you safe while running away from the problem," he said after a thoughtful pause. She ignored the double meaning. "I'm no good at it."

"Then where do you suggest we go?" Normally, she knew exactly where Rory would end up—out on the range where he could disappear without a trace. He was most comfortable there and he knew this area of Texas better than anyone. Even the Butlers knew less about their land, which was saying a lot considering the fact that they'd grown up on it and it was part of their souls. Of course, when she really thought about it, Rory had, too.

She remembered the day he'd shown up at the ranch as vividly as if it had happened yesterday. He wasn't a day more than fifteen years old. His hair was curly, a little too long, and his eyes a little too wild. He reminded her of the best of the land, untamed and beautiful in its own right.

Her heart squeezed a little more thinking about what her father had said about him… That he reminded him so much of himself at that age. That he could be lost forever if someone didn't intervene and look out for the kid.

She didn't see any similarities between her father and Rory.

She'd had a crush on Rory from the minute he strolled—too casual a word for what he'd done, romped over her heart was more like it—into her life. Of course, she'd been his best friends' little sister. Three years age difference had meant a lot at twelve and fifteen. Now, it seemed like nothing.

"I have no idea," he said, but his voice lacked his usual certainty.

"There was a guy who came into my room before the nurse. I think he was a janitor," she said.

"How well did you see his face?" he asked.

"Not well. He kept his chin to his chest and he was wearing a ball cap." She pinched the bridge of her nose, trying to force a picture. "I didn't think much of it before because he blended in but after what happened with the nurse, the timing of his visit strikes me as odd."

"It does me, too," Rory admitted. "What else do you remember about him?"

"He was shorter than you and my brothers," she remembered. "I'd say he was five feet ten inches if I had to guess. He had on jogging pants underneath a gray shirt. But he looked like every other guy. I mean, he was pushing a mop and he took the trash can out."

"I saw him. He's the reason I rushed into your room," Rory said.

"Do you think it was Dex?" Cadence's voice cracked with tension.

"It's possible."

"How could he know about the nurse's kids?" she asked.

"That's easy enough to figure out at her area at the nurses' station," Rory said. "She most likely had pictures up and he figured he could use them to get to her. Whoever this guy is, he thinks on his feet."

"These are the kinds of people you deal with on a regular basis, aren't they?" Cadence asked, realizing how much he knew how to think like them. Would that be enough to keep her and the babies safe?

AFTER DRIVING FOR two hours straight, Rory pulled off the road at a familiar campsite. It was remote and hardly anyone knew about it, which was just the way he liked it. When he'd first walked out of Cadence's life, this is where he'd come to get a grip on his emotions so he could move on.

"Stay in the cab. I'll set us up," he said to Cadence.

"Are we camping in this cold? The radio said it was going to dip below freezing tonight," she said with a look of horror.

Rory suppressed a laugh. "No, I'm not going to let you freeze. Believe it or not, I'm damn good at my job and I wouldn't be if I got frostbite and lost my fingers or toes." He wiggled his fingers and smiled. The break in tension was needed to regain perspective. More often than not, perspective came with patience and silence.

He could admit that living on the range had lost some of its appeal lately. Being alone with no one to talk to after being with Cadence and not being able to stop thinking about her had made him soft. Doing his job meant keeping a sharp mind and everyone at a safe distance.

Cadence had made that difficult. Being with her made him think he had to make a choice between living on the range that he loved or being with her.

He climbed out of the cab and took in a deep breath. Being out of town and away from all the cars and activity, he could finally breathe again. It didn't help as much as he would've liked.

A world without Cadence had lost its appeal.

He was too young for a midlife crisis but feeling a complete loss of identity was the best way to describe what it had felt like to leave Cadence. He'd figured getting back on the range in the job he loved would be enough to fill the void. It hadn't been and he'd been wrong on both counts.

The tent on the back of his conversion vehicle was set up and ready to go in less than ten minutes. He'd done it so many times he could set it up in his sleep. He'd built the platform for a foam mattress long ago. He'd even rigged an extra battery to his truck's heating system for those freezing nights when he was too far from civilization to get back and needed a few hours of shut-eye.

There was a stash of power bars and coffee. He had supplies to make a fire and the setup for a pot to boil water.

Early in life, being on the range had been his solace. The feel of a light summer breeze on his skin had brought a sense of peace he'd never known with people, until Cadence.

Had she rocked his world? *Hell, yeah.*

But watching his parents had taught him that love was toxic, too. His parents probably didn't fight from day one, either. There'd most likely been a honeymoon period in which they'd gotten along before having kids.

Speaking of which, Rory wondered where his sister had landed. Was she still on the road with what's-his-name? Was she trapped in a bad relationship? Marriage? The last thing she'd said before she left home was that she'd rather die than end up like their parents.

Rory couldn't agree more.

"That's quite a setup," Cadence said, and the sound of her voice caught him off guard.

He hopped out of the vehicle's bed to help her climb inside.

She took his hand and he ignored the electricity shooting up his arm and the heat pinging between them.

"It's warm in here," she said, rubbing her hands together.

"Afraid all I have is coffee to drink." Warm liquid would soothe her throat and he wanted to give her as much comfort as he could.

"I'd take hot water right now," she said.

"Then hold on." He could do that. He gathered a few supplies and hopped out of the truck bed.

Fifteen minutes later, he was handing her a cup of warm liquid.

"I'm impressed, Rory," she said, taking the offering. "It's easy to see why you're the best at what you do."

"Being alone has its disadvantages. It doesn't always make me the easiest person to get along with," he admitted. He'd need to learn to give-and-take to make co-parenting a possibility with Cadence.

"We do the best we can, right?" It was a peace offering he would take.

He needed a minute to mull over his thoughts about what had happened at the hospital. All that stress couldn't be good for the baby, correction, *babies.* Rory couldn't even go there right now about suddenly having two lives depending on him.

Cadence's physical description of the janitor matched Dex's.

An idea popped about how Rory could find out. Local poachers may have seen Dex and his cohorts. One of the poachers could possibly lead them to Dex's location. Rory needed to find a way to infiltrate a poaching site while bringing Cadence along. That wasn't going to be easy. She didn't exactly fit in out there with her manicured nails and ivory skin, and especially not while she was pregnant.

But nowhere was safe and especially not in the city. The person or persons targeting her wouldn't expect her to be out on the range and that's most likely why Dex had started there. Rory could circle back to the original campsite for clues as to who this guy really was. There was another consideration. Dex might be a gun-for-hire but his identity could help lead them to his boss. Sheriff Sawmill needed an update, too. It was too risky to take Cadence to his office.

"What's going on? What are you thinking?" Cadence asked, breaking into his thoughts.

"I have a crazy idea."

"It can't be worse than sleeping in the back of a conversion vehicle in the freezing cold," she joked. He'd missed that quick sense of humor. He'd missed her smile, too, but this wasn't the time to make a laundry list of all her good qualities.

"This is going to seem like The Four Seasons compared to what I'm about to recommend," he admitted.

"Oh, no. It *is* worse, isn't it?" she asked on a laugh.

"I can always take you back to the ranch," he suggested.

She shook her head and she was right. He was just throwing it out there to feel like he was giving her an out. There was no out. There was only catching the guy involved and forcing him to talk. Rory reminded himself that he'd been doing a terrible job of keeping her safe so far. She had the cuts, scrapes and swelling to prove it.

A fresh sprig of anger sprouted, welling up inside him at his failures.

"Hey. Remember that time I was in the barn when you first came to the ranch? I was cornered by a rat and completely freaking out," Cadence said before taking a sip of water.

"I think you asked me to go get your dad." He chuckled. "You were practically climbing the walls."

"Do you remember what you told me?" she asked.

He thought about it for a while. "Knowing me, it was probably something stupid like stay put until I take care of it."

She practically pinned him with her stare. It was the one she had that said she could see right through him and wasn't buying anything he said.

"You told me that I was wearing your favorite color.

Blue. Like the sky." She sounded a little offended that he didn't recall. "And that I should focus on that while you took care of things."

"And did you listen?"

"Yes. It kept me from panicking. I was able to calm down while you did whatever it was that you did to get rid of that thing," she said. "Ever since then I think of the color blue when I get scared. I think of the beautiful Texas sky and it calms me down."

Well, damn. How was he supposed to respond to that? "I was a know-it-all kid back then. I would've said anything to keep you quiet and hold on to my job. As I remember, you told your father about the rat and he gave me a pat on the back. Told me I'd done a good job."

If his off-hand comment surprised her, she didn't immediately show it.

The warmth on her face faded when she said, "Guess you'll say just about anything to get your way."

"Is that what you think?" Rory bit out through clenched teeth. He didn't like being called a liar and he especially didn't like the fact that all he could think about was kissing Cadence since he'd seen her.

There was so much heat between them that when she leaned forward he could almost taste her. She smelled like flowers and he figured she'd washed up while in the hospital.

Emotion overtook logic and Rory closed the gap between them until their lips pressed together. He couldn't ignore the pull she had, so he stopped fighting it.

He kissed her tenderly, afraid of doing anything that might hurt her.

She parted her lips and welcomed his tongue inside

her mouth. She tasted sweet and exactly like he remembered—a fact that he'd thought about far too many times in recent months while alone on the range.

He brought his hand up to her neck and felt her pulse pounding at the base. The tempo matched his own as need stirred inside him.

On some level, he knew this was a mistake. It would only complicate matters between them and make him want things he shouldn't. But he couldn't care about that while she brought her hands up to tunnel her fingers into his hair and deepen the kiss.

Their breaths quickened as she scooted onto his lap and repositioned until her full breasts were flush against his chest.

Rory dropped his hands to her sweet hips, which were fuller than before.

But that put the brakes on for him because it also reminded him that she was pregnant.

Running with his emotions instead of using his brain had gotten him into this mess in the first place—the one where his mind was convinced that he couldn't live without her and that scared him more than any physical threat he'd faced.

Plus, she was so damn sexy. He was already stiff and his length pulsed against her, so that made pulling back more difficult than climbing a rock covered in honey.

"Cadence." His mouth moved against her lips when he spoke.

She pressed her forehead to his. "Yes."

"Is this a good idea?"

"Probably not."

Silence sat between them, thick with sexual tension.

It felt a little too good to be right where he was, to be holding her.

Cadence finally blew out a slow breath, the kind meant to garner strength. And then she climbed off his lap.

Cold air blew through the tent the minute she pulled away. Or was it just his imagination playing tricks on him? Either way, he retied the straps of the small cloth window meant to let light inside and tossed on another layer before exiting the tent.

He'd almost let his emotions run wild and now all he could think about was that kiss. Just how much he'd missed Cadence was a punch to the gut.

Maybe they'd both be better off if he made other arrangements for her. Being this close was messing with his mind.

Was being this close to her a good idea?

If it only involved him, he'd say *no* and move on with his life. But there were other lives to consider now.

Could he be this close to Cadence and not fall for her again?

Not kiss her again?

## *Chapter Ten*

Seventy-two hours of rest in a tight space had Cadence ready to climb the walls. Three more days passing also meant that Christmas Eve was tomorrow. Thinking about her father not being there for the holiday caused a physical ache. Everything was going to be different this year.

Her entire life had changed in less than half a year.

She placed her hand on her belly. Technically, next year would be her babies' first Christmas but ever since she'd felt one of the little bugs kick in her stomach, they were real to her. Before that, she'd felt like she had the flu for a few months and the reality of the pregnancy hadn't been able to sink in while she spent most of her time trying to keep food down.

"Good morning," Rory said as he slipped inside the canopy. She hadn't heard him leave, or return for that matter. But when she'd opened her eyes a few minutes ago she knew he was gone because his side of the mattress was empty.

Cadence stretched sore arms and legs. The swelling in her ankle had gone down, which felt like a miracle.

"What time is it?" She felt lost without her cell phone or any of her usual comforts from home.

"Half past ten," he said, handing her a cup of warm water. "Wish I had something to put inside to give it flavor. Didn't you used to drink chamomile with lemon?"

"Sometimes." She was surprised he'd noticed those little things about her.

"This is better than nothing."

"What's it like out there?" She'd only left the pop-up tent to use the bathroom and take short walks. But she was amazed at how well Rory knew how to take care of injuries. He was used to relying on himself, on not having an ER on every street corner and she admired his independence. She always had and that was most likely part of the draw she felt toward him. That, and his ridiculous good looks. He had that rugged cowboy image nailed and his kiss had practically imprinted on her lips. She'd thought about it more than she wanted to admit in the last forty-eight hours.

"Cold." He smiled. It was the sexy out-of-the-corner-of-his-mouth smile and her heart free-fell.

Then again, maybe she'd spent too much time in a confined space. She was losing it.

"What's the plan? My ankle is better today and so is my foot," she said. He'd stopped off and bought a few supplies to make life more comfortable, one of which was hiking boots for her.

"Sticking around in one place too long is how poachers end up caught. So they're always on the move."

"That's poachers. We're looking for a murderer," she said.

"This guy used the same tactics I would've. I underestimated him before and that nearly cost us everything." There was so much self-recrimination in his voice.

"But we're okay. We're alive and I'm already healing nicely." Was he as hard on everyone else as he was on himself?

"My mistakes nearly killed you." Anger boiled up and she was close enough to see his steel eyes darken. He fisted his coffee mug and his knuckles were white.

There was no getting him to see reason when he was in this dark of a mood, so she didn't try. Instead, she grabbed the small bag of bathroom supplies he'd made for her and headed out of the pop-up camper.

This shouldn't have come as a surprise to her. She knew Rory better than he probably knew himself. Not long after he'd come to work at the ranch, he'd accidentally given cold water to a few of the horses after exercising them and that had made them sick.

He couldn't have been there longer than six months when it happened and Carl Hambone—or Bony Carl as everyone like to call him—had covered for him before chewing him out royally. Cadence remembered stopping at the barn door when she'd heard shouting. Bony Carl was an old hand and it took a lot to rile him.

She'd already had a crush on the young new hire, so she couldn't help but listen to what Bony Carl had said to her father. She'd been shocked that he'd taken full responsibility. Said he'd gotten distracted with a sick calve and then took the fall, saying he gave the horses cold water after exercise. They'd come close to losing two due to colic.

Rory must've heard, too, even though she didn't

catch him listening at the time. The very next morning, he was up early and had packed his stuff. He didn't own much more than the clothes on his back. His entire life's worth of items barely filled his rugged, worn denim-style backpack.

She'd stormed into his room in the bunkhouse and had demanded he tell her exactly what he thought he was doing.

Rory had told her that he had to go. That he'd done something wrong and it was time to move on. He'd told her to leave it at that.

She'd planted her balled fists on her hips and dared him to try to get past her as she blocked the door.

"You'll listen to reason and that means owning up to your mistakes, Rory Scott," she'd said as she blocked the door.

"Is that right?" he'd asked.

"Yes. There's no use running from your mistakes. You have to face them or they'll just follow you and grow bigger than you can imagine," she said all full of sass and spice.

"That's what you think I'm doing? Running away?" he'd asked.

"That's what it looks like to me," she shot back, thinking she'd just nailed it.

"I told your father what I did," he'd said.

"And then what happened?" She was tapping her foot like an angry schoolteacher staring down an out-of-control class.

"I got fired."

Her jaw fell slack and she couldn't hide her mortification. "There's no way. I'll tell him he can't do that—"

"Your father has every right to take care of every animal on his property. He can run the place as he sees fit." Rory threw his backpack over his shoulder and stalked straight toward her. "Are we done here?"

And because she'd somehow convinced herself that he actually wanted to kiss as much as she did him, she threw her arms around his neck, closed her eyes and leaned forward to plant a big one square on his lips.

She could not have misread the situation any more.

Embarrassment flamed her cheeks just thinking about it. He'd turned his head to the side in time for her to miss. And then he'd gently taken her wrists and peeled them off him.

"Are you trying to get me shot?" he'd asked incredulously.

"No," she'd defended.

"You're twelve, Cadence," he'd said with that same self-recrimination she'd heard a few minutes ago in his voice. "I'm a teenager. It's not right for me to kiss a sixth grader."

She didn't figure this was the time to point out to him that he hadn't. And she'd known even then that he was being gracious by saying so.

Years later, when they shared a proper kiss, she'd pointed out that she'd been waiting a long time to kiss him.

"That's a lot of pressure," he'd said. And then he kissed her until her heart pounded her ribs and she had a difficult time catching her breath.

By then she was a grown woman and he a virile man. And the age difference from twenty-seven years old to thirty didn't seem like such a wide gap anymore.

She flushed thinking about how hot the sex had been.

The past three nights she'd slept with him, bodies pressed against each other for warmth.

Sleep had been fitful, worrying about what might happen, or if Dex, Wiry and Athlete, or someone else, stumbled upon their makeshift campground.

And then there was her heart. She'd moved on from Rory.

So why did her thoughts keep circling back to that kiss?

RORY DISASSEMBLED THE pop-up tent in less than ten minutes.

After hanging around the camp for a few hours, it was time to go. Especially after waking for the second time with Cadence's soft body against his, remembering how incredible the feel of her silky skin was as she lay next to him.

Besides, his thoughts kept wandering back to the kiss they'd shared the first day they'd arrived at the campsite. He performed a mental headshake to clear the image of her pink heart-shaped lips. The memory of how they felt moving against his wasn't helping.

Suddenly, the cold shoulder she'd been giving him seemed like it was for the best.

This was business, not personal. It was his job to keep her safe while the sheriff tracked down the person or persons hunting her. After three nights at this location, she hadn't come any closer to figuring out who could want to harm her. He'd cut them off from the world and her disappearance would be news.

One day until the will was going to be read.

"I know where we can go," Cadence said, returning with her bag filled with water, a toothbrush, soap and a washcloth.

"Where's that?" he asked.

"The barn."

Dozens of memories involving her and her family's barn tried to crash his thoughts. The bunkhouse had been the first place she'd made herself known to him. The thought of kissing a twelve-year-old when he was fifteen had felt all kinds of wrong, no matter how cute Cadence had been. Annoying, but cute. At fifteen, he'd felt like he was more of a man than a boy and she seemed so much like a kid in her highlighter-green halter dress and matching sandals.

He stared at her, trying to look deep.

"Think about it. It's perfect. Where's the last place anyone would expect me to go right now?" She wore the expression that said she knew she was right. Fist on right hip. Bottom lip in a slight pucker. It was damn sexy.

"Nowhere seems safe to me, but especially not the barn," he admitted. Again, a fist of guilt punched him. "That's my fault, Cadence."

"That's one way to look at it," she said. "As far as I can tell, you're the only one who's been keeping me and the babies alive so far. On our own—" she paused "—I don't even want to think about what would've happened."

Her gaze dropped to the ground and it looked like she was trying to hold back tears.

"I don't know if I expressed it before but I'm truly sorry about your father. He was a good man."

Cadence rolled her eyes and made a grunting noise.

"I think we both know that's not necessarily true. I mean, don't get me wrong, he was my father and I loved him but he was no saint."

"He wasn't perfect. There's a difference. Most of his big mistakes were made when he was young," he said.

"Like having multiple children close in age? You know what that means, right? He wasn't faithful to my mother, and I've always wondered if that was the reason she took off or if she just knew she could never love us. And let's not forget the fact that someone hated him enough to want him dead." He moved close enough to see tears welling in her eyes. She turned her face away to hide them.

"It's okay to be emotional, Cadence. You don't always have to put up a strong front."

"Is that what you think I'm doing?" she shot back, her voice full of that spice he loved. Missed. The band around his heart tightened.

She was gearing up for a fight based on her disposition. Fists down at her sides were clenched so hard her knuckles were white. Her normally full pink lips compressed into a thin line.

He closed the distance between them and stood there. "Your mother leaving had nothing to do with you."

"If that's true, why does it still hurt so much?" She blinked up at him. He never realized the impact her mother deserting her could've had on her, the effect being abandoned would have on her self-esteem. He'd always seen the Butlers, and especially the girls, as being confident and privileged. He knew them well enough to realize their lives weren't perfect but he'd totally underestimated just how broken they could be deep down inside.

Rory recognized the emotion in Cadence because it was the same one he'd felt his entire life. That he was broken and no one noticed. The world around him kept on spinning. His parents kept on hurting each other and by extension him and his sister.

"I know how it feels." His words were meant to offer comfort, reassure. He was surprised by a sob escaping before she buried her face in his chest.

"What kind of parents can we possibly be to these babies, Rory? Neither one of us had a role model worth looking up to in the parenting department, and we don't even get along anymore."

"We can learn a lot from our parents' mistakes." This wasn't the time to debate their parents' failures. "They don't define us."

"I hid the truth from you. I know you, Rory. You'll never trust me again," she said. "How are we supposed to be good parents when we can't trust each other?"

She didn't say that he'd run away from her when their relationship had heated up. She didn't have to. He was already saying it to himself. And he was more convinced than ever that it had been the right move. Sure, it had hurt. He had the internal scars to prove that it had almost brought him to his knees. And yes, a weak part of him had wanted to show up on her doorstep more than a dozen times in the past five months. That was part of the reason he'd kept tabs on her whereabouts. His sensible side always kicked in and kept him from making a stupid mistake like that. He'd done that once when he let his feelings grow too strong for Cadence.

He would only hurt her.

Holding her in his arms, feeling her shaking, he knew that she deserved better.

Cadence deserved commitment, a white-picket fence, hell, a minivan if she wanted one. She needed a man who would walk through the door every evening without fail. With his job, and it was the only life he knew, he couldn't guarantee that.

When he really thought about it, the babies deserved more than that, too.

The thought of another man with Cadence and his children shot an angry fire bolt swirling straight down his spine. He had no right to feel that way if the two of them had no plans to get married and to bring up these children together. The fire bolt didn't care about logic. It burned a scorching trail down his back.

"There are two things I know for sure," he began. "One. And this is probably the most important. You are going to make an amazing mother."

She looked up at him with those big eyes and his heart stuttered.

"Two. We'll figure out how to take care of those babies together. We'll make mistakes but they won't be the same ones as our folks. I can guarantee that much."

"How are we going to do that, Rory?" There was a straight-up challenge in her eyes.

He didn't say by keeping a safe distance from her or by not kissing her again.

Because that's exactly what he did, kissed her.

"You're not making this easy." He said the words low as his mouth moved against hers when he spoke.

But great sex wasn't going to help the situation.

And the sound of a twig crunching nearby sent his pulse racing.

# *Chapter Eleven*

Rory took Cadence's hand in his, linking their fingers. She followed him to the conversion vehicle that was ready to go. Her heart raced and she worried about the babies. She'd been under enough stress recently, between losing her father and the pregnancy, and now someone wanted to kill her.

She placed her free hand protectively over her stomach. Whatever else was going on between her and Rory, she was glad he was the one helping her. Granted, he'd been shocked to learn he was going to be a father and he had every right to be upset. But he also cared as much as she did about protecting the little ones. She'd already seen the look in his eyes.

"Get in." He motioned toward the passenger side as he released his grip on her hand.

Within a few minutes, they were clear of the camp, and they spent the next several hours driving around killing time. Her heart still thumped wildly but this time it was because she was thinking about the few kisses they'd shared. She needed to get a firm handle on her feelings for Rory, which had the annoying habit of careening out of control without notice. Hitting the wall in a fiery crash was certain if she let herself slip onto that racetrack again.

Cadence liked to think she learned from her mistakes. She and Rory needed to get to a good place with each other and that would begin with letting him know how much she appreciated everything he was doing.

"You've had a lot thrown at you all at once," she began. Admitting she was wrong wasn't the difficult part. Finding the right words to truly express it was more complicated. "I don't think I've thanked you for what you're doing for me and the babies."

"There's no need," he said without so much as a pause to consider her words. But that was Rory. He did the right thing like it was just expected, like everyone would. She knew it was part of his Texas upbringing, his cowboy code. Rory was not most people. No man from her past dating life had held himself to the same incredibly high standard.

"I'd like to anyway. I'm sorry that I didn't reach out to you sooner to tell you about being pregnant," she continued, wanting to explain but not make excuses. "I was so sick the first trimester." She saw his brow shoot up and realized that he wouldn't have experience with pregnancy lingo. "The first three months," she clarified.

He nodded his understanding.

"To be completely honest, I was terrified when I found out. You were gone, and I'm not blaming you for taking off and abandoning me. I could've handled the whole situation better." She understood him better than he thought. He would die a slow death if he couldn't be out on the range. She'd known it from that first summer he came to live on the ranch. He was almost as wild as the quarter horse her father had bought when he went through a horse-racing phase. The stallion her father had bought had a similar fire in his eyes as Rory. It was the first thing she'd noticed about the new hire when he'd come to work and live on the ranch.

Rory checked the rearview and she realized he was watching to see if anyone had followed them. That his gaze shifted back and forth a few times reminded her of the danger they were in.

"What did Sawmill say after your father was murdered?" Rory changed the subject. She could tell by his demeanor that she'd made progress and it was time to give the topic a breather.

"Everyone, including Sawmill, speculated that he'd gotten involved with a married woman because of the way in which he died," she admitted. "Sawmill explained that he was looking at someone close to our father or to the family because the murder was personal. It occurred while he was in his own bed in his room in the barn."

"Landry didn't see anyone coming or going." He stated the obvious. He was thinking out loud, which was the way he liked to talk through an issue.

"No. But my father didn't like to bring women in the house around his children and he also didn't like security knowing his business. He was private about his personal affairs. The main house was for family. His place in the barn was for..." She made eyes at him. "You know. His *other* activities."

"Who else did he suspect early on? Did he say?" Rory pressed.

"He said that it could've been a jealous ex or his

current girlfriend. I spoke to my sister about that, and we can't imagine that Ruth would've done something like that and there was no evidence to prove she did. Besides, my sister and I had the feeling that Dad was going to announce their engagement soon. He must've been killed before he could ask her because Ruth didn't know anything about it. She said he'd been acting different lately and he'd hinted that he'd be making a big announcement soon. Ella and I thought the same thing."

"I can't think of a bigger announcement or lifestyle change than an avowed bachelor getting married," he stated.

"You made your views on relationships pretty clear to me five months ago," she retorted, wishing she could take the words back the minute she heard them coming out of her mouth. There was no reeling them in now.

He held up a hand in surrender. "I was talking about your father."

It still stung and her pride wouldn't let her admit that she'd ever wanted more from him than a casual relationship. So she shrugged it off, trying to come off as noncommittal. "Let's just move on."

"Fine by me." His voice was deep and tight. She'd hit him in a sore spot.

"A few of us were speculating that he was going to take a step back from some of his day-to-day responsibilities," she admitted, softening her voice.

"I'm surprised there wouldn't be some kind of communication trail that would give away what he was thinking. Emails? Receipts for an engagement ring?" Rory's tight grip on the steering wheel relaxed a notch, which was good. No matter what else was going on with them personally, they needed to be able to work together. Now, for her and the twins' safety. Later, because the two of them would have to learn how to co-parent. Tension between them would affect their girls and Cadence didn't want that.

"The sheriff didn't uncover anything in his investigation. Honestly, I wasn't all that surprised, considering how secretive my father was. We didn't even know that we had two other siblings until he brought them to the ranch through Ed," she stated. "All this time, we've had a sister and a brother and didn't know it. Dad kept his secrets until he was ready to reveal them and he'd been keeping those my entire life."

"I'm guessing that Sawmill didn't find anything unusual in your father's business accounts," Rory stated.

"Nothing so far. He brought in a few experts to examine Dad's accounts and then he sent them off to another agency for a favor. They're still trying to untangle his relationships but there's nothing obvious there." She was already shaking her head. "You know my dad, Rory. His business, like his life, was complicated and private."

"A MAN DOESN'T amass the kind of fortune your father did by keeping things simple or blabbering about his plans to anyone who would listen." Rory should know. He'd spent more time than he cared to admit in the past five months trying to figure out how to do the same. After being with Cadence, he'd realized how lonely his life had become. In order to be able to go out and do the only job he was good at, he'd been forced to walk away from her for his own protection. He knew he was doing her a favor. But hearing the heartbreak in her voice when she talked about the breakup was a face punch.

"Ed's been checking into all the paternity claims that have come up since my father's death. And there have been quite a few." He noticed that she couldn't bring herself to say *murder* this time.

"Again, he must be drawing blanks or he would've arrested someone by now," he said.

"Sawmill has interviewed everyone on the ranch. He put the ranch hands through hell. Carl and Dale have been with us the longest so they took the news hard. Anthony and Rupert were hired by my dad in the last year but they were both sick about the news. No one had any ideas of what could've happened. Of course, half the community thinks they know who would want my father gone but no one seems able to agree on a name," she said. "Hence, the reason I balked when you said my father was a good man the other day. If he was, there wouldn't be so many possible suspects."

"On any given day, people will love or hate you. When it comes to your father, ask one of his ranch hands how they felt about him," he stated after a thoughtful pause.

"They're loyal to my father. They would never say anything bad about him," she argued.

"True. But why are they loyal? None of them are stupid."

"Because he gave them a job." Her forehead wrinkled like that should be obvious.

"Have you ever worked for anyone who was a jerk?" he asked.

"I've only ever learned how to run a ranch," she admitted, and her cheeks flushed with embarrassment. "But I had a few pieces-of-work-type professors in college."

"Tell me about one of them," he said.

She rolled her eyes. "My history professor was the worst. He would come to class and only want to talk about current events but all his tests were from the test bank from the book. There were never questions from class discussions. He'd tell us something was important but it wouldn't show up on the test. It was infuriating."

"How often did you complain about him while you were taking the class?" Rory glanced at her quickly before returning his focus to the road.

"Pretty much every day," she admitted. "So I see your point."

"Your father gave jobs to a lot of good men over the years and he treated them—*us*—better than any other owner we'd ever worked for," he admitted.

"I think Rupert comes from a tough background. He's young. I think Dad wanted to give him a chance to make something of himself," she said.

"He might've been tough but we always knew where we stood with him. And he gave a few of us opportunities that no one else would've."

"He fired you for making a mistake six months after you arrived," she pointed out.

"True. And it was him who showed up after you left the bunkhouse and admitted that he was the one who'd made a mistake. Said he appreciated my honesty and gave me a raise because of it," he stated.

"I thought he hired you back after I yelled at him that night." An emotion flickered behind her eyes. Was it admiration for her father's actions? He hoped so, because it would be wrong to look at the bad side of her father and ignore all the good. Okay, Rory bit back the irony of that statement when it came to his own family. As for his father or any other man who got physical with a woman, even if she started punching first or baited him into it, had no honor.

"Sorry to disappoint you or make you doubt your ability to throw a good temper tantrum at age twelve," he said with a chuckle. "It was your father who showed me how to be a man and own up to my mistakes. It sure as hell wasn't mine." The last part came out with so much disdain it caught him off guard.

"Tell me something about your family, Rory. Why did you run away?" She turned the tables on him.

"My parents fought all the time. We couldn't take it anymore—"

"Hold on a second. Who's *we*?"

"Me and my sister," he stated.

"You have a *sister*?" Shock echoed from her voice. "And you never told me?"

"Guess it never came up," he admitted.

"I thought I knew you, Rory. How could I if I didn't even know you had a sister?" Cadence turned toward the window and crossed her arms.

He released a heavy sigh. Talking about his family wasn't easy.

"She's two years older than me. Her name's Renee. It was just the two of us growing up with our folks. I already said they fought nonstop. Mostly verbal but it got physical at times." He paused, trying to deflect the feeling of knife stabs in his gut as he dredged up the past. "Renee and I tried to convince our mother to leave him."

"And?"

"She refused. Said their fights were how she knew he loved her." He took in a frustrated breath. "There wasn't much we could do, so after a rough dust up Renee took off with a guy in a band she'd been sneaking around with. I didn't last long without her there, so I was next to go."

"Since you never mentioned this before and your family had trouble, I'm guessing you and your sister lost contact," she said.

"Yep. I'm not much on technology and didn't have one of these at fifteen anyway." He held up his cell phone. "I still don't have a social media account."

"Easier to stay under the radar that way," she guessed, and he nodded.

"I'm more of a light-a-fire-under-the-canopy-of-a-clear-night guy anyway." He shrugged. "So, no, I haven't spoken to my sister."

"Why didn't you look her up once you got older?" Cadence asked. It was a damn good question.

"I could say the same for her."

"So it's because you're stubborn," she said.

"You could say that. Last time I checked the phone rings both ways," he countered.

"Do you miss her?" she asked.

"We were close once."

"I'll take that as a *yes*." Cadence nodded toward his phone. "You know, it's not hard to look someone up on the internet these days. I can show you how to do it."

"I think I can figure out how social media works.

What would be the point?" He pocketed his phone. "She could do the same thing and hasn't."

"You're a little harder to find for one. You track people for a living, Rory. And part of your job is making it as difficult as possible to find you, and yet you're mad at your sister because you think she hasn't even tried. You don't even know for sure and you don't see the irony in any of that?" She was walking on dangerous turf. An annoying voice in the back of his mind reminded him that the truth often hurt.

"What would be the point of getting in contact?" he asked.

"Seriously? Did you just ask me that?" Her voice was incredulous.

"She walked out on me as much as she did them. We both put the past behind us." It was easier that way. "What good would it do to dredge up those painful memories?"

"My father could be tough to deal with and he was especially hard on the boys. I don't know what we would've done if we hadn't banded together. We'd probably all be crazy by now." She shot him a look. "Sorry. I'm not saying there's something wrong with you."

"Let's talk about something else. Like who might be trying to kill you." He needed to change the subject because this was hitting a little too close to home.

Cadence sat there for a long time without speaking. When she finally did, she said, "Rory, I'm sorry about your folks. That's not fair to you or your sister. We didn't grow up in a house full of fighting and I bet that was hard on you."

Rory pulled into a pay-cash-as-you-go-type motel.

The rooms-available sign had a couple of bulbs knocked out. "You'll be okay in here for the night?"

"Of course. A warm shower sounds amazing right now." Cadence sat there in the passenger seat as the sun dipped below the horizon.

"I'll be right back." He could keep an eye on the vehicle from the pay window.

He walked up to the thick plastic window, which looked like he was buying tickets for the state fair. A guy who was probably in his late forties looked up from the small screen he'd been watching.

"What can I do for you?" he asked.

"Need a room for the night." Rory kept his chin tucked to his chest because he didn't want to give away his identity. Not that—he read the guy's name tag—Phil seemed to mind.

"That'll be seventy dollars." Phil pulled a key ring with a plastic tag and held it out in front of him.

Rory took money from his wallet. He always carried cash. Staying off the grid helped in his line of work. Tomorrow night they'd be back in Cattle Barge. Rory couldn't deny that there was a certain feeling of rightness in thinking about being with Cadence on the ranch again. It was most likely because Hereford was where they'd met when they were just kids.

At fifteen, Rory might've thought he was grown. Experience had taught him a lesson about how much he had to learn before he'd be considered a man.

He slipped the exact amount through the metal slit at the bottom of a drawer.

When he returned to the vehicle, silence sat thickly

between them. Rory didn't want to talk about his family with her, with anyone.

"Speaking of sisters, we should give yours a call," he said.

## *Chapter Twelve*

Room number three had a metal door and a large window with royal blue curtains. There were two beds inside. One looked like it dipped in the middle and Cadence didn't want to think about how many bodies it would take to create such a dent. There was a desk, a lamp and an old TV.

"This place isn't much." Rory handed her the throwaway cell phone.

"It'll do." She was determined not to make a big deal. Besides, a shower was a shower. The thought of a warm shower went a long way toward making this place seem better.

Cadence punched in her sister's number. Ella picked up on the first ring as though she'd been waiting for the call.

"How are you?" There was so much worry in Ella's voice.

"We're good," Cadence responded, hating that her sister and the rest of her family were going through this again. She knew what it was like to stand by helplessly when someone she loved was in danger and it was the worst feeling. "Rory's taking good care of us."

She didn't look up at him when she said it because her cheeks flamed. She shouldn't be embarrassed giving him a compliment. Trying to deflect her reaction she added, "It's easy to see why he's considered the best at what he does."

Ella sighed in relief. "I'm grateful to him."

"Tell me what's going on at the ranch." She put the call on speaker.

Besides, she needed to change the subject. Going down that slippery slope of feelings for Rory wouldn't do her a bit of good.

"Preparations are being made for tomorrow night's will reading. Terrell and his team are on high alert and we brought in reinforcements to secure the perimeter," Ella supplied.

"That's smart. We'll need all the extra help we can get to keep everyone safe," Cadence confirmed.

"Who did you hire?" Rory asked. This was his field of expertise and he would most likely know the players.

"The Janson Brothers," Ella supplied.

"Good. They know what they're doing," Rory said. "How about the sheriff?"

"He's sending reinforcements. We're planning to get plenty of eyes on the ranch over the next few days. We also sent all our employees home to celebrate the holidays with their families. No one is even allowed on the property aside from May, of course." Hereford was home to May and she'd been a mother figure to the Butler children. It only made sense that she would stay for the reading.

"How'd they react to that?" Cadence asked. Everyone had been on edge since their father's murder.

"They were surprised at first, as expected. And then they were concerned. There were a lot of questions and speculation. You know how close we all are," she continued. "Everyone's worried about our well-being and no one wanted to leave. Ed did a great job convincing them that we'd all be safer if the ranch was cleared out over the holiday."

Hereford was family to everyone who lived there. The ranch hands and Carl developed brother-like relationships. Many of them had worked on the ranch for years. It took time to develop bonds like they shared.

"Will extra security make it more difficult for us to come home?" Cadence asked Rory. She couldn't imagine that they'd waltz through the front gate and announce their presence.

"We can postpone the reading if you can't make it back safely," Ella offered.

Cadence knew it would require skill.

"We'll be fine," Rory said and she could tell by the tone of his voice that he already had a plan.

Ella heard, too, because she said, "Let me know if that changes. Otherwise, we'll plan to see you both tomorrow night at eleven thirty."

"We'll be there," Rory stated.

"Thank you for taking care of my sister," Ella said to Rory.

Normally, a comment like that would've been fingernails on a chalkboard to Cadence. In this case, she appreciated how many people were looking out for her because it was plain to see her sister was coming from a place of love.

"I love you, sis," Cadence said. She didn't say those words nearly enough to the people she cared about.

"I love you, too," Ella responded.

Rory stepped back, away from the receiver as though he'd intruded on a private family moment. He tucked his chin to his chest and turned his face away. Was he thinking about his sister, Renee?

Cadence and Ella exchanged goodbyes before ending the call.

"Where are we headed next?" Cadence knew he had their next move mapped out and she figured they would need to be close to Cattle Barge if they were going to be at the will reading.

"To Hereford."

"Right now?" She knew with one look in his determined eyes that he was serious.

"Ella said employees have been sent home. Anyone watching will expect us to show tomorrow close to the time of the reading." He made a good point. "I know how to get in and out of that bunkhouse unseen. I spent ten years of my life there." His jaw was set and his folded arms told her all she needed to know.

"Okay. Let's go home," she said with a certainty she didn't feel.

THE BUNKHOUSE HAD a common living area and kitchen with four bedrooms. Each had locking doors. No one ever used the locks but they were there.

Rory knew the layout better than the back of his hand. He'd spent many a night there in his formative years.

Hereford had saved his life and he owed the ranch

and its owner a debt of gratitude that he couldn't make up in a lifetime. Where would he be if not for the ranch? Prison? Dead? And that's the reason he could set aside his personal feelings about Mr. Butler telling him that he wasn't good enough for his daughter. Hell, Rory already knew that. One look at Cadence told him all he needed to know about where he stood. He couldn't figure for the life of him why she'd taken a shine to him when she could've had any male in the area at the snap of a finger.

Rory could name a dozen guys who would have made her much happier if she'd given them a chance. Men with normal schedules who could guarantee they'd be home every night instead of leaving her waiting in some two-bit shack like the place he owned. And yet the thought of Cadence with another man sent pure fire shooting through him.

His eyes had long ago adjusted to the dark.

He picked up the spare key to the back door of the bunkhouse from underneath a boulder next to the back porch. Ranch hands might be able to account for every member of a herd but ask any one of them to keep track of a set of keys and that was a whole other story.

After unlocking the door, he led her inside. It was past midnight and pitch-black outside. "We can't turn on any lights."

Cadence had been quiet on the journey over and he figured she must be exhausted. He'd taken her on a trail he used to ride every morning. It was the best way onto the property near the bunkhouse.

"I know we were just sitting but my legs are tired," she'd said.

"An hour's a long time to be in one spot." He'd had to be certain there was no one in the area before he would take her the final quarter of a mile to the bunkhouse.

"A warm shower and decent night of sleep would be amazing right now," she said.

"My old bathroom is on an interior wall and there are no windows in that hallway. As long as you keep the lights off, you should be good." He didn't want to think about her naked body in the next room.

"Not a problem. I remember when this place was built. I used to play on the slab of concrete before the walls came up. I know every inch. Don't need light to see." She disappeared down the hall.

Rory dug around and found clothes for both of them.

"Found a clean sweatshirt and jogging pants for you. They'll be too big but you can tie the waist off," he said, placing them on the counter.

He made himself a cup of coffee while she finished showering and dressing. And then he popped into the shower for a quick rinse before joining her in the living room.

"I still can't believe there were so many spare toothbrushes," she said.

"May keeps the place well stocked. Leave it up to the guys who live here and it'd be a sad state," he admitted with a chuckle.

"Too bad she didn't keep women's clothes in here," she said with a laugh.

The oversize shirt hugged her curves—curves that were sexier than he knew better than to let himself dwell on.

"Are you thirsty?" He'd managed to get a decent

meal of burgers and fries in her earlier but that was hours ago.

"A cold glass of water would be nice."

He fixed another cup of coffee for himself and brought her ice water.

"Are you tired?" he asked, joining her in the living room. There was another thing he didn't want to think about and that was the day she'd stood at that door, fisted hand on hip, demanding he stop running. She'd been so full of sass and confidence. And then she'd tried to kiss him, which had given him a good chuckle at fifteen. She'd been a kid then. But the few they'd shared since seeing each other again were so damn hot he started stirring every time he thought about them.

The heat in those kisses had a habit of popping into his thoughts when he needed to stay focused on keeping her alive.

Speaking of which, he couldn't help but think the family would most likely be targets during the will reading.

Rory had every intention of ensuring that Cadence made it through the next few days alive.

Once this was over, it was going to be difficult to walk away again. Leaving her the first time had almost done him in. But now, with the babies, it was going to hurt punch-in-the-gut-like pain. The coil around his heart tightened and he took a minute to catch his breath.

This seemed like a good time to remind himself that he had a job waiting for him in Wyoming. A life on the range that he loved.

"Rory..." Cadence said, and he picked up on something reverberating low in her voice as she scooted over next to him on the couch.

"What is it?" he asked.

"I'm scared." Her chin jutted out in defiance and he knew it took a lot for her to admit that.

"Nothing's going to happen to you or those babies on my watch," he swore.

"I believe you," she said. He could hear it in her voice that she didn't but he decided not to challenge her on it.

Instead, he asked, "Then what is it?"

"Don't let us end up like your folks," she said.

"That won't happen to us." That was a promise he could keep.

"What makes you so sure?" she asked and quickly added, "I know you would never lay a hand on me. I'm talking about the arguments. Words can be as damaging as a fist and that hurts kids just as much as when they hear their parents fighting. You know?"

"I do." Experience had taught him that was true.

She leaned into him, resting her head on his shoulder. It was most likely his being caught up in the moment but he wanted to be able to show her that he meant his words and kept his promises.

So he didn't debate his next actions. He put his hand under her chin and lifted it until her eyes met his.

And then he dipped his head down and tenderly kissed her.

She parted her lips and deepened the kiss. He slid his tongue inside her mouth, tasting her sweetness, which only intensified his hunger.

Primal need had him rearranging her until she was

facing him on his lap. She eagerly complied, and his body had an instant reaction. Damn, she was sexy.

Heat ricocheted between them as her hands tunneled in his hair and her breath became ragged.

He wrapped his hands around her hips as she settled on his groin. His erection strained the second he realized she wasn't wearing panties. He dug his fingers into those sweet hips as she teased him with her rocking movement.

"Cadence," he said through quick breaths. His pulse raced at a staccato beat, pounding at the base of his throat.

He brought his right hand up to wrap around her neck and grazed his thumb across the base, a matching rhythm to his thumped against the pad.

"Do you really want to talk right now, Rory?" She froze long enough to look into his eyes. Even in the dark, he could see that hers glittered with need.

When she put it like that, she had a point. "No."

"Good. Because I want you to make love to me right now, Rory Scott."

That was all the encouragement he needed to keep going.

Until he thought about the babies.

"I don't want to hurt you...*them*."

"I'm not a fragile doll, Rory. I won't break and they aren't much bigger than my fist. There's no way you can hurt them." She crossed her arms and gripped the hem of her oversize shirt, freeing her generous breasts. He issued a primal grunt as he took one in his hand and then the other. Her nipples beaded against his palms as her mouth found his again.

He rolled her nipples between his thumb and forefinger, causing her to moan.

She brought her hands to the waistline of his jeans, fumbling around for the snap. She lifted herself off him, giving enough room for him to remove them. His stiff length ached to be inside her.

Her jogging pants hit the floor next, and she stood there naked and beautiful and everything he wanted in a woman. Her body was perfection but there was so much more to their chemistry. She was the perfect mix of spunk, intelligence and kindness.

He barely had his T-shirt off before she'd straddled him. Not long after that, she was guiding him inside her, *home*. Her silky skin against his rough hands nearly did him in, so he distracted himself by thinking about something else—anything else—besides how soft her skin was.

"You better slow down if you don't want this finished before it gets good, Cadence," he warned.

And that made her laugh. It was a sexy, throaty sound that came from the excitement of her being in total control and knowing it. She loved taking the lead in the bedroom.

"From what I remember, your stamina was never in question, Rory."

"It's been a few months," he defended. "And I missed the hell out of you."

As far as his heart went, Rory didn't normally go there but this was Cadence. She was his weakness and he was man enough to admit it.

Yeah, he was pretty much putty in her hands when it came to sex. And yeah, Cadence was the only person who had that effect on him. And then there was the simple fact that their sex had been beyond any experience he'd had in the bedroom, which was saying a lot because there'd been plenty of good sex before her. Since had been the downer. He'd gone on a few dates, none of which had netted anything more than boredom and a reminder of how much he missed her quick wit.

After being with someone he could really talk to and care about, having sex for sex's sake had lost its appeal.

And he didn't want to examine the reasons.

Rory didn't want to do anything but bury himself deep inside Cadence and finally find his way home again. He wrapped his arms underneath her legs and stood. She wriggled her hips, burying him deeper and he released a guttural groan.

"I missed you, Cadence."

"I missed you, too, Rory."

He walked over to his old bedroom. The door was open so he dropped to his knees at the foot of the bed and set her sweet round bottom on the edge. She tightened her legs around his midsection and dug her nails into his shoulders as she gripped him. Her body was flush with his and her breasts pressed into his chest as she rocked back and forth, as he met her thrust for thrust.

Deeper. Harder. She drove him into a fever pitch.

Rory wrapped lean fingers around her hips, driving faster until both of them were gasping for air, climbing…tension building…muscles cording and straining with a need for release.

He could feel her muscles clench and release around

his shaft and that rocketed him toward the edge as she flew over.

His body became a battlefield of electrical impulse.

Bombs detonated inside him, releasing all the pent-up tension.

Cadence's mouth found his and kissed her hard.

"I love you," he said low and under his breath when they finally broke apart in order to catch some air. And that was the problem. He did love her. And sex was tainting his thoughts, confusing him because right then, he wanted to find a way to make a relationship work.

It wouldn't.

And his heart was about to be ripped apart a second time.

## *Chapter Thirteen*

"Wake up, sweetheart." Rory's voice was a soft whisper in Cadence's ear as he woke her up from a late-afternoon nap the next day.

She blinked her eyes open slowly.

Rory's face filled her field of vision and her stomach flip-flopped like a champion gymnast. He smiled out of the corner of his mouth but she could see tension written across the lines of his forehead, reminding her of the harsh reality waiting for her.

She didn't want to focus on that now. She'd had a few hours of happiness and she wanted to hold on to that for as long as she could.

"What smells so good?" she asked.

"I made tacos."

"Seriously?" Tacos after the deepest sleep she'd had in months and the best sex of probably her life. She'd have been even more thrilled if she wasn't facing down the reading of her father's will in—she checked the clock on the nightstand—an hour and a half. "You cook?"

"Not a lot. But I can manage a decent meal." He didn't kiss her and she could tell from his expression that he'd constructed a wall. Was he distancing himself because of the threat they faced in a little while?

Rory held up a finger and then returned a few minutes later with a plate and a glass of ice water. He handed over the offerings before making another trip. When he returned he was white-knuckling a coffee mug as he took a sip and sat down on the edge of the bed.

"This looks amazing." She wasted no time taking a bite. It was cooked to perfection. Why didn't she know this about him before? Because neither had ever stuck around long enough after sex to find out, a little voice said. She didn't want to go down that road again. "It's even better than it smells."

Normally, he would at least smile at the admission but he studied the wall next to her like it was a treasure map.

"Everything okay?" she asked, figuring he wouldn't tell her but she wanted to ask anyway. Rory had always held his cards to his chest, even with her.

"I need to protect you and I keep making mistakes that put you at risk," he admitted.

Was he talking to her about something real instead of brushing her off?

"Is it too obvious to point out that I wouldn't be alive if it weren't for you?" She touched his arm and half expected him to pull away. When he didn't, she took it as a positive sign that he wasn't completely shutting down on her. He'd done that, she'd noticed, right before he told her that he couldn't be in a relationship with anyone. The fact that he'd quickly added, *If I could, it would be with you*, had done little to stem the pain.

He shot her a look of appreciation. There was something else behind his eyes, an emotion that looked a lot like shame, and she knew him well enough to realize that he believed he was letting her down.

"You're the best at what you do and I realize this whole situation is in reverse for you. Normally, you're on the offensive and this is pure defense. But I'm alive because of *you* and the babies are safe because of their *dad*." She brought her hand over her stomach protectively. "If there's a problem in all this, it's me. I'm not doing a good enough job remembering. I've been thinking that I might be the key. I mean, if someone's after me then I have to have done something to them, right?"

He'd angled himself toward her and was listening intently. The old Rory would've held tight to his anger and put up a wall too high to climb. She could work with this and they could come up with a solution together.

As he seemed to be taking a minute to soak in what she'd said, she cleaned her plate. After downing a glass of water, she felt more like herself than she had since losing her father.

Was being around Rory calming her overactive mind?

She'd bet on it. As a matter of fact, she'd go all-in. Forgetting him before had been torture and the thought of co-parenting, being close without being together, set her nerves on edge. She'd fallen for Rory the minute she'd seen those wild eyes and untamed hair. She'd also known anything short of setting him free to roam the range would be like placing a choke collar around his neck and chaining him to a tree in the front yard.

But it was his sadness, his loneliness that had touched her somewhere down deep. It had left an imprint on her heart that wasn't so easily shaken off. As much as she didn't want that to be the case, she couldn't deny what she felt.

There was no man who had made her feel smart, sexy and beautiful in the same way Rory had. Even being around him now with no makeup and hips that seemed to grow wider by the day made the world feel right in so many ways. He made her feel desirable.

The heat in the kisses they'd shared blew her mind and had been missing in every other kiss her whole life before him.

Even she knew that they couldn't repeat what had happened last night. *Technically, this morning.* That was obvious. And it was most likely the danger she faced, the reality that Dex or whoever was tracking her might catch up to her that had her craving another night with Rory. That made her want to reach out and touch him, get lost in his arms again.

She excused herself to go to the bathroom to freshen up so she could regain perspective. Because right now, she wanted to pull him down on top of her for another round of mind-blowing sex.

After washing her face and brushing her teeth in a real sink for a change, she returned to the bedroom.

Rory was bent forward, elbows on his knees. He looked up at Cadence; those wild eyes seemed so lost to her. His hair was disheveled and there was stubble on his face. He was in beast mode, detached, and she could see determination on his face.

"What's the plan?" She knew there was one.

She stopped in front of him and he took her hands in his.

"Run away with me. Let's get as far away from Cattle Barge as we can," he said, and there was so much pleading in his steel eyes.

"I want to more than I can say. But if I don't show up tonight, good people, honest people would lose their ability to earn a living. These guys have families and they can't afford to stop working. This is what they know and Hereford is their home."

RORY ADMIRED CADENCE'S sense of sacrifice. Even on her worst day, she was better than most people could ever hope to be.

"I hear what you're saying," he admitted. "Nothing in me wants to march you into that house where I'm afraid there's going to be a trap set. One I might not be able to save you from. You understand what I'm saying?"

She nodded. Standing there, beautiful and determined with the fire in her eyes that said she had to do the right thing, caused the viselike band around his heart to tighten.

"How would I ever sleep at night if Dale's niece had to be pulled out of the preschool she's in because he couldn't afford to send money to his sister? You know Sara's just starting to match the development of her classmates. That costs money and these men deserve to be paid. They sacrifice so much of their lives living at Hereford instead of living in their hometowns with their families and yet they've always looked after me. Dad has helped a lot of young men, like Rupert Grinnell, our newest hire. If he's off the ranch for too long or out of work, who else will hire him? He's still young but he deserves a chance." She made a lot of sense.

"I can see you've put a lot of thought into it," he admitted.

"Believe me when I say that I'm torn between doing right by you and right by them. The minute I start putting my needs above everyone else's is the day I stop caring about anyone but myself. I definitely don't want these girls to grow up thinking their problems are the only ones that count in life," she said.

Rory snapped his face toward her. "Our girls deserve everything we can give them, and that includes perspective."

It was going to take a minute for him to digest the fact that he was having twin daughters. For now, he had to keep the information on the back burner.

"You think Dex or whoever is after me is going to make his move tonight, don't you?" she asked.

There was no use lying or trying to hide what he knew at a gut level. She deserved to know what she was about to face. "Yes. I think he's going to come in with everything he's got to stop you from walking inside that house. There could be so many things that we can't account for. Extra foot patrols will help but that might not stop them from setting booby traps on the ranch. A lot can go wrong because he's in control, not us. We can do our best to control access to the environment but once a target's location has been identified, the rest becomes easy."

"And we already know he can shoot from a distance," she agreed.

"That rifle would have never been set up like that if he couldn't."

"Do you think Dex is our man? What about those guys who tracked us to your place? How many more can there be?" She was firing a lot of questions at him that he couldn't answer.

"It's an unknown variable, which is an enemy in a situation like this." Rory's cell buzzed. He fished it out of his pocket and checked the screen. "It's Sawmill."

"I have news," Sawmill started right in.

"Okay. I'm putting you on speaker. I have Cadence Butler with me," he informed the sheriff.

"Good. You'll want to hear this, too, Ms. Butler." He issued a sharp breath before continuing. "We got a hit on the descriptions you gave us of the pair of men in the woods after my deputies canvassed the area. Does the name Martin Jenkins or Randol Fleming sound familiar?"

Cadence looked to be searching her memory. She compressed her lips and her gaze darted around. "No. Not at all."

"They're kin to a new hire on the ranch. Young man by the name of Rupert Grinnell," he informed.

All the color drained from Cadence's face as she whispered, *"Rupert."*

It was impossible to believe that a ranch hand would be involved and especially with how close everyone was.

"He was Dad's last new hire. But how could he possibly be involved?" she asked. "And what problem could he possibly have with me? I didn't know the guy from

Adam before he came on board at the ranch. And all the men were interviewed after Dad's death."

"Mr. Grinnell has an association with a man by the name of David Dexter Henley, who sometimes goes by the name of Dex," the sheriff informed.

So, Dex didn't use a fake name like Rory thought he would have. The man must've panicked and given his nickname.

"Rupert, Martin and Randol are related," Rory pieced together. "Dex is…what?"

"All we know so far is the four men are linked. Means, motive and opportunity are still open for question," Sawmill stated.

"Although, with Grinnell working on the ranch, it's possible that he let the others in," Rory said.

"And that could end his involvement right there. We suspect he might not've given them access knowingly based on reviewing the file of interviews. We're considering all possibilities at this point in the investigation," Sawmill informed.

"Do you have any theories?" Cadence asked.

"I was hoping to gain more information from you in order to fit the pieces together, Ms. Butler." Sheriff Sawmill's radio beeped and buzzed in the background. "We're in the process of tracking down last known addresses and making a list of family members to investigate. I know this doesn't sound like much and I'd like to be able to give you answers, but this is a big break. It's only a matter of time before we piece the story together and make an arrest."

"Where's Rupert?" she asked.

"We were hoping you could tell us that," he said.

"The information about his family members and address when not on the ranch should be in our files. Ed Staples can provide everything." Cadence was cracking her knuckles and her gaze was darting around wildly, her nervous tics.

"Sometimes witnesses remember something later. If that's the case with you, please call my number directly," Sawmill informed.

This phone call was about to be over.

"I wish we had some idea of why Rupert would be involved in this," Cadence said. "He never struck me as a criminal and our office is good at vetting out unstable people. I know his background is shady but he seemed like an honest kid."

"Hereford has a great reputation for treating employees well and it's widely known that it's not an easy job to get," Sawmill agreed.

Cadence's father had a weak spot for young men who needed a hand up. In Rory's case, he would never have betrayed Mr. Butler. Okay, the irony of that thought smacked him square in the nose. He'd walked out on his relationship with his former employer's daughter and had gotten her pregnant. That wasn't much of a thank-you to the man who'd saved Rory's life.

Rory thanked the sheriff and ended the call.

One look at Cadence and he could see that her mind was reeling from the news.

"How old is Grinnell?" Rory asked.

"He's young," she admitted. "He was barely eighteen when we gave him the job and that was about nine months ago."

"Seems odd a young guy could take the heat of being

investigated," Rory said, thinking out loud. "It has me wondering if he knew at the time that he'd allowed someone on the ranch."

"It's possible that he could've been used and not known it. He's a sweet kid who I felt didn't belong in the system," she informed.

"The sheriff will send a deputy to turn this place upside down at any moment," Rory stated.

"I don't like the fact that there'll be so much chaos on the ranch during the will reading," she admitted.

"Me, either." He put his arm around her and she leaned into him for support. It felt a little too right and she felt his muscles tense. Was he thinking the same thing as she was? Getting too close was going to hurt like hell when this was over. If a criminal had his way, that would be tonight.

That old wall erected between them and she could feel the detachment growing. Was he distancing himself so it would be easier to walk away tomorrow? *Like he'd done before?*

Cadence was an idiot to let her emotions get away from her twice. Especially when Rory had already proven he could disappear at a moment's notice and not look back. The only reason he was in Cattle Barge and at Hereford was because her brothers had summoned him. And she was certain he was itching to get back to the land he loved.

She wasn't being fair to him and on some level, she knew it. Rory hadn't exactly said he wanted to leave.

"Sawmill has a direction and a few names. Now, it's a matter of tracking those boys down and fitting the pieces together," he stated.

"The sheriff initially said that the top reasons people murder are for greed, anger and revenge," Cadence stated as she stepped away from him. A look of hurt darkened his eyes, but what had he expected? He wasn't the only one who could play the made-of-ice game. Plus, she needed to keep her emotions in check and maintain focus. "If I isolate greed, what could any of these boys hope to gain from Dad's death?"

"Anger seems like it would be more heat-of-the-moment. You come home to find your spouse in bed with the neighbor and lose your cool. You grab the gun in the cabinet before reason can set in and *boom* everyone's life is changed forever," he speculated.

"Revenge is killing someone in cold blood while they slept on their ranch," she said. "Rupert would've had access to my father. But everyone, and I mean *everyone*, was interviewed by the sheriff or one of his deputies. How could he have come out clean? He's young and that's a lot of pressure for someone his age to pull off. He never struck me as a coldhearted criminal and he'd have to be in order to murder the man who was giving him a chance at a better life."

"That's all true and everything depends on his background. There are world-class thieves and liars younger than eighteen," he stated. "Rupert could be in trouble. Someone could've paid him to look the other way."

"Seriously?" She'd read news that supported his accusation but it was almost impossible for her to believe someone like that could slip through Hereford's hiring system.

"I know it's difficult for someone like you to believe," he said.

"What does that mean, *someone like me*?" she scoffed.

"Someone who grew up in the main house," he informed.

"Don't you mean someone who was born with a silver spoon in her mouth?" she snapped.

It was the stress of the situation causing her temper to flair.

"I didn't say that," he defended.

"Why not? Am I too fragile to know the truth of how you really think about me?"

# *Chapter Fourteen*

Cadence could feel her temper rising. It wasn't good for the babies. It wasn't good for her. And it wasn't good for her relationship with Rory. Why did she let his words cut right through her?

"I'm not sure what's going on but I don't want to fight with you, Cadence." Instead of giving as good as he got, Rory's voice was a study in calm. There was compassion there, too.

"Same here."

"The sheriff has names. He finally has suspects. The investigation is about to break apart and your father's murderer will be brought to justice." He glanced toward her belly. "We might have a long road ahead of us and a lot to work out personally between the two of us, but I don't want them to feel stress when they hear you talking to me anymore. I have no idea what they can sense or remember, but we need to be on the same page when it comes to them."

Everything he said made sense. Her emotions were about as overclocked as they could get, which wasn't all Rory's fault. It wasn't right to take out her frustration on him. "I owe you an apology for—"

"None needed," he cut her off.

"Let me finish," she insisted.

He nodded.

"You made a good point. I have no idea what the real reason was for my parents' divorce. Did they fight? Was he unfaithful because of it? I don't even know what my mother was like. We never spoke about her. It was like some unwritten rule that she could never be brought up in conversation. And why? What happened that was so bad?" She paused to stem the flow of emotions and gather the rest of her thoughts. "You and I have a chance to do better. We can get this right for our girls." She paused to take another breath. "I know what we did last night was a mistake and can't happen again. I think we both know how much sex complicates the situation between us."

He nodded but an emotion flickered behind his eyes. Regret? Sadness? Feelings aside, they both knew what she said was for the best. He'd instinctively pulled away from her, even if he hadn't fully acknowledged it yet.

"I'll always care about you, Rory. We've known each other since we were kids. Nothing's going to change that." Beyond that, her feelings were a hot mess, and she figured pregnancy and hormones were amplifying them.

"Everything you said makes sense," he said after a thoughtful pause. "Kissing you when we're this close is as natural as breathing to me. But that muddies the water and we won't just be hurting ourselves anymore if we go back and forth between friends and…" He looked to be searching for the right word before adding, *"More."*

"We owe it to these girls to find common ground," she stated, hoping her heart would catch up. Everything they were saying was logical.

He glanced at her belly. "I think we did the day we made those two."

There was a huge positive emerging out of all this. Rory seemed to be coming to terms with the fact that he was going to be a parent. It had taken Cadence months to do the same.

"Right now, our main focus needs to be getting you through the next few days until the sheriff can get those boys off the street and get to the bottom of what's happened." There was so much sincerity in his voice.

"Agreed." Her heart fought against the idea of settling into a friendship with Rory. But their feelings were volatile and being a good parent had to come before everything else in her life. "It's about time to go to the main house."

"As soon as I cover our tracks here," Rory said, turning toward the kitchen.

"What if there's evidence here?" she asked.

He stopped midstride. "I'll text Sawmill to let him know where we've been hiding. He'll be able to figure out how to best move forward with his investigation and, hopefully, keep our names out of the report until Grinnell is found."

"It's so tempting to look through his things to see if we can figure out why he would be involved in something like this," she admitted.

"You were right before, though. We can't risk damaging evidence. Not only is it illegal but it can hurt the investigation. I don't want to do anything to make this harder."

Cadence glanced at the clock on the microwave in the open-concept room. "It's getting late."

The severe look that crossed his features before he forced a smile worried her. It meant that the normally confident man was hiding something. Fear? She'd never seen him afraid of anything in his life. In his job, he'd stared down death countless times. But then there'd never been so much at stake before, she thought as she touched her belly.

Rory fished his cell out of his pocket. He punched in a number she recognized as Dalton's.

Her brother picked up on the first ring. He and Rory exchanged greetings and confirmation that she and Rory were safe and doing well.

"There haven't been any attempts on any of us at the ranch," Dalton confirmed. His tone was guarded with Rory now and Cadence regretted insisting on keeping their fling a secret. Her brothers and Rory had been close once and she could see that this had hurt their relationship. Since she was having Rory's daughters, he would be in their lives as family no matter what. She made a mental note that she would have to smooth things over with her family once this was all said and done. She prayed she'd be around to be the one to do it.

"You hear about Rupert Grinnell?" Rory asked.

Dalton issued a grunt along with a strong word under his breath. "Yes."

"Any idea where he is?" Cadence interjected.

"No. He's probably damn lucky I don't," Dalton responded.

Rory glanced at Cadence before asking Dalton, "Where are you right now?"

"I'm heading home. Why?"

"Are you coming from the east or west?" Rory didn't answer Dalton's question yet and Cadence immediately picked up on the reason.

"West." Dalton's voice was tentative.

"Mind a couple of extra passengers?" he asked.

It sounded like it took a second for everything to click in Dalton's mind. "I see what you're saying. Where's a good place to pick up my extra cargo?"

"What's the situation with the reporters?" he asked.

"They're lining the street half a mile on either side of the gate. Seems like they want to be certain they get a shot of anyone coming or going tonight so they're sticking closer to the main entrance," he admitted, and Cadence didn't like the sound of the word *shot.*

"We can make it to the road two miles out and coming in from the west side in twenty minutes," Rory promised. "That work for you?"

"I'll see you both then," Dalton said. Before ending the call, he added, "Cadence…"

"Yes, Dalton."

"I know we gave you a hard time growing up but Dade and I are proud of you. Everyone wants you to know how much we love you."

"I love y'all, too." Tears welled in her eyes. An onslaught of emotion nearly drowned her. Cadence steeled her determination. Crying wouldn't do any good. Focus would. "And I'll see you in twenty minutes."

The call ended with a bad feeling. She didn't like the tone in her brother's voice. It was filled with regret and had a quality that made her think he was afraid he'd never see her again.

THE NIGHT WAS pitch-black and cloudy. A cold front was blowing through and the temperature was expected to drop twenty-five degrees in the next hour. Cadence would be inside the main house long before then, warming up by a nice fire.

Being outside on such a chilly night reminded her of all the times she and her brothers or Ella would sit out back and roast marshmallows over the fire pit.

There was a large tire swing off to one corner of the yard. She'd spent a good portion of her childhood on it during lazy summer days.

When she really thought about her life growing up on a ranch, she remembered how wonderful and different it had truly been. There were so many good times with her siblings. There were fights, too. She never doubted any one of them would have her back if she needed a hand.

If she got bored with her siblings, there were always animals around. The best part about being at Hereford, though, was being surrounded by so many people she loved. What would her life have been like if she hadn't? Would she have felt lonely? Granted, her girls would always have each other.

The thought of bringing up twins on her own while Rory disappeared for weeks, sometimes months, on end hit her like stray voltage. Would she feel lonely?

Alone? The freedom that was supposed to come with moving to Colorado was sounding more like a recipe for isolation. Babies were a lot of work. Could Cadence take care of them on her own?

She would do what she had to, a little voice said.

Would their lives be better at Hereford? May would be here. She would be the closest they'd have to a grandmother since Rory didn't speak to his family. Now she understood his reasoning and she wouldn't try to push him into doing anything he'd be uncomfortable with. Besides, it wasn't her business anyway.

She couldn't help but think it would be nice if the girls had grandparents in their lives, though. Having none was far better than someone who was abusive, don't get her wrong. Since Rory clearly had been close with his sister when they were young, Cadence could urge him to locate Renee. Family was family and she'd take all she could get.

Especially now that she was having a change of heart about living at Hereford. There was plenty of land on which she could build a house for her and her girls. She wanted her babies to have more than her and Rory. Growing up in a loving environment like Hereford would give them a safety net. The past few days had taught Cadence that she couldn't guarantee she would be around.

She didn't want to think about that while she traipsed through the chilly woods again. Rory cut a path for them. He knew exactly what he was doing and where he was going at all times on Hereford.

It might be cold outside but she and Rory had borrowed warm coats from the bunkhouse and only her hands were cold. She blew on them while rubbing them together to stave off the chill.

Rory's phone dinged, which was the signal that Dalton was nearing the pickup spot.

"Let's pick up the pace," he urged.

She followed in his footsteps to keep branches from smacking her in the face as they cut through the woods.

The hum of an engine, the bright lights caused her to gasp.

Nearing the road, seeing the headlights of her brother's vehicle coming toward them, brought on another wave of nostalgia.

Rory linked their fingers before jogging toward it.

The thought of going home to the main house caused a surprising onslaught of emotion to crash down on her.

And then it dawned on her. It was Christmas Eve and her father wouldn't be coming home.

Soon, everyone would know his final wishes.

She put a hand on her belly as the passenger door opened and she slid inside the back of Dalton's vehicle.

"It's good to see the two of you." Stress deepened her brother's voice. "Stay low and I'll get us through security. I pulled a blanket out of the back so you can pull it over your heads. You'll blend in back there and no one will be the wiser."

"Thank you, Dalton. For always looking out for me." She might not have always appreciated her brothers nosing in her business and overprotecting her. Looking back, she realized that their hearts were always in the right place, even if some of their actions were misguided.

Judging her brothers harshly for always having her

back seemed overly sensitive now. The pregnancy had changed her perspective on life and family.

She made herself as small as she could on the floorboard, working around the protruding bump without putting undue pressure on her midsection.

"Comfortable?" Rory whispered, readjusting himself in order to give her more room. He took up a lot of space. He was a big guy.

"It's not far. I can make it until we get home," she responded.

Now, all she could do was hope they made it inside the gate safely. Of course, based on what Rory had said about the possibility of the place having traps set, that was only the first step. She had no idea what was waiting for them.

BEING AROUND CADENCE for the past few days reminded Rory of all the reasons he'd fallen for her in the first place, not the least of which was her spunk.

As long as he kept his emotions under control, he figured the two of them would get along fine. But he and Cadence were gasoline and fire when they were together. That same spark made for great conversation and even better sex, both of which had to be tempered now that they were going to be parents of twin girls.

As much as Rory knew better than to let the babies affect his judgment he was already getting attached. The thought of losing Cadence or his girls to some creep sent his blood pressure through the roof.

Since learning he was going to be a father, he'd started thinking about the possibilities of getting more out of life. Could he have a wife and a happy marriage?

Was a real family even an option for someone like him? Someone with his background?

Hearing Mr. Butler's words inside his head every time he thought about a future with Cadence wasn't helping. Rory wasn't good enough for her and it would only be a matter of time before she figured it out and left him.

And once again, he reminded himself that his parents were the worst possible fit for each other because of their differences.

Having grown up in what felt like a war zone, he'd vowed long ago never to allow that to happen if he ever had a kid. He was more resolved than ever to keep his feelings for Cadence in check and his eye on the prize—happy children.

That would make her happy, too, in the long run. But then he also realized the irony of his trying to rationalize his feelings toward her. Was it too late?

In walking away from her before he'd not only hurt her but he'd put himself through hell. He'd wanted to forget her, to put her out of his mind, but that had been impossible.

Seeing the way she glowed when she talked about the babies wasn't helping him keep perspective.

People co-parented all the time without letting their feelings for each other run out of control, he reminded himself. He and Cadence could do the same.

Couldn't they?

## *Chapter Fifteen*

Slipping onto the ranch and avoiding journalists seemed like a simple enough plan. Cadence was surprised at how easy it turned out to be. She was reminded of one of May's most frequent sayings that most of the time the simple plan was the right one.

Being home brought so many memories crashing down around her. Cadence exhaled slowly as she heard the garage door closing. Facing Hereford without her larger-than-life father was hard. A band tightened around her chest. For a split second, she wanted to escape. Until she saw his old pickup truck in the bay next to them.

She smiled as she remembered spending a good chunk of her childhood sitting next to him while he drove on the property. He'd tell her to scoot next to him and instruct her to take the wheel just before putting his hands high in the air.

Air from the open windows had blasted her, whipping her hair around as she squealed and gripped the steering wheel.

"It feels good to be home," she said, pulling the rest of the blanket off.

"This is where you should be," Dalton said. It felt so right to hear those words.

"How much time do we have before the reading?" she asked her brother.

He checked his watch. "Ten minutes."

Rory smiled at her. Without much fanfare, he pressed a kiss to her lips. It was tender and sweet and was more intimate than making love in a strange way.

"You're going to be okay. Dalton and your family will make sure of it," he said and then slipped out of the vehicle.

"Wait a minute. You're not coming inside with me?" she asked and then it dawned on her that he was going to check the perimeter and do what he did best…track people.

"I know exactly who I'm looking for and I won't be far," he promised before turning to Dalton, who was standing off to the side. "I owe you and Dade an apology for seeing your sister behind both of your backs. I hope you know that I'll do right by her and our children."

"Children?" Dalton asked with shock in his voice.

"She's pregnant with twin girls," Rory informed him. "I have every intention of being the father they need."

"I never questioned it," Dalton said, and she saw Rory exhale out of the corner of her eye. "Just so you're aware. We were given clear instructions from Ed Staples. Our father requested your presence at the reading."

Rory's jaw fell slack and his eyebrows knitted. "What reason could there possibly be for *me* to be there?"

"Those were the instructions. I have no idea the rhyme or reason. You know my father," Dalton said with a shrug.

"Did he call for other ranch hands?" Rory asked.

"Not to my knowledge and we would've received word before we sent everyone home," Dalton stated.

Leave it to her father to throw a fast-pitch when everyone was expecting a curveball.

"I'd rather be outside, watching the perimeter," Rory admitted.

"There's some kind of stipulation that if you don't show, the envelope is not to be opened. Ed said he'll have to destroy it," Dalton said. "Aren't you at least a little curious about what our father wanted to say to you?"

Rory stood there for a long moment. There was so much emotion playing out in his features that she could only imagine what was going on inside his head. Her father had been a mentor to Rory. By Rory's account, her father had saved his life. By contrast, Cadence was in danger and that would weigh heavily on Rory's mind. Although he would never speak it aloud, he would never forgive himself if anything happened to her. He was already giving himself a hard enough time for the pregnancy and feeling like he'd backed Cadence against a wall by not being there for her.

"Can the reading start without me?" he asked.

"I believe so. It shouldn't hurt anything if you're late," Dalton said.

"I promise I'll be there," he said to Cadence before slipping out the door.

Rory was a pro. He tracked dangerous men for a living. This was no different.

So why had her nerves tensed?

"Are you ready for this?" Dalton asked with a glance toward her stomach.

"I'm not going to lie. It's hard to be at Hereford without Dad," she admitted, and there was so much relief in finally saying that out loud to one of her family members.

"Holidays are making it tougher," he agreed with a nod.

"It won't be the same without him," she said. "It doesn't even feel like Christmas. Between the pregnancy and…everything that's happened, I haven't done anything to feel in the holiday spirit. I doubt there's anything I could do this year to make it feel normal."

"Same here." Dalton paused in front of the door leading into the main house. "I'm thankful the rest of us are together, though."

He made a good point.

"It might not be the same without him but we have a lot of new family members to look forward to spending the holiday with." Dalton glanced at her stomach with a smile.

"Look at how much has changed in less than a year," she said. "We have a brother and sister we never knew about. And don't even get me started about all the love that's come into everyone's life." She tried not to think about the fact that she was the only single Butler now. Besides, she was thrilled her siblings had found true love and life partners. It didn't bother her not to be married. Being around all that love made her realize what she was missing in her life, what she would never have with Rory… Stability. He would always have a need to take off and live off the land. Whereas, she wanted a nice house on the ranch and plenty of space to bring up her daughters while being surrounded by the same love she'd known as a kid.

"This past year has taught me how important family is. I guess I've always taken it for granted that we'd be here for each other. Are you still thinking about staying on in Colorado?" he asked.

"How'd you know that?" The only person she'd admitted that to was Rory.

"After all the time you were spending there, it seemed like the next logical step for you," he admitted.

"Not anymore. I'd like to build a small house for me and the girls right here at Hereford, where we belong."

"Sounds like the best idea I've heard all day," he said with a genuine smile before opening the door to their family home.

Ella rushed to the kitchen and wrapped Cadence in a warm hug. May followed, as did the newest Butler sister, Madelyn. Cadence embraced her soon-to-be sisters-in-law, Carrie, Meg and Leanne. Her new brother, Wyatt, wrapped an arm around her and gave her a quick peck on the forehead followed by a protective look. "No one's getting through here while I'm around."

Wyatt fit right in with Dade and Dalton, she thought.

Ed Staples, the family's attorney, padded into the kitchen next. After a hug and a greeting, he glanced up at the clock on the wall. "It's midnight. Time to get started if everyone's ready."

That meant it was Christmas. For a long moment, no one spoke.

Cadence got lost in memories of waiting up with her brothers and sister every Christmas Eve. When the clock struck midnight, they would gather in the main living room, scattering around the Christmas tree. May was there right alongside them with a tray of freshly baked cookies and glasses of milk. Their father would hand out presents and she could see the gleam in his eyes so clearly even now. It was the one time he went overboard and treated them to a stack of presents. He was like a kid himself for that brief time when he helped put together train sets or Hot Wheels tracks and then beamed as he sipped coffee and watched each of his kids with smiles plastered on their faces. They'd stay awake until the sun came up and then crash until supper.

She might not have her father anymore but she had those memories. In an odd way, remembering him made it feel like he was still present and it comforted her.

An instant later, it was like everyone in the room had the same idea at exactly the same time. Synchronicity.

"Merry Christmas," Cadence said to her brother Dade, who had moved next to her before embracing her in a warm hug.

"Merry Christmas, little sis," Dade said before they both moved on to pass holiday greetings onto someone else. Ella and Madelyn hugged and a few tears were shed.

Eventually, everyone filed into the main living area and took seats. Cadence glanced around, wishing Rory was there, too. There was no telling what dangers he faced outside and a thought struck her that something could've happened to him.

He might've encountered Dex or one of the others.

A tree branch scraped across the window, causing her to gasp. Others froze.

It was easy to see that everyone was on edge.

"Thank you to everyone for being here," Ed said. "I know your father would hate to miss a gathering like this and especially on Christmas."

"He always did like a good party," Ella agreed, and those who knew him best chuckled at the fond memory. It was true.

"And he loved to be the center of attention. Although, he'd never admit it," Cadence added.

Heads nodded and smiles brightened everyone's faces. She glanced at Wyatt and Madelyn before realizing they had no memories of their father. How sad was that? To grow up never knowing who their father was. She could help them in that department if they'd let her.

Ed held up a yellow legal-sized envelope and opened the clasp. On a sigh, he said, "Let's begin."

The ticking clock made Cadence's pulse kick up. Where was Rory?

She focused on Ed, trying to block out the fear that something had happened to him.

> "To my family,
>
> "First of all, I'd like to wish y'all a Merry Christmas. I'm sorry that I won't be there this year to join you for presents and our traditional meal."

Shocked gasps echoed throughout the large space.

"How on earth is this possible?" Cadence asked under her breath, but others said similar things. "Could he have known all along that he was being targeted for murder?"

Ed gave a noncommittal shrug. "He never said anything to me about it."

When she really thought about it, it was the only thing that made sense. He'd left letters for most of the others that had given them the closure they needed to be at peace with their complicated relationships with him.

But one part didn't add up. Her father had never been the roll-over-and-die type. Why would he let a murderer prance onto the property and shoot him in cold blood?

Logic said he might not've known how or when exactly it was going to happen. But had he expected it? Had he seen it coming somehow?

Once the room quieted down again, Ed continued reading.

> "I've never been a sentimental man, but I have loved every one of you in my own way. My biggest regret in life is that I wasn't a good enough father. It's my final hope that you can find forgiveness in your hearts for a foolish man who learned what was truly important a little too late in life."

Ed paused, clearly becoming emotional. He mumbled an apology before continuing.

> "To each of my six children I leave equal division of the ranch and my assets with the exception of a million dollars in cash and the main house, both of which go to May Apreas. Her faithful years of service, kindness and generosity have gone well above and beyond the call of duty. I thank you from the bottom of my heart, May."

Smiles wrapped everyone's faces who'd been touched by May. The gifts to her were so well deserved.

Ed explained that rights to the main house would revert to the children following May's death.

> "To Dade. I was the hardest on you and could never figure out how to fix it. You are so much like me that it scared me. I didn't want you to make the same mistakes I did. My failed attempts to build a bridge of communication recently are not your fault. They belong to me. I failed you, not the other way around. I am sorry. Forgiveness for my sake is too much to ask. So, do it for yours. It's taken a lifetime for me to figure out that forgiveness is a gift we give ourselves, not the other way around. I hope you can be free of the same burdens I carried that kept me from being able to let everyone know how dear y'all are to me. How proud I am of each one of you."

Sniffles filled the room and there wasn't a dry eye. Not even with the new additions to the family, some of whom had never met him.

Dalton threw an arm around Dade in a brotherly hug and it looked like a weight had been lifted from Dade. He and Cadence were the only two who hadn't received personal messages. Cadence was happy for Dade because he carried around the biggest burden from their childhoods. He and their father had never seen eye to eye or found common ground. The look on Dade's face right now said he had found peace with the past.

Cadence was hoping that her father would be able to

shed light on why Dex and the others might have murdered him. How Rupert was involved.

And, selfishly, she wanted to know where her mother was and if he'd stayed in contact with the woman who'd given birth to four of his children.

Ed allowed a few minutes to pause and let everyone gather their emotions. His ruddy cheeks were wet with tears and she figured he missed their father, his friend, as much as everyone else did. In some ways, Ed was probably even closer to their dad, being his best friend and confidant.

He glanced around the room, searching each face, seeming to wait for approval to keep going. He swiped at a tear and nodded before refocusing on the page in front of him.

> "I didn't talk about your mother much. Losing her when Cadence was still so young weighed on my conscience. I thought it was best to tell you she'd moved away because I didn't know how to explain to little kids that their mother was never coming back. I thought it would give you hope that you'd see her again someday instead of breaking you down like it did me. It was my guilt eating away at me. Not only was I a bad father but a no-excuse husband. When I lost her, I didn't know how to talk to you about death. I thought it would take away hope.
>
> "Life is odd.
>
> "Now that I'm facing mine, so much more makes sense to me."

Their father knew he was dying? That was the big secret he was going to reveal? The reason for the big changes in his life?

Questions swirled. Their mother had died? She hadn't run off?

Did Ruth know? She must not've because she would've said something. Right?

> "When I found out that the pain in my side turned out to be more than a pulled muscle or lower back injury, I realized life is short for everyone. Enjoy your time. Don't waste it on hurt or sorrow. Celebrate more. Let others win sometimes.
>
> "I've wronged a lot of people in my life, including the people who mattered most. A few men will most likely come for me and I'm not going to stop them. Believe me, whatever death they have planned will be so much shorter and less painful than the one nature has dealt. I'm not excusing anyone's behavior. No one should get away with murder. But it's my hope that you can forgive the one who gets to me first. Live your life on your terms and make them good ones.
>
> "I couldn't be prouder of any one of you. Hereford is in the best possible hands.
>
> "With all my love,
>
> "Your father."

Cadence glanced up in time to see Rory standing in the doorway. She pushed up to her feet, met him halfway across the room and buried her face in his chest.

His strong arms wrapped around her and she finally felt like she was home.

"I heard everything," he said low enough for only her to hear. "Your father's right. We have a chance to be better people than our parents. It's time to forgive them and ourselves, and move on."

## *Chapter Sixteen*

Out of the corner of his eye, Rory saw Ed Staples making a beeline toward him. Emotions had been running understandably high in the room and Ed showed that intensity in his expression.

Mr. Butler had been clear in person. Was he worried that Rory hadn't gotten the message to leave his daughter alone? Under the circumstances, Rory wondered if Mr. Butler would feel the same way now that Cadence was pregnant. Guess he'd know in a few seconds.

"This is for you, Mr. Scott." The family lawyer handed Rory an envelope. He glanced at Cadence—for reassurance?—before opening the letter as Ed excused himself from the conversation. He must've realized this needed to be a private moment.

Rory was thankful for the consideration as he unfolded the handwritten note.

> Rory,
> You remind me so much of my younger self. I've been hard on you. I tried my best to push you away. But the fact that you're reading this now shows me how much you care about my daughter.

It's been obvious to everyone that she took a shine to you the minute the two of you met. She was too young and needed a chance to date other people so she would know you were the one if she came back to you. I did everything I could to keep the two of you apart and give her time to grow into herself. I even sent her away to college, hoping she'd meet someone else there.

True love stands the test of time and I knew if the two of you ended up in the same room long enough that you'd find a way to be together.

You'll never know how much time you have with a person. Don't waste it.

And should you and Cadence decide to spend your lives together, I hope you'll take your place alongside the others on the ranch. I'm proud of Hereford. Not because of the money it made. It's done well enough. But for the people I've been able to help along the way. In the beginning, I bought a ranch to make a successful business. I'll admit it. Recently, I've realized that it was the home we built there that has mattered the most.

You have my blessing.

Mr. Butler had been good to Rory. The man was the reason Rory had stayed on the straight and narrow. Having her father's blessing lifted a heavy weight off Rory's shoulders. He needed to find a way to convince Cadence to marry him. He loved her with all his heart and he would trade his life if it meant protecting her and the babies.

With Cadence tucked under his arm, Rory felt like he was finally home.

Now, it was time to figure out why Dex and the others were after Cadence and put them behind bars for their involvement in Mr. Butler's murder. Rory wanted to give that gift to the family for taking him in and always making him feel a part of something real. He figured family was as much a choice as it was a birthright.

Dalton's cell phone buzzed and a hush fell over the room. He glanced at the screen. "It's Terrell."

This wasn't going to be good news.

Dalton answered the call and said a few *uh-huh*'s into the phone.

"Hold on," he said and then lifted his mouth away from the receiver. "There's been a breech. Someone's in the house."

A palpable wave of panic rolled through the room as Rory tucked Cadence behind him.

Everyone backed up until they were huddled together in the center of the space and could see every entrance into the room clearly.

Rory pushed himself up to the front so he could watch the hallway leading to the bedrooms and the laundry room doorway on the other side of the kitchen. Of course, they were all sitting ducks and a good sniper could pick them off one by one.

The sound of glass breaking whirled his attention toward the front window.

The crack of a bullet split the air.

"Get down," Rory commanded as he made himself as large a target as he could by puffing up his body.

Shock registered and he ignored the white-hot pain in his shoulder.

"Get everyone out of here and off the property," he said to Dade and Dalton.

The twins immediately bolted into action, moving the group toward the garage. Rory ducked behind a sofa and belly crawled toward the shooter that he was sure was Dex.

Dex would change locations now that he'd given his position away, so Rory needed to stay low and behind as large of an object as he could find.

One of the twins had the presence of mind to tap the light switch on his way out, plunging the living room/kitchen areas into complete darkness. Rory couldn't see his hand in front of his face. It would take a minute for his eyes to adjust.

Right now, he had the advantage, so he tucked and rolled toward the broken window, knowing full well Dex would've changed positions by now.

It was a chess match. The one with the best moves would win.

The stakes for Rory had never been higher. The Butlers had given him a real family with a real home. He was in love with Cadence and wanted to spend the rest of his life with her bringing up those babies. Being on the range in Wyoming without her had been miserable.

His life had been full of darkness and Cadence was the light.

In facing the possibility of losing the people he cared most about, life became crystal clear. Rory would do what it took to make his family safe. Nothing else mattered.

Rory pulled his backup weapon, a Sig Sauer, from his ankle holster. Sharp stabs of pain radiated from his right shoulder. That would be tricky for a couple of reasons. For one, he already knew he was bleeding badly. He ripped off a piece of his T-shirt to tie off the injury. Felt like the bullet had hit bone but that was the pain talking. Another problem was that being shot on the right shoulder could affect his aim. He needed a steady hand in order to hit his target at a safe distance. He might not have either.

Shouting echoed from the garage and it dawned on him what Dex and his boys were doing. Herding. They'd isolated him from the group and then attacked. He released a string of curse words as he popped to his feet and blasted toward the kitchen. He caught the corner of the solid wood coffee table on his shin, which caused him to stumble.

Quickly regaining his balance, he bolted toward the kitchen door. His eyes didn't need to be completely adjusted to the dark. He knew the layout of the house as well as he did his own cabin. He'd grown up at Hereford. It was home. And it was under siege.

Rory dropped to a crouched position, opened the door leading to the garage and then slipped inside.

A shot blasted his ears and there was more yelling. The sound of a car door slamming shut echoed.

Frantic, he searched the immediate area for the shooter. He dropped down onto his stomach to check for shoes, peeking under the carriage of the trucks. Cadence had had on the hiking boots he'd purchased for her. He scanned the area for any sign of the brown boots. Hope died in his chest when he saw there were none.

He couldn't shout at anyone because that would give away not only his position but also anyone's who answered.

Popping to his feet burned his thighs but it was his shoulder that was causing the blinding pain.

Progressing forward, he located a small group that was huddled together.

"Where is she?" he whispered to Dalton who was protecting the small group.

"With Dade maybe?" Dalton responded in a hushed tone.

Rory located Dade next and asked the same question. His heart clenched when Dade told him to ask Dalton.

All commotion had ended and silence belted Rory across the face like a physical punch.

A full search of the garage revealed she wasn't there.

Cruiser lights along with sirens lit up the night sky as Rory ran outside. His gaze darted across the expansive yard, searching for her. There was nothing. He checked the ground for any signs of her.

Did she break away? Run?

It was almost too much to hope that she'd gotten away and was biding her time until Dex and his men were caught.

Or was it? She knew the land as well as anyone.

He picked up on a set of footprints going out to the barn. The imprints in the heels were a match to Cadence's boots. The deep imprint suggested she was running. So this was recent.

The image of her hunkering down against the frigid

night air, trying to keep herself from freezing, assaulted Rory. Other images crossed his mind that he couldn't allow to take seed because they had her in a trunk somewhere with a bullet in her forehead.

Rory focused on the first possibility. The one that had her sleeping outside at night with no coat or covers. So much for improvement.

And then he realized the tracks stopped. He scanned the area for a second set or any signs of a struggle.

The doctor had told her to rest and he worried that more stress could cause her to lose the babies, *their babies.* Waves of anger vibrated through him.

A noise to his left sounded. Rory froze. It wasn't much more than wind whistling through barren trees but he heard it.

The unmistakable sound of a heavy shoe on a branch caught his attention next.

Rory crouched low, his movement soundless. Based on the weight of the footsteps, Rory was dealing with a male. He could also tell the person was being quiet intentionally, signaling the man was hunting. The man—Dex?—would take a few steps and then listen. After another few steps, he would stop to listen again.

What if Dex or one of his men were watching Rory?

And that's when Rory realized that tracking Cadence could bring the killer right to her.

Rory had a decision to make. His instincts said go after Dex and stop him. The sheriff hadn't caught him yet and if Rory walked away now, Dex could go free.

Before Rory could debate his next actions, Dex came into his field of vision. It was clear that Rory had the element of surprise on his side because Dex didn't so much as tilt his ear toward him. Dex liked to hide in the woods and shoot, which convinced Rory that he didn't trust going one-on-one with an opponent. Rory had him in height and build.

He waited until he could see Dex's chest move when he breathed before he made his move. And then Rory burst from behind the tree, tackling Dex at the knees. The smaller guy toppled over and Rory landed on top.

A fist connected with Rory's chin. His head snapped back and it took a second to register the pain radiating from his jaw. The loss of blood combined with the constant bite coming from his shoulder weakened him. He needed to make a mental adjustment for that as Dex bucked, trying to tip him off balance.

Rory threw a punch but his right side was too weak to make the impact he wanted. He felt around for a rock, anything he could use to knock Dex out.

Dex got off a few punches to Rory's midsection.

Thinking that this was the man who was trying to take Cadence away from him and harm his children gave Rory the burst of adrenaline he needed to power through the blinding pain and focus on stopping Dex.

He fired off several punches, connecting with Dex's face, chest and upper arms.

Dex's head snapped from side to side, taking the impact of everything Rory had left inside him to give. After a few more jabs, Dex finally dropped his arms and fell slack.

To make sure he'd debilitated his enemy, Rory fired off one more punch. When he was certain that Dex was not a threat, he rolled off and onto his back. His breathing was ragged and all he could see was dots.

He fished out his cell phone and called Sawmill to give his location before he passed out. Sawmill answered on the first ring. Rory immediately relayed his location.

"Rupert Grinnell turned himself in an hour ago. He had no idea his cousins were involved last summer with this character who goes by the name Dex. According to Mr. Grinnell, David Dexter Henley's mother claims to have had a relationship with Mr. Butler. Mr. Butler refused to acknowledge Dex as his child and she had a difficult life bringing up the child on her own. Dex talked to his associates about having a DNA test that confirmed he was an heir to the Butler estate. His associates said that he later said that Mike Butler needed to pay for walking out on Dex and his mother. They're assuming he murdered Mike Butler in order to draw the inheritance his father threatened to tie up in court should Dex try to claim it. Mr. Grinnell stated that Dex walked right past Cadence when she was leaving the barn the night of her father's murder." Sawmill paused.

"Meaning as soon as she realized it, she'd be able to positively ID him and testify," Rory said.

"The man became obsessed with tracking her down and said she needed to die so she couldn't identify him, according to his known associates. Mr. Grinnell said his cousins came to him once they realized how far the situation had gotten out of control and the three of them hatched a plan to disappear. David Dexter Henley had threatened them into doing his bidding in the first place and they were afraid of disobeying his orders."

Rory sighed in relief. The others were in custody. Dex was three feet away from him, still knocked out.

And then he heard a noise.

"Is one of your men near me?" he whispered into the phone.

"No," Sawmill admitted.

"Then I gotta go."

Rory listened intently, trying to discern the noise that could mean the difference between life and death.

The footsteps were definitely softer this time, so he hedged that it might be Cadence. Maybe he was hearing what he wanted—plain and simple hope—because he was about to pass out and his life might depend on being the one to wake first. Law enforcement was on its way. Rory fought against the blackness overwhelming him as he strained to listen.

More soft steps.

And then he heard the gasp that could only belong to Cadence.

His heart felt bigger than his chest, barely contained by his rib cage when her beautiful face came into view.

"Are you hurt?" he asked.

"No. I'm fine. Cold but good," she admitted. A look of panic crossed her features when she scanned his body and he instantly knew he must look in bad shape.

"Rory." She dropped down to his side. Her gaze shifting between Dex and Rory.

"It's done. A deputy is on his way. Rupert's cousins confessed and all three went to the sheriff's office to turn themselves in. All three are in custody. Rupert had no idea what was going on," he informed her. The look of relief on her face was short-lived.

"What about you, Rory?" Her gaze surveyed his shoulder and then his face. "Are you in pain?"

Tears welled in her eyes but her chin jutted out in defiance. She was trying to be strong for him.

He stared into her eyes so she would know just how serious he was about what he planned to say next. "I'll be fine the minute you agree to be my wife."

Her chin faltered.

"Before you answer, hear me out." His face pinched in pain as he tried to move his right arm to take her hand in his. Contact sent a bolt of lightning straight to his heart.

"You're hurting, Rory. Don't move." More tears welled in Cadence's eyes, a few spilling over and staining her cheeks.

"I wanted to ask your brothers first," he began and she shot him a warning look.

"I'm perfectly capable of making my own decisions about who I spend time with," she countered.

He smiled at her spunk, even though it hurt like hell.

"Believe me, I know. But I want to do this the right way. No more going behind people's backs. I already have your father's blessing." He patted his jeans pocket with his left hand.

At least she smiled at that, though it didn't reach her eyes.

"If you'll have me, I'm asking you to marry me. You're all the family I need in this life. You and those babies *are* my life. You're the only person I want to come home to every night. The one I can't wait to see first thing in the morning. I want us to be an official family, Cadence." His normal confidence waned. "What do you say? Will you do me the honor of becoming my wife?"

Tears free-fell now and he couldn't tell if that was a good thing or not. His breath stuck in his throat.

"I've loved you since the day I met you, Rory Scott. But I have to ask, what's changed? You still love the outdoors and you'll always see me as some sort of princess."

"That's where you're wrong. I've always treated you as an equal. I never thought I was good enough for you before. If you tell me that I am, I promise to believe you. All I really need to know is that you love me. I want to do right by you, Cadence. My life for the past five months without you has been pure hell. There's nothing on the range that can compete with the way I feel for you. You and those babies are all I really need for a good life, a happy life," he said.

Cadence's face broke into a smile. "I love you. I know who you are and I'll be your wife on one condition."

"Which is?"

"You have to stay true to yourself. I love you the way you are and I wouldn't dream of keeping you indoors or changing you in any way." Her tears stemmed. "Plus, if you change for my sake, you'll resent me."

"That's where you're wrong, Cadence. I'm changing because I'm in love and I want to be with you. And there's no better place than holding you when going to bed at night, comfy sheets and all."

The sound of hurried footsteps broke into the moment.

"So much has changed in the past year," she said. "The family has suffered a terrible loss but I realized something earlier. We've gained so many new faces and so much love. I don't want to dwell on the past. I want to walk toward our future. Together with our girls."

"I love you, Cadence Butler," Rory said as the squawk of a deputy's radio cut into the night air.

"Save your energy," Cadence said. "Help is almost here and I want you back to full form soon so I can marry you."

"As long as you agree to let us keep Boots," Rory said. His heart filled with love for the woman by his side as she smiled.

"I insist we keep him," she said.

"Merry Christmas, Cadence."

"Merry Christmas." She leaned toward him and pressed her lips to his.

He kissed her as he touched her belly. This was his family. He was home.

# Epilogue

Rory turned to his wife. He'd never openly admit the look was meant to steel his nerves. Admitting weakness had never been his strong suit. Seeing Cadence's face and quiet strength offered the reassurance he needed to take the next couple of steps toward the old bungalow-style house that needed a fresh coat of paint.

While April showers brought May flowers in many parts of the country, the first of May promised plenty of thunderstorms in Texas and the skies were welling up with clouds. The air was thick and heavy. His hospital visit and recovery were long behind him.

Cadence looked even more beautiful—if that was possible—holding their eight-week-old daughter Katie in her arms. Rory held the other bundle, Kelly, who was swaddled in a pink blanket. Two miracles. Three counting his wife.

Rory wasn't sure how he'd gotten so lucky, but he didn't plan to waste his good fortune.

"I can't wait to meet them," Cadence said. She'd taught him so much about forgiveness in the past five months.

"I hope it turns out to be a good thing." In forgiving

others, the darnedest thing happened. He was finally able to forgive himself. For all of it. For the feeling of letting his mother down by not being able to stop his father from hurting her. For the feeling that he'd let Cadence down.

Rory stepped onto the porch. The boards creaked under his weight. The whole place could use some repairs, he noted. Easy enough to send a contractor over to help out if his parents would agree. He had no idea what mood they'd be in and part of him—a big part—had been holding off on making this house call because he hadn't wanted to expose Cadence and the girls to his parents' unpredictability. Cadence had made the phone call asking to meet his parents. He'd been planning to do it, putting it off, but she'd beat him to the punch. That summed up his wife on so many levels. She wasn't one to shy away from a difficult situation. She'd put up with him and had agreed to spend the rest of her life with him. Again, he thought about how lucky he was.

Before he could knock, the door swung open and his mother stood there with a wide smile on her face. She looked surprisingly good. She wore a sleeveless dress. His gaze immediately swept her arms for bruises. There were none.

"Come inside," she said, opening the door wide.

Rory saw his father standing behind his mother. He, too, wore a big smile. Everything looked copacetic but looks could be deceiving.

"Do you want to come in, son?" his father asked, seeming to catch on to his hesitation.

Rory glanced at the grouping of rockers on the porch. "How about sitting outside?"

He wasn't ready to walk into that house again, a house that had brought so much pain, frustration and sorrow.

His mother nodded, still smiling as she wiped a tear from her cheek.

"You okay?" he asked, stepping aside so she could come out.

"It's just so good to see you again," she said as more tears sprang to her eyes. She quickly apologized as he wrapped an arm around her.

"Same here," his father grumbled. He seemed to be fighting emotions, too.

"This is my wife, Cadence." There was so much pride in his voice that he could hear it.

Cadence beamed at his parents. "So nice to meet you both."

She was warmth and sunshine wrapped up into one as she exchanged greetings with his parents.

"It's wonderful to meet you." His mother beamed right back. "She's beautiful, Rory. Looks like she can keep you on your toes."

His father introduced himself before giving her a hug. It was odd to Rory but he liked what was happening with his folks.

"Who do we have here?" his mother asked, nodding toward the baby in his arms.

"Kelly. And over there is Katie." He nodded toward the other pink bundle.

His father shoved his hands in his pockets and shuffled his feet as he moved next to Cadence.

"Please, take a seat wherever you want," he said before smiling at his own wife. He took his right hand out of his pocket and put his arm around Rory's mother.

"Those are our grandbabies," he said quietly and with a reverence Rory had never heard from his father before. Was it true? Had the man changed? Rory wanted to believe it was possible and signs pointed toward it being true.

He searched his mother's arms for bruises again and saw none. Relief washed over him, because he was no longer a child and wouldn't be able to hold his tongue as a man.

Was it possible his parents had changed?

Rory took a seat after Cadence. His parents took a bench, sitting next to each other as they held hands.

"Do you talk to Renee? I plan on tracking her down next," he said as his mother peered at Katie with a huge smile practically plastered on her face.

"We found her last year. She's making music in Nashville with Rodney," his mother supplied.

"She followed her dream. That's cool." It was cool, and he applauded his sister for making good on her plans.

His mother shrugged. "You should hear them. The band's called… Oh, shoot, Henry, what's the name?"

Rory's father put his hands together in his lap. "What are they calling themselves now? Sudden-something."

"No, I think that was the name of the last one. The lead singer took off. They'd been doing backup vocals and making good money, too. But he wanted to take his act solo, so they decided to do their own thing and jobs lined up for them," she supplied. "Oh, I know. It's called, Double Dose of Dixie."

His father was rocking his head.

"She and Rodney have a son. He's the cutest thing with curls for days." His mother's eyes lit up when she talked about Renee and her family.

"How old is he?" It was strange to think of his sister as a mother. Rory almost laughed. No stranger than him being a father when he really thought about it.

"He's five-years-old. They call him Rory Daniel," his father supplied.

That news punched him in the chest.

"I should've stayed in touch," he admitted.

"She says the same thing," his father said. He fished his cell phone out of his pocket.

"Oh, yeah, show him the pictures," his mother urged.

After a few swipes on the screen, his father handed over the phone. Cadence leaned in and Rory marveled at the five-year-old kid with the gap-toothed smile.

"He looks just like your pictures at that age," his mother said proudly.

"He's beautiful," Cadence agreed. "I hope our girls get those curls."

Being back at home was nicer than Rory had expected it to be.

"She happy?" he asked his mother.

"I believe so," she responded. "I mean, look at them. They live in Nashville and she's making music. They're doing pretty well financially. It's not like they're making the kind of money some of the bigger acts make but it's enough to make a good living, to make a home."

"And how about the two of you?" he pressed. "Are you happy?"

His father leaned back and slowly put his arm around

his wife. "Losing our kids taught us a thing or two about how our actions affect everyone around us. I quit drinking not too long after you left."

His mother perked up. "He went to one of those AA meetings and before you knew it, we were in counseling." Her eyes sparked in a way he'd never seen before. She seemed happy. "We would've reached out to you a long time ago but we had no idea how to reach you."

"I've been out of touch. I used to be a tracker. I hunted poachers. Not being able to locate me told me I was doing my job well," he admitted.

"Doesn't matter, son. You're here now. And your mother and I..." He hesitated. "*I* owe you an apology. When I should've been a father, a husband, I was too busy trying to hide my own pain. Guess I thought I could drink it away, but that only made it worse." He leaned forward and rested his elbows on his knees. "I'll never be perfect, but I'd like to be part of your life. I understand that might take some time after the wrongs I did. I've changed and... I hope that someday I'm half the man you turned out to be."

"As far as the apology goes, I accept," Rory said. "Forgiveness is something I'm learning from my wife. I'm still a work-in-progress. But getting to know the two of you sounds good to me."

"I should've made iced tea so we can toast," his mother said. "Well, here goes nothing." She held out her hand as though holding on to a glass. "To second chances."

"And new beginnings," Cadence said, pretending to clink the imaginary glasses. "And most of all, to love."

She looked at each of his parents and then beamed at their daughters.

Rory could toast to that. To love. To the loves of his life.

And to the future ahead of them, which was something he'd always believed would be out of reach for a man like him—a real family.

* * * * *

# DELTA FORCE DADDY

CAROL ERICSON

# *Prologue*

Pain seared through his left ankle as he put weight on it. He listed to the side, throwing out a hand to wedge it against the rocky wall of the cliff face. As the gritty surface abraded the skinned flesh on the heel of his hand, he sucked in a breath.

Sinking into a crouch, he extended his injured leg in front of him and surveyed the rocky expanse below. Even with two steady legs, hydrated and nourished, this landscape would pose a challenge to navigate. Parched, weakened by hunger and with a bum ankle, he didn't stand a chance.

He eyed the gray skies, scuffs of cloud rolling across the expanse, promising rain and relief—and more challenges. He dragged his boot over the rocks coated with dirt. Once the rains started, rivulets of water would wash the grit from the stones, joining forces in a muddy stream, making his path to the bottom of the mountain a slippery—and dangerous—proposition.

He'd already witnessed one of his men take a tumble down the side of a mountain. Had Knight survived that fall? If he knew anything about his Delta Force team, he'd lay odds on it. But even if Asher Knight had made it through, the men who had double-crossed them would've finished off Knight.

They wouldn't have left any witnesses.

He took a deep breath and swiped the back of his hand across his mouth. "Did you think it was gonna be easy going AWOL in Afghanistan in the middle of enemy territory, Denver?"

His voice sounded rusty to his own ears, but it was strong enough to startle a bird from its hiding place. The bird scuttled and flapped before taking wing and soaring up to those threatening clouds. He watched its ascent with something like envy roiling in his gut.

He willed himself to stand up—he owed it to Knight and the others to persevere. He stomped his bad foot and secured the laces on his boot—the tighter, the better for support. He hoisted his backpack and belted it around his waist. He strapped his rifle across his body. Couldn't afford to lose that if he took a fall.

The first step jolted his bones, and he gritted his teeth. The next step felt worse, but at least he didn't slide down the mountain.

Several more yards of jerky movement and his face broke into a sweat, which dripped into his eyes, blurring his vision. Maybe this descent would work better by touch and feel than sight, anyway. He didn't need to see the view if he pitched off a cliff.

Something scrabbled behind him, dislodging several small stones that tumbled down and peppered the back of his legs. He could get lucky and ride down with an avalanche.

"Meester."

Ripping his sidearm from its holster, he whipped around and took aim at…a boy. The boy looked down at him from several feet above, clinging to the side of the mountain like a goat.

Denver's muscles coiled, and he spat out in guttural Pashto, "Who are you? Where did you come from?"

The boy's eyes grew round, crowding out the other features in his gaunt face. Then he raised an old Russian rifle, pointed it at him and said, "American soldier. You die today."

## *Chapter One*

"I'm sorry. Lieutenant Knight doesn't remember you." The army officer on the line cleared his throat. "But he doesn't remember much of anything. He didn't mention your name. That's for sure. Are you positive you're engaged to him?"

Paige's hand shook as she tried to hold on to her phone. "That's crazy. Do you think I'd make up some phony engagement to an injured Delta Force soldier?"

The army officer on the line paused, and a burning rage sizzled through Paige's veins. She released it as a hiss through her teeth.

"I—I'm sure you are engaged and Lieutenant Knight will remember soon enough. The doctors are confident he'll remember everything."

"Oh, that's encouraging." Paige took a deep breath and closed her eyes. "What else has he forgotten?"

"Well, ma'am." The officer coughed. "If he's forgotten it, how would he be able to tell us about it?"

Her fist clenched in her lap. "You must know details of his life. Does he remember them?"

"I'm just the messenger, ma'am. I don't know much about Lieutenant Knight's condition."

*That's for sure.* Paige took a gulp of water from the

glass on her desk. "Can I talk to his doctors? I'm a psychologist myself."

"Ma'am, since you're not next of kin, the doctors won't speak to you."

She ground her back teeth together, suppressing the scream that ached in her throat. "His mother is dead, his father's in prison and he's an only child. Whom exactly is the doctor speaking to about his care?"

"I don't know, ma'am. We called you because Lieutenant Knight had your name and number in his phone. Yours was the only number listed in his favorites."

"There!" She was his favorite. Didn't that mean something? "Obviously, I'm the person he'd want you to contact in an emergency. Can I fly out to see him?"

"No, ma'am. We can't allow that—yet."

The soldier's words punched her in the gut, and she doubled over. She had to speak to Asher, had to see him. Once they were back in each other's arms, he'd remember everything.

"How much longer will he be in Germany?"

"Again, ma'am, I'm not at liberty to discuss any of the particulars of the lieutenant's recovery with you. I got the order to call you out of courtesy...because you're a favorite."

She wished he'd stop saying that word. "Can you at least tell me he's not badly injured physically? Will he make a full recovery?"

"He's strong. As far as I know, he's doing fine physically and is expected to make a full recovery. And, ma'am?"

"Yes?"

"That's off the record."

When the call ended, Paige sank to her chair behind the desk and placed her hands flat on the surface. What did this mean? Just because Asher had amnesia and couldn't recall the details of their relationship...or her, did that mean it never happened? What were those doctors in Germany doing to help him recover his memories?

A light blinked above her door, indicating her next client had arrived. How in the world could she help anyone right now when she couldn't even help herself?

She dragged herself out of the chair, straightened her shoulders and strode to the door. Plastering a smile on her face, she swung it open.

"Come on in, Krystal."

Her next client sashayed into the room, flicking her long hair over one shoulder and wiggling her hips in a tight skirt that she must wear to impress her johns—which she wasn't supposed to have anymore.

She smacked a piece of paper on Paige's desk and tapped it with one long fingernail. "Can you sign now? Only two more sessions after this one before I satisfy the terms of my probation."

Paige scribbled her signature on the form. "I hope you've gotten more out of these sessions than just the completion of your probation."

"I have." Krystal sat in her usual chair and crossed her long legs. "You've been great, Paige."

Paige took the seat across from Krystal and nodded, which Krystal took as a signal to launch into a recitation of her sad life story.

Her words filled the room, and Paige tried to catch one or two to get the gist, although she'd heard most of it before.

"So, do you think I should call my father?"

Paige blinked and dropped the pencil she'd been tapping against the arm of her chair. She dipped forward and patted the carpet to buy time, to hide her confusion at the question that seemed to have come out of left field.

"It's right next to the leg."

"Huh?" Paige looked up, her face flushed with heat.

"The pencil. It's next to the left chair leg."

Paige's fingers inched to the left and curled around the pencil. "Got it."

Krystal arched one painted-on eyebrow. "So, do you? Do you think I should call the scumbag?"

Clearing her throat, Paige folded her hands in her lap. "What do you think?"

"I knew you were going to say that." Krystal slumped in her chair and clicked together her decorated nails. "Why do you always answer a question with a question?"

"If you did call your father, what would you say?"

"I'm not sure." Krystal chewed all the lipstick off her bottom lip. "I don't want to remember any more stuff about him."

"Any more stuff?"

"I know you helped me with the repressed memories and all that, and remembering my father's abuse really did help me deal with my issues and figure out why I thought hooking was a good way to make a living, but I think there might be more." Krystal dashed a tear from her face, leaving a black streak on her cheek. "I have a funny feeling in my gut that he did more to me, and I'm afraid seeing him again is gonna make those memories bubble up. And I don't want them. I don't want them anymore."

Paige hunched forward, her knees almost touching Krystal's, and shoved a box of tissues at her. "You want me to tell you what to do? Screw it. Don't talk to him. Don't see him."

After Krystal left her office, all smiles and thanks,

Paige plopped down in her desk chair and scooted up to her computer. She brought up her calendar on the monitor and placed her first call to cancel her appointments for the next two weeks.

If just seeing her father would prompt memories for Krystal, maybe seeing her would do the same for Asher.

She felt guilty canceling on her clients, but she'd just gotten her most important client ever.

ASHER WEDGED HIS boots against the railing surrounding the porch and squinted into the woods beyond the clearing. The doctors here must be wary of him going postal or something, because he could sense them spying on him. Spying? That was what his intuition told him, anyway.

He huffed out a breath and watched it form a cloud in the cold air. Funny how he could remember all the skills he'd learned as a Delta Force member, including that last mission—the one that had thrown him for a loop and wiped out all his previous memories—but he couldn't recall the rest of his life.

The doctors had assured him it would all come back, not that he had much of a family to come back to—mother dead, father in federal prison for bank robbery and no siblings or even aunts and uncles. No wife.

He glanced at his left ring finger and wiggled it. No ring tan and the docs had assured him they'd perused his army files and no wife was listed—even though it felt like he could have one. Something—or someone—more than just his memories felt missing.

The guys who might know more about him than anyone else—his Delta Force team—couldn't be reached right now. Their commander, Major Rex Denver, had gone AWOL. He should know—he'd been there the moment Denver had escaped.

The man he'd trusted with his life, had looked up to, had followed blindly, that man had shot and killed an army ranger and had pushed Asher over the edge of a cliff before escaping. Asher had been rescued by a squad of army rangers, surviving the fall with minor injuries… because his head had taken the brunt of the impact.

Asher ran a fingertip along the scar on the back of his head where his hair had yet to grow back. That moment, that scene when Denver had shot the ranger and then turned on him and pushed him into oblivion was etched on his brain, but he couldn't remember his own family.

The doctors in Germany had tried to fill him in on his background, so he knew the outline, hadn't even been shocked by the details of a dead mother and a father imprisoned for bank robbery. On some gut level that life had resonated with him, but he couldn't recall the specifics.

The docs showed him pictures of his Delta Force teammates, had even allowed him a phone call with Cam, who'd been on leave.

Asher scratched the edges of his scar. That phone call hadn't gone well. Cam had accused him of lying. He didn't have a chance to get into it with him because the psychologist ended the call. The doc had shrugged off Cam as a hothead, and that definitely rang a bell with Asher.

An ache creeped up his neck, and Asher tried to massage it away. The doctors had warned him about trying too hard to remember, but what else could he do in this convalescent home? The army called it a rehabilitation center, but Asher didn't feel rehabilitated. He needed… something. He couldn't put his finger on it, but a big piece of his life was missing.

He snorted and dropped his feet from the railing, his boots thumping against the wood porch. *Most* of his life was missing right now, and if he wanted it back, he'd be well-advised to keep taking his meds and going to his sessions with the shrinks. Shrink. Shrinky-dinky.

Where had that come from? He shook his throbbing head. The stuff that popped into his mind sometimes convinced him he'd already gone off the deep end.

A flash of light glinted from the trees, and Asher squinted. As far as he knew, no roads ran through that part of the property. A new symptom, flashes of light, had probably just been added to his repertoire of strange happenings in his brain.

He rubbed his eyes, and the light flickered again, glinting in the weak winter sunlight. He cranked his head around to survey the buildings behind him. Most of the patients here napped after lunch and the staff took the time to relax. He had the place to himself—as long as his spies were on break.

When the third flash of light made its way out of the dense forest, Asher pushed back from his chair and stretched. Investigating this would take his mind off the jumble in his brain.

He zipped up his jacket and stuffed his hands into his pockets. This felt like a mission and his fingertips buzzed, but he felt stripped bare without his weapon. He wouldn't need it for what would probably turn out to be something caught on the branches of a tree, but at least he had a mission.

He strode across the rolling lawn, scattered with chairs and chaise lounges, abandoned in the wintry chill of December. He glanced over his shoulder, expecting someone to stop him, although he didn't know why. He wasn't a prisoner here. Was he?

Hunching his shoulders, he made a beeline for the forest at the edge of the grass. When he reached the tree line, he tensed his muscles. His instincts, which seemed to have been suppressed by the drugs he got on a regular basis, flared into action.

He stepped onto the thick floor of the wooded area, his boots crunching pine needles. Where had the light gone? It had flashed just once more on his trek across the lawn, like a beacon guiding him.

The rustle of a soft footstep had him jerking to his right, his hand reaching impotently for a gun. "Come out where I can see you."

A hint of blue appeared amid the unrelenting greens and browns of the forest, and then a head, covered with a hood, popped out from behind the trunk of a tree.

"Asher?"

He swallowed and blinked. Had the docs chased him out here, too?

The figure emerged from behind the tree and the hood fell back. A tumble of golden hair spilled over the woman's shoulder, and Asher had a strange urge to run his fingers through the silky strands.

"Asher, it's me." She held out a hand, keeping one arm around the trunk of the tree and leaning out toward the side as if approaching a wild animal. "It's Paige. Do you remember?"

Paige? Her voice sounded like cool water tumbling over rocks in a stream. A sharp pain lanced the wound on his head, and he rubbed his fingers along the scar to make it stop.

She hugged the tree with one arm, her other arm stretched out toward him in a yearning gesture that made his heart ache.

"Are you in pain, my love?"

His mouth gaped open. "I-is this a joke?"

Her eye twitched, but her smooth face remained impassive. “No joke, Asher. I’m your fiancée.”

“My fiancée? But…”

A million emotions coursed through his brain in a tangled mess. *Ivy. Shrinky-dinky.* He tried to latch on to one, but something stung the back of his neck. As he clapped his hand against his flesh, the beautiful face before him melted away and he sank into darkness.

# *Chapter Two*

As Asher hit the ground, Paige gasped and lurched forward.

Loud voices and a crashing noise had her jumping back behind the tree.

"What the hell, Granger? Did you have to shoot him with a dart?"

Paige backed up and scrambled for cover behind a clump of bushes and a rotting log. She flipped up her hood and smashed her face into the mulch, the smell of moist, verdant dirt filling her nostrils.

"Don't give me that, Lewis. If that guy gets away, it's your ass and my ass."

"I don't think he was running for the hills or anything. Where would he be going? Besides, he's got enough drugs pumping through his veins that he wouldn't get far, anyway."

Paige held her breath as two sets of footsteps marched closer to her hiding place. She couldn't see the two men and she hoped to God they couldn't see her.

The other man, Granger, snorted. "You're gonna count on that? This dude's big, and even though his mind's messed up, he's still in Delta Force physical condition."

"That's exactly my point." The underbrush crackled and rustled as if the two men were hauling a tree trunk.

"You brought him down, and now we gotta carry him back. We coulda just told him the Ping-Pong tournament was starting or something."

A bug crawled across Paige's face and she squeezed her eyes closed, willing it away from her nose. These two men could not catch her here, as much as she wanted to save Asher from their clutches.

"We didn't know what he was up to or his state of mind. I don't trust any of these guys, and I'm not gonna lose my job or risk getting my ass kicked by any of them—especially this one."

Huffs, puffs and curses replaced the conversation of the two men, and when the forest had gone silent once again, Paige raised her head and peeked over the crest of the log.

She crawled on her belly in the opposite direction, every cell in her body screaming at her to turn back toward Asher. Would he remember their meeting when he came to? Would he understand what they'd done to him? Would he know to keep her a secret?

By the time she reached the end of the wooded area and scrambled downhill to the access road, tears streamed down her face. What were they doing to Asher and why?

He was a hero who'd risked his life for his country, and that very country now held him captive, held his mind captive.

She hiked along the side of the access road, her boots scuffing the dirt. She couldn't go to the police. She couldn't go to the army. She might be putting Asher in danger if she did.

Before she hit the main road, she glanced over her shoulder at the hillside covered with trees. She'd be back.

She'd be back to get Asher and get him the hell out of that loony bin—after all, she was the fiancée of a D-Boy.

ASHER GROANED AND shifted to his side. His tongue swept his bottom lip and he tasted dirt. The forest. The woman.

A chipper voice pierced his brain. “Coming to?”

He peeled open one eye and took in the form of a sturdy nurse in pink scrubs. It wasn’t this woman—Tabitha—he’d seen in the forest. How come he could remember her so well?

“What happened?” He cupped the back of his head with his hand, flattening his palm against the scar.

“You got a little too ambitious.” She shook a finger at him and he wanted to chomp it off, but the sentiment floated away before it even registered.

“While everyone else was napping, you decided to take a walk across the lawn and collapsed midway.”

Asher ground his teeth together, mashing the dirt in his mouth. *You’re lying, Tabitha.*

“I remember heading across the grass.” He massaged his temple with two fingers. “I don’t remember much after that.”

As he struggled to sit up, Nurse Tabitha sprang into action and perched on the edge of the bed. “Let me.”

She curled a strong arm around his shoulders, hooked the other around his chest and helped him sit up. “There.”

“How’d I get back here?” He straightened up farther, hoping to dislodge her hand resting on his chest.

She curled her fingers, briefly digging her nails into his pec before releasing him. “Granger and Lewis went out to move the lawn furniture and saw you sprawled on the grass. They got you back to your room.”

Asher ran his tongue along his dry teeth and recognized the cotton mouth associated with the meds they gave him—the meds he’d chucked this morning. His gaze wandered to the window, the curtains open to the dark night.

"Did I pass out? Have a seizure? It was daytime when I took that walk, or at least late afternoon."

Tabitha's translucent eyelashes fluttered. "Just a little overexertion, and because of your…brain injury, the doctors thought it best to medicate you."

Of course they did.

Asher scratched the scruff on his jaw. "Thank God for Lewis and…"

"Granger."

"Right."

Tabitha hunched forward, her pink tongue darting out of her mouth. "I could shave you if you'd like."

He'd rather grow a beard down to his knees. "I'm…"

"How's the patient feeling, Tabitha?"

The nurse leaned forward and pressed a warm, clammy hand against his forehead. "He's awake and feeling fine, certainly looking fine, and I'm sure he's ready to eat. Are you hungry, Lieutenant?"

Asher threw back the covers, realizing for the first time he was naked beneath a hospital gown that gaped open in the front. Who'd done the honors of taking off his clothes? He sure hoped it wasn't Nurse Touchy-Feely.

His gaze darted around the room, looking for his missing clothes. "I am ready to eat. Too late to grab something in the mess hall?"

"Not so fast there, Lieutenant Knight." Dr. Evans stood by the bed, hovering over him. "I'd like to run a few tests and then bring Dr. Goshen in to see you."

"The shrink?" He swung his legs over the side of the bed, almost taking out Tabitha. "I'm fine. I passed out. I didn't have a hallucination."

Did he? Was Paige, his fiancée, all an illusion? Nobody had said anything yet about finding a woman in the woods. If she hadn't been a dream, he hoped she got away, because he had a feeling she wouldn't be welcome here.

"Your passing out could've been psychological. We don't want to take any chances." The doctor jerked his thumb at Tabitha. "While we're poking and prodding your body and mind, Tabitha can go down to the kitchen and put in an order for your dinner." The doctor adjusted his glasses. "You can have dinner in bed and we'll give you something to ensure you have a good night's sleep."

Asher's blood boiled and his hand clenched into a fist. Then he closed his eyes, dragging in a deep breath. If he kicked up a ruckus now, they'd never let him out of their sights again.

"You know, that sounds good about now."

"Of course it does. Tabitha, help the lieutenant back into bed. I'll do my thing and go round up Dr. Goshen."

Tabitha reached across him, her right breast brushing his arm, and fluffed up his pillows. "We had some delicious pork chops and mashed potatoes tonight. I'll have the cook fix you up a special plate and have him add an extra dessert."

"That'll work." He eased back onto the bed, his gown hitching up to his thighs.

Tabitha tugged on the edge of the material, her fingers dangerously close to his crotch, and then twitched the covers back over his legs. She tucked the covers around his waist, and her hands lingered next to his hips.

"Anything else I can get you before ordering your dinner?"

"I'm fine, Tabitha. Thanks." He even managed to crack a smile in her direction.

Wrong move.

The nurse turned pink up to her strawberry blond hair. "We're going to make sure you stay that way… Asher."

When Dr. Evans returned with the psychiatrist, Dr. Goshen, Tabitha squeezed Asher's thigh and gave him an encouraging nod.

He endured their invasion of his body and mind with a smile on his face and an agreeable tone in his voice. When Tabitha returned with a tray groaning with steaming food, Dr. Goshen shook out two blue pills next to the plate.

"Take these when you get some food in your stomach, and you'll be back on track."

Back on track to crazy town? The only track he wanted to be on was the one back to the forest...and Paige.

PAIGE RAN HER fingers through her damp hair and collapsed on the hotel bed. He really didn't know her. His dark green eyes had been vacant when he looked at her. Maybe he suffered from more than memory loss.

She'd worked with enough people suffering from PTSD to know it could take many forms. Maybe he was a danger to himself and others and that was why the army had him stashed away here—captive. Maybe he'd been trying to go AWOL, like Major Denver. Maybe they were just holding him here until he got better before they court-martialed him.

She rolled over onto her stomach and pounded the pillow with her fist. No way. She had a hard time believing Major Denver turned, but apparently Asher himself had confirmed it. He'd been the lone survivor of the disastrous mission that had resulted in the death of an army ranger, the defection of Denver and Asher's fall and subsequent amnesia.

If Asher were in trouble with the army, wouldn't they just tell her? That would be enough to keep her away. Her inside army source, Dad's friend and now Mom's confidant Terrence Elder, hadn't mentioned anything about an arrest or court-martial. Terrence had pulled in a few favors to find out where Asher had been sent after Germany. That was how Paige had tracked Asher down to the convalescent facility, Hidden Hills, here in Vermont.

Asher's own teammates had been no help at all. If they'd returned her calls, and only a few did, they denied any knowledge of Asher's whereabouts and weren't too concerned about finding him. They'd viewed his accusations against Major Denver as the supreme betrayal of the man and the team.

But Asher would always do the right thing. With his father in federal prison for bank robbery, Asher followed the straight and narrow path. If he saw any wrongdoing, he'd report it—no matter who it was or how much it pained him to do so. She had firsthand knowledge of that.

If Asher said Major Denver killed that army ranger, pushed Asher off a cliff and took off, that was what happened.

But Asher had amnesia. How did he remember all that and not remember his fiancée? And if he didn't remember her, he didn't remember…

Her cell phone rang on the nightstand and she swept it off and answered. "Hi, Mom. Everything okay?"

"We're fine. Everything okay there? Did you see him?"

"Sort of. It's a long story." She tapped her phone's display. "You're not using FaceTime. Is Ivy still awake? It's three hours earlier there."

"I'm sorry, honey. Ivy went down for a nap right after dinner. Do you want me to do the face thing when she wakes up?"

"That's all right, Mom. I'm exhausted."

"I-is Asher okay? Do you think you can help him?"

Paige scooped in a big breath. "I do. I think I can help him."

"All by yourself? Maybe you should come home, Paige. You don't need this stress. Let the army handle it."

"I can handle the stress, Mom. Don't worry about me. It's Asher who needs help this time, and I'm not going to abandon him."

Her mother clicked her tongue. "Don't push yourself. You don't do well under pressure."

After that comment, Paige ended her call with Mom sooner rather than later and stretched out on the bed, staring at the ceiling.

She'd better start doing well under pressure, because the only way to help Asher was to get him out of that hell-hole and restore his memory of her…and their daughter.

THE NEXT MORNING after breakfast, Paige shook out a clean pair of jeans. She'd wear the same hooded jacket as yesterday, since it seemed to have kept her hidden in the forest. Those two goons had no idea she was hiding in plain sight.

Asher had been on that porch by himself after lunch, so she'd aim for the same time again. Would he follow her signal? Would he rat her out—just like he'd ratted out Denver?

At least nobody had come into the small town of Mooseville looking for her. If she could get back to that wooded area again, she'd be safe. She just needed Asher to trust her.

Could he trust a…stranger? She clutched the jeans to her chest and bowed her head. She and Asher could never be strangers. Her love for him soaked every pore in her body.

When he found out she was pregnant, he'd swept her

up in his arms and swung her around and around, even though the pregnancy had been a surprise and she wasn't quite…ready. He'd wanted nothing more than a family of his own…and now he couldn't even remember he had one.

She wiped the back of her hand across her tingling nose. She had no time for tears and no time for Mom's doubts. She had to rescue her man, if he'd let her.

After lunch, Paige parked her rental car in a turnoff on the main road, tucking it away and out of sight. As she hiked up the road to the access trail, she tilted back her head and studied the sky. The sun still shone through the clouds, enough for her to catch its beams with her mirror and signal Asher, as she'd done yesterday.

She ducked onto the access road and pumped her legs up the hill as the terrain grew more challenging. A steep angle and a few bushes didn't faze her. She'd hike through fire and brimstone to get to Asher.

The trees became denser, but Paige had marked her way the day before and those bits of blue yarn guided her back toward the compound perched on the hill.

She located her lookout tree and jumped to catch the lowest branch. She swung herself up and clambered from branch to branch like a clumsy monkey to reach her perch.

She shrugged off her pack and pulled out the binoculars. She scanned the desolate lawn. Maybe the action perked up in the warmer weather months…or maybe this retreat kept its patients drugged up and chained in the basement. Clenching her teeth, she shivered.

Fifteen minutes later Asher rewarded her patience by appearing on the porch, taking the same chair as yesterday. She focused the lenses on him, and her heart filled with joy. He looked healthy, if…lackadaisical.

As she reached into the inside pocket of her jacket, the door behind Asher opened and a nurse stepped onto the porch.

"Damn." Paige's whisper stirred the leaves on the branch hanging next to her face.

Were they watching him now? They must've been watching him yesterday to notice he'd left the porch and loped across the grass.

Her jaw ached with tension and disappointment. She might just have to go through the front door and demand to see him.

She refocused on Asher and the nurse and pressed her lips into a thin line. Was personal massage part of Asher's recovery?

The nurse, standing behind him, had her hands on his shoulders, massaging and rubbing him. Each time she reached forward, her hands slid beneath his jacket and moved against his chest.

Either Asher liked it or he was too zoned out to care. Each time the nurse's hands slid farther and farther down his chest, working toward the inevitable happy ending.

Asher turned his head and said something, and she stopped. Had he gotten the feeling his fiancée was watching?

When the nurse retreated inside, Paige grabbed the mirror and caught the weak sun. She tilted it back and forth, and Asher raised his head.

He'd seen it.

Paige's soaring spirits crashed a minute later when Nurse Grabby-Hands returned to the scene, this time pushing a wheelchair ahead of her.

Paige held her breath as the nurse helped Asher from the chair to the wheelchair. He listed to the side, and the large woman wrapped both of her arms around his body to right him. She kept her arms around him, putting her face close to his while talking to him.

Paige growled. "Get out of his face."

The nurse tucked a blanket around his legs and aimed the chair down the ramp.

If Asher needed a blanket on his lap, he'd be too weak to accompany her through the forest and down the hill. Squinting into the binoculars, Paige tracked their progress across the lawn. The nurse pushed the chair with one hand, her other resting on Asher's shoulder.

They made it about midway and stopped. Paige swore when she noticed Asher's attire. He did have a jacket on against the cold, but he wore it over a hospital gown. No wonder he had a blanket draped over his lower extremities. He was in bigger trouble than Paige imagined and a sob burst from her chest. She'd never get him out of here like that…especially with Nurse Ratched hovering over him.

Suddenly both of their heads jerked in unison. The nurse turned to face the building with the porch where Asher had been sitting.

Paige swept her binoculars toward the building and zeroed in on a doctor standing and waving. Paige tracked back to Asher and the nurse on the grass. The nurse jumped to her feet and waved back.

Leaning over Asher, the nurse smoothed the blanket across Asher's lap and tucked it under his thighs. Then she ran her hands over his chest before pulling his jacket closed. Finally, she turned and scurried back to the building.

Paige watched the doctor and nurse team go inside and shut the door behind them. She jerked the binoculars back to Asher and held the mirror up to the sun again, tilting it back and forth.

But what could he do in a gown and a blanket? He didn't even have shoes.

Asher sat quietly for several moments, and then Paige's heart slammed against her chest as he rose from the wheelchair. The blanket fell from his lap and he bunched it up and stuffed it into the chair. Then he shrugged out of the jacket and wrapped it around the blanket. From behind and from a distance, it might just look like someone slumped over in the chair.

Without looking behind him once, Asher took off in a jog across the lawn.

Paige stashed the binoculars in her backpack and scrambled down the tree. She hit the thick carpet of mulch just as she heard Asher crash through the trees.

"Are you here? Are you here? Paige?"

Her heart took flight. He remembered her. All he needed was to see her once.

"Here! I'm here!"

He emerged through the trees, the hospital gown flapping around his bare legs, a pair of socks the only barrier between his feet and the sharp needles and twigs that formed the forest floor.

She rushed to him. "Asher. Oh my God, Asher."

He grabbed her hands and held her off from throwing herself in his arms.

"You've gotta help me. You've gotta get me out of this place…whoever you are."

## *Chapter Three*

His words chipped off a piece of her heart, but she squared her shoulders and stepped back from him. "We have to go through these woods and down a steep hill. Can you make it dressed like that?"

"I could make it naked with one arm tied behind my back to get out of here. Lead the way."

"Let's go. You should've kept that jacket though."

"That jacket might buy me some time if someone happens to look out the window at the drugged-out invalid to make sure he's still drooling in his chair."

"You're not drugged?"

"I've been spitting them out—and pretending."

She held a branch to the side for him. "They still didn't trust you enough to give you clothes."

"They underestimated me." He charged after her. "Don't worry about clearing a path for me. Just go. I'll follow you."

"Your physical health is okay?"

"Strong as an ox." He nudged her back. "Stop talking. You're wasting energy."

She scrabbled and stumbled her way to the forest's edge. When they reached the path down to the access road, she made a half turn. "You can make it down?"

"I survived a tumble off a mountain in Afghanistan. I can traverse a wooded hill in Vermont."

He didn't need her to show him the way anymore, and he barreled past her into the descent, reaching back with one hand. "Keep up now."

As his gown gaped open in the back, her eyebrows shot up. "You're naked under that thing."

"Their way of keeping me tame. Like I said. They underestimated me." He craned his head over his shoulder. "If you're really my fiancée like you said, my bare backside shouldn't shock you."

"I'm not shocked." She twisted her fingers out of his grasp. "And stop dragging me or we'll both end up in a freefall to the bottom of this hill."

They had no words left as they negotiated their way down. When they hit the access road, Asher peeled off his socks, now decorated with dirt, small pebbles and pine needles.

He bunched them in his hand and stuffed them into the pack on her back. "I don't want to leave any evidence."

He hung back as the access road spilled onto the main drag. "It's too exposed here."

"The car's less than half a mile away. Wait here and I'll pick you up."

As she started to turn away, he grabbed her hand. "You'll be back?"

"I didn't come all the way out here to leave you behind, Asher Knight…even if you don't know who the hell I am."

Paige ran to the car, the pack jostling on her back. She wished she had some clothes in there for Asher. She never would've imagined she'd be rescuing him in a hospital gown and nothing else.

When she reached the car, she lunged at the door and

threw it open. She gunned the engine and swung into a wide U-turn.

The empty road in front of the access entrance stretched before her, and a wave of panic washed through her body. When Asher stepped out from behind a bush, a sob escaped from Paige's lips.

"Get hold of yourself, girl." She flipped a U-turn again and pulled over.

Before she even stopped the car, Asher had yanked at the door and jumped inside. "Go!"

She didn't have to be told twice—or even once. Her foot punched the accelerator and the little rental roared in protest before switching gears and lurching forward.

The tires ate up the road, and Asher put a hand on her arm. "Slow down. We don't want to get a ticket."

Glancing in the rearview mirror, she eased off the gas. "But if we do get pulled over, we can tell the police what's going on. You're not a prisoner. You haven't been committed."

"Really?" He cocked an eyebrow at her. "I don't know what the hell is going on right now. That's the US Army, the United States government. They can tell the cops whatever they want and, I guarantee you, I'll be back in their clutches."

Paige's heart flip-flopped, and she tried to swallow her fear. She was the daughter of a police officer, had always trusted law enforcement, had always trusted authority. Now she had to rely on herself.

Asher jerked his head toward her and braced his hands against the dashboard. "Unless that's what you want? Where are you taking me?"

Paige drew in her bottom lip. Great. Now she had to deal with Asher's paranoia. Was it real or imagined? She slid a sideways gaze at him. Maybe his mental issues involved more than amnesia. Maybe he'd been kept naked and drugged because he *did* pose a threat to himself… and others.

She could feel his hard stare boring into the side of her face. A stranger's stare.

"Is that it? Are you one of them?"

His harsh voice grated against her ear, and she took a deep breath. If he could listen to reason and think logically, that would tell her a lot about his mental state.

"I'm taking you to my motel right now. We should leave as soon as I can check out. This is a small town and the people at that house of horrors will most likely fan out there first to look for you."

He nodded, his mouth still tight.

"Why would I contact you secretly and help you escape if I were in cahoots with the hospital and planned to deliver you back to them? What would be the plan? To test you? They don't need to test you. They have you captive and a pharmaceutical cornucopia to keep you complacent."

His firm jaw softened and he blinked his eyes.

"What did they tell you about the woods yesterday? Because I can tell you right now, one of those stooges who came after you, Lewis or Granger, shot a dart in the side of your neck to take you down."

Asher clapped his hand against the left side of his neck. "They said I passed out."

"Yeah, like a lion passes out after a few hundred blow darts sink into him."

"I suspected something but didn't let on." He touched the back of his head. "I'm still pretty confused, but I pretended everything was great so that I'd have another opportunity to go outside…in case you came back."

"Well, I did." She reached for his thigh and stopped

herself. He still thought of her as a stranger, but she planned to remedy that.

She grabbed the bottle of water in the cup holder instead. "Do you want some water?" She shook the bottle and the water sloshed back and forth. "It's not laced with anything—except my germs."

His hand hovered near the bottle for a couple of seconds and then he snatched it from her. He downed the rest of the water. "Sorry. Those damned drugs make me thirsty."

She looked away from the road and pointed to his feet. "We're going to have to take care of those."

"My feet are the least of my worries right now—and I have plenty."

About a half hour later, they hit the outskirts of Mooseville and Paige tapped Asher's shoulder. "You should slump down in about five minutes, just until we get through the town. My motel is tucked away from the main drag. I can sneak you inside without a problem."

"I'm not going anywhere sitting in this car."

"Excuse me?" She always did have to deal with Asher's stubbornness, but his stubbornness combined with amnesia and fear just catapulted it to another dimension.

"It's too risky. Pull over now and I'll get in the trunk."

"The trunk?" Her gaze swept his large form, unchanged from weeks of captivity and bed rest.

"I can squeeze in. I'm not taking any chance of anyone seeing me in this town. Is it really called Mooseville?"

"It is and I will." She pulled over and popped the trunk from the inside of the car. They both got out and she lifted the lid of the trunk. "Make yourself comfortable."

"Looks like heaven compared to that hospital bed."

He crawled inside the trunk and his hospital gown spread open, revealing his mighty fine backside.

"Here, let's get you decent." She tugged the gown around his thighs, her fingers skimming his cold skin. She started to remove her jacket.

"Leave it on. You shouldn't look any different from when you left… Shut it."

Paige slammed the lid of the trunk on Asher, curled into a fetal position. She could do this, despite what her mother believed.

She drove through the sleepy town of Mooseville and pulled up to her room at the motel. She shouted over her shoulder. "I'm back at the motel. I'll just grab my stuff and check out."

After Asher gave his muffled assent, Paige slid from the car and pushed the door closed with a click. It took her ten minutes to throw her stuff in a bag. She dumped the three bottled waters from the fridge into a plastic bag, along with her leftover sandwich from the day before.

She strode to the motel office, swinging the room key from her finger. The bell on the door jingled when she swung it open.

Charlie, the motel's proprietor, peeked around the corner of the back office. His eyes widened when he saw her. "You'd better get out of here."

The key flew off her finger and her jaw dropped. "Why?"

"They're looking for you."

Goose bumps rippled across her flesh. "Who?"

"Those folks at the rest home on the hill." Charlie looked both ways as if the two of them weren't the only ones in the room. "Government folks."

She stooped to pick up the key and smacked it on the counter. "They're looking for me by name?"

"You…and others." He swept the key from the counter and dropped it in a drawer. "They came charging in here asking about this one and that one—mostly men—but then they mentioned your name, Paige Sterling. Said you also might be using Paige Knight."

Paige gripped the strap of her purse. "They asked for me by name? What did they want to know?"

"If you'd been here, checked into the motel."

She glanced over her shoulder at the parking lot and her rental car with one big Delta Force soldier stashed in the trunk. "And you said…?"

Charlie folded his arms and narrowed his eyes. "Told 'em they'd need to come back with the cops and a search warrant if they wanted to see my guests' names. I did tell them I didn't have any single women staying here."

"Thank you, Charlie. I'm not involved in anything illegal."

He waved a hand. "I don't trust that bunch up there. Wouldn't give 'em the correct time of day if they asked."

"I don't trust them, either. I'm out of here. You can put the balance for the room on the credit card I used."

"Will do. Too bad I already ran it. That can be traced now."

"When I checked in here, I didn't realize…" She shook her head. "It's all right."

"Safe travels."

She slammed the office door harder than she'd intended and jogged to the car. She opened the back door and tossed her suitcase and pack onto the seat. When she slid behind the wheel, she turned her head to the side. "They're already looking for me, and others. They must realize you had help. The guy at the motel didn't tell them anything, so they can't know I'm the one who's here."

A thump resounded from the trunk, and Paige knew Asher had heard her.

She squealed out of the parking lot and raced toward

the town. As she turned down the main street, she said, "Can you pound on the trunk again or something so I know you're still alive back there?"

Another loud thump answered her but did nothing to calm her nerves. "As soon as I get the chance, I'll let you out of there. We need a place to go."

She pulled up behind a white van at the one stoplight in town. The red light turned green, and she removed her foot from the brake pedal and held it above the accelerator as the car rolled forward.

The van hadn't moved, and she slammed on the brake. The car heaved forward and back. "Sorry, but there's some idiot who won't move."

Her hand slid from the steering wheel and rested on the horn in the center of it. "I'm going to give this guy two more seconds."

In less than a second, both doors of the van swung open and a hulking man dressed in the scrubs of a hospital orderly burst out of the passenger side and into the street.

He pinned her with a menacing glare and started to charge toward her.

"Oh my God, Asher. It's them. They found us."

# *Chapter Four*

Adrenaline pumped through his body, and Asher's limbs jerked with the power of the sensation.

Paige screamed and he flushed with rage. She had to get out of here, had to move the car. Unless they had her boxed in. A car in front and one in back that she didn't notice?

He pounded on the roof of his prison with his fist. The car jumped in Reverse, and his head whacked the side of the trunk. He didn't even care. They were in motion.

He heard a man shouting. Sounded like that giant oaf Granger. The tires squealed and the smell of burning rubber assailed his nostrils.

The car jerked to the left. Asher felt like he was on some amusement park ride that kept you in the dark so you couldn't see the next turn of the track.

Paige must've floored it, because the car leaped forward and then the back fishtailed. As the car picked up speed, a crash echoed outside the trunk. Asher braced his body for an impact, wedging his bare feet against the side of the trunk…but none came.

The car hit a bump and then…nothing. It sailed forward. "Paige. Paige, can you hear me?"

Several seconds passed, and then he heard the sweetest sound ever.

"We're in the clear. The van that was blocking me crashed into another car."

Asher's lungs ached as he released a long breath in the close confines of the trunk. "Get as far away from here as possible and head south. Can you do that?"

Maybe Paige didn't have any breath left to answer, but as long as the car kept going forward he'd leave it in her capable hands.

Because his…fiancée had proved herself to be more than capable. In fact, she was a badass.

They traveled for what must've been at least thirty minutes before the car slowed down. It bumped and rumbled over rocky terrain before coming to a stop.

Paige threw open the trunk, and Asher blinked his eyes at the daylight.

"Are you okay?" They asked the question in unison, so he answered first.

"I'm fine. What the hell happened back there?" He uncurled his legs and swung one outside the trunk and then rolled out.

"Do you need to stretch out before getting into the passenger seat?"

"I just want out of this area." He picked his way to the front door of the car as pebbles and twigs attacked the soles of his feet.

Paige got behind the wheel and cranked up the heater. "You must be freezing."

"Hadn't noticed…until now." He rubbed his arms. "Are you going to tell me what went on with that van?"

She cranked her head over her shoulder and backed out of the outlet she'd pulled into. "Came up to the lone signal in Mooseville and pulled behind a white van. When the light changed, the van didn't move. I was about to pull around it when two goons in scrubs burst out of the van. I knew right away who they were. They must've been waiting for me—or any of your other friends on their list—to show up. They must've had my picture, and when they recognized me, they made their move."

"Now they know who helped me." And they knew that Paige was connected to him in some way. His fiancée. "How did you get away?"

"I reversed, and they jumped back into the van, but they weren't paying attention. The light had changed, and another car T-boned them." She smirked. "That van isn't going anywhere."

"Buys us some time."

She flicked her fingers at him. "We have to get you some clothes...and food. Are you hungry?"

"Not at all." He tapped on the window. "Not sure where we're going to buy clothes in the middle of nowhere."

"We're not exactly in the middle of nowhere. See those mountains?" She tipped her chin forward. "There's a ski resort up there, and it's open despite the lack of snow. They're manufacturing it now and expect the weather to cooperate in the next day or two for the Christmas holidays."

"You know this area?"

"No. Why would I know this area when I'm from Vegas?" She stopped and bit her bottom lip. "But you don't know that I'm from Vegas, do you?"

He reached out suddenly and touched her wrist. "No, but I'll remember. You'll tell me everything."

A smile wobbled on her lips. "Looking forward to it."

He pulled his hand back and dropped it in his lap as guilt nibbled at the edges of his mind. Touching her had been a calculated move on his part because he'd sensed her grief at his memory loss. His amnesia might even be worse for her. At least he didn't know what he was missing.

It had to be devastating to look into the eyes of someone who was supposed to love you and see a complete lack of recognition or feeling.

He stared out the window. Not a complete lack of feeling. Even locked in the trunk, he'd experienced an overpowering urge to protect this woman when she'd been in danger. Maybe that was normal under the circumstances, but he'd felt a tug at his heart when he first ran into her in the woods, too.

He'd get it all back. From what he'd seen of Paige so far, he had great taste in women.

"How much longer to the ski resort and do you think you can make it to a store before it closes and pick up some clothes for me?"

"Maybe an hour away. I know your sizes. Don't worry." A crease formed between her eyebrows. "Do you think it'll be safe? Would they have any reason to track us there?"

"Hell, I don't know. I don't even know why they'd *want* to track me down. What do they want with me?"

"I was hoping you could tell me. All I wanted to do was visit you, and the army officer who called me wouldn't tell me where you were. Didn't believe I was your fiancée."

"Why'd he call you?"

"I called the army trying to locate you when I heard about the incident. One of your team members called me to tell me about it, but he wouldn't tell me much. The army finally returned my call after they found my name and number in the favorites on your phone." She flexed her fingers on the steering wheel and then renewed her grip. "What happened, Asher? Do you remember?"

"That's what's weird." He scratched his jaw. "I do remember what happened right before my fall."

"That *is* unusual."

He jerked his head toward her. "You think so, too?"

"Since you don't know anything about me," she said with a sniff, "you don't know I'm a psychologist. I handle a lot of PTSD cases and repressed memories."

He raised his eyebrows. "That's convenient… A shrink. A shrinky-dinky."

She jerked the steering wheel. "Why did you say that?"

"Shrinky-dinky? I don't know. The silly phrase keeps coming to me every time I say or hear the word *shrink*." He studied her profile—the slightly upturned nose and the firm chin. "Why?"

"When I finished my hours and got licensed to practice, that's what you'd call me." She licked her lips. "You remembered that on your own."

"I did. Thank God. It's all going to come back, isn't it?"

She dropped her chin to her chest. "I can help you, Asher. I can help you recover your memories. It doesn't sound like the damage to your brain is permanent if a nickname came to you like that. Did the doctors mention anything about a permanent injury?"

"No. They kept assuring me that I'd fully recover my memory."

She let out a sigh. "That's good. It is strange though that you happen to remember the incident itself. What *did* happen? Can you tell me?"

"I can tell you. It's not classified or anything, and if it were, I guess I can't remember the classification level, anyway." He poked her in the side and got a smile out of her. "There are a few advantages to memory loss."

"There can be." Her pale cheeks flushed. "So, what happened out there in Afghanistan?"

"My commander, Major Rex Denver, was supposed to be having a meeting with a snitch from one of the groups that holds control of that area. The guy wanted to start feeding us intel and Denver was the man. He took me along and an army ranger. While we waited for the contact to show up, Denver took control. He shot the army ranger and then came at me. He took me off guard and pushed me off the edge of a cliff. I fell—" he tapped his head "—hit this thing and blacked out. An army ranger unit rescued me. Somehow, I managed to escape any severe physical injury, but I had a gash on the back of my head and I couldn't remember a damned thing when I came to."

"Except the incident that sent you over the edge."

"No."

"No?"

"I didn't remember that right away, either. That unfolded for me when I got to an army hospital in Germany and much more when they got me to Hidden Hills."

"Hidden Hills is an unfortunate name for that place." Paige lodged the tip of her tongue in the corner of her mouth. "That kind of selective memory is unusual."

"I stayed in Germany for a month before they shipped me to that crazy place. The hospital in Germany dealt more with my physical injuries—my head wound."

"And your Delta Force team members? Did they ever come to visit you?"

"No." Asher curled his hands into fists. "They didn't like what I had to say about Major Denver. Didn't believe me and blamed me because Denver went AWOL."

"I tried calling a few of them, too, with no luck." Paige

drummed her thumbs on the steering wheel. “Denver went AWOL after what happened with you?”

“Right after. Apparently, he took off after he attacked me. Left me for dead, but at least he got word to someone that my body was lying at the bottom of that drop-off.”

“He did? He reported your location and condition?”

“Yeah, great guy, huh? He thought he’d killed me.”

“D-do you remember Major Denver and the others?”

His eye twitched as pain throbbed against his temple. “No. I only recall Denver in that moment. I don’t remember anything about him or working with him… or the others.”

“Maybe it’s your defense.” She lifted her shoulders. “He did such a terrible thing to you, you’ve blocked out anything good about him to protect yourself.”

“I don’t know.” He squeezed his eyes closed as the pain spread across his forehead.

“Grab my purse in the back seat.” She jerked her thumb over her shoulder. “I have some ibuprofen in there. That plastic bag on the floor has some bottled water and a leftover sandwich if you’re hungry.”

He reached around and dragged her purse into the front seat. “Where?”

“The bottle’s in the makeup bag.”

He unzipped the little leopard-print bag and plucked a small bottle from it. He shook three gel caps into his hand and tossed them into his mouth. He chased them with a gulp of water and eased his head against the headrest. “I’m going to try to rest my eyes.”

“Go ahead. I’ll wake you up when we get there.”

“I don’t think I’ll be falling asleep.”

As much as he tried to keep his eyes open, closing them soothed the pain in his head and he allowed his heavy lids to drop. He would drift off, but something urgent kept prodding him and he'd jerk awake with a start.

In a short time he'd become dependent on the drugs that had eased his passage into sleep each night. He didn't want that anymore. He didn't claim to be any expert, like Paige apparently was, but being drugged up had to be interfering with his memories. How could he remember his past when half the time he couldn't remember what he'd eaten for lunch?

"Give in to it."

"What?" Opening one eye, he rolled his head to the side and pinned her with his gaze.

"You've been nodding off and jerking awake for the past forty-five minutes. Is it that you can't fall asleep or don't want to?"

"Maybe a little of both. Maybe I snore and drool in my sleep."

"You don't drool—at least not when you're sleeping."

He twisted his lips into a smile. This woman who knew him…intimately could do more to restore his memory than all the drugs and doctors in the entire US military.

Why had they tried to keep her away from him?

The signs that flew by the car window announced cabins and lift tickets and ski rentals. "We must be close."

"We are." She snatched her phone from the cup holder and tossed it at him. "First things first. Can you look up a clothing store? Even if it's a ski shop, I'm sure it'll have pants and shirts, jackets and boots."

He tapped the phone's display and then shook it. "No internet connection yet. We may have to drive straight to the ski resort to get connectivity. I'm sure there are stores there. Any reason you don't want to shop at the resort?"

"Those people from the prison… I mean rest home, might see this as a logical place for us to land."

"Probably, but we have a head start on them, and how do they know you didn't have clothing and an escape plan waiting for me?"

"I should have." She skimmed her hand along the side of her head. "When I saw the situation yesterday, I should've put more thought into breaking you out of there."

"I'd say you did a pretty good job." He plucked at the hospital gown barely covering his thighs. "You didn't know they'd have me stripped and defenseless."

She snorted. "If they thought taking your clothing was enough to render you defenseless, they don't know Asher Knight like I know Asher Knight."

Tilting his head back and forth, he loosened the knots in his neck for probably the first time since he'd regained consciousness. Somebody knew him, and that deep pit of abandonment in his gut ached a little less.

He heaved out a sigh.

"Underwear, T-shirt, socks, jeans, long-sleeved shirt, boots and a jacket. Do I need to write that down?"

"You're the one with the memory problems, not me." She poked him in the side and grinned. "Like I said, I even know all your sizes. You stay slumped down in the seat while I go inside. I'm going to have to use my credit card though. I want to save the cash I have for later. Do you think the army is going to track me down through my credit card?"

He pointed out the window to the turnoff for the resort. "Very real possibility, but there's not much we can do about it. I have no money. No cash. No cards. No memory. No life."

She veered right onto the ramp and swiveled her head

in his direction. "That escalated quickly. Are you okay? I mean other than the obvious?"

"Just a little brush with self-pity." He smacked the side of his face with his palm. "I've recovered now."

"You've shown zero self-pity. I think you're allowed a second or two."

"We need to come up with a way to get our hands on some cash. Maybe my old man stashed some away for a rainy day."

"Actually—" she slid him a sideways glance "—the feds thought he had, but he never copped to it."

"If he ever told me about it, I would've forgotten that along with everything else." He rubbed the goose bumps on his arms. The temperature had been steadily dropping outside and the heater inside hadn't kept pace with it.

Paige cranked it up higher. "We're not going to wait to find piles of cash somewhere while you freeze to death with no clothes."

The car bounced as she drove into a large parking lot for the ski resort. "We'll get you dressed and then maybe just get out of here. You don't really think it's the US Army that's after you, do you?"

"At first I took everything the army told me at face value. In Germany, my physical wounds were treated and everything seemed okay, except for the fact that my Delta Force unit wanted nothing to do with me because of my allegations against Major Denver. It's when they started messing with my mind and then sent me to that so-called rehabilitation center that things started rubbing me the wrong way."

"Let's put that on hold for now." She hunched over the steering wheel and peered through the windshield. "I see a clothing store on the periphery of the shops. Start scrunching down or it's back in the trunk with you."

He pushed the seat all the way back and slid down. "Go for it. This hospital gown is getting old…and baby blue is not my color."

She swung into a parking space. "Look at you, making jokes. You must be on the mend—and you look good in any color…or nothing at all."

Before he could think of a comeback, she slammed her door and the car shook.

How were they going to go anywhere under the radar if the army really was tracking Paige through her credit card? He didn't even know if he had any money. Let alone how to access it. His doctors had told him he was from Las Vegas. He must've met Paige there. Had he known her for a long time?

Even if he had money, they were about as far from Vegas as they could get.

He closed his eyes, although his instincts told him to keep watch. The orderlies in the van couldn't have gotten out of that mess fast enough to determine he and Paige would head for this ski resort and then give chase.

They might've sent word back to Hidden Hills and sent someone else up here to look for them though. He and Paige had made it easy for them, but the doctors at Hidden Hills had made it hard for him. Where else was he supposed to get clothes?

One thing he did know was they couldn't use Paige's credit card to check into some lodge or hotel here. They'd be sitting ducks.

A shadow passed over the car, and Asher's eyelids flew open. He inched his head up and pinned his gaze to the rearview mirror. A figure moved behind the car.

Asher ducked his head, clenching his fists, holding them at the ready. They were the only weapons he had and wouldn't be very effective against a gun—not that his jailers at Hidden Hills could get away with murdering him in a parking lot. Could they?

In the silence of the car as he waited, his heart hammered in his ears. The rush of adrenaline ebbed and flowed in his body and he fought off the dizziness it caused.

If the guy had spotted him in the car, why hadn't he made a move? Asher scooted up in his seat and looked in the rearview mirror first. The man had moved on—probably just someone making his way through the parking lot.

Asher sat up straighter and his gaze swept the lot. A shuttle bus waited at the curb at the base of the broad steps that led to the shops and ultimately the ski lifts. A few people were milling around the steps. When the shuttle pulled away, two women and a solo man were left behind.

The women seemed to be conferring about something over their phones, but the man watched…and waited.

Asher kept his eye on him as the man's head swiveled from the parking lot to the shops. Was he waiting for his wife?

He could be the man who'd passed by Paige's car. Asher didn't see any other single men in the parking lot and not another man in red plaid.

Asher locked on to him, studying his every move. When Paige appeared at the top of the steps laden down with shopping bags, Asher sat up, every sense on high alert.

The stranger seemed to come to attention, too. He turned his back to the parking lot to watch Paige's descent, his hands shoved in his jacket pockets.

With his fingertips buzzing, Asher clicked open the car door. His first step on the cold asphalt with his bare foot sent a shock through his system, but it only served to jolt him into action.

He left the car unlocked and then weaved through the parked vehicles, ducking and crouching in case the man decided to peel his eyes from Paige.

As she hit the last step, her vision and movement hampered by the bags swinging from her arms and clutched to her chest, the stranger made his move.

He reached his arm out to Paige as if in assistance… but Asher knew better. He shot forward, shouting and waving his arms.

"I'm here. I'm here. I'm the one you want."

# *Chapter Five*

Paige had been moving away from the man and now she turned her face toward Asher barreling down on both of them. Her mouth dropped open and she stumbled to the side, away from the stranger and his outstretched hand, the rest of his body twisted in Asher's direction.

His right hand still out of his pocket, the man swiveled around to face Asher. He swayed to his left and in a split second Asher took advantage of his imbalance.

He charged the man, his hospital gown flapping around him, and shouted. "Run, Paige!"

With a few feet between him and the stranger, Asher made a flying tackle at him that would've made his friend Cam the football player proud. Before the man could reach into his pocket for whatever weapon he had, Asher drove his shoulder into the guy's chest, knocking him backward onto the steps.

The two women several feet away screamed.

The man's hand clawed at his pocket, but Asher pinned the hand with his knee, driving it into the cold cement. He grunted, and Asher gave him more to grunt about as he smashed his fist against the man's nose. Blood spouted and Asher followed up with a punch to the gut.

A woman was screeching behind him. "We're calling the police."

Asher landed another punch to the side of the man's head. As he drew back his fist for another onslaught, a car horn blared behind him.

He twisted his head over his shoulder, and Paige's rental car squealed to a halt at the shuttle stop. His hand jerked to a stop in midair, and he plunged it into the man's pocket. His fingers curled around a syringe.

He pulled it out as Paige honked again. The man groaned beneath him and Asher jabbed him in the side of the neck with the needle.

A few more people had gathered at the top of the steps and Asher knew the cops wouldn't be far behind. He pulled the needle from the man's neck, staggered to his feet and jumped into Paige's car, which she'd already put into motion.

She floored it out of the parking lot, and the car bounced like it was in a movie chase scene when she rolled off the curb into the street.

"Oh my God. You're bleeding."

"I think that's his blood."

"No." She reached over and rubbed his burning knuckles. "Your hand is bleeding."

"That's from hitting him. I took him by surprise and he didn't get many shots in." He held up the needle. "He was counting on using this."

Paige gasped. "Throw it out the window."

"So somebody else, maybe a kid, could pick it up?" He dropped it on the floor of the back seat. "I'll wrap it up and dispose of it later."

"I screwed up. We shouldn't have come here." She slammed the heel of her hand against the steering wheel. "Of course this would be the first place they'd look."

"We had to come here. We didn't have a choice."

She pressed her fingers against her cheek. "And your

poor feet, running around out there in the cold, fighting in a hospital gown."

"Don't worry about me. I should've never sent you out there on your own. I should've realized someone would be staking out the ski resort."

She lifted her eyebrows. "You couldn't exactly go shopping in that getup."

"I need to get out of this." He plucked at the hospital gown. "I need to start feeling human…and then there's going to be hell to pay."

PAIGE GLANCED AT him as she smoothed her hands over the steering wheel. They'd finally stopped shaking, but Asher's words sent a new jolt of adrenaline through her system.

"What do you mean?"

"I'm going to figure out who's doing this to me and why, and I'm not going to stop until I have all the answers…and all my memories."

"Where can we go now?" She adjusted the rearview mirror and released a small breath.

"There's no real snow yet, right? There must be hundreds of cabins in this area, vacant for at least a few more weeks until the holidays."

She swallowed. "You're suggesting we break into someone's empty cabin and make ourselves at home?"

"Just until we can get our bearings, and I can put some clothes on." He jerked his finger over his shoulder. "Whoever that guy was back there, he's out. His associates are going to figure we've fled the area."

"We should flee the area."

"Let's do the unexpected." He tapped on the window. "Make the next turn."

For the next twenty minutes, Asher guided her through

mountain roads and turnouts like he knew the place. After surveying and abandoning several prospective cabins, he had her follow a road into a heavily wooded area where a single cabin nestled against the side of a mountain.

"This one."

"How do you know someone's not living here?"

"Do you see any vehicles? Any pets? Any life at all?"

Her eyes darted around the property. "No, but it doesn't mean there won't be."

"We'll play it by ear."

She jabbed his thigh with her finger. "I think you forgot how cautious you used to be."

"I was Delta Force. I couldn't have been that cautious."

"You *are* Delta Force, and I guess *cautious* is the wrong word. Maybe I mean organized. You like to plan."

"This *is* a plan. It's the only viable one right now except to go on the run."

"In a hospital gown."

"Right. Park in the back."

She swung the car to the right on the dirt road that curved around the house and continued through the trees in the back. Luckily the snow had held off so far this season, or it would've piled up in front of them. Now they just rolled over cold, frozen ground.

Ducking her head, she peered through the windshield. "Do you think they have security cameras?"

"If they do, I'll have to disable them."

As Paige stepped out of the car, her shoe crunched the gravel and the sound seemed to echo in the woods. She tipped her head back and scanned the edges of the roof for security equipment.

Asher appeared next to her. "I don't see anything, do you?"

"No." She pointed to his feet. "You could've at least put on the boots I bought for you."

He curled his toes into the gravel. "I'm getting kind of used to being barefoot."

"I'll get them." She buried her head in the back seat of the car, where she'd tossed the bags in her mad rush to get back to Asher fighting with the stranger. She backed out of the car with the bags hanging from her arms and turned to face the cabin, leaving her own suitcase and laptop on the seat.

Asher waved from the cement slab behind the cabin. "I think I found a way in."

She strode toward him, the bags banging against her thighs. "I feel like a thief."

"We're not going to steal anything…except some soap and water." He rubbed his hands together. "And maybe some firewood."

A few minutes later, Asher had jimmied the lock on the back door. He rested his hand on the doorknob. "Are you ready?"

"For flashing lights and guard dogs?"

"Something like that." He eased open the door.

Paige held her breath, but nothing came at them. A hushed silence even emanated from the woods behind the cabin. Would they finally get a moment's peace? She had so much to tell Asher.

He widened the door, and they faced a mudroom, four pairs of ski boots lined up against one wall.

Paige nudged the toe of one of the boots. "Doesn't look like they've been worn recently."

Asher snapped the door closed behind them and locked the top dead bolt. "I think we're safe…for now."

"That'll be a first since you arrived in Vermont."

"I think that'll be a first since I left on that assignment with Major Denver."

Asher led the way into the kitchen, clear of clutter and dishes, waiting for its inhabitants to bring it to life.

Paige grabbed the handle of the fridge and yanked open the door. Empty shelves greeted her.

"They clean out at the end of the season." She plucked a bottle of ketchup from inside the refrigerator door. "Unless you feel like some ketchup."

"I'm guessing they turn off the gas." Asher cranked a knob on the stove. "Yeah, that's going to be one cold shower."

"There is a potbellied stove with a little wood stacked up next to it."

"Are you planning to heat up buckets of water and pour them in the tub for me like a pioneer woman?" He dropped the bags at his feet.

"No, but you can warm up once you get out of your cold shower and get dressed."

"I think I'll skip the full shower and just wash up in the sink."

"Just get out of that hospital gown." She felt the heat wash into her cheeks. "And get into those clothes."

He tilted his head. "I know it's an awkward situation between us, but you don't have to blush like a schoolgirl and clarify every double entendre."

"You're right. It's awkward and I'm awkward, so I'm going to cover by looking for some first-aid supplies. You could use some antiseptic on those feet."

"Let me get that fire started first."

"Go." She flattened her hands against his broad back and gave him a small shove. "Clean up and get dressed. I'll worry about the fire. I was a Girl Scout, remember?"

He lifted one eyebrow. "If you say so."

She smacked her hand against her forehead. "I am so sorry. It's just..."

"Don't worry about it." He encircled her wrists with his fingers. "You don't have to watch what you say around me. Treat me like a normal person, and I might just start feeling like one."

Even this light touch from him felt like coming home, and her body ached to fall against him and have him take care of everything like he always did. She shook her head. They were way beyond that.

It was her turn to take care of him now, get him back on track. She could do it.

He released her wrists as quickly as he'd claimed them. "I'm going to leave the fire in your capable hands, Girl Scout."

"There must be a full bathroom upstairs in the loft." She jerked open a door below the stairs. "This one's just a half bath."

"Maybe that's all I need." He hunched his shoulders in the thin material of the hospital gown. "I'm not going to soak in a cold tub."

"No, but you need to dip those feet into some water—cold or not."

"Yes, ma'am." He saluted and took the stairs two at a time while clutching the robe behind him with one hand and holding the shopping bags in the other.

Paige crouched before the potbellied stove and wadded up some newspaper from the stack next to the woodpile. She glanced at the date before crumpling the next one in her fist and mumbled, "Last year. Place has probably been empty for that long."

She shoved pieces of wood into the stove on top of her kindling and lit the corner of a paper with a long match. She touched the match around the edges of her pile and sat back on her haunches as the flames lapped toward the wood.

With the fire crackling in the stove and the water running intermittently upstairs, Paige searched a closet under the stairs. She pulled out a blanket and tucked it under her arm. Standing on her tiptoes, she felt the top shelf for a first-aid kit but came up empty.

Hugging the blanket to her chest, she raised her gaze to the loft. Maybe there were some medical supplies in the bathroom upstairs.

She was engaged to Asher, had lived with him and would've thought nothing of barging into the bathroom with him in it. And if he were in the shower, nine times out of ten he would've pulled her in with him.

Her nose tingled, and she swiped her hand across it. She'd have to take it slowly. Asher didn't know her from one of the crazy nurses at Hidden Hills. She'd have to gain his trust and had already come a long way in that direction after the events of today. She'd also have to use her professional skills on him to help him recover his memories. It wasn't just their love that depended on it now—it was Asher's life.

She shook out the blanket and placed it on a rug in front of the stove, now cranking out heat like a little ball of burning lava.

"Feels warmer already."

She tipped her head back to see Asher leaning over the wood railing that bordered the loft, dressed in jeans and a green flannel shirt that matched his eyes. She'd recognized the color immediately in the store.

"Could you look for some bandages and ointments in the bathroom?"

He held up a square red bag and dangled it in the space above her. "Already found it."

"Come on down, then. It's getting cozy." Did that sound like a come-on? "I mean it's warm down here. B-by the stove."

She'd just shut up now.

"On my way."

He jogged down the stairs with more energy than he had a right to have. He hit the bottom step and tossed the red bag to her. "That water was cold, but it felt good."

"Seems like it energized you. Maybe you should roll around in the snow." She waved her hand at the window.

"It's snowing?" His stride ate up the distance between the stairs and the front window and he flicked back the drapes with one finger.

"I mean if it were. Looks like it's coming soon."

"Whew." He stepped back. "We don't need snow right now bringing people back to this cabin."

She unzipped the first-aid kit. "How are your feet? Let me take a look."

"Not bad, considering what I put them through."

She sank to the floor in front of the stove and patted the seat of the chair she'd drawn up to the heat. "Sit."

He folded his large frame into the chair and stretched out his legs. "The clothes are a good fit. Waist is a little big on the jeans, but nothing a belt won't fix."

"I didn't get you a belt." She took his right foot and propped it on her knee. "You probably lost a little weight while in…captivity."

He whistled. "That's exactly what it was."

"You have a few slivers on the soles of your feet." She reached behind her for her purse, dragged out her makeup bag and poked around for her tweezers. "Aha."

Pinching them together, she held them up. "These should do the trick."

She traced the bottom of his foot, the skin soft from

the soap and water, and located the three slivers lodged into the epidermis. She swiped an antiseptic wipe across the tips of the tweezers and aimed for the first sliver. When she'd pulled out the third one, she tapped his other foot. "Let me get this one while I have the tools ready."

He switched feet. "Don't tickle me again. I'm very ticklish."

She whispered, "I know."

She plucked out just one sliver from his other foot. She then dabbed all the raw spots on his feet with another antiseptic wipe. "I don't think anything needs bandaging."

"I hope not. I wouldn't be able to walk much less run with my feet bandaged."

"You planning to do a lot of running?" She peered at him over his toes.

"Oh, yeah. Until I can figure out what the hell is going on with my life."

"I can help with that, too." She tapped the side of her head. "I'm going to start by hypnotizing you, Asher."

"Let's do it." He pulled his legs back beneath him, and hunched forward, arms crossed on his knees.

"I don't work on an empty stomach. I don't know about you, but I need to eat something first. It's past dinnertime."

"Did you see anything besides ketchup in that kitchen?"

"I didn't look in the cupboards, but I picked up some trail mix, nuts and beef jerky in the store when I was shopping for your clothes."

He snorted. "Do I look like a squirrel?"

"Would you be happier with cold beans from a can, or whatever they might have in the cupboards?"

"Actually, beef jerky sounds pretty good right now."

She hopped to her feet, her proximity to Asher making it hard to concentrate on food or anything else. She grabbed one of the plastic bags and dug through it. "It's actually turkey jerky. Is that okay?"

"Bring it on."

She tossed him the bag of jerky on her way to the kitchen. "I'm going to wash my hands. Do you need anything?"

"Water." The plastic crackled as he ripped into the jerky bag. "Do you think you can do it?"

"What? Get you water?" She cranked on the faucet and opened a cupboard to look for a cup.

"Hypnotize me."

She let his words hang in the air as she filled a glass with tap water. She approached him with the water in one hand and a bag of trail mix in the other. She dangled the trail mix in front of him, but he shook his head.

"You're susceptible to hypnosis. I can do it."

He ripped off a piece of jerky with his teeth and chewed for several seconds. "Can I tell you what I want to remember first, or is it just a free-for-all of memories?"

Shaking open the bag of trail mix, she scoped out all the cashews and took her time answering. "I can pinpoint memories through suggestion. What do you want to remember first?"

He dropped the jerky and wiped his fingers together. "I want to know what happened on that ridge in Afghanistan."

His answer pierced a little hole in her heart. He didn't even know about Ivy.

"I'm sorry."

"N-no. I understand. That was the moment you lost your memory. Why not start there?"

"I think understanding what happened at that moment is imperative right now. Knowing what occurred will keep us safe. Maybe it holds the clue as to why I was locked up at Hidden Hills."

"Of course." She plucked out a few more cashews and glanced up. "What?"

"When do we get started?"

"You didn't finish your—" she waved her hand in his direction "—dinner."

"I'd rather start working on regaining my memories… All of them eventually."

Her heart fluttered. She should just tell him about Ivy. She didn't have to wait until he remembered his own daughter. Of course, if she told him they had a four-year-old together, he'd wonder why they hadn't gotten married yet.

Then she'd have to tell him all that other stuff.

He clasped his hands and pinned them between his knees. "The sooner the better."

She knew Asher had a stronger desire right now to find out what happened on that mission with Major Denver than to learn about his life with her, and as much as she wanted to tell him all about their romance and their beautiful daughter, she wasn't in any hurry to divulge the rocky road their relationship had taken. Now she had an excuse to keep it hidden a bit longer.

"That's not going to happen with you sitting all hunched over like that." She licked some salt from her fingertips. "I'm going to wash my hands and find an object of concentration to use. You sit back in that chair and relax."

She rose from where she'd parked herself on the arm of the sofa across from Asher and peered out the front window.

Asher shifted in the chair, twisting his head over his shoulder. "See anything?"

"No, and no snow yet, either." She twitched the curtain back into place. "I think we're still safe."

"Even if they think we stayed in the area, they have a lot of cabins to search. Doesn't mean they won't find this one though."

She turned from the window and flicked the back of his head with her finger, avoiding his neat scar. "You're supposed to be relaxing, not thinking about the next attack."

"Attack—that's what's going on, isn't it? Hidden Hills wants me back."

"And maybe we can find out why." She jerked open a drawer and the stainless-steel utensils inside rattled. "This should do it."

Asher's eyes widened when she walked toward him with a knife. "Is that supposed to help me relax?"

"Exactly. You need something to watch, something to focus on."

"You mean like a swinging pendant, Shrinky-dinky?"

She pointed the blade of the knife at him. "You can wipe the smirk off your face. That's how it works."

Stretching his arms in front of him, he rolled his shoulders. "I'm ready."

"Okay. It shouldn't be too hard for you to clear your mind, so breathe deeply and think of something pleasant." She pulled her chair forward and sank into the soft cushion, her knees almost bumping Asher's.

Too bad that something pleasant wouldn't be her.

"Breaking out of Hidden Hills was about as pleasant as it gets." He blinked. "Should I close my eyes or leave them open?"

"Open." She held up the knife. "Watch the shiny object for a while first, listen to my voice, keep breathing. If you begin to feel like you want to close your eyes, do so."

He leaned back, the muscles in his face relaxing, and she realized how taut he'd been holding himself. He must be in a world of hurt and confusion right now. She couldn't even imagine being in the limbo he must be experiencing.

"Watch this." She held up the knife, and it caught the flickering light of the fire, which made the knife look like a wand glinting with magic. She hoped it could work some magic tonight.

"I'm watching."

"Listen to my voice, and pay attention to your breathing—in and out. Make sure your breathing is consistent."

For several minutes, Paige led him into a deep state of subconsciousness and then snapped her fingers.

His head lifted, his eyes still closed.

"You can open your eyes, if you like. I'm going to take you back to that mission in Afghanistan with Major Denver. Who else was with you?"

Asher's mouth opened and then closed.

"It's okay. You can talk, answer my questions."

"Army ranger. We were with an army ranger named Dylan Curran."

"What was the mission? What were you doing there?"

"It was secret."

"You can tell me." She touched his knee.

"Major Denver was meeting with an insurgent, someone playing both sides. He had information for Denver, important information."

"Did you ever meet this insurgent?"

"We were waiting for him."

"While you were waiting for him, Major Denver shot the ranger?"

"No." Asher's chin dropped to his chest.

"Don't fall asleep. If Major Denver didn't shoot the ranger, what happened to Dylan?"

"He was shot."

A frisson of fear whispered across the back of her neck. "Who shot him? D-did you shoot Dylan?"

"No."

She released a small breath between puckered lips. "So, Major Denver shot Dylan and then he pushed you off the cliff?"

"No. No. Stop." Asher's body stiffened, and his face contorted. "Shots fired. Stop. Take cover. Stop."

"It's okay, Asher. You're not on the cliff anymore. I'm bringing you out now." She snapped her fingers.

His shoulders dropped, and his chest rose and fell rapidly.

The hypnotic state should've relaxed him, but he'd become agitated as she took him back to that place. It was best to bring him out, even if he didn't get as far as they'd wanted.

She squeezed his thigh. "Are you okay?"

His eyelids flew open and he pinned her with a burning gaze. "I remember. I remember what happened."

"You do? That's great. A great first step." Now maybe she could get him to remember her and their daughter.

"Great? I don't think so."

"Why?" That fear crept back across her flesh.

"They lied to me, Paige. Major Denver never shot that army ranger. Never pushed me off the cliff. It was all a setup…and they used me and my amnesia to perpetrate it."

# *Chapter Six*

Asher shook his head, trying to escape the fog from the hypnosis.

Paige snapped her fingers again, and the crack penetrated his brain like a bolt of lightning.

"You're awake now." She spoke the words as a command, not a question, and it dragged him all the way back to consciousness.

She handed him his glass of water. "Why would those doctors at Hidden Hills implant false memories in your brain? Memories that would implicate Major Denver?"

"I have no idea, but that's exactly what they did. Right? They must've put those scenes in my head." He dug his fingers into the indentations of both temples. "They're obviously after me, after us now, because they don't want me to remember the truth."

"When you were under, you stopped answering my questions and I brought you out of your hypnotic state because you were getting agitated. You must've been going through the scene on your own. If it wasn't Denver, do you remember who *did* shoot the ranger and attack you? Was it the insurgent you were supposed to meet?"

"I don't know. We never saw Denver's contact. He never showed up."

"Did you see who shot Dylan?"

"No. I heard the shot and Dylan dropped. Denver and I looked at each other, and the shooter took a shot at me and missed. Denver *did* push me, but he was pushing me behind a boulder. Nobody pushed me off that cliff. I slipped when I was trying to avoid the bullets raining down on us."

"*Could* it have been the guy you were supposed to be meeting, shooting at you from a distance? Maybe he and Denver arranged for him to kill you and Dylan. Maybe that's what the army doctors were driving at."

"He saved my life, Paige. Major Denver saved my life, and there's no way he'd kill a ranger." He drove his fist into his thigh. "How could I ever have believed that?"

"When you woke up, you didn't know Major Denver from Colonel Sanders. You wouldn't have remembered his character or anything else about him."

Clasping his hands behind his neck, Asher asked, "What the hell is going on? Why would anyone try to set up Denver? And if I hadn't rolled off the side of that cliff and injured my head, would I be dead right now?"

Paige lifted her shoulders, about the only answer he could expect to his rhetorical question.

"I need to find out who was behind setting up Denver, setting me up. Did they really think they could get away with implanting those false memories in my head?"

"In a way I'm glad they did."

"Why?" He sat up in the chair and studied her face, a face too beautiful to ever forget.

"Think about it. Whoever shot that army ranger and shot at you didn't plan on leaving any witnesses. The people behind this setup must've panicked when they realized you survived that fall—until they found out you had no memory of the events." She leveled a finger at him. "Your amnesia saved your life."

Paige was happy he had amnesia, even though he couldn't remember her, remember their life together?

"Saved my life and strengthened their narrative. Who better to implicate Major Rex Denver in a traitorous plot than one of his own loyal Delta Force men?"

"And now they've lost you." She twisted her fingers together. "They're never going to allow you to tell the real story. They'll do everything in their power to discredit you."

"You and I both know they're going to do more than discredit me." Asher pinched the bridge of his nose and squeezed his eyes shut. "They want me back."

"They, they, they. Who is they?"

"If I knew that, I'd be halfway to recovery. When people in the government, the army, people you're supposed to be able to trust, turn on you, anyone can be the enemy."

"Anyone but me." She dropped to her knees in front of his chair and took his hands in hers. "I hope you know that, even if you don't remember me."

"I know that. You've proved yourself over and over today." He squeezed her fingers. "Should we get going on those memories now?"

"You mean through hypnosis?" She shook her head from side to side. "Not tonight. You've had enough."

"Why don't you just tell me, then? Tell me a story about how a fearless psychologist wound up with a messed-up Delta Force soldier."

"Fearless? Messed up? I think you have us confused." She tipped her head back and laughed at the ceiling. "You were far from messed up, Asher."

"I do know my father is in prison for bank robbery. My mother is dead. Doesn't exactly sound like a prescription for sound mental health."

"You fought through it."

His brows shot up. "Were you my therapist?"

"No. That would've been unethical." She released his hands and crossed her legs beneath her. "We met at a party. You came with a buddy who was friends with my friend's cousin."

He rolled his eyes. "I'm going to need hypnosis again just to straighten that out."

"It was a birthday party at one of the hotels on the Strip. It got kinda crazy and you saved me."

"I did?" He hunched forward, burying his chin in his palm as if listening to a story about two strangers...which he was. "Tell me more."

"The party was out by the pool and...some drunken idiot got the bright idea to take the party *into* the pool. People started jumping in, with and without their clothes, and someone pushed me in, fully clothed, holding a drink. My arm hit the side of the pool and my glass broke, cutting my hand. You jumped in and rescued me."

"I was watching you from across the deck."

"You remember?" Her cheeks flushed and her blue eyes brightened.

He didn't want to disappoint her, but he didn't want to lie, either. "No. I'm just embellishing the story. I saw a pretty blonde across the pool deck, kept my eye on her, and when I saw her flailing in the water, I did my Delta Force thing and jumped in. I must've thought it was a stroke of good luck that she needed my help."

She tilted her head to one side. "I don't believe you're that conniving."

He wiggled his eyebrows up and down. "Maybe I am."

"You just like saving people." She hit his kneecap with her fist.

"You do, too."

"Me?"

"You're a therapist. You help people every day." He tapped the side of his head. "You just helped me. Why do you work with people who have PTSD?"

She drew her knees to her chest and wrapped her arms around her legs. "My dad was a cop. He suffered from PTSD and wound up…dead."

Sympathy flared in his chest, and he put his hand over his heart. "I'm sorry. Seems crazy the daughter of a cop would want to go out with the son of a criminal."

"You're not your father." She wrinkled her nose. "And I'm not mine."

"Why wouldn't you want to be like him? Cops are heroes, straight up, every day."

Paige sucked her bottom lip between her teeth. "My dad committed suicide."

His stomach dropped. How much pain could this woman endure? And he was just adding to it.

He slid off the chair and crouched in front of her on the floor. "I'm sorry, and here I am making you go through all this again."

She met his gaze with her blue eyes that held all the keys to his life.

"You know what? You responded to this news with all the same sincerity and compassion you're showing now. That's when I knew I wanted you forever, and nothing's changed…for me."

He drew one finger along her smooth cheek and touched her trembling bottom lip. "Nothing's going to change for me, either, Paige. What you've done for me already, getting me out of Hidden Hills, is enough to show me what you're made of, what we had together. And we'll have it again."

Her lashes fluttered, and her lips parted in invitation.

He wanted to kiss her, but it felt false. Did he have a right to kiss her? Leaning in, he closed his eyes and stopped analyzing.

Brushing her lips with his sent an electric current charging through his body. That had to mean something. He rested his forehead against hers to steady himself, and her warm breath bathed his cheek.

She turned her head and whispered against his ear. "I do have something to tell you about us, something you need to know."

His muscles tensed as he prepared for another betrayal. Had this all been some kind of setup?

He jerked away from her and held up one hand.

"Y-you don't want to hear it yet?"

"I want to hear everything you have to say, Paige, but I think there's someone outside the cabin."

She scrambled to her feet, bumping his chin with her head. "It's either the owners or someone tracked us down. What did you hear?"

He pushed up from the floor. "The engine of a car—too close for a vehicle passing on the mountain road."

Hunching forward, he crept to the front window, lifted one corner of the curtains and peered into the black night. "I don't see anything, no lights, although they wouldn't come driving to the front door."

"They would if they were the owners of the cabin." Paige had come up behind him and stuck her fingers into his pocket.

"Around the back, then. There's another road to this cabin through the woods." He shifted away from the window and headed to the mudroom that led to the back door of the cabin. He pressed his ear against the door, his hand on the doorknob.

"Anything?" Paige hovered at his shoulder.

"You stay here. Scream if someone tries to come through the back. I'm going around to try to surprise him."

"I'll do more than scream." She picked up a ski pole and thrust it in front of her. "Anyone coming through that door is going to get the sharp end of this."

"Be careful." He squeezed her arm on his way out of the mudroom.

He grabbed his new jacket, went to the front door and eased it open. He scanned the empty gravel drive in front of the cabin before stepping out onto the porch.

He sniffed the air like a wolf on the hunt and then slipped around the side of the house. When he rounded the corner, he stumbled to a stop and braced his hand against the side of the cabin.

A figure dressed all in black hunched over the driver's side of Paige's rental car, and another car was parked behind it—it must have come from the woods.

An energy force slammed against his chest and he launched himself at the stranger. The man squeaked as Asher crushed him against the car.

Asher grabbed the intruder by the back of the neck and swung his body around, lifted him off his feet before slamming him to the ground.

The man groaned and rolled over.

Asher stomped on his flailing wrist in case he had a weapon nearby, although Asher didn't see any weapons.

Paige materialized beside him, panting and brandishing the ski pole. "I saw the other car from the window in the back, and then I saw him lurking around my car. Who is he?"

His galloping heart slowing to a trot, Asher leaned

over the figure writhing on the ground and ripped the ski mask from his face.

Paige gasped. "What the hell?"

The woman on the ground choked out, "Please, Asher. I want to help. I—I love you."

## *Chapter Seven*

Paige jerked her head toward Asher, his foot still firmly planted on the woman's wrist. "Do you know her? Who is this?"

"A nurse from Hidden Hills—Tabitha Crane." Asher bent over and hauled Tabitha to her feet. He spun her around and shoved her against the car. "Any weapons?"

He patted her down in a way she must've relished if she really did love Asher. He hadn't touched Paige that intimately yet.

The woman sucked in a breath, obviously still hurting from the rough treatment. "I don't have any weapons."

Asher yanked Tabitha against his chest, his arm around her neck. "Anyone with you?"

"I'm alone. I swear, Asher. There's nobody else."

Her voice hitched on a sob, and Paige caught the double meaning of her words, even if Asher didn't.

He released her and shoved her toward the open door to the mudroom. "Get inside. You have some questions to answer."

Tabitha moved slowly, her right arm dangling beside her. She tripped over the door's threshold and Paige instinctively caught her arm to steady her.

That earned Paige a scowl from Asher, and she

shrugged. If they wanted to question Tabitha, they couldn't allow her to collapse.

When they got to the living room with the heat emanating from the potbellied stove and the wrappers from their makeshift dinner littering the coffee table, Tabitha's eyes widened. "What is this place?"

Asher shoved her into the chair he'd vacated earlier and growled, "We're asking the questions."

"Do you want some water?" Paige tapped her own chin where Tabitha's had an abrasion.

"Yes, please. Who are you?"

Asher stepped between them and pointed a finger at Tabitha. "Be quiet, and the water can wait until she's answered a few questions."

Paige knew all about Asher's no-nonsense approach. She'd been the recipient of it and she didn't kid herself about what he did as a D-Boy, but his tone with Tabitha still made her flinch.

Paige pulled up the other chair close to the stove and rubbed her hands together. "We want her to be able to answer questions."

"Oh, she'll answer our questions." He loomed over Tabitha and crossed his arms. "How did you track us here?"

Tabitha's head swiveled. "Where's the hospital gown?"

Asher took a deep breath, his chest expanding, which made him look even more imposing. "What does that matter?"

"That's how I tracked you." Tabitha blinked her eyes, her light-colored lashes giving her a surprised look.

But Asher seemed like the surprised one. "What do you mean? How did the hospital gown lead you to me?"

"Go get it, and I'll show you."

Afraid Asher would rebuff Tabitha again, Paige bounded from her chair. "I'll get it. It's upstairs in the bathroom."

She rushed up the staircase to the bathroom and scooped up the hospital gown Asher had dropped in the corner. For a few seconds, Paige pressed it against her face to inhale his scent.

She dangled the gown in front of her as she scurried back down to the interrogation. "Here it is."

"Check the hem." Tabitha tipped her head toward Paige and winced, grabbing the back of her neck.

Paige felt along the hem of the gown and felt something hard sewn into the material. "What is it?"

"It's a GPS tracker."

Asher lunged for the gown and snatched it out of Paige's hand. With his bare hands, he ripped the material apart and pinched a small, black device between his fingers. "Is this still active?"

"It is." Tabitha held up her hands. "But I'm the only one who can track it, nobody else."

"You put a GPS tracker on me?" Asher spit out the words and then tossed the device into the fire, where it popped and sizzled.

Tabitha ran her hands through her stringy hair. "Better that than injected in your body."

Asher narrowed his eyes. "What do you mean?"

"The doctors had orders to inject a tracker under your skin after the incident in the forest." She pulled back her shoulders and folded her hands in her lap. "I convinced them you'd notice, as you'd already recovered from your physical injuries. I suggested the GPS be sewn into the hem of a hospital gown and that we keep you in it."

"Had orders?"

Asher had latched on to the same words that had jumped out at Paige—well, that and the fact Tabitha seemed quite pleased to keep Asher in a hospital gown under her watchful eye.

Spreading her hands, Tabitha said, “Don’t ask me whose orders. I don’t know.”

Paige cleared her throat. “Tell us about the facility. Hidden Hills is supposed to be a rehab center for injured soldiers, right?”

“Yes, but not physical injuries. There is some of that, but we handle soldiers suffering from PTSD and other psychological traumas.”

“Are they all prisoners, like Asher?”

A flush crawled from Tabitha’s neck into her face. “Prisoners? Asher wasn’t a prisoner. Who are you again?”

“Not a prisoner?” Asher snorted. “GPS trackers, drugging, implanted memories. If those things don’t scream imprisonment, I don’t know what does.”

“Implanted memories?” Tabitha’s eye twitched and Paige almost believed her.

Asher uncrossed his arms and rolled his shoulders. “Okay, we’ll play it your way—for now. What did the doctors tell you about me?”

Tabitha’s tongue darted from her mouth as her gaze shifted from Asher to Paige and back again. “They told me you might be involved in traitorous activity involving Major Rex Denver and an insurgent he was meeting. They thought you might be lying about your amnesia to avoid answering questions.”

“Damn them.” Asher smacked a fist into his palm. “Instead of implanting memories to implicate myself, they manufactured a remembrance that would crush Denver. But why?”

Paige smoothed her hand down Asher’s corded forearm where his veins popped out from his flesh. She turned toward Tabitha, who had her gaze pinned to Paige's hand.

Paige snatched her hand back. Maybe they should allow Tabitha to believe she had a chance with Asher to get more info out of her. The woman couldn't really believe Asher felt anything but contempt for her, could she?

She studied Tabitha's light-colored eyes, gleaming with light as they rested on Asher, and felt a stab of pity. Tabitha adored her fiancé, and it didn't resemble a normal attraction. They'd have to watch this woman. She might even be lying to them right now.

There was one sure way of finding out. Paige tucked her hand through Asher's arm and snuggled in closer to him, watching Tabitha's face blanch.

Paige cleared her throat. "What did you hear about Major Denver at Hidden Hills?"

"What?" Tabitha dragged her gaze away from Paige's contact with Asher, who hadn't moved a muscle.

"Major Denver. What did you hear about him while you were at Hidden Hills?"

"J-just that he was a traitor. He killed an army ranger, pushed Asher… Lieutenant Knight off a cliff and went AWOL—probably working with the insurgents he was secretly meeting."

"That's all garbage, all lies." Asher's muscles tightened until he felt like a coiled spring beside her. "Those shrinks at Hidden Hills manufactured my memories—whether you know that or not—to fit their story about Denver. It didn't happen that way. I don't know who shot the ranger, but it wasn't Denver, and he didn't push me. I slipped."

"How do you know that?" Tabitha's Adam's apple bobbed in her slender neck.

"Because Paige—" Asher slung an arm around her

shoulders and pulled her close "—my fiancée, hypnotized me."

Apparently, the only word Tabitha heard was *fiancée*, because she repeated it. "Fiancée? Fiancée?"

Enjoying the warmth of Asher's body next to hers even if it was for show, Paige rested her head against his arm. "The doctors at Hidden Hills didn't even tell Asher he had a fiancée. Don't you find that odd? Shouldn't they be doing everything in their power to help him regain his memories, including filling in the pieces of his life for him?"

"Maybe they didn't know about you." Tabitha scooted to the edge of the chair.

"If they had access to his army files, they knew about me."

"Of course they did." Asher curled his fingers into her upper arm. "Wives, fiancées, children, it's all there. Paige should've been contacted immediately after the incident—she wasn't."

"Paige." Tabitha gave her the once-over, her gaze sweeping from the top of her head to the toes of her boots. "You helped Asher escape."

"Of course."

"I was going to help you, Asher." Tabitha pinned her hands between her knees, raising her broad shoulders to her ears. "That's why I wouldn't allow them to shoot you up with a tracker. I was going to get you out of Hidden Hills."

"You had a strange way of helping me, Tabitha, keeping me drugged up and confused. Taking away my clothes." He shook his head. "I don't know if I can trust you."

Tabitha flung her arms out to the sides. "I came alone. I tried to protect you."

The nurse opened her mouth again and snapped it shut.

Paige held her breath. Had she been about to repeat her proclamations of love and thought better of it?

Asher's nostrils flared. "How did you plan to protect me? And protect me from what? Why are they after me now, on whose orders and what are they going to do with me when they get me?"

"I was going to protect you by making sure they didn't take you back." Tabitha stood up but stayed close to the chair, her fingers brushing the padded arm. "I have a place, or my family does, not far from here. I was going to take you there. I didn't realize you had help…didn't realize you had a fiancée, but I can still take both of you there. You'll be safe. I already stocked it with food. You can stay hidden until…"

"Until what?" Asher turned his back on Tabitha. "I have to get to the bottom of this morass. I can't hide out forever. I have a life."

Tabitha plunged her hands into the pockets of her knee-length, black down coat. "It will at least give you some time out of the public eye to start making inquiries. Unless you start driving now, miles and miles away, you won't be able to get food. You can't show your face. You'll never know who to trust." She shuffled away from the chair. "Am I right, Paige? You know I'm right."

Paige hated to admit this woman with the slightly manic edge and a huge crush on Asher had a point, but she had a point. But the mania and the crush made it hard to trust her.

Without turning around, Asher dragged one hand through his hair and said, "If you really want to help, Tabitha, go back to Hidden Hills and try to find out some information for me. I need to know what's behind the frame-up of Major Denver."

"I'm not sure I'd be safe if I returned to Hidden Hills." Tabitha inched closer to Asher's back, her body stiff.

A shaft of guilt lanced the back of Paige's neck, and she made a half turn toward the kitchen. "You must be hurting, and I never got you that water. I have some ibuprofen, too."

Now level with Asher, Paige ignored his eye roll and took another step toward the kitchen.

"I'd like that, Paige."

The breathless quality of Tabitha's voice made Paige take a quick glance over her shoulder.

In a blur, Tabitha lunged at Asher, her clenched fist raised.

Asher heard Tabitha's approach at the same time Paige screamed, "Look out."

Swinging around, his leg extended, Asher swept Tabitha's feet out from under her. She took a hard fall on her side, her head landing inches from the potbellied stove, her hand still fisted.

This time it was Paige's boot that came down on Tabitha's wrist…and she felt no sympathy. "What do you have in your hand?"

"Be careful, Paige." Asher crouched next to the nurse and pried open her fingers. He pinched the needle between his thumb and forefinger and held it up. "More sedation? This is how you're going to protect me? Who sent you?"

Tabitha's head whipped back and forth. "Nobody. I'm here on my own. You're not well. You have more drugs swimming in your body than you know. I can take care of you."

"Yeah, like some demented fan. What next? You're going to bash in his kneecaps?" Paige ground the toe of her boot against Tabitha's hand.

Asher's eyebrows shot up. "Paige, go check the mudroom for some rope."

"What are you going to do?" Tabitha's voice squeaked.

"You can't be trusted. That's the last time you try to inject some poison into my body."

"It's not poison, just a sedative, a mild sedative."

"In that case." Asher flicked his fingers against the glass tube of the syringe and plunged it into Tabitha's thigh, right through her jeans.

She gasped and her eyes widened.

The effect of the drug was instantaneous. Her mouth went slack, and her hand slid from her leg.

Paige covered her mouth. "Oh my God. If she'd stuck you with that thing, you would've been a goner and I would've been left alone with her."

"Eh." Asher nudged one of Tabitha's arms with the toe of his boot. "I think you could've taken her down."

"What now?" Paige hugged herself and rubbed her arms. "I don't want to be here when Tabitha comes to. I've heard enough from her."

"How do you think I felt being trapped in that place with her yammering in my ear night and day?"

"She thinks she's in love with you, Asher."

"She's just obsessed. This has nothing to do with love."

"We can't stay here now, and Tabitha was right about one thing." Paige scooped up a handful of wrappers. "We need to get out of this area so we can buy some food and other supplies."

"We also need a base where I can start investigating this conspiracy—against me and Major Denver." He jerked his head up. "And start getting my life back with you."

Paige swallowed. That always seemed like an afterthought for him that he had to throw in there for her benefit. "What are we going to do with Tabitha?"

"She said it wasn't poison. We'll keep her in front of the heater. Her car's out back and she can leave when she wakes up."

"Without you."

"Thank God, without me." Asher bent down on one knee next to Tabitha and dipped his hand into her jacket pocket.

"What are you looking for?"

"Anything—phone, keys, more drugs."

"Just watch out for any more syringes. You could poke your finger."

"I will." He dragged his hand from the pocket, dangling a key chain from his finger. "Looks like car keys, house key, cabin key, so she wasn't lying about that."

"How do you know that's a key to her parents' cabin?"

"Could be the piece of tape across the top that says 'cabin.'" He plucked one of the keys from the key chain and held it up.

"Are you thinking what I'm thinking?"

He raised one eyebrow. "Probably not."

Tilting her head at him, she said, "Tabitha said there was food there. Maybe we should raid her cabin before she comes to."

Asher slid the key from the ring and tossed it to her. "You can be in charge of cabin raiding. Did she say where it was located?"

"Have you found her phone yet? Maybe she has it on her phone's GPS."

"She had me on a GPS, why not the cabin?" He unzipped the other pocket and reached inside. "Nothing in here except a couple of bucks."

"Let's keep it. She owes you, big-time." Paige thrust out her hand, palm up.

Asher slapped the bills into her hand and then squeezed it. "I guess I must feel comfortable with criminals."

"What she stole from you is worth a lot more than a few bucks." Paige winked. "Besides, if she's so crazy in love with you, she won't mind."

Asher wagged a finger at her. "Justification. My dad had all kinds of excuses for his behavior."

Paige froze midway to stuffing Tabitha's money and key into the front pocket of her jeans. "He did? Do you remember that? Do you remember his excuses?"

Asher glanced up from rummaging through Tabitha's pockets, and a new light gleamed from his eyes. "I remember something. My mind flashed on a conversation with my father. I even saw him in my head."

"That's great news, Asher. Without all those drugs running through your system, you have a good chance of recovering your memories. What did he look like—your father?"

"A lot like me." He brushed his hand over the top of his short, brown hair. "Except no hair, shaved head."

Her heart did a little flip in her chest. "That's him. I've seen pictures of your father—handsome devil, handsome, crooked devil."

"That memory just came naturally to me in the course of our conversation. When I launched myself at the guy at the resort, I also recalled that Cam Sutton played football, too. Do you think that's how it's going to happen for me?"

"I think it's a great start."

He patted an inside pocket of Tabitha's jacket. "Phone. This could yield some important information."

"Like if her visit here was an outing planned for her by Hidden Hills?"

"Exactly." He tapped the phone. "Password protected."

"Let me have it. I have some ideas. If you were her obsession—and you were—her password might be easy to guess."

"You have no idea how that creeps me out."

"Your devastating charm and hunky good looks worked to your advantage in this case." Paige cupped the phone in her hand and started trying some obvious passwords. "Well, at least her password isn't your first name, last name or any combinations of those."

"That's a relief." He jingled Tabitha's car keys in his hand. "Since we can't access her phone right away, I'm going out to her car to see if she has anything in there, maybe directions to the cabin."

"Okay, I'll keep trying the phone's password in here where it's warm."

Asher went through the mudroom to the back, and Paige perched on a stool in the kitchen, wanting to keep as far away from Tabitha as possible. The woman could reanimate like one of those villains from a horror movie and grab her ankle.

She murmured to herself as she tried one password after another. "Delta Force, D-Boy, Lieutenant Asher."

Her finger hovered over the letters, and the back door crashed open. She jumped from the stool and spun around. Her heart slammed against her chest.

Asher charged from the mudroom and grabbed her arm. "Let's go. They're here."

Paige didn't ask one question. Curling her fingers around Tabitha's phone, she allowed Asher to drag her from the cabin as she couldn't keep up with his long stride.

The cold air hit her face and made her nose run instantly.

Asher still had her car keys, and he gave her a little push toward the passenger side. “Get in. I’m taking that small access road through these woods. It’s our only chance. As soon as they hear this engine start, they’ll know we’re out here instead of inside.”

Paige shut the car door without slamming it. As Asher hopped in beside her and shoved the keys in the ignition, she held her breath and twisted her head over her shoulder to watch for anyone coming after them.

In an instant a flash of light lit up the night sky. The cabin exploded behind them. They didn’t want to capture them… They wanted to kill them.

# *Chapter Eight*

Asher cranked the engine and floored it, navigating between two tall pines that ushered in the access road behind the cabin.

The people after them would never hear it. The explosion and fire would mask any sounds from the car.

The flames shot up toward the clouds, and Paige dug her fingers into Asher's arm as the car bounced over the rough road. "Tabitha!"

"She's dead, Paige. Did you get a look at that inferno?"

She covered her face with both hands. "Oh my God. They thought we were in there. They don't care to get you back anymore. They just want to kill you."

"Us." He clenched his jaw. "They want to kill *us*."

"How did you know someone was there?"

"I heard an engine when I was going through Tabitha's car. I peeked around the corner of the cabin and saw a vehicle pulling into the driveway. I knew it had to be trouble, but I had no idea they were going to firebomb the cabin—with Tabitha in it."

"If you hadn't gone out to her car, it would've been us in there." She cranked her head over her shoulder. "Do you think they're coming after us?"

"I don't think so. They figured we were inside, and now they think we're burning to a crisp." He tightened his hands on the steering wheel as they hit another bump. "That fire saved us. If they'd been about to surround the cabin, they would've heard the car. They would've known we survived the blast. Instead they think they caught us off guard."

"If they think we're both dead, it does buy us some time. They're not going to be hanging around waiting for the fire department to find out how many dead bodies are in the cabin. They probably won't even stay long enough to check out the cars in the back."

"A flying, burning log crashed through the windshield of Tabitha's car as we pulled away. It's probably burning as we speak. Maybe it even exploded."

Paige twisted in her seat to stare out the back window. "I see a lot of black smoke billowing up into the air. If they left right away, will we meet them on the main road?"

"We'll wait before we hit the road, see if any cars pass by. Watch for the emergency vehicles."

"Then what?"

"We're going to Tabitha's family's cabin."

"What?" She turned to stare at him.

"Before I heard the engine from the road, I found the address to the cabin in Tabitha's car's GPS. Then I wiped it clean, although the fire may have done a better job of that."

"Do you think it's safe to go there now? Even if we don't have to worry about Tabitha showing up—" Paige's voice hitched in her throat "—the people she worked with must know her family has that cabin. Once her family hears about her death, they'll probably head out this way, too. It all sounds risky."

"If the people after us think we died in that fire, they're not going to be looking for us in Tabitha's cabin or any other cabin. Since the cabin that just blew up was not Tabitha's, the arson investigators are not going to be able to identify the body immediately. They'll most likely have to use dental records, and that's even if someone reports Tabitha missing. Do you think Hidden Hills is going to report one of its nurses missing if its employees are the ones responsible for her death? Not likely. Tabitha's cabin is our safest bet right now. Nobody's going to be looking for us right away, and nobody's going to be looking for her. We need to stay out of sight for now."

Paige settled back in her seat and held her hands splayed in front of her. "Yep, still shaking."

"My God. That was close. If I hadn't gone out to Tabitha's car and heard the approaching engine, we would've still been inside that cabin when they firebombed it."

"How did they know Tabitha was there? Do you think she lied and was working with them all along?"

"Nope."

"You trust her?" Paige clasped her hands in her lap to stop their trembling.

"I trust nothing and no one but solid evidence. After I located the GPS information, I searched the outside of Tabitha's car and found a tracking device stuck to the undercarriage."

"So, Tabitha was following you using a GPS on your hospital gown and the friendly docs at Hidden Hills were following Tabitha with a GPS on her car." Paige raised her folded hands to her lips, pressing them against her white knuckles.

Asher clicked his tongue. "I'm gonna give the lovestruck Tabitha the benefit of the doubt here and assume she didn't know about the tracker. They used her."

"She led them right to us…and to her own death."

Paige shivered, and her teeth chattered. "If Tabitha hadn't been conked out, she could've gotten out with us."

Asher clasped her knee with his warm hand. "That's not our fault. She came to the cabin to sedate me, and God knows what she would've done to you once she had me under."

The car slowed down as they approached the main road. Asher pulled over on the access road with a view of the action and idled, headlights out. "Let's see what's what before continuing."

Paige cracked her window a few inches. "I think I hear sirens."

The wails got louder and louder until the emergency vehicles passed before them on the main road.

Asher threw the car into gear. "The people who started the fire have already left. Tabitha's cabin is just a few miles ahead off another access road."

Paige didn't relish the thought of staying in the cabin Tabitha had planned for her and Asher's love nest, but if she could turn it into a love nest for the two of them instead, she could live with it.

She slid a glance toward Asher. He'd remembered details about his father and Cam. Details about her and their daughter couldn't be far behind. She'd been ready to tell him about Ivy right before Tabitha interrupted them.

Of course, once she told him they had a four-year-old together, she'd have to explain why it was they were engaged instead of married.

And right now she was enjoying his ignorance.

ASHER HUNCHED OVER the steering wheel when they arrived at Tabitha's cabin and peered through the windshield of the car. Although it looked deserted, he cut the lights and swung the car around the back.

He and Paige hadn't had two minutes together where they hadn't been under a threat or some kind of pressure. Maybe once he had a chance to catch his breath, the memories would start rolling in.

He wanted to give this woman what she wanted, what she deserved. He wanted to love her. Hell, he was already half in love with her now, even though she was a stranger.

He parked and held up his hand to her as she reached for the door handle. "Stay in the car until I give you the all-clear signal."

"Do you think it might be a trap?"

"It could be anything. Let me go first and check it out. This place looks bigger than the other one."

"I hope those owners had insurance. We're responsible for the destruction of their cabin."

"We didn't blow it up." He pinched her chin. "Wait here."

Asher crept up to the back door, on the lookout for cameras, dogs and laser trip wires. He made it to the door unaccosted and shoved the key into the dead bolt. When he heard the click, he relaxed his shoulders. At least they had the right place and the right key.

He opened the door and poked his head inside…listening. He stepped inside and the warmth of the cabin enveloped him. Moving through the cabin, he did a quick search and then went to the back door and waved to Paige.

He waited for her and swung the door wide. "This one looks a lot more comfortable than the previous cabin."

"That's because Tabitha had prepared it for you." Paige swept past him and made a beeline for the kitchen.

Cranking on a burner on the stove, she said, "The gas is turned on."

"And the fridge is stocked." He hung on the open refrigerator door, taking in the bottles of water, juice, wine, eggs, milk, vegetables—enough food to feed a family of six for a week.

Paige joined him, looking over his shoulder. "Wine? She really had a cozy getaway planned for the two of you."

"Yeah, with me drugged out of my mind and strapped to a bed. That would've been worse than Hidden Hills."

"Do you want to eat something? I can cook a quick meal—scrambled eggs and toast, at least."

"It's late. You must be exhausted."

"Actually, I'm wired."

"Have a glass of wine—or two. I'll keep watch. I've had enough sleep to last me the next six months."

Two red spots formed on Paige's cheeks, and she pressed one hand against her chest. "I—I don't drink."

"Maybe there's some hot tea instead." He flung open a cupboard door and looked over his shoulder. "Do I?"

"Do you drink?"

"Isn't that strange? I don't even know what I like and don't like." He shrugged and swept a box of tea bags from the shelf.

"You do drink sometimes, but we don't drink together. It's not something we do."

"I need to keep my wits sharp, anyway. At least as sharp as they can be under the circumstances." He shook the box of tea. "Do you want a cup?"

"No, thanks. I'll scope out the sleeping arrangements, unless you think we should stay down here." She tipped her head back and surveyed the loft above them.

"You can check it out upstairs, but I'll definitely be bunking down here. Do you want me to get your bags from the car?"

"Please. I'd like to get on my laptop and see if there's any news."

"It's a lucky break we didn't bring your stuff into the first cabin. It would've all been destroyed."

"Along with Tabitha."

"Are you all right, Paige? Are you sure you don't want some tea? You still look rattled." He strode to a couch in the room and dragged a blanket from the back of it. "Why don't you lie down? I'll bring you your laptop."

"You're the patient here. I'm taking care of you, remember?"

"I do remember." He shook out the blanket and placed it on the couch. "And you did a helluva job, but I'm getting better and better, so you can take a break."

"Maybe we can both take a break."

"I'm more than ready." Asher left Paige standing next to the couch and returned to the car. The stillness of the air and the gray skies signaled snow on the way. Soon the resort would be crawling with skiers and snowboarders, and they'd be just two more people holed up in a mountain cabin.

He gathered Paige's bag and laptop case from the back seat of the car and brought them back to the cabin.

He dropped the bags on the floor and jerked back as Paige faced him holding a shotgun. "Are you pointing that at me?"

"Of course not. I found it in the closet." She leaned it against the stone mantel. "It might come in handy though."

"You don't look relaxed at all." He grabbed the strap of her laptop case and hauled it over his shoulder. "Do you think they have Wi-Fi here?"

"My phone has a connection. I'm sure all the lodges and hotels have service, so it makes sense they'd have it out here."

He swung the case onto the coffee table. "Give it a try. I want to start doing a little research tomorrow."

"Research?" She leaned forward and pulled her computer from its case.

"On Major Denver. I want to see what the official story is. You must know all my Delta Force teammates, right? I want to try to contact them. They wanted nothing to do with me once I implicated Denver."

"That's what the mad scientists at Hidden Hills told you, anyway. You can't be sure they even contacted your teammates, other than to tell them you survived."

"If they had, and I had made contact with them, would they have told me about you?" He collapsed in the chair across from the sofa and studied her face, which seemed to take on a guarded look.

"Yes, of course. I've met all your team members, including Major Denver." She pointed at him and circled her finger in the air. "Do you still suspect me of being a fake fiancée?"

"I never suspected that. At least I don't think I did. There was something about you from the very beginning when I stumbled on you in the woods."

He drew a cross over his heart as she began to protest. "Honest. I'm not just telling you what you want to hear, and then your actions backed up my initial instincts. You rescued me."

She waved her hands in the air, as if fanning her hot cheeks. "Believe me, that's a switch for us. I'm usually the one in need of saving."

He stretched his legs in front of him, propping them on the coffee table between him and Paige. "You sure you don't want to try some of that hocus-pocus on me tonight?"

"I think you've had enough for one night. We both

have." Her fingers flew across her laptop's keyboard. "I don't see anything about the fire, but then I'm not quite sure where to look online for local news."

"You don't see anything about a soldier going AWOL from a rehabilitation center, do you?"

She snorted. "Some rehabilitation center, but no, nothing about that, either."

"Any stories about Major Denver?" Despite his interest in her answer, Asher yawned and stretched his arms over his head.

"That story is top secret, not for public consumption. I only know about it because the army told me when they were explaining your incident to me."

"I imagine my situation will stay under the radar, too."

"I'm keeping you from your bed." She scooted off the edge of the sofa. "Unless you want the loft."

"It's best if I stay down here, and now I have a weapon." He jerked his thumb at the rifle leaning against the fireplace. "You go upstairs and try to get some sleep once you're done on the computer."

"I do want to check some emails just in case my clients are having any difficulties."

"I'm sure you left them in good hands. You'd be that kind of therapist."

She peered at him over the top of her computer. "Don't go putting me on a pedestal. You'll be sorely disappointed."

"I will keep my expectations low and my teeth clean, thanks to you leaving that other bag in the car." He stood up and reached for the ceiling. "The only things we lost in that cabin were my hospital gown and some food and water."

"And Tabitha."

"I know." He came around the back of the sofa and placed his hands on her shoulders. Her soft hair tickled the backs of his hands. "I don't mean to sound callous, but I don't think Tabitha had anything good in store for either of us."

"I know. I just..." She flicked her fingers at him. "Go brush your teeth. I'll vacate your bed in a few minutes."

He snatched up the bag containing the toiletries Paige bought him and crumpled it in his fist. He didn't want Paige to vacate his bed, but sleeping together tonight would only emphasize the awkwardness of their situation.

Maybe it was too much to ask, but he wanted their love and relationship to develop naturally as he began to recall things, not to have an insta-fiancée because it was part of some life he couldn't remember.

In one dark corner of his mind he couldn't banish the thought that just because he'd been in love with Paige once didn't mean he was going to remember that love, and they'd be back in the same place.

Was that what she feared, too? Something was spooking her about him recovering his memories. Why wouldn't she just jump right in and tell him everything about their life together?

After brushing his teeth, he wiped his mouth on the clean towel Tabitha had provided. As he hung it back up, a gasp from the other room caused him to miss the rack and drop the towel on the floor.

Asher bolted from the bathroom. "What's wrong?"

"I got an email from one of your Delta Force teammates."

"That's good, isn't it?" His eager stride ate up the space between them, and he crowded next to her on the sofa.

"Not—" she shoved the computer onto his lap "—necessarily."

As he scanned the words on the screen, he read them aloud. "'If you know where that traitorous SOB is hiding, you can tell him to rot in hell.'"

## *Chapter Nine*

Asher's eyebrows shot up. "That's kinda harsh, isn't it?"

Paige clicked her tongue. "That's Cameron Sutton—opens his mouth before he thinks anything through."

"Cam." Asher rubbed the stubble on his chin. "That sounds thought-out to me—and decisive. It's what they must all be thinking, isn't it? Cam just put voice to it."

"He must know you left Hidden Hills."

"If he knew I was there at all." Asher drew his brows together. "I don't like him calling you out though."

"No offense taken." She reached past him and wiggled her fingers over the keyboard. "Should I give him the good news?"

"Wait." He cinched her wrist with his fingers. "I'm assuming your laptop isn't encrypted or secure in any way, besides your password. Someone, somewhere may be waiting for some communication from your email. They might be able to track you down, or at least know you're still alive. It's too soon."

She snatched her hands back and pressed one to the side of her head. "You're not kidding, are you? Someone might be monitoring my email."

"I'm erring on the side of safety. No reason to tip off anyone that we're still alive when the minions from Hidden Hills think we were in that cabin." He held up a finger. "Cam is feeling chatty."

Draping an arm over his shoulder, she leaned toward the laptop, her soft breast pressing against his arm. "He said he's found evidence that Denver was set up."

"Him and me both." Asher trailed his finger across Cam Sutton's words. "Says he has proof the emails that first implicated Denver were planted."

Paige drummed her fingers on the laptop as they waited for more from Cam, but the next email to make it through was an ad for online coupons.

"I think Cam's exhausted all his words for now." Paige sighed. "I wish I could call him. Would that be safe?"

"Nope."

She slid a gaze to her phone charging on the table. "You mean they could be tracking my phone, too?"

"They could get your number and ping it. They can look at your calls. Any call coming from your phone right now wouldn't look good for us."

"We're going to be holed up in here with no communication with anyone."

"It doesn't mean I can't do a little research on your laptop." He flicked a finger at the screen. "And if we can pick up a temp phone, we could make that call to Cam."

She snapped her fingers. "Every mom-and-pop grocer carries phones these days. I'm sure I could venture out tomorrow in some kind of disguise and find a phone."

"We'll figure it out." He handed the computer back to her and pushed up from the sofa, away from Paige's warmth. "It's late. This day started a long time ago."

"I know." She logged off her laptop and scrambled from the sofa. "I can see a bathroom upstairs. I'll head up to the loft, brush my teeth and hit the sack. I haven't even been up there yet."

Backing up, Asher tilted back his head. “There’s at least one bed up there and what looks like a sleeper sofa next to the bathroom. I’ll keep watch down here.”

“You need your sleep, too. We could take turns keeping watch.”

“Okay, I’ll take the first shift.”

She put a foot on the bottom step and wedged her hand on her hip. “You don’t fool me for one minute, Asher. Your shift would never end and mine would never begin.”

“Don’t worry about it. You’ve done enough worrying about me. I’m fine, and I’ll be better once I figure out what the hell is going on.”

Paige tossed her head and jogged up the stairs. Her voice floated down. “Wow, you’re not gonna believe what’s up here.”

Asher’s hand clenched reflexively. “Something bad?”

“Depends on your perspective.” Paige leaned over the loft’s railing and dropped something over.

Pink rose petals floated to the floor, a few landing on his shoulder. He brushed them off. “Dead flowers?”

“Tabitha was getting ready for your visit. Rose petals on the bed, candles all over the room—” a drawer opened and slammed “—condoms in the nightstand drawer.”

Asher whistled. “That woman was seriously delusional. I feel sorry for her now.”

“I know. I almost feel like a voyeur pawing through all this stuff—evidence of her obsession. Apparently, she also has an obsession for cats, unless this cat theme is her parents’ idea of great cabin decor.”

“On the plus side, you can now sleep on rose petals.” Asher grabbed the shotgun, saw it was loaded and stationed it on the floor next to the sofa. “I thought you wanted your laptop with you.”

"I'm tired. I'm going to sleep—without the rose petals. I shook them off the bedspread."

The light went off in the loft, and Asher turned off the lamp next to the sofa. "Good night, Paige. Thanks for rescuing me."

"Good night, Asher. Glad to return the favor."

He pulled the blanket up to his chin and closed his eyes as he inhaled the sweet scent Paige had left behind.

He didn't need rose petals, but he was beginning to realize he needed Paige—if she'd only help him remember.

THE NEXT MORNING, Paige rolled from the bed and padded to the window. Her gaze followed the puffs of snow as they fell from the gray sky and kissed the branches of the pines.

Snow meant people flooding the area, not that she and Asher could stay in this cabin forever hanging on to some sort of suspended thread of time. Asher had to get his life…and his memories back.

The smell of coffee wafted up to the loft, and Paige turned away from the window. She crossed the room and hung over the railing. "The coffee smells good. I'll make some breakfast to go along with it."

Asher shuffled backward out of the kitchen, his head tilted back. "I took care of breakfast. Pancakes."

"Ooh, I'll be right down." Paige tugged at the hem of her nightshirt—hardly sexy, but should she change into clothes? She smoothed the material over her thighs and headed for the stairs. That man downstairs was her fiancé—whether or not he remembered.

She pulled a stool up to the counter as Asher put a plate in front of her stacked with pancakes.

He held up a bottle in each hand. "We even have a choice of maple syrup or blueberry syrup."

"What's a visit to Vermont without maple syrup?"

He shoved the bottle toward her. "You should check out the local news on your laptop. I'm curious as to what the authorities are calling that fire at the cabin and if they've discovered Tabitha's body yet."

"If they report just one body in the cabin, we're going to have to get moving. The people after us are going to realize we weren't in the cabin."

Asher stabbed his fork into four layers of pancakes. "But it felt good to slow down and now it feels good to eat some real food."

"Did you sleep okay on the sofa?" She jerked her thumb over her shoulder at Asher's bed for the night.

"I probably had my best night of sleep since the incident."

"You didn't keep watch? I noticed the rifle was your sleeping companion." She knew she wasn't.

"I'm a light sleeper, especially now. I figured I could catch some shut-eye, and if anyone tried to break in, I'd wake up."

"So, on the agenda today—pack up and get out of here, get a burner phone and call Cam—" she tilted her head to the side "—and maybe get you a few more clothes."

"If you say so. I'd rather pack up some of this food Tabitha put aside for our rendezvous." He licked some syrup from his lips. "And I'm ready for another hypnosis session when you are. This time, I want to know everything that happened in my life *before* that hillside in Afghanistan."

"Maybe tonight when we get settled somewhere." She made little crosses in the syrup on her plate with the tines of her fork. "Where *are* we headed? I suppose it's not a good idea to go back to Vegas. They'd look for us there."

"I'd like to stay close to the action, close to DC. I can't exactly waltz into army headquarters somewhere and tell them my memory of the incident with Major Denver was a lie and try to correct the story. I need to know who's behind the machinations at Hidden Hills, who wanted that version of the story to come out."

"You have to be careful, Asher. Whoever is behind that story is one hundred percent invested in it. We both know this whole thing was not engineered by a couple of shrinks at Hidden Hills. They had orders."

"I wonder how high up the chain of command this goes." He dropped his fork on his plate and swept it from the counter. "I think Cam Sutton can help."

"As soon as we tell him you're not a traitorous SOB."

"The kid has a hard head, but his heart's always in the right place."

Paige pressed two fingers to her lips. Asher's memories and feelings were seeping in naturally.

Asher dropped their plates in the sink with a crash. "How about that? I remembered that about Cam's personality."

"I noticed. It'll all come back to you in time without the interference from the Dr. Frankensteins at Hidden Hills and their cocktail of drugs."

Asher dried his hands on a paper towel and then leaned across the counter and traced the edge of her jaw with one fingertip. "I knew you, too, Paige. When I first saw you in the woods, I knew I could trust you."

"That'll all come back to you, too—all of it." She blinked her eyes and pasted a smile on her face. "If you don't mind, I'm going to take a shower first and get dressed. I have more to pack than you."

"Would you mind checking the news on your computer first? Then I'll clean up in here, put everything back the way we found it—except the food. I'm taking what we can."

"Tabitha bought it for you, anyway." Her stomach dropped and she flattened one hand against it. She still couldn't quite believe they'd left a dead body behind in that cabin.

Crossing his arms over his chest, Asher wedged his hip against the counter. "Tabitha was playing with fire, Paige. She was a nurse. As a mental health professional, would you have gone along with some crazy scheme to imprison a soldier who'd just been through a trauma? Trick him?"

"No way."

"Like I said, playing with fire."

Paige unplugged her laptop and brought it to the counter. "What do you think? Vermont news? News for this ski resort?"

"I'd enter the name of the resort."

Paige typed in the resort name. The screen populated with weather reports and ski conditions, and then she saw it. "Cabin fire. They have it."

His hands in the sink washing dishes, Asher glanced over. "What does it say?"

"They think it's arson." She traced a finger across the words of the brief article. "Nothing about a body."

"I can't believe the firefighters didn't find her. They're just not reporting anything yet, or maybe just not in that article. Is there anything else?"

Paige clicked for the next screen of search results. "I don't see anything else."

"Then the people who set the fire don't know, either."

He draped the dish towel over the oven door handle. "And that gives us a little time."

Paige blew out a breath. "I'm going to take that shower now."

"Don't use all the hot water." He threw open a cupboard door. "I'm going to get some supplies for the road. The less we have to stop in at stores around here, the better."

Paige showered and got dressed in record time. She didn't like being here in Tabitha's cabin—and it wasn't just because she feared being tracked. The whole place gave her the creeps.

She stomped on one of the dried rose petals. They needed to get out of here.

By the time she got downstairs, dragging her suitcase behind her, Asher had packed up a few bags of food. He glanced up at her approach.

He pointed at her computer. "I took the liberty of looking up a few places nearby where we can get our hands on a phone, but it might be best to head to the capital. Finding a place to stay is going to be harder. We don't have enough cash to book a hotel room, and we don't want to use your credit or debit cards."

"I might be able to get my hands on some cash."

"No banks."

"Where's your father when you need him?" She put a hand over her mouth as her eyes flew to his face. "I'm kidding. Y-you got to the point where we could joke about your father."

"I would hope so. I don't think a little amnesia has made me overly sensitive."

Paige watched Asher as he walked upstairs to take a shower. She hoped a little amnesia hadn't made him overly judgmental, either.

THE SNOW HAD stopped falling by the time they'd packed up everything they needed from Tabitha's cabin.

Asher crouched next to the back door and slid the key beneath the mat. "Tabitha's parents are going to wonder what she was doing in that other cabin when theirs was two miles away."

"They should be wondering why someone would want to kill their daughter."

"That investigation will go nowhere. The authorities will connect her to Hidden Hills, but the doctors there aren't going to reveal Tabitha's fascination with a missing, damaged soldier."

As Asher hoisted her suitcase into the trunk, she put a hand on his arm. "Is that how you see yourself? Damaged?"

"I'm not whole, am I? I won't be whole until I remember everything, and I won't be whole until I figure out why Denver was set up." He handed her the keys. "You drive, and I'll navigate."

"Where to? Did you make a decision?"

"Head south, and we'll buy a phone as soon as it feels safe, more populated."

"Hopefully the whole bunch at Hidden Hills thinks we're dead and gone."

"For now. I'd still like to get out of this general area."

Paige accelerated in agreement. She wanted to put as many miles as possible between them and the burned-out cabin—and Tabitha's body.

About an hour later, Asher directed her to take one of the turnoffs for Montpelier. "Not a huge city, but we're not going to stand out, either."

Paige pulled into the parking lot of a big multipurpose store. "We can get a phone here, clothes and even more food."

"Are you going to use your cash for this or use that card again?"

"I'm going to retire the credit card now. Back in Mooseville, once I decided I was going to break you out of that hellhole, I made two visits to the ATM over two days and took as much money as I could out of my…our savings." She patted her purse. "I have enough for this shopping spree, anyway."

"And the rest? You mentioned before you could get your hands on some cash—without robbing a bank."

"My mother's…friend. He was Dad's army buddy, and he and Mom have been spending a lot of time together. I think they're a couple. They just haven't admitted it to me yet. Anyway, Terrence is the one who found out where the army was keeping you. I think he could get us some cash."

"He's not going to be loyal to the army?"

"Are you loyal to the army after what they did to you and Major Denver? Terrence is loyal to me and my mom. He's going to do whatever it takes to protect me…and you."

They wandered around the store, picking up a temporary phone and a few more items of clothing for Asher.

As she stood beside Asher in the checkout line, with some cheap jeans and a few flannel shirts draped over his arm, Paige covered her smile with one hand.

He lifted his eyebrows. "What's wrong?"

"In the real world, you wouldn't be caught dead in those duds. You're a very sharp dresser—one of the good things you learned from your father."

He held the clothes away from his body and inspected them. "Even more reason for me to stay alive—so I can wear my own clothes again."

When they got to the car, Asher ripped into the phone.

"We need to find a coffeehouse to charge this thing up and start making a few calls."

"We seem to be in a commercial area, should be able to find something around here."

A half mile out of the parking lot, Asher pointed at the windshield. "Up there on your right."

She parked in front of the coffeehouse, and they found a seat inside. While they sipped their coffee, they let the phone charge up.

Digging her own dead phone from her purse, she said, "I'm going to have to turn this on to get Cam's phone number."

"That should be okay. If our enemies do decide to ping your phone later, we'll be long gone from this location."

Paige swallowed. "Enemies?"

"What would you call them? These people are trying to kill us."

"Yeah, enemies will work." She powered up her phone and went to her contacts. "Might as well jot down all these numbers and program them into the new phone. I don't have anyone's number memorized anymore."

"Neither do I."

As she shot him a glance, he cracked a smile. The first she'd seen from him since Hidden Hills. She smacked his biceps, still hard and ready, with the flat of her hand.

"If the army doesn't want you back, maybe you can have a career as a stand-up comedian."

"The army had better want me back." He tapped the table in front of the burner phone. "It's charged."

Leaving the phone plugged in, Paige took a deep breath and entered Cam's phone number. "He's probably not going to pick up from an unknown number."

"Probably not." Asher picked up the phone. "Let me leave the message."

He paused for several seconds and shook his head. “Cam, this is Asher. I’m with Paige and heard your message about me. I’m retracting my version of the events that led to Major Denver going AWOL. I was set up just as surely as he was and we need to talk.”

Asher paused and rubbed his eyes. “Give us a call back at this number. It’s a phone…a burner phone.”

He broke off, and Paige studied his face. A light sheen of sweat glistened on Asher’s forehead.

His jaw worked and he started talking again. “Trying to keep Paige’s phone off. Long…long sto—”

“Asher!”

His eyes rolled back in his head. The phone slipped from his grip and fell to the floor…just before he hit the table.

# Chapter Ten

Paige looked around the coffeehouse, her gaze darting from the occupied tables to the people standing in line. Thank God for people's addiction to their phones. Nobody had noticed Asher collapsing at the table.

Leaning forward, Paige swept the phone from the floor and then pretended she was talking to Asher—just in case someone looked up from texting long enough to notice.

Cam's voice mail was probably still recording, so she whispered into the phone. "Cam, it's Paige. Asher just collapsed. I'm going to need some help. We're in Vermont… Montpelier, but probably not for long."

She ended the call and folded her arms on the table, resting her chin on her hands. With her lips close to Asher's ear, she whispered, "What's wrong, Asher? Can you hear me?"

He answered with a soft moan. At least he wasn't dead.

What *had* happened? Had someone poisoned the coffee? She popped the lid off her own cup and eyed the liquid as she swirled it around. Nobody could've poisoned their coffee but the barista, and she doubted the doctors at Hidden Hills had compromised a couple of baristas in Montpelier.

Maybe he was just ill, still suffering from his head injury. God knew what kind of treatment he received for his physical injuries. Those doctors had been more concerned with his psychological responses—and how to tweak them.

She brushed his hair back from his clammy forehead. She couldn't risk calling 911 for him, but she couldn't risk not calling. She'd rather see him back at Hidden Hills than dead, although another stint at Hidden Hills might end in his death.

"Think." She pressed her fingers to her temples. She'd helped more than a few drunks out of bars. Could this be any different?

She grabbed Asher's wrists. "We're getting out of here. I'm going to help you, but you're walking out of here. Got it?"

Asher's eyelids fluttered and he moved his lips.

"I'm gonna take that as a yes." She shoved the phone in her purse and strapped it across her body. She crouched beside Asher's chair and dragged his arm over her shoulders.

"On the count of three, I'm going to straighten up and you're coming with me." She braced her feet on the floor. "One, two, three."

She pushed up and Asher made a move to join her, which made hoisting up easier than she thought. So, he could hear her and respond in some way.

Once on her feet, Paige began to shuffle toward the door. A couple walking in gave them a wide berth but held the door open.

Paige nodded her thanks and half dragged, half carried Asher across the threshold.

A young man jumped from his chair in the coffeehouse and followed them outside. "Do you need help? Is he sick?"

"Yes, he's sick. I just need to get him to the car."

"Should I call 911?"

"No. He has the flu. I just need to get him home."

"I'll help you."

The man got on the other side of Asher and together they dragged him to the car and loaded him into the passenger seat.

The customer's friend had run out after them—too late to be of any help.

Paige rushed around to the driver's side. "Thanks so much."

Before she closed her door, she heard the man's friend say, "What's wrong with him?"

The man who'd helped her snorted. "Junkie."

As she slammed the car door, anger burned in Paige's chest—for just a second. Could it be a drug in Asher's system? Something put there by the Hidden Hills's doctors earlier to release at a later time? Was that possible? Something Tabitha had given him to make sure he'd stay compliant?

She snapped Asher's seat belt across his body and checked his breathing—still steady.

She drove out of the parking lot, just in case someone at the coffee place got the bright idea to call the cops or an ambulance.

She pulled up next to a park, its swings and slides deserted in the chilly air.

Could Asher be on something he hadn't told her about? She wouldn't blame him if he were after what he went through, but he had a strong aversion to drugs of any kind.

She pulled her old phone from her purse, turned it on and scanned through her contacts until she found Elena Morelli's number. As Paige didn't have the authority to prescribe medication, she often referred clients who needed drugs to Elena, a psychiatrist who worked in the same building.

Paige almost sobbed with relief when Elena picked up after the second ring.

"Hi, Paige. I thought you were out of town."

"I am. I need your help."

"I'm great. How are you?"

"I'm sorry, Elena. This is urgent."

"Shoot."

"I'm with a…friend, and he passed out. I think it might be some kind of narcotic, but I'm not sure. I need to know the best way to bring him out of this if it is a drug. Is there any such thing as a timed-release drug? Something injected that takes effect later?"

"Whoa." Elena whistled. "You just gave me a lot to chew on. Why not bring this friend to the emergency room? You're not in trouble, are you, Paige? Are you in a…situation?"

This could certainly be called a situation, but it wasn't the kind Elena meant.

"I'm fine, Elena. But my friend… It's a long story. I can't bring him to the hospital right now. I just want to make sure he's okay and see if there's anything I can do to speed up his recovery."

"I can't be much help if I don't know what drug he took. How's his breathing?"

"Steady, slow."

"Is his skin dry to the touch? You know what I mean? Parched?"

Paige shoved up Asher's sleeve and rubbed his fore-arm. "Doesn't seem to be."

"Peel up his eyelids. How do his eyes look? Blood-shot? Pupils dilated?"

Paige shoved back her seat so she could turn and face

Asher in the passenger seat. Placing her thumb against his eyelid, she pushed it up. "His pupils are dilated."

"You don't have any idea what he took? Does he have anything on him?"

"It's not like that, Elena. He was drugged, but there's no way someone could've slipped him something before he passed out. That's why I asked about a timed-release drug."

"This is too weird, Paige. What kind of trouble are you in? Do you need to call someone in the program?"

"No. I'm fine, Elena. I just want to help my friend."

Elena took a measured breath over the phone. "The best thing you can do for your *friend* right now is get him comfortable, lying down, preferably. Let him sleep it off, keep him on his side. When he starts to come to, and he will, give him lots of water and then get him to a Narcotics Anonymous program."

Paige closed her eyes and breathed deeply through her nose. Elena wasn't going to believe her anyway, so she might as well plunge right in. "So, is it possible to administer a delayed-reaction narcotic?"

"Yep, it's possible." Elena's clipped tones cut through the phone.

"Then that's what happened. How long could this last?" She couldn't have Asher passing out on her every twenty-four hours.

"I don't know. It depends on the drug. You're being totally serious, aren't you?"

"I am."

"You're going to have to take your friend to a doctor."

"I'll try." Paige brushed Asher's hair from his forehead and pressed her palm against it. "Thanks, Elena. If anyone asks if you've heard from me, tell them you haven't."

"Of course. Paige, are you okay?"

"I will be."

Paige ended the call. Where should they go? She didn't want to go back to Tabitha's cabin.

She pounded the steering wheel in frustration. The man who'd always helped her, the man with all the answers was now slumped in the seat next to her.

She shook her head. She'd had an idea before how she could get cash. Using her own phone, she called Terrence, her father's best friend and now her mother's… best friend.

Asher stirred and mumbled.

"Asher?" Paige squeezed his shoulder. "Asher? Come out of it."

Terrence answered the phone, his voice sounding strong and sure—just what she needed. "Paige? Are you okay?"

"I'm fine, Terrence, but I do need to ask you another favor."

"I'm just about ready to head out for a three-day desert hike, Paige, but I'll do what I can."

What could he possibly do from the desert? "I need money—cash."

"Where are you? Still in Vermont?"

"Yes, but I can leave at any time." She took a side glance at Asher. Could she?

"Let me get on the phone with a couple of contacts out there before I leave." Terrence cleared his throat. "Did you see Asher?"

"He's with me, Terrence. I took him out of there."

"I'm assuming he didn't have their approval to leave if you need cash. How is he?"

"He's fine." She didn't want to worry her mother or Terrence. She'd put Mom through too much already. "We just really need that cash to get around without using my credit or debit cards."

"You *are* using your phone, Paige."

"Just to make a few calls. We have a temp phone."

"Then use it. Call me back on that phone later tonight and turn off the one in your hand. Do you have enough cash for tonight?"

"Yes."

"Good. Call me later—on that other phone."

She ended the call and powered off her phone. She dropped it in the cup holder and then started the engine. She had the cash right now to get them a hotel room. Asher had wanted to stay near DC, so she'd start driving south now.

Paige cast an anxious glance at Asher, still slumped in the passenger seat. He looked like he was asleep, but if he didn't come to soon, she'd have to take him to an emergency room—even if that meant he'd be recaptured.

Her muscles became more and more relaxed and her grip on the steering wheel looser and looser the farther she drove away from Hidden Hills.

Finally, as she sped out of Vermont, the temp phone rang. Keeping her eyes on the road, she felt for the phone and propped it on the steering wheel in front of her. Her heart jumped when she saw Cam's number.

"Cam, it's Paige. Don't hang up on me."

"Why would I hang up on you? I just called you back, or I thought I was calling Asher. Has he come to his senses?"

"Did you hear my part of the message?"

"I just heard Asher's message. What's going on?"

Paige slid a sideways glance at Asher. "Asher's in trouble. They've been messing with his mind, Cam."

"Can I talk to him?"

"H-he's out."

"Out? Out where?"

Paige scooped in a big breath. "He's knocked out, drugged, whatever. I don't know."

Cam let loose with a string of expletives. "What are you talking about? Is he still at that rehab center in Vermont?"

"I broke him out of there. They were the ones jerking him around, Cam. They're the reason he came out with that statement about Major Denver. The doctors at Hidden Hills planted those memories in his head."

"Paige, slow down. What's wrong with him now? He just left me a voice mail a few hours ago."

"If I had to guess, I'd say the docs at the rehab center injected him with some timed-release drug to try to control him. They didn't even tell him about me. They haven't been trying to help him at all. They only wanted him to tell their story about Major Denver."

"Unbelievable, but I know there's some setup involving Denver. I just learned that the original emails implicating him were bogus. Are you going to take Asher to the emergency room? Where are you, anyway?"

"We're on the road." She eased off the gas pedal. She didn't need to get pulled over for speeding now. "I don't want to take him to a hospital, Cam. I don't think he'd want that. It could lead to his recapture."

"Are you sure he's okay?"

Paige reached over and pressed her hand against Asher's chest, slowly rising and falling. "He's still breathing. He doesn't seem like he's in distress—no foaming at the mouth or jerking limbs."

"Well, that's a plus. Are you still in Vermont?"

"Just left it. Can you help me, Cam? Help us?"

"I'm leaving the country, Paige. You're gonna have to do this on your own. Can you do this on your own?"

She flushed and snapped, "Of course."

He clicked his tongue. "It sounds like you've been doing a great job so far… At least you got him out of Hidden Hills. Do you have money? A place to stay? You can't leave an electronic trail. You can't let the army track you down."

"I'm working on it. We're heading south. Before Asher…passed out, he told me he wanted to go to DC. He wants to figure out who's behind this."

"So do I. About how far are you from DC now?"

"Maybe another nine hours."

"I have an idea for you. My girl has a family home on Chesapeake Bay, about an hour outside the capital."

Paige blinked. "You have a girl?"

"Yeah, long story. It's her mother's home, but there's nobody there now. You and Asher can stay there and we can arrange to have money and resources there for you, including a doctor."

"Really? I would feel so much better if Asher could see a doctor."

"Martha has a lot of contacts in the area. We can do this as long as you can get Asher to Chesapeake in one piece. Can you do that, Paige? Can you do that without falling apart?"

If Asher's friends couldn't trust her, how could Asher with all his memories fresh in his mind?

She clenched her jaw and ground out the words. "I'm fine, Cam. I'm not falling apart. Just give me the address and I'll get Asher there if I have to die trying."

"Okay, okay."

Cam rattled off the address and instructions for getting a key. "Text me when you get there. And, Paige?"

"Yeah?"

"When Asher wakes up, tell him we have his back."

PAIGE DROVE ON into the late afternoon and the beginning of the evening. She listened to music, talked to herself, talked to Asher.

He stirred a few times, and she drove through a fast-food place to have food and water on hand when he woke up—because he *would* wake up.

Halfway through Delaware and the first verse of a song, she got her wish. Asher had been shifting his body for the past several miles, and now his eyelashes fluttered and he stretched his legs.

He mumbled and swiped the back of his hand across his mouth.

"Asher? Asher, are you awake?"

She couldn't wait to tell him the good news about Cam and that they were on their way to a safe place—and she'd arranged it on her own.

He scooted up in his seat and rubbed his eyes, cranking his head back and forth as if to work the kinks out of his neck.

He muttered, "God," and then his hand closed around a water bottle in the cup holder.

Paige released a sigh. "*Thank* God. I was so worried about you, but I didn't call 911 and we're on our way to a safe house. You're even going to see a doctor there. There's food in the back, just burgers and fries, and we're halfway to DC."

Paige drew back her shoulders and waited for Asher to say more, maybe how he felt or what he thought happened to him.

Instead he downed the water and gazed out the window.

"Asher?" He seemed awake, but was this some kind

of suspended state of consciousness? She waited for several minutes that stretched into an eternity.

"Asher? Did you hear me? We're on our way to a safe house." She touched his cool hand.

He snatched his hand away from her, screwed on the lid to the empty bottle, placed it back in the cup holder and finally turned toward her, his green eyes dark and unfathomable.

"When the hell were you going to tell me about our daughter?"

## *Chapter Eleven*

Paige jerked the steering wheel, and the car swerved across an empty lane. She righted the car and hunched her shoulders.

"Y-you remembered? Everything?"

"Everything that matters." Asher's eyes narrowed, his jaw settling into a hard line.

"I thought piling that on when you still have unnamed forces after you…and your mind would be too much for you to handle."

"Really? Didn't you come out to Hidden Hills to see me so that you could help me get my memory back? Make me whole?"

"I did, but that was before I knew the full extent of what they were doing to you. I still don't know the entire story—and neither do you. I had to haul you out of that coffee place earlier because you just passed out. Do you remember that?"

"I remember leaving a message for Cam, and then… nothing."

"Exactly. Do you understand why I didn't think it was a great idea to tell you about Ivy?"

"Let's get real, Paige." He gripped his knees. "You didn't think it was a great idea to tell me about Ivy because you didn't want to reveal the circumstances of her birth and everything that followed."

Her nose stung, and she tried to swallow the lump in her throat. "Okay, maybe I thought that was too much for you to bear. You didn't remember me, didn't remember what I went through. I didn't want you to worry about putting your faith in a woman, a stranger really, who'd had…issues."

"Who was an alcoholic who relapsed after the birth of our child. An alcoholic who put that child in danger. An alcoholic I couldn't trust with my daughter."

The road swam before her, and she blinked her eyes, dislodging a tear from her lashes. "I could've told you the whole story about my recovery and my path to sobriety, but it would've just been words to you, hollow words if you couldn't remember the ups and downs and the feelings."

Closing his eyes, Asher ran a thumb between his eyebrows. "I remember. God, I remember."

She skimmed her clammy palms over the steering wheel. "So, you conked out, and when you woke up, your memory had returned? That's not the effect they'd counted on, I'm sure."

He sliced a hand in the air to cut her off. "How is Ivy? Who's taking care of her? Your mom?"

"Mom has her and Ivy's doing great. She misses her daddy. I kept telling her you were coming home soon—and then you went on that assignment with Major Denver."

"Do you have pictures on your phone? I want to see her. I want to talk to her."

"Of course." She tipped her chin toward her phone on the console. "My phone's there."

He grabbed it and then folded his hands around it. "We still shouldn't turn this on."

Paige licked her lips. She didn't want to tell him she'd used her phone to call Elena and Terrence. She'd fallen into old habits so easily…keeping things from him.

"I'm truly sorry, Asher. I… Maybe I wanted you to keep me on that pedestal for a few more days. It was wrong. I should've told you everything."

The words came to her lips easily and willingly. She'd spent years apologizing to Asher.

He rubbed his eyes. "I can't believe I didn't remember Ivy. She's everything to me."

"I know that." Paige dropped her lashes. "I promise I'll give you a complete update on Ivy, but what do you think happened in the coffeehouse? Had you experienced that before at Hidden Hills?"

"The only time anything like that occurred at Hidden Hills was the time I ran into you in the forest, when Granger and Lewis shot me with the dart. Complete blackout."

"Well, that didn't happen back in Montpelier. I keep thinking it must've been a timed-release drug. I called my friend Elena Morelli, a psychiatrist, and she told me there are such things."

"I can believe anything of those docs at Hidden Hills. If they can implant false memories in my brain, they can inject something into my system that will affect me later."

"But why would they do something like that?"

"Who knows?" He rubbed the back of his head where his dark hair was growing in over the wound. "If I had escaped and been on my own and collapsed like that in public, someone would've called 911 and they'd have me in their clutches again."

"I did the right thing not bringing you to an emergency room? I wasn't sure."

"You did the right thing." He cleared his throat. "Thanks."

She nodded her head, the pleasure in any compliment from him dulled by the knowledge that he resented her for keeping Ivy from him. Had she been wrong to want to bask in his pleasure at having a kickass fiancée who'd sprung him from captivity?

Even after she'd recovered from her addiction, she always looked for the acknowledgment of her weakness in Asher's eyes. She'd been sensitive to every nuance in his voice, every glance at her when she had Ivy in her arms.

Yeah, she'd been wrong. That hadn't been her call to make. She squared her shoulders. "I'm sorry. I should've told you everything about us and our daughter. I should've put you under hypnosis and brought you back—all the way back to the day we met at that party—when I was drunk and fell into the pool, fully clothed and clutching a margarita for dear life."

His lips twisted. "I still felt an overpowering urge to rescue you, drunk or not."

"And you did. You rescued me in every way imaginable." She covered one of his hands with hers. "I'm so glad you got your memory back."

"I am, too, but when am I going to pass out again and where? Maybe next time the drug will erase any memories I gained back and put me at square one." He pounded his knee with his fist. "I can't afford to be back at square one, Paige."

"I know that, but I meant what I said about the doctor."

"Doctor?"

Of course he couldn't remember what she'd said about their destination and the money and the doctor and Cam.

He'd been remembering their whole tumultuous relationship together and what a bad mom she'd been.

"I talked to Cam—on the temp phone." She slipped her hand from Asher's and flicked on the windshield wipers. "We're heading to his girlfriend's place on Chesapeake Bay. They'll have money for us there and send a doctor over."

"Wait, wait." He held up his hands. "Maybe I don't have all my memories back. Cam Sutton has a girlfriend? A girlfriend with a place on Chesapeake Bay?"

"He told me it was a long story, so we didn't get into it. He also told me he's on his way out of the country, so maybe another deployment."

"I wonder where he's being assigned with Denver and me out."

"He didn't say, but the house will be empty. He gave me instructions. I also have Terrence working on getting us some cash."

"Terrence needs to be careful. He's retired. He doesn't need to be getting into any trouble with the army."

"He knows what he's doing. He has contacts in Atlantic City who might be able to help us out, too."

"You did good." Asher ran his fingers along her arm. "You saved me again."

"I think I owe you a lot of saves to pay you back for all the times you saved me."

He tapped the heel of his hand against his head. "It's a strange feeling knowing someone is controlling you remotely."

"Could your blackout have been a result of your injuries? You remembered everything when you woke up. Could it have been your body's way of healing you?"

"That sounds a lot better than some timed-release drug ready to bring me to my knees every twenty-four hours."

He cocked an eyebrow at her. "How the hell did you get me out of that coffee place?"

"You were still on your feet. I half dragged, half carried you out." She winked. "Don't forget. I've had a lot of practice hauling drunks out of bars."

"You always were the best sponsor in AA."

"Full disclosure." She held up two fingers. "Another customer helped me through the parking lot and into the car."

"Another customer? Someone you could trust?"

"He wasn't going to turn around and call the police or EMTs, if that's what you mean. He thought you were a junkie." She bit her bottom lip.

"He's not so far from the truth." Asher thumped his fist against his chest. "I don't know what's coursing through my veins."

"Maybe Martha's doctor friend can figure it out."

"Martha?"

"Cam's girlfriend."

"Cam's girlfriend." He shook his head. "God help her."

NOW THAT HIS memories had returned, Asher couldn't turn them off. Everything he and Paige had been through with her addiction to alcohol rushed back in every painful detail. He'd made it clear to her that she had to choose between him or the booze—she'd chosen the booze but then found out she was pregnant.

That had scared her. She'd stayed sober during her pregnancy but had fallen off the wagon after Ivy was born. He'd reached the end of the line with her, threatening to take the baby away from her unless she got help.

She loved Ivy as much as he did, and she got to work, with a vengeance—AA, therapy, cutting off drinking buddies. The process spurred her on to become a marriage, family and child counselor, and she attacked that course as vigorously as she had dealt with her addiction.

He understood why she'd want to keep all that from him a little while longer, but when he remembered he had a daughter and realized why she hadn't told him about Ivy, he'd gotten that sinking feeling in his gut—the same one he'd felt when Paige had tried to get sober the first time…and failed. She'd lied to him, hid things from him, made excuses. It had almost torn them apart—almost.

From the driver's seat, he glanced at her, head tipped to one side, mouth slightly ajar. They'd bonded over their dysfunctional family lives.

His father, a convicted bank robber serving time in federal prison, and hers, a disgraced cop who'd taken his own life, but her trauma had gone a step further.

As a teenager, Paige had found her father in the family's garage, his brains blown out. How did a kid recover from that? Paige had numbed it with alcohol.

Asher had dealt with his own…disappointment by becoming overly regimented in all aspects of his life. Fate had led him to Paige, just when she needed him and he needed her. Nothing could disrupt your life quite like an alcoholic.

Taking care of Paige had satisfied that driving need in his life to impose order on all things. It also taught him compassion and forgiveness—emotions that had been absent in his psychological makeup until that point. He needed to find those again.

Paige jerked awake, her eyes wide-open immediately. "Where are we?"

"We're already through Jersey. We have less than an hour to get there. Cam's girlfriend must be rolling in dough with an address like that."

"Cam said it's her mother's house."

"Where's the mom?"

"He didn't say, just that the house would be all ours."

"It'll be a good base for our operation, and now that the boys are back on my side, maybe I can get some help from them. I need to talk to Cam again and find out more about those emails he mentioned. I don't think my imprisonment had anything to do with me, and everything to do with Denver. I was just a tool for them."

Paige yawned. "Now that you have your memories back, do you remember anything more about the mission?"

"I remember the name of Denver's contact—Shabib. He had information for the major that he had to communicate in person. It was something Denver was expecting, something he'd been investigating—something big."

"Apparently, it was so big, he had to be neutralized."

"But they didn't get him, did they?" Asher watched the rain lash the windshield and the wipers flick the drops off as fast as they fell. "Denver's out there somewhere, and he's going to be counting on us—his team members—to help him."

"Where are you going to start?"

"At the beginning. I'm going to track down Shabib, one way or another."

"Turnoff in less than two miles." Paige hunched forward and peered through the rain. "This is an out-of-the-way place."

"The more remote, the better."

"The farther from Hidden Hills, the better."

"They're still probably trying to figure out what happened in that cabin."

Paige hugged herself and rubbed her arms. "I hate thinking about it."

"It all worked in our favor—fate."

"That was Tabitha's fate? To die in a fire in that cabin?"

"She etched it out herself." He aimed the car down a long driveway. "And this house on the bay is ours right now."

Asher slid out of the car and used the code on the garage door to open it. He drove the car into the garage and closed the door so it still looked like a deserted house.

Paige followed Cam's directions on the location of the key, and ten minutes later, they entered a lavishly decorated house, clean and well stocked with food.

Asher whistled as he hung on the fridge door and surveyed the contents. "We could probably hole up here for six months."

"Let's hope we don't have to." She kicked a duffel bag she dragged from beneath a chair. "Cash. I already called Terrence to let him know we had another source."

Asher shook his head. "I can't believe Cam orchestrated all this. He's not exactly a planner."

"I know, but his new girlfriend must be. He was on his way out of the country. Martha must've made these arrangements."

"We'll have to thank Martha if we ever meet her."

Paige looked up from pawing through the money in the bag. "Is that because you don't think they'll last…or you don't think we'll last?"

"Oh, I plan to be alive to meet any and all of Cam's girlfriends, and you're coming along for this ride. Speaking of staying alive—" he pointed at the duffel "—is the gun in there?"

She buried both hands in the bag and withdrew a .38, holding it by its barrel. "Just like Cam promised."

"I'm starting to revise my opinion of that hothead." Asher crossed the great room and took the gun from Paige. "Bullets?"

"I felt a box at the bottom of the bag."

"Money, weapon, food and your computer. I'm ready to get to work."

"I'm ready to go to sleep." Paige ran her hands through her hair. "And maybe take a shower."

"I'm ready to see pictures of Ivy." He raised his eyebrows. "You didn't think I forgot, did you?"

"Of course not." She retrieved her laptop and brought it to the kitchen counter. "I have a bunch from Thanksgiving. I sent some of those to you. Those bastards at Hidden Hills must've seen them on your phone and still didn't bother to tell you about your daughter." Two red spots flared on Paige's cheeks. "I didn't, either."

"Two different motivations."

"Both selfish."

"No argument from me." Asher felt the anger tighten in his chest again and filled his lungs with air. At least he understood Paige's motivation, and it wasn't like she planned to keep Ivy's existence a secret from him forever. She'd just wanted a little breathing room away from his judgment and censure.

He joined her at the counter as she powered on the computer. "I never had my phone, anyway."

"They never gave you your phone?" Her fingers clicked across the keyboard. "Of course they didn't."

"My phone was never recovered—at least that's what they told me."

"Do you believe them?" She double-clicked a folder on her desktop and his daughter came back to him in living color.

He put his face close to the monitor and traced a finger around Ivy's face. "How could I have ever forgotten this cute little button?"

"You didn't have a choice." She clicked open another

folder. "Here are the ones from Thanksgiving, which are on a phone somewhere in Afghanistan."

"Yeah, I wonder where it really is."

They spent the next fifteen minutes looking at pictures while Paige updated him on Ivy's latest antics. But he remembered these photos now, remembered that Ivy had started singing into a hairbrush, had her first ballet recital, was begging for a puppy.

Paige was a good mom and even across the miles had kept him informed about Ivy's activities.

Guilt tweaked the edges of his mind. She kept him apprised of every detail because she still felt as if she had to prove herself to him. Prove that she was a good mother.

No wonder she'd wanted a brief respite from his accusing eyes.

He turned to her suddenly and cupped her face with one hand. "You're doing a great job with Ivy. She looks happy and healthy. And all this... You did this. You got us here to safety."

Paige's lips curved into a smile. "Technically, Cam and his girlfriend got us here."

"Cam's not here. You are." He brushed his thumb across her lips. "You got me out of that coffeehouse. Hell, you got me out of Hidden Hills. I'd still be rotting away in there, thinking Major Denver was a traitor."

"Did you think I'd let you languish at Hidden Hills and get out of our engagement? When the guy on the phone told me you didn't remember me, I thought it was a convenient way for you to get out of marrying me."

"As if I'd want to do that." He kissed her, really kissed her, for the first time since they'd reconnected, and the touch of her lips felt like coming home.

He buried his hands in her hair and deepened the kiss as they connected over the pictures of their daughter on the computer screen. He whispered against her mouth, "I love you, Paige."

She pressed her hand against his chest, one finger resting in the hollow of his throat where his pulse galloped. "I've been waiting so long to hear those words from you."

"Let's not waste any more time." He cinched her wrists lightly with his fingers. "We haven't even checked out the sleeping arrangements yet, but I'm not spending another night without you."

Digging her fingernails into his chest, she whispered, "I wasn't planning on that, either, but I need a quick shower before I crawl into bed with anyone."

He kissed her forehead. "You do that. Find us a bed and I'll make sure everything is secured down here—including that money."

"Bring the gun with you…just in case."

She slipped away from him and he drank in the photos of Ivy for several more seconds before shutting the laptop. He hauled the bag of cash into the kitchen and stuffed it into the cabinet under the sink.

He heard water running through the pipes, so Paige must've found the shower.

If he hurried, he might be able to join her. He grabbed a couple of bottles of water from the fridge and tucked them under one arm. As he flicked off the light and pivoted toward the staircase, Paige screamed.

"Asher, they're watching us."

# *Chapter Twelve*

Asher charged into the dark bedroom, and Paige shouted, "Leave the lights."

His forward motion propelled him onward and had him tripping over a piece of furniture, banging his shin on something hard. "What the hell, Paige? I nearly killed myself getting here. Who's watching us?"

Turning back to the window, Paige hooked her finger on one of the slats of the blinds. "There's someone out there on the boat dock, and he has a pair of binoculars trained on the house."

Asher's adrenaline flared and then receded. He caught his breath. "Did he see you?"

"I don't think so, not from this window, but he must've seen the light from the bathroom." She adjusted the towel around her body with one hand, causing it to slip farther off her chest. "I came in here from my shower, and on my way to the light switch by the bed, I stopped to peer out this window. I figured the house had a view of the bay. I saw the bay, all right, but I also caught a glimpse of something shiny by the boat dock. It was a figure, a man, turned toward the house and holding something to his face—I'm sure they're binoculars."

"He's still there?"

"Yes. Is it possible we were followed?"

"Anything's possible, but if he were after us and knew we were here, why's he waiting outside in plain view? And if he were following us, how did he get here before we did?"

Paige let the slat drop. "That makes sense, but what doesn't make sense is that guy spying on the house from the boat dock."

"It's not surprising. If a soldier is on the run, who's he going to contact for help?"

"The members of his unit, but this isn't even Cam's house."

"Because Cam's house is nowhere near this area."

"I guess everyone, including the bad guys, knew about Cam's new girlfriend except us."

Keeping away from the window, Asher perched on the edge of the bed and rubbed his shin. "Is your phone up here? I'm going to give Martha a call. Cam told you to call her when we got here anyway, right?"

Paige stepped away from the window, her back still rigid, fear still etched on her face. She yanked her sweater off the chair and dipped her hand in its pocket. "It's here, and I have Martha's number programmed into it."

She handed it to him, and he slid off the mattress to the floor. "We don't want to show any more light in here than we have to."

He tapped the phone for Martha's number and held his breath through two rings.

A soft voice answered. "Hello?"

"Martha, this is Asher Knight, Cam's friend." He put the phone on speaker and nodded to Paige.

"Y-yes. I recognized the phone number Cam gave me. Did you get to the house okay? Is it stocked with food? Is the money there? I arranged everything, and my mother won't be home for another few months. A doctor should be showing up tomorrow—unless you need him right now."

"No. Everything's fine…except there's a man watching the house with binoculars from the boat dock."

She gasped. "Cam was worried someone might be watching him…us. This conspiracy is so deep and wide, I still don't feel safe."

"You don't?" Asher raised his brows at Paige, sitting on the floor next to him, and she shrugged her shoulders.

Martha said, "I'm the one who received the fake emails implicating Major Denver. Cam and I even proved the emails were phony, but it didn't stop the locomotive that's barreling forward to nail Denver for treason."

"This is messed up." Asher ran a hand over his mouth. "So the guy watching your house now may just be trying to get lucky on the chance that Cam is helping me."

"That could be it, unless you think someone followed you or tracked you. I have an idea. My mother has a cleaning lady who comes by the house all the time. She's the one who laid in the food supplies. If she were at the house now and noticed someone watching it, she'd call the police."

"Martha, this is Paige. You want us to call the police?"

Martha answered, "I'll do it and pretend I'm her. The cops will go out there to investigate and chase the guy off, and maybe he'll believe the only person at the house is my mother's cleaning lady. He wouldn't figure you two would call the cops…unless he already saw you."

Asher glanced at Paige and she shook her head. "Not that we know of, but if the police chase him off, he'll be back and I'll lose an opportunity to get my hands on someone who could give me some answers."

"Get your hands on him?" Paige's eyes widened in her pale face. "I don't think that's a good idea."

"I think it's a great idea." Asher smacked a hand on the floor. "Martha, is there a way I can get from the house to the boat dock without being seen by someone down by the water?"

Paige poked his leg, but he ignored her.

"You can get down to the water from a path next to the house. He won't see you coming that way—until you reach the bay. He's going to see you once you start approaching him from the shoreline."

"Unless I come up from the water."

Martha responded, "He'll hear a boat coming, even if it's a rowboat."

"I'm not talking about hitting the water in a boat."

Both women gasped at the same time—in stereo.

Paige jabbed his leg again. "You are *not* going into that water and swimming up on some guy who probably has a gun."

Martha joined in as soon as Paige left off. "The bay will be freezing cold."

"I won't be in there long…and Paige can warm me up once I'm back inside."

"Not if you're dead." Paige scowled at him.

Martha sighed. "If I've learned anything about you D-Boys after hanging out with Cam these past few months, I know you can't be dissuaded once you've made up your minds."

"You'd think my fiancée would know that by now, too." He ran a hand down Paige's leg.

"Then that's the way to go. Slip out the side door and duck through the fence on that side of the property. Take the path straight to the waterline and slip in from there. You'll know when you're at our dock because of the pilings in the water. I know Cam will be disappointed he wasn't there to help you."

"He helped us plenty. And tell that hothead to keep being a hothead. He should talk it up about how I'm a… traitorous bastard. I think those were his original words. If the agents behind this setup believe Cam still thinks I'm accusing Denver of sabotage, maybe they'll leave him—and you—alone."

"I'll tell him when I can. Be careful… These people will stop at nothing to keep spinning the lie about Major Denver, and we don't know why or who's behind it."

"We'll watch our backs."

Asher ended the call and crawled to the window. "I'd better make sure he's still there and not on the porch instead."

Paige blew out a breath. "This is bigger than we thought. Bigger than a few doctors at Hidden Hills."

"I always thought it was. I'm just sorry you're involved."

"I was always going to be involved, Asher." She scooted on the floor and joined him under the window. "Let me look. I can keep watch while you're on your way. If he makes a move toward the house, I'll start turning on all the lights. That'll be our signal."

"Okay. I'll keep an eye on the house on my way to the water. If I see the lights go on, I'll head back." He gestured toward the gun. "You keep that with you here. I can't take it in the water anyway."

She lifted the bottom of the blinds. "He's still there. You know, if they're watching Cam and his girlfriend, they would've been watching me."

"Probably." He crawled to the bedroom door. "Stay here. With any luck, I'll be bringing our prey back with me."

Putting one hand over her heart, she nodded. "I'll be ready. Be careful and don't do anything stupid."

"I think those two might be mutually exclusive."

Paige blew him a kiss from her position under the window. "I'd give you a real one, but I don't want to give that guy out there a target."

"I don't think he can see us behind the blinds in a dark room—" he reached out as if to snatch her kiss from the air "—but I'll take this one to be on the safe side."

Asher jogged down the stairs and exited the side door of the house. Staying in the shadows, he hopped the fence that separated the property from the public path to the beach and his boots crunched against the sandy dirt. He'd have to lose the boots before he entered the water unless he wanted to sink to the bottom of the bay.

He hunched forward and made a beeline to the water's edge, occasionally casting a glance over his shoulder at the house to watch for the signal. The house remained in darkness.

About ten feet from the shore, he dashed for a small boathouse with the stranger on the other side. He shed his jacket and pulled off his boots. On his hands and knees he made his way to the water's edge, the rocks biting into his kneecaps and palms.

He held his breath and rolled into the frigid bay, his insides curling up as the water embraced him, soaking into his clothing and his flesh.

He swam beneath the surface, frog-kicking his legs, keeping his left hand outstretched to feel for the pilings of the boat dock. When he reached the other side, he rose to the surface, tipping his head back to take a sip of air.

With his face out of the water, he paddled around to face Martha's house. The stranger had his back to the bay, silently watching the house. His powerboat bobbed in the water and Asher used it for additional cover.

Asher didn't have any room for error. If the man heard

him coming out of the water and he took too long to get out, he'd probably wind up with a bullet in the head and this bay would be his watery grave.

He floated to the edge of the dock. In one movement, he hoisted himself out of the water and launched at the man.

The cover of darkness, the element of surprise and the fact that the man had both hands on his binoculars all worked in Asher's favor.

Before the stranger could react, Asher had tackled him and smashed his face against the binoculars.

The man grunted and struggled beneath him, trying to free his right hand pinned between his body and Asher's knee. Asher helped him out and shoved his hand into the pocket the man was trying to reach.

His fingers curled around the handle of a gun and he whipped it out and pressed it against the man's temple. "Who the hell are you and why are you watching the house?"

The man grunted and swore. His body bucked beneath Asher's.

"It's not gonna go that way. You're gonna answer my questions, or you're a dead man."

The man narrowed his eyes and spit out of the side of his mouth.

"Your stubbornness is gonna get you killed." Asher pushed off the man's body and rose above him, aiming the gun at his chest. "Get up."

The man staggered to his feet, the binoculars swinging from his neck.

Asher ripped them off and kicked the back of the man's legs. "Get moving—toward the house. If you try anything, I'll shoot."

They walked in silence, one ahead of the other, the

swishing, sloshing sounds of Asher's wet clothing the only noise.

As they approached the back door, the patio lights illuminated their way. Then the door swung open and Paige greeted them with Asher's weapon pointed at them.

"You did it."

"I surprised him. He hasn't said a word yet…but he will."

Asher prodded the man into the house as Paige slammed the back door behind them. She scooted past Asher and his prisoner and settled a dining room chair on the hardwood floor. "Have him sit here. I found rope and tape in the garage."

Asher searched the man's pockets and pulled out a phone and a set of keys. Placing a hand on the man's shoulder, he shoved him into the chair. As Paige held her gun on their captive, Asher tied the man's ankles to the legs of the chair and secured his hands behind him.

"Let's start over." He put his face close to the other man's. "Who the hell are you and why are you watching this house?"

The captive licked his lips. "Why are you doing this? Why didn't you just call the police?"

Asher kicked the leg of the chair and the man's head snapped back and forth. "I'm asking the questions. What are you doing here?"

"I'm casing the place." He lifted his narrow shoulders. "This is a ritzy neighborhood and I heard this house was empty."

"Then why are you out there watching it instead of breaking in?"

"Wanted to make sure it was empty. I came by boat, saw a light go on upstairs, and that stopped me."

"Stopped you, so why didn't you go away? Find another house to burglarize?"

"This is the one I was told to hit."

Paige jerked her head toward Asher. "*Told* to hit? Someone commissioned you to burglarize this property?"

"Not like that." The man shook his head back and forth, the ends of his scraggly hair spewing droplets of water from Asher's watery takedown. "Just heard a rumor around town about some of these fancy beach houses and the ones left vacant. This was one of them."

"That still makes no sense. I don't know many thieves who would stay back from a property they wanted to break into and watch it with binoculars."

The man snorted. "You know many thieves?"

Asher growled. "You have no idea."

"Are you acting alone in this plan?" Paige still held the gun, but she'd let it slip from her tight grip. "Is there anyone else out there?"

The man's dark eyes flickered. "Just me."

"I don't believe you." Asher's jaw ached from tension and shivering. How the hell was he going to get information out of this guy…especially with Paige here watching?

"Believe it or not, buddy. Why aren't you calling the police? Did you two break in here, too?" He laughed, and the laugh turned into a hacking cough.

"And what if we did? What would the police discover about you? Some nobody who doesn't exist anywhere? A fake ID? Fingerprints leading to no one?"

A muscle twitched in the corner of the man's eye.

He knew something. Asher lunged at him and closed his hand around his throat until the man's eyes bulged from the sockets. "Tell me who you work for and what you were doing outside this house."

The man choked and his body squirmed in the chair.

Asher released him suddenly, and the chair tipped on its back legs. "Answer me."

Asher felt Paige's hand on his back, and his spine stiffened. He couldn't properly question the man with Paige looking on in judgment.

The man's eyes watered and one tear slipped from the corner of his left eye. "Go to hell."

Gritting his teeth, Asher stalked to the kitchen and pulled a knife from a block on the counter. He returned to his prisoner, avoiding Paige's wide-eyed stare.

He loomed over the man, wielding the knife at his throat. "You're going to tell me what I want to know, starting now."

The man's Adam's apple bobbed as he swallowed, but he pressed his lips together and closed his eyes. "I already told ya."

Asher flicked the blade against the man's flesh, and a drop of blood beaded on the side of his neck. "You can die from a thousand paper cuts just as assuredly as you can from a slice across your jugular."

Paige sucked in a breath behind him.

"Take your best shot, buddy."

Asher tapped Paige's right arm, the gun dangling from her fingers. "Keep your weapon trained on him. I'll be right back."

Asher strode to the door leading to the garage and flipped on the light. He scanned the tool bench against the wall, noting the drawers Paige had left open in her search for rope, and slid a hammer and a pair of pliers from the hooks on the wall.

He returned to the dining room, untied the man's hands and grabbed one, splaying his fingers on the arm of the chair.

"Hey, hey, hey." The man tried to snatch his hand back, but Asher drove his fist into the back of his hand.

Then he brought the hammer down on one of the man's fingers and the guy let out a howl, which blended with Paige's cry.

"Why are you here and on whose orders?"

The man's mouth twisted. "You think you can do anything worse to me than they can?"

Asher's heart skipped a beat. "Now we're getting somewhere. Who's they? Who sent you to watch this house and why?"

The man curled his good fingers into the arm of the chair. "You already know why I was sent here. I was told to watch this house, the house of Cam Sutton's girlfriend, to keep an eye out for you."

"Why? What are they trying to do to Asher?" Paige squared herself in front of the man, crossing her arms over her chest.

Asher raised the hammer again—this time over the man's kneecap.

His leg bounced. "I—I think you know that already, too. They want him to implicate Major Rex Denver. They want him to report that it was Denver who killed that ranger and Denver who pushed him over the cliff."

"He's right, Paige." Asher lowered the hammer but kept a firm grip on it. "We already know why they're after us and what they want me to do. The question is, who's behind all this? Who's behind the setup of Major Denver and why?"

"That I don't know." The man hunched his shoulders. "But it's big."

"I-is anyone else coming here? Did you contact your backups?"

"I haven't contacted anyone. I saw a light on in the

house and started watching. I didn't know if it was Martha Drake back in the house or her mother or the cleaning lady."

They already knew a lot about Martha. Asher pointed to the phone he'd dropped on the floor. "Check it out, Paige."

She swept the phone up from the floor. "Password?"

The man dropped his chin to his chest.

Asher nudged his shoe with his bare foot and held up the pliers in his other hand. "You know I'll use them. The way I was treated in Hidden Hills? Made me kinda crazy."

Paige nodded beside him and held up the phone. "Give me your password. There's nothing I can do to stop him."

The man licked his lips and reeled off a four-digit code.

Paige entered the password and the phone came to life. "His name's Peter. Last text was from an hour ago—about the time I spotted him outside. Just says 'lights on in the house.'"

"Who'd he text?"

"A contact named Linc."

"Who's Linc?" Asher kicked the chair leg.

The man's head snapped up. "He's my guy. The one who gives me orders. The one I report to."

"Any calls, Paige?"

"An incoming call a few hours ago, just a number, no contact name."

"What is this organization? Who are you working for?"

"I dunno, buddy. I just do what I'm told."

"You're lying. If you were some grunt, you wouldn't know about Major Denver and our failed meeting with his contact."

"I'm the muscle, nothing more, but it doesn't mean I don't ask questions."

Asher tipped his head toward Paige. "Text Linc back and let him know it was a false alarm—nobody at the house."

The man in the chair gurgled. "If they ever find out about this, I'm a dead man and they'd have more than hammers and pliers to use."

"Sounds like a highly organized group, a group that doesn't fool around. Is it linked to the US government? It has to be with the personnel installed at Hidden Hills. What names have you heard? What else has Linc told you?"

"I don't know. I can't think." He bucked in the chair. "I have to use the bathroom. Just give me a break here, man. I don't have any more weapons on me. I'm cooperating, right?"

Paige nudged Asher's back.

Trading the tools for a gun, Asher said, "I'll let you get up and use the bathroom, but I'm coming with you. If you try anything, I'll shoot you."

While Asher held the man at gunpoint, Paige untied his ankles.

The man rose to his feel slowly, rubbing his forearms beneath the long sleeves of his shirt.

"Move." Asher waved the gun toward the half bathroom next to the garage door.

The man took a tentative step forward and covered his mouth with one hand.

"I thought you were desperate to use the head. Get going before I decide this is a ploy and shoot you."

The man took another stumbling step and then dropped to his knees.

Paige gasped. "Is he going for a weapon?"

Asher aimed a kick at the man's back and he pitched forward, his head turning to the side.

"Shoot him, Asher. Stop him."

Asher crouched down, rolling him to his side. The man's eyes bugged out and his tongue protruded from his mouth. Asher rested two fingers against his pulse.

"I don't have to shoot him, Paige. He's dead."

## *Chapter Thirteen*

Paige gripped the handle of the gun, still pointing it at the man's head. When he'd dropped to his knees, adrenaline had flooded her body and it still coursed through her.

"H-how? How is he dead?" She stared at the man's slack mouth and bugged-out eyes.

"I'm not sure, but I think he took something. He was reaching into his sleeves when he got up. He covered his mouth."

Her own mouth dropped open. "He poisoned himself?"

"It looks like it." He pointed to the tongue, now turning bright red.

"He committed suicide rather than tell us any more about this organization."

"He must've had orders to do so. Once his bosses found out he'd been compromised, lost his phone, gave up his phone's password—they probably had a little homecoming planned for him that would make a few broken fingers look like child's play."

She'd been afraid when Asher had dragged this man back to the house. She hadn't wanted to watch as he brought the hammer down on his hand, and she didn't want to think about where this would all lead.

She swallowed. "Would you have let him go?"

"I don't know." Asher swiped a bead of water from his forehead.

"What are we going to do with his body now?"

"Bring it back to the water. He has a boat at the dock. That's how he got here. We can leave him in the boathouse. Nobody's going to find him there at this time of year."

Paige shivered. "Leave him for Martha's mother to discover?"

"She's not due back for a while. We'll let his cohorts know the location of his body later, and they can pick him up. They're not going to allow the death of one of their own to be investigated by a local PD."

Crossing her arms, Paige cupped her elbows with her hands. "Do you think we're safe here?"

"No."

"We're going to have to hit the road again, aren't we?"

"At least we have a bundle of cash now."

"The doctor. You need to see the doctor, Asher. I can't have you collapsing on me again."

"We'll stay here for what's left of the night and get him out here tomorrow morning. Then we leave."

Paige glanced at the dead man's phone on the dining room table. "Linc hasn't responded yet, but maybe we can convince him that this house is a dead end."

"At some point his bosses are going to have another assignment for this guy." Asher nudged the man's foot. "What's going to happen when he doesn't show up? Doesn't respond?"

"We can pretend to be Peter for a little while. It could buy us some time in this house."

"We'll see." Asher crouched next to the dead man. "I'm gonna get him out of here first."

"I'll help you."

"You sure?" Asher raised his brows.

"He's my problem, too. In fact, I probably want him out of here more than you do." She spun toward the kitchen. "I am going to get a pair of gloves first."

"At least there's no blood to clean up."

Paige stuck her head in the cupboard beneath the kitchen sink and found a pair of rubber gloves. She pulled them on and joined Asher, who'd already heaved the man's body over his shoulder.

"Get the doors, clear a path for me and use the light from the cell phone to guide us."

Paige scurried ahead of Asher lugging the body of a dead man and opened the back door. She led him down to the boat dock and swung open the door to the boathouse.

"There's a light. Should I turn it on?"

"No. You never know who might be watching out here."

Paige flicked the little beam of light around the boathouse. "Let's wrap him in this piece of canvas. It's big enough, probably meant for a boat."

"Good idea. Spread it out." Asher stepped into the boathouse, panting in the small, close place.

Paige unrolled the canvas. As Asher ducked and started to slide the man off his shoulder, Paige grabbed lifeless arms dangling to the floor.

Together, they heaved him into the middle of the canvas.

Asher stepped back and brushed his hands together. "That's some kind of devotion to off yourself for the cause—whatever that cause is."

"Maybe he didn't do it for the cause. Maybe he did it out of fear of what they'd do to him after getting caught."

"Either way, it's extreme."

Paige studied Asher's profile in the dim light. "Would

you do it? If the enemy captured you, would you kill yourself rather than give up information?"

"I'd suffer torture rather than give up intel. But call me an optimist, I'd never give up hope that I'd be rescued." His jawline hardened to granite. "That's why we can't give up on Denver."

For the next ten minutes, they busied themselves with rolling up the body in the sheet of canvas and shoving it to the back of the boathouse.

Paige puffed out a breath. "I really hope nobody finds his body before his associates come and collect him. This looks more like a murder than a suicide, and we've probably implicated ourselves in a hundred ways in that house."

"That's why it's best we leave him in here instead of dumping him in the water. We don't want him washing up on the shore somewhere, and nobody's going to come out here in the dead of winter. The house is isolated enough that no neighbors are going to be reporting a foul odor."

Paige wrinkled her nose. "Let's go back to the house and clean up there just in case."

"I'm anxious to see if Linc has responded yet. In fact, I'm looking forward to playing a few games with Linc. He's our best lead yet."

They took the public beach path back to the house, and Asher picked up his boots and jacket. When they got back, they wiped down the hammer, the pliers and all the tools they'd used to subjugate their intruder and put them away.

Then Paige turned to Asher and plucked at his damp shirt. "You need to take a warm shower. I'll dump these clothes in the washing machine."

While Asher undid the top two buttons of his flannel, the cell phone on the dining room table buzzed. He lunged for it and held it up. "The password?"

She gave him the four numbers and he tapped the phone.

"It's Linc. 'Confirm position.'"

"How are you going to respond?"

He spoke aloud as he typed the text. "'Still at house, no movement.'"

Paige put a hand over her mouth as she waited.

Five seconds later, Asher read, "'Roger. Keep watching.'"

"There. That's a sign that you can take a shower and we can get some rest. Nobody followed us here. Nobody knows we're here except Cam and Martha. The dead man in the boathouse was assigned to watch this house just in case."

"I could use a shower and some dry clothes, but I'll feel a lot better if you keep that gun in your hand and keep watch."

"As much as I'd rather be in that shower with you, I'm on it."

He undid the rest of his buttons and sloughed off the shirt. As he handed it to her, he grabbed her hand. "Paige, you continue to amaze me with your strength. I couldn't ask for a better partner."

She brought his hand to her lips and pressed them against his knuckles. "Ditto for me. You've always been my strength, Asher. It comes off you in waves and I just soak it up free."

He slipped away from her and charged upstairs, calling over his shoulder, "I won't be long. Stay vigilant."

Paige peeked out the front window, but nothing stirred out there. Nobody in this little wealthy enclave had a clue that they'd stashed a dead body in the boathouse.

She crept upstairs and through the bedroom to the bathroom, filled with steam. She could still make out Asher's naked body behind the glass shower door.

"Just here to get the rest of your wet clothes."

He opened the shower door and sluiced a hand across his wet hair. "All quiet out there?"

"Uh-huh." Her gaze dropped from his face and skimmed down his body.

"When you look at me like that, it makes me wanna pull you in here with me."

"I would take you up on it, but—" she pulled the gun from the back of her waistband "—vigilance."

"Yeah, just don't wave that thing around in here…or any lower."

She swept his clothes from the top of the toilet seat, where he'd piled them up, and tucked them under her arm. "I'll take care of these. Then maybe we can get a little shut-eye before we start the day."

He'd ducked back under the water and didn't seem to have heard her.

Sighing, she trudged down the stairs. If the man with the binoculars hadn't been spying on them, she and Asher might be tucked into bed together right now…and that man would still be alive and maybe getting ready to break in.

She stuffed the clothes in the washing machine and checked for a message from Linc when she reached the kitchen. Nothing. At this time of the morning, he must be sleeping. He must be convinced Peter hadn't seen anyone at Martha's house. How long could they keep up the ruse?

She used the charger from her old phone to plug in Peter's phone to keep it juiced up. They didn't want to lose connection with Linc.

She left her phone turned off. She'd already called Terrence to let him know they'd found another source of money.

While the teakettle whistled, Asher poked his head into the kitchen.

"Tea?"

"No, thanks." He stepped out, fanning a blanket around his shoulders. "No pajamas, but I feel one hundred percent better after that warm shower."

She poured the boiling water on the tea bag in the cup. "Do you think we can get a little sleep?"

"Sure, so why are you drinking that tea?"

"It's herbal." She flicked the tag hanging over the edge of the cup. "It's just for warmth and comfort."

"I guess I haven't been much good for warmth and comfort." He spread out his arms, opening the blanket. "Come here."

She moved toward him like a magnet and stopped inches from his body.

He enfolded her in his arms, wrapping the blanket around her. He kissed the top of her head. "You need some sleep. I'll keep watch."

"We'll both keep watch. If you can't sleep, I'll stay awake for support."

"I can sleep in the car or at our next stop—provided that one's not compromised like this one."

She wriggled free from the cocoon of his embrace. "I'll drink my tea to stay awake."

"You just said it was herbal." He strolled to the sofa and sat down in one corner.

"It is, but it'll keep me occupied." She dropped the tea bag into the trash and cupped the mug with both hands. Then she joined Asher on the sofa, curling her legs beneath her.

He draped his arm and one edge of the blanket around her shoulders.

She took a sip of her warm brew and rested her head

on Asher's shoulder. "I can't wait to go home and see Ivy. She'll be so excited to have her daddy home."

"It's gonna happen, Paige. We'll all be together, safe." He stroked her hair, and she closed her eyes.

The cup felt heavy in her hands, and she must've communicated this to Asher, because he took it from her. She didn't even make an attempt to hold on to it.

Her eyelids grew as heavy as the cup had been, and she struggled to open them, but Asher's warm touch continued down the side of her neck and shoulder, caressing her, soothing her as only he could.

As she drifted off to sleep, she had one last surge of energy and she blinked her eyes. She mumbled, "I'm supposed to be taking care of you."

"Shh, it's my turn now."

And for the first time, she felt worthy of his protection.

THE SMELL OF bacon tickled her nose, and for a few seconds Paige imagined she was at her mom's house with Ivy. Then she peeled open her eyes, took in the room with its lavish decor, and reality hit her smack between the eyes.

She sat up on the sofa, and the blanket slipped from her shoulders. "Asher?"

"I'm in the kitchen, making breakfast. You were sleeping so soundly—" he hunched over the counter "—I didn't want to disturb you. Good news."

"The guy in the boathouse is still dead and nobody has found him yet?"

"Yeah, that, too." He held up one of the phones charging on the counter. "Linc has agreed to a meeting."

Paige blinked. "What? Agreed to whose meeting?"

"Our meeting?"

"You set up a meeting with Linc?"

"How else am I going to start working my way up the chain of command to get to the top dog?"

"When and where is this meeting taking place?"

"Don't have all the details yet. Maybe we'll meet him right here." He held up a plate of bacon. "We have everything we need for now."

"I don't know." Paige scooted off the sofa and stretched. "You shouldn't have let me fall asleep. I'll bet you didn't get any."

"I'll sleep later. Who knows? Maybe blacking out like that stored up my energy."

"Which reminds me." She snapped her fingers. "We need to call Martha's friend this morning—the doctor. What if you pass out before our meeting with Linc?"

"Not optimal." He pinched a piece of bacon between his fingers and bit off the end. "Pretty good. I made eggs, too."

She pulled a stool up to the counter and straddled it. "I see you dried your clothes and got dressed. How long have you been up?"

"Just over an hour."

"Nobody snooping around the boathouse?"

"I don't think we have to worry about that, Paige. The boathouse is on private property. Nobody has any reason to suspect anything. Even Linc doesn't know Peter's current condition."

She pulled Peter's phone toward her by the cord, entered his password and read the text exchange between Linc and Asher. "So, he made contact first?"

"Asked for an update. As you can read, I told him no movement and inquired about our next move."

"How's this going to work?" She nodded as Asher held a spatula full of scrambled eggs over a plate.

"Not sure yet. Maybe an ambush."

"With all your busy texting, did you contact the doc yet?"

"No. Do you want to do the honors?"

"He needs to get here before Linc does if we're meeting him at this house." She wrinkled her nose. "And if we are, that boathouse is going to get pretty crowded."

"As long as we're not among its inhabitants." He winked and dumped the eggs onto her plate.

An hour later, Martha's friend knocked at the door. As Paige put her eye to the peephole, the doctor took a step back and displayed his hospital ID with his name printed on it.

Grabbing the handle of the door, she glanced at Asher hovering to her right, his gun drawn. "He's legit."

Asher pocketed his gun, and Paige swung open the door with a smile. "Dr. Tucker? Thanks for coming out."

"Call me Preston. Martha and I go way back to our prep school days, and I'd do anything for her."

"Can I get you something to drink?"

"Something hot. It's getting cold out there." Preston clamped his black bag between his body and arm and rubbed his hands together.

"Hot tea?" She jerked her thumb at Asher. "He's the patient. Asher, Preston."

As the two men shook hands, Asher said, "I don't know how much Martha told you…"

Preston held up one hand. "I don't need to know the how or why. Martha explained your issue to me, and I believe I have a remedy. I'm going to need to take some of your blood, and I'm going to give you a shot as a counteragent if it's what I think it is. If after looking at your blood, it turns out to be something else, I'll let you know."

Asher narrowed his eyes. "If it's not what you think it is and you give me the shot anyway, is that going to have some negative effect on me? Kill me? Make me impotent?"

Paige snorted.

Preston shoved his glasses up the bridge of his nose, all business. "If it's not the drug I believe to be running through your system, this antidote is harmless. If I analyze your blood and find something else… I'll have to do more research."

"And he'll continue to be affected." Paige laced her fingers in front of her and squeezed them together to keep from fidgeting nervously.

"He may continue to pass out at random intervals." Preston's thin lips eked out a smile. "But let's think positive thoughts."

His head flicked from side to side like a bird's. "Can we sit at the dining room table?"

Paige retrieved a clean dish towel from beneath the sink and spread it on the table. As Preston readied his tools of the trade, Paige put on the teakettle.

"Asher, do you want some water?"

"Yeah, thanks." He looked up from rolling the sleeve of his shirt and exposing his veins for Preston.

She placed a glass of water on the table next to Asher as Preston swiped an antiseptic pad over the inside of his elbow. "Your tea is coming up."

Preston nodded and then held up a vial between two fingers. "I'm not going to take much. Just enough to fill this vial."

Paige turned away as the needle plunged into Asher's arm. The teakettle's whistle saved her and she scurried to the kitchen, anxious to get away from the sight of Asher's blood pumping into the glass container.

She prepped the tea and returned to the dining room table, carrying a mug in each hand. "Good, I missed the gory stuff."

Asher raised his brows at her and her cheeks warmed. Of course, they'd just hauled a body from the house, but Peter hadn't been bleeding anywhere, which made rolling him up in canvas a lot less icky than seeing blood trickle down the side of a glass vial.

Setting the mug in front of Preston, she asked, "Milk or sugar?"

"Black is fine." Preston capped the vial and slipped it into a plastic bag. "One more needle, if you can take it."

"I have to admit, I've had my fill of needles, but if this is the last one, I can take it." Asher presented his other arm. "How's it going to make me feel? Any immediate reaction?"

"It might feel like you just drank five energy drinks, but that will subside." He tapped the water glass with the needle. "Keep drinking water."

"And if I still pass out today like I did yesterday?"

"It means my diagnosis and assessment were wrong, and you should call me immediately."

Paige took her tea and wandered to the back door, staring out at the boat dock. They hadn't done anything wrong. Peter had killed himself. They couldn't have saved him even if they'd called 911.

She pressed the warm cup against her face. Second house, second dead body. Would Linc be a third? What would Asher have done with Peter if he hadn't offed himself? What would he do with Linc if he didn't get the answers he wanted?

"All done, chicken."

She glanced over her shoulder. "I don't mind injections, but I don't like the blood."

"I'm finished." Preston peeled the gloves from his hands. "I'm confident we did the right thing here."

"What do we owe you?" Asher gulped down the rest of his water and pushed back from the table.

"Nothing. If you're a friend of Martha's, you're a friend of mine." Preston cupped the mug in his hands and slurped a sip of tea. "You're military, like Martha's new guy?"

"Yeah."

Preston squinted at Asher through the steam rising from his tea. "That's it. Don't look so fierce. I'm not going to interrogate you. I told you I didn't need the details."

Paige studied Preston's face. Had he been crushing on Martha before that big, tough D-Boy Cam Sutton had come in and swept her off her feet? "Did you have a thing for Martha?"

"Me?" One side of Preston's mouth turned up as he took off his glasses and wiped them with a cloth. "She's a darling girl, but I'm gay. That's how we got close in school—just a couple of misfits in that environment."

"We appreciate your help, Preston." Asher pressed a hand against his chest. "You weren't kidding about the adrenaline rush."

"Are you okay?" Preston reached for his bag. "I can take your blood pressure."

"I'm okay." Asher held up his water glass. "I'll keep drinking this stuff, right?"

"It'll pass within an hour or so. You can reach me at the number you called before if you need help. If that blood test doesn't yield the result I expect, I'll be calling you." Preston took a few more sips of his tea. "Is that all you need?"

"What else do you have in that black bag?" Asher

leveled an unsteady finger at Preston's medical bag on the table.

"A full complement of medical supplies…and some drugs. What is it you're looking for, Asher?"

Paige's eyes popped open as she watched Asher pace to the window and back. Had he become dependent on those drugs he'd been getting at Hidden Hills? She wouldn't put it past that bunch to get Asher addicted.

"If you have it, I'd like a syringe or two of something that can knock someone out—fast, put 'em out like—" Asher snapped his fingers "—that."

"No lasting effects but fast-acting and total?"

"That's it."

"I have just the thing." Preston unzipped his bag and plucked two plastic wrapped syringes from an inside pocket. He smacked them down on the table. "The effects of this should last a good twenty-four hours. Best administered in a large muscle, like a thigh or buttocks."

"Through clothing?" Asher returned to the table and nudged the needles with his finger.

"As long as the needle goes through." Preston drained his teacup and clicked it back onto the table. "Now, before I let my feelings for Martha get me into any more trouble, I'll leave you."

Paige handed Preston his coat at the door. "Thank you so much, Preston."

"Thanks, man." Asher thrust out his hand. "And remember, discretion."

"Do you think I want anything I've done today to get out? I'm asking for the same."

"We never heard of you."

When they sent Preston on his way, Paige spun toward Asher. "What are you going to use those for?"

"Might come in handy for Linc or anyone else who decides to make a move on us."

She placed both hands on his shoulders. "How are you feeling? Still hyped up?"

"Yeah. Maybe I should take a jog along the bay to work it off."

"Don't you dare. We don't want anyone to spot us here. If the police find Peter's body before his associates do, we could be investigated for murder. Fingerprints, fiber—Homicide would have a field day with all the evidence."

"But we didn't kill Peter. He killed himself." Asher wrenched away from her to take a lap around the family room.

She tracked him with her gaze. "I don't know about you, but I don't even want to go down that road."

"Paige, that's the least of our worries. The people setting up Major Denver, the people after us are never going to allow one of their own to become the subject of a murder investigation or even a missing person's investigation."

She put a hand to her head. "I'm getting anxious just watching you. Are you sure you're okay? Can you sit down for a minute?"

"I'm fine—agitated, just like the doc warned."

"I don't want to have that meeting with Linc until you're…unagitated. There's no telling what you'll do to him in this state."

"Preston said this will last just about an hour. We have plenty of time. I'd rather get Linc out here in the cover of darkness."

"How are we going to spend the rest of the afternoon?"

"Oh, I don't know. Our enemies are off our trail for the time being, it's cold outside and warm inside, and I'm hopped up on something that's giving me an incredible sense of vitality." He wiggled his eyebrows up and down. "I can think of the perfect way to spend an afternoon alone with my fiancée."

"I don't know if I'll be able to keep up with the Energizer Bunny." Paige tilted her head and pursed her lips, but her heart had started racing.

"There's only one way to find out." He swooped in and swept her off her feet.

She screamed and kicked her legs, a sense of relief flooding her body with the thought that maybe they could find some normalcy in this unnatural situation.

Asher stooped next to the coffee table and her legs dipped down as he grabbed his gun. "I hope this doesn't kill the romance for you."

"The fact that you want to keep me safe only heightens it." She tucked her head in the crook of his neck. So much for normalcy.

Asher carried her up the stairs effortlessly and eagerly. Either he couldn't wait to make love or his current manic state was driving him.

One way or the other, she didn't care. Instead she squealed when he kicked open the bedroom door.

He dumped her on the bed and she scrambled to her knees, tugging on the hem of Asher's T-shirt. "You've been teasing me with this bod for days now—playing peek-a-boo with your backside in the hospital gown, taking showers with your clothes off."

"Imagine that." He spread his arms so she could roll his shirt up his torso.

"Go ahead and pull it off. I can't reach that high."

He yanked the shirt over his head and tossed it over his shoulder.

Paige skimmed her hands over his chest and hooked

her fingers in the waistband of his jeans. "I knew there was a good reason why I didn't buy you a belt."

He tapped his foot while she undid the buttons of his fly. "You can't move any faster than that?"

"You'd better slow down, mister. I've waited a long time for this moment, and I'm not going to be rushed."

His chest expanded as he took a big breath, and his lashes fluttered closed. "I'll try."

Paige opened his fly and peeled his jeans from his hips. She ran her hand across the front of his briefs. "Do you think that antidote is going to give you a ramped-up erection, too?"

"I think I'm already there."

Paige clicked her tongue. "I told you to slow down."

"I think daytime sex should be rowdier and faster, don't you?"

"Oh, is that the problem? It's too light out for you?" Paige scooted off the bed. "I'm going to close these drapes and trick you."

She bounded to the window and grabbed handfuls of the drapes on either side of the window, her gaze automatically shifting to the boathouse with the dead guy inside—or so she thought.

A chill gripped the back of her neck and she choked. "My God. It's Peter."

"Someone found him?"

She whipped her head around, clutching one side of the drapes to her body. "No, he came back to life."

# *Chapter Fourteen*

Asher pressed his face to the glass, fogging it up. He wiped a circle with his fist and swore again.

His gaze locked onto Peter, or someone who looked a lot like him, standing outside the boathouse staring at the bay.

"Maybe it's not him. Maybe it's someone else."

"Which could be almost as bad. I don't understand. Peter was dead." Paige's eyes took up half her face. "Wasn't he?"

"Let's ask him." Asher yanked up his jeans and dived across the bed to grab his T-shirt and gun. As he raced down the stairs, he heard Paige coming in fast after him. He twisted his head over his shoulder when he reached the first floor. "Stay here."

"Are you kidding? I've never seen a man come back from the dead before."

Asher pulled on his boots and struggled into his jacket as he lunged for the back door.

With his gun in his pocket, he charged across the back lawn toward the water's edge. If Peter had all his faculties, he wasn't using them.

The man gazing out at the bay didn't even turn around, didn't make a move.

Asher scooped in a deep breath and grabbed Peter

from behind with one arm. Although the man in his grasp wasn't dead, his icy-cold flesh might fool a coroner.

Peter staggered forward and then twisted around, wielding a knife.

Paige screamed. "Look out."

A second later, Asher jabbed the syringe he had in his fist into Peter's thigh through the denim of his pants.

Peter dropped immediately.

Asher looked up and down the shoreline, squinting at the other houses. "God, it's broad daylight. Is there anyone out, Paige? Did anyone witness this?"

"There's nobody. Martha said the nearest house is vacant, and the other house is too far away to see anything, unless someone has binoculars trained on us—and why would they?"

"I would've liked to have questioned him some more, but he didn't give me a choice." Asher kicked the knife that had fallen from Peter's hand into the bay.

"Preston did say the stuff in the syringe would last up to twenty-four hours, didn't he?"

"Yep. That means we'll have to get out of here after we meet with Linc."

Paige pointed to Peter's inert form on the ground. "I suppose we'd better get him back into the boathouse. I still don't understand what happened. He was not breathing when we carried him out here the first time. He didn't have a pulse."

"That we noticed." Asher crouched and slid his hand beneath Peter's arms. "The mad scientists at Hidden Hills have proved themselves to be adept at concocting a variety of strange-acting drugs. It's not a stretch to think these...agents are equipped with one that simulates death."

"He's one lucky guy." Paige backed up to the boathouse door, which Peter had left standing open. "What if we had dumped his body in the bay? He would've died for real."

"I guess it was a chance he was willing to take. He probably thought we would leave him right there in the house and make our escape."

"Maybe we should have." Paige held the boathouse door open for him as he dragged Peter back inside.

He dumped him on top of the canvas. "We don't need to wrap him up. I'm surprised he didn't suffocate in there."

"You still have the other syringe, don't you?"

"It has Linc's name on it."

After they stashed Peter in the boathouse and hooked a padlock on the outside, they returned to the house.

The antidote that had been racing through his system seemed to have diluted. After the excitement of seeing a man rise from the dead, his heart rate had returned to normal and unfortunately his raging erection had subsided.

He took a quick glance at Paige, twisting her fingers in front of her and peering through the window of the back door every ten seconds. That erection would've gone to waste, anyway. Paige's anxiety had gone through the roof.

Asher approached her from behind and touched her back. She jumped.

"He's not going to make a comeback, Paige. I trust Preston and his pharmaceuticals."

"You're going to contact Linc now, aren't you?"

"Sunset is early. The sooner we get him out here, the better. Then we can hit the road. They still don't know where we are, but when two of their grunts go missing checking out Martha's mother's house, they're gonna come calling."

"Go missing?" Paige licked her lips. "What are we going to do with them, Asher? If you kill them…"

He stroked her back. "I'm not going to kill them, Paige—unless they try to kill us first. Who knows how this group after us could spin the murder of a couple of men? Instead of being accused of going AWOL, I could be accused of murder. I'm not going to chance that."

Her shoulders slumped. "Okay. That makes me feel better—not that they deserve our mercy, but I don't want to be responsible for someone's death."

"Of course not." He swept her hair from the back of her neck and pressed his lips against the top knot of her spine.

"Tabitha…"

"We weren't responsible for that. She chose to track me down even knowing others were on my trail. She was playing a dangerous game." He let her heavy hair fall against her back. "I'm going to text Linc."

"How are we going to play this?"

"Peter's boat is still on the bay. I'll ask Linc to meet in the boathouse. After all, why would Linc think Peter has access to the house unless he broke in? And I don't think that was part of their plan."

"Okay, so we set up the meeting for the boathouse." She pivoted from the door and leaned back against it as she crossed her arms. "Then what?"

"We ambush him. I'll make sure I check his sleeves for any hidden pills so I have a chance to question him. Then we get some answers, maybe we find the next person up the ladder, someone with some authority, some knowledge."

She smoothed her hands across his chest. "When we have enough, we have to take this to someone. Your name has to be cleared."

"Major Denver's name has to be cleared." He grabbed one of her hands and kissed her wrist.

He returned to the kitchen with Paige right behind him. He entered the password for Peter's phone and tapped his messages. Nobody had sent Peter any messages since the one from Linc earlier.

Asher read his text aloud for Paige as he entered it in the phone. "'No sign of anyone at house. Meet me here at the boathouse behind the house at five.'"

They both stared at the phone for several minutes, and then Asher shrugged and tucked it in his pocket. "He'll respond."

"I suppose we should have some lunch." Paige stood in the middle of the kitchen, hands on her hips. "There's no telling when we'll get dinner if Linc shows up at five and we have to deal with him."

"We should also plot out our next move—literally. We need to hit the road again after we see Linc, although where we go will probably depend on what he tells us."

Standing on her tiptoes, Paige reached into a cupboard and pulled down a can. She turned it toward him. "Soup?"

"Sounds good. I saw stuff for sandwiches this morning when I was whipping up breakfast. I'll get to work on those."

Fifteen minutes later, they sat down with a plate of sandwiches and two bowls of tomato soup.

Paige slid one of the cell phones charging on the counter toward her. "I never did find out Tabitha's password. We also don't even know if they found her body yet in the cabin. I'm going to check on my computer after we eat."

"I'm sure they've found a body by now—whether they've ID'd Tabitha or not is another matter." Asher blew on a spoonful of soup and slurped it up, the rich tomatoey taste filling his mouth. "I'm sure the doctors at Hidden Hills have figured it out by now."

"I wonder if she left them a note or something. Do you think she was planning to return to work after she had you safely stashed away? I'm beginning to wonder if Tabitha's the one who injected you with that timed-release drug to control you once she had you at her cabin."

"I wouldn't put it past her, and if she wanted to return to Hidden Hills, she wouldn't have clued them in that she'd aided and abetted my escape from the center." He shrugged and took a big bite of his sandwich.

While he was chewing and Paige was going on about Tabitha, the phone in his pocket vibrated. He held up a finger to get Paige to stop talking. "Peter's phone."

He pulled the phone from his pocket and dropped it on the counter as if it burned his hand.

"What's wrong?"

"It's a call from Linc, not a text." He poked at the phone, nudging it away from him.

"Damn." Paige covered her mouth with one hand. "What are we going to do?"

"Well, I'm not going to try to pass myself as Peter, if that's what you're thinking. We don't know how well these guys know each other." He brushed his hands together and took a gulp of water. "Let it ring. I'll respond with a text later."

While he finished the last sandwich, Paige put her dishes in the sink and retrieved her laptop from the living room.

"I'm going to look for a story on that cabin."

Asher slid off his stool and took the rest of the dishes to the sink to wash them.

Paige whistled behind him. "Here's one. Explosion…cabin…gas leak. Yeah, right. Body found."

"Did they identify her?" Asher grabbed a dish towel and wiped his hands as he joined Paige and hovered over her shoulder.

"No. The article says the owners are accounted for and don't know who could've been in their cabin. The authorities are wondering if the person was a trespasser or transient. God, they don't even know if the person was a man or a woman." She raised her glassy eyes to his face.

"That was an intense fire, and there's no reason for anyone to suspect Tabitha to be in that cabin."

"What was Tabitha's last name?" Paige wiggled her fingers over the laptop's keyboard.

"Crane. Tabitha Crane. What are you going to do?"

"Look her up. See if anyone has connected her to that cabin yet."

Paige clicked away on the keyboard while Asher returned to the dishes. "How long should I wait before I text Linc back?"

"Here she is. I found her on a medical professional's site. Tabitha Carly Crane, Tabby Crane. She sounds so normal on here."

"Did you expect her to list her interests as being a lovesick stalker on a professional website?"

"Maybe you're the one who drove her mad for love." Paige peered at him over the top of the computer. "You had all the girls hot for you at that party…and you wound up with the most unstable one of all."

"I didn't see you that way, Paige. You were hurting. Anyone with half a brain could figure that out." He clenched his fists in the soapy water. Why did she have to keep dismissing herself?

She had wanted to keep him in the dark because she didn't want to relive *his* reaction to remembering his fiancée had been a drunk he didn't trust with their baby.

She'd kept the truth from him because she knew she'd have to pick up that role again—constantly downgrading herself before he could do it.

"Lots of people figured out I was hurting, but nobody wanted to deal with it—except my other wild friends who had their own addictions. And we dealt with it in our own way."

"And now that part of your life is over and we have a beautiful daughter together. Let's make sure we both get home to her safely."

She rubbed one eye and pushed the laptop away from her. "What excuse are you going to give Linc for not picking up the phone?"

"I'm in the middle of nowhere, camped out in a boathouse on the shore of the bay—the reception is bad." He dried and stacked the dishes and then dug the phone from his pocket. "I think it's about time. It's almost two thirty."

Asher straddled the stool, cupping Peter's phone in one hand. "How does this sound? 'Missed your call. Reception bad on the bay. Meet at five?'"

She tipped her chin to her chest. "Go for it."

Asher entered the text and this time they didn't have to wait long. Linc responded almost immediately, as if he were waiting for Peter's communication.

"What does it say?" Paige tugged on his sleeve, leaning against his body.

"'See you at five.'"

"Great." Paige turned and looked at the room. "We should get packed up in case we need to make a quick getaway."

"Is there any other kind?"

They spent the next hour washing and packing their clothes, loading the trunk of the car with nonperishable food and stashing the bag of cash next to the food. They cleaned up the kitchen, stripped the sheets of the bed for the housekeeper and got ready to meet Linc.

Asher handed Peter's gun to Paige. "You take this one. I'll keep the one Martha left."

"The syringe?"

He patted the pocket of his jacket. "Right here, along with Peter's keys. I can put them back in his pocket. I'm bringing a flashlight this time."

"And there's rope, a knife and tape in the boathouse."

"Everything we need to subdue Linc—and get him talking if we have to."

Paige's eye twitched and he squeezed her shoulder. "Don't worry about it. Leave the rough stuff to me. Remember, I'm a soldier, and as far as I'm concerned, this is war."

Asher locked up the house and killed all the lights except the lamp in the front room, which was on a timer. He locked the back door behind them, and they made their way to the boat dock, holding hands.

Paige laced her fingers with his. "It looks like Preston was right. You haven't had a repeat performance of losing consciousness today. How are you feeling?"

"Seeing Peter rise from the dead and running out here to subdue him worked out the rest of that antidote. I feel fine—so far. But then I felt fine in the coffeehouse just before I slumped in my seat."

"Don't say that." She bumped his shoulder with hers. "If something happens to you during this operation…"

He pressed his finger against her lips. "You'd carry on just fine. I have faith in you to get me out of any scrape."

She puckered her lips and kissed the end of his finger. "Let's do this."

Asher unlocked the boathouse and peeked around

the corner. "I wanna make sure Peter hasn't had another resurrection."

Paige flicked the beam from her flashlight over Peter, still stretched out on top of the canvas sheet.

"Keep that light on him." Asher crouched beside the sleeping man and felt his pulse. "He's still alive...and still out."

"Hopefully, he'll stay that way." She aimed the flashlight at the ceiling. "On or off?"

"Linc isn't going to know where the boathouse is and he wouldn't expect Peter to be sitting here in the dark. Leave it on." He checked Peter's phone. "T-minus twenty."

Asher took up his position on one side of the door and he directed Paige to wait in the back corner. In case this guy came in hot, Asher wanted Paige well away from the door.

Paige drew her gun first. "I'm ready. If you can't bring him down on the first try, I'm going to shoot first and worry about it later."

"I thought you wanted to avoid any unnecessary violence."

"If someone's attacking my man, that's very necessary." She widened her stance like she meant every word.

He liked her new tough swagger—turned him on.

They waited in the semidarkness, every breath they took sounding like a whoosh of air in the stillness of the boathouse.

Asher stole a glance at the phone and then whispered, "Ten minutes."

They didn't have to wait that long. Peter's phone buzzed and Linc's text came through. Asher read it to himself. I'm here.

He flashed the phone at Paige and nodded.

He texted back, Boathouse on the bay shore.

Asher's muscles coiled and his eye twitched. With his foot, he eased open the door, which swung outward.

As Linc left the grass and hit the gravel, Asher could hear every footstep down to the water's edge.

A harsh whisper echoed in the night. "Peter?"

Asher nudged the door again and it creaked on the rusty hinges. He growled, "Over here."

As Linc approached closer…and closer, Asher curled his fingers around the edge of the door. Then he took a deep breath and pushed the door out.

It met the solid object of Linc's body, and the man grunted.

Asher slammed the door against Linc once more before whipping around and driving his shoulder into the man's midsection.

Linc rocked for a moment like a bowling pin before toppling over.

When Linc hit the ground, Asher dropped to his knees beside him and checked his hands and pockets for weapons. He pulled a gun from Linc's waistband, and a knife from a leg holster. He was collecting quite a stash of weapons. Asher slipped his fingers up Linc's sleeve in case he was carrying a poison pill like Peter had been, but it looked like he was more cowardly than Peter.

Asher rose to his feet and pointed his weapon at the prone man's head. "Don't move. In case you can't see it, I have a gun pointed at you, and in case you didn't feel it, I divested you of all your weapons."

Linc groaned and drew his knees to his chest in a fetal position. "Where's Peter?"

"Crawl into the boathouse and you'll see."

Linc's head jerked up.

"That's right. He's dead. Start crawling or that's gonna be your fate, too."

Asher exchanged a quick look with Paige, who'd ventured outside. Might as well instill some fear into the guy from the get-go.

Linc army-crawled on his belly into the boathouse. His eyes widened when Paige trailed her light across Peter, serenely oblivious to the fact that he was playing possum again.

Linc rolled to his back, and his eyes got even wider. "You're Asher Knight."

"In the flesh."

"You got the jump on Peter? Took his phone?"

"You're a genius." Asher kicked the man's boot. "Now you're going to impart all your knowledge to me. Peter over there wasn't very cooperative."

"Peter doesn't…didn't know anything to tell."

"Too bad for Peter." Asher hunched his shoulders. "I hope you know more."

"Wait, wait." Linc waved his hands in front of his face. "Who's the woman? Is that Tabitha Crane?"

Asher narrowed his eyes. "What do you know about Tabitha?"

"Nothing, nothing."

Paige kept the light away from her face and shrank farther into the corner. If Linc thought she might be the nurse, let him think it.

"If you think Tabitha is here with me, then you must know something about her. What are they saying at Hidden Hills?"

"That she helped you escape. That's how they found you at that cabin. They didn't trust Tabitha and put a GPS tracker on her car. She led them right to you, but we know

now there was just one body in that cabin. They were hoping it was yours."

Paige sucked in a breath.

"But then you have your fiancée with you, too, don't you? Granger and Lewis saw her in that little hick town." Linc snorted. "Before she slipped out of their grasp and they ended up crashing the van. So, which one of your women is this one?"

Asher's jaw tightened. "You seem like you're in a talkative mood. That's good. Keep talking. Who's setting up Major Denver? Who gave the orders to mess with my mind so that I would implicate Denver?"

"Those are some heavy questions."

"I hope you have more answers to them than Peter did."

Linc's eyes rolled sideways to take in his associate. "It's high up. That's all I know. Your amnesia was just one piece in the puzzle—the only piece I know about."

"C'mon, Linc. You can do better than that."

To be more convincing, Asher picked up a pair of pliers and studied them. "You know, even though Delta Force doesn't use torture methods in our operations, it doesn't mean we don't know all about them."

Linc scrambled up to a seated position. "No need, man. Peter and I belong to a web of people who have certain services for hire. That's all. It's not my fight, not my ideology."

"He felt differently." Paige aimed a toe at Peter.

"He's young." Linc shrugged. "Me, I don't care as long as my employers don't think I ratted them out. That's not tolerated. We're even ordered to carry a pill on us, one that simulates death, if we're captured or compromised. Screw that."

"Your employers. Who are they?"

"Wish I could help you with that. I really do, but I take orders from a nameless, faceless text message." He raised one hand. "What I do know is that the setup of Denver goes high up."

"High up where? The military? The government?"

"Both. I think both."

"I need a name, Linc."

"I can't give you a name, but I can give you a hot tip. Can you get the gun out of my face?"

"Gun stays where it is." The man was cooperative, but Asher still didn't trust him. "Let's hear this hot tip."

"The conspiracy against you is laid out in a computer file at Hidden Hills. If you got your hands on that, you could clear your name and come out of hiding."

Asher blew out a breath. Not the bombshell he was expecting.

"Yeah, sure. I can just waltz back into Hidden Hills and ask for my records."

"You might try asking someone else for them."

"The army?" Asher snorted.

"That nurse."

"Tabitha Crane?"

"Yeah, I thought she might be the one standing over there, but now I realize if she was and she really wanted to help you, she'd have given you that file."

Paige asked, "How do you know Tabitha has the file?"

"They all know it now. We have orders to track her down just like you—and that's the reason. She's become public enemy number two."

"I have a question for you, Linc." Paige stepped from the shadows. "What are you supposed to do with Asher when you find him?"

Linc's gaze darted to the barrel of the gun and back to Paige's face. "Kill him."

The wooden wall across from Asher splintered. Cold air rushed into the boathouse.

Asher lunged in front of Paige and grabbed her hand, yanking her to the floor.

"Get down! They're shooting the place up."

## *Chapter Fifteen*

When Asher had pulled her down, he covered her body with his as the bullets rained above them.

She squirmed beneath him. "Asher, I can't breathe."

He rolled off her and leveled a finger at Linc cowering in the corner. "Did you bring them here? Did you know?"

"No, no. I swear."

"Leave him, Asher."

"His bosses are not going to be as generous as I was." Asher scooted toward the door and kicked it open. "Our only chance now is Peter's boat. Those shots are coming from the house. Follow me."

Paige gritted her teeth as Asher crawled outside. Every cell in her body was screaming, but she pushed past her fear.

When she joined him on the short dock, he shocked her by pushing her off. She rolled into the small powerboat, even as another wall of the boathouse ripped open.

Asher jumped in next to her, flattening himself on the deck of the boat. He jammed the key into the ignition and pulled on the throttle. The engine roared, churning up the frigid water of the bay.

The boat leaped forward and Paige's head banged against the side.

"Hold on, Paige. I don't know where I'm going and I

can't see anything. I don't want to put on the lights until we're farther along."

The boat skimmed across the water, away from the shore, away from the bullets. Paige rubbed her head, tracing the knot already forming there.

After several minutes, the boat's course evened out and Paige realized Asher was upright at the helm.

She dragged herself up, leaning against the inside of the boat, still holding her hand to her head and feeling slightly nauseated, which had nothing to do with seasickness.

Asher's head jerked to the side. "Are you okay? My God, were you hit?"

"No. My head banged against the side of the boat during our escape." She squinted at the distant lights on the shore. "We did escape, didn't we? We got away?"

"We did."

"Y-you weren't shot, were you?"

"No."

"I'm glad you held on to Peter's keys instead of putting them back in his pocket." Paige covered her eyes with one hand. "But all our plans—the car, our clothes, the money—all gone. We're back to square one."

"We're alive." He stretched his hand out to her. "And you're with me."

She wrapped her fingers around his. "You remember me, remember our engagement, remember all the ugliness and you're still here."

"Where else would I be?" He brought her hand to his lips and kissed the tips of her fingers. "I don't know. Square one feels good to me."

His words created a warm bubble around her, and she just wanted to float in that bubble, but they weren't in the floating stage yet.

"Do you think Linc knew he was walking into a trap? He didn't act like it."

"Maybe he was told to play along. He did seem accommodating, but I just had him pegged as a coward." Asher eased off the throttle and the boat's nose lowered in the water. "Or maybe his employers were tracking the phones and noted the unusual activity. Linc looked as surprised as I felt when the bullets started flying."

"Maybe he figured the cavalry coming to rescue him would at least wait until he was out of the way before starting to blast away."

"There's little honor among thieves—another lesson I learned at my father's knee."

"Do you think Linc was telling the truth about your file and Tabitha stealing it?"

"That part makes sense, doesn't it? Linc might've felt he could tell me the truth because he figured I'd be dead ten minutes later."

"Then we need to get our hands on that file. You can take it to the army. There might be a few traitors, but I refuse to believe the entire army and Delta Force unit are after Major Denver—unless he's really guilty."

"He's not."

"Showing what the doctors at Hidden Hills tried to do to you will put you back on track, anyway. They wouldn't be able to claim you were crazy or a traitor or AWOL then, could they?"

"Somehow I think sneaking back into Hidden Hills is going to be harder than sneaking out."

"Unless we find Tabitha's copy of the file."

"We could return to her family's cabin and look there. My guess is if she has it, she was planning to use it to blackmail me to bend to her wishes."

Paige huddled into her coat. "I don't recall seeing a computer there. It was probably in her car."

"You still have her phone, right?"

"Which I haven't been able to access yet." Paige tried to snap her cold fingers and gave up. "She might have her email on the phone. Maybe we could get some information from that."

"It can't hurt." Asher pointed to some lights along the shoreline. "We're going to have to get off this bay sometime."

"Where are we going to go and what are we going to do without money?" The reality of their situation punched her in the gut, and she folded her arms across her midsection.

"I wouldn't say we have *no* money." Asher patted the pockets of his jacket. "I didn't want to keep going into the bag in the trunk for cash, so when we were packing up I crammed my pockets with the stuff. We'll be okay."

Paige threw her arms around his neck. "You're right. We're safe for now and we're together. All we need is Ivy to make us whole."

"We'll get there, Paige…and we'll be stronger than ever."

SEVERAL HOURS LATER, after ditching Peter's boat, hitching a ride with a trucker and picking up a pizza, Paige fell across the bed in the dumpy motel they found outside of DC.

"I think I might be too tired to eat—bullets, boats and trucks can do that to a girl." She hoisted herself up on her elbows and watched Asher dig into the pizza. "Another spot of good news is that it doesn't seem like you're going to have a relapse of going into a drugged stupor."

Asher pounded his chest with his fist, a piece of pepperoni pizza in the other hand. “I feel great.”

“I texted Martha again about the mayhem at her mother’s house, but she hasn’t responded. I hope she’s okay.”

“She wasn’t planning to go to the house. I’m sure she’s fine.” Asher wiped his hands on a napkin and held up a can of soda. “If you’re not going to eat anything, have something to drink.”

“I think I will have a piece.” She slid off the edge of the bed and pulled a slice out of the box, pinching off a string of cheese with her finger. “Do you think the men with the guns went into the garage and found our car with all our stuff? My laptop’s in there.”

“I doubt they wanted to stick around that long. They probably swarmed the boathouse, thinking they killed us or trapped us, and found Linc and Peter instead.”

“I wonder if they killed Linc…or Peter for that matter.”

“Don’t waste your sympathy. Do you think either one of them would’ve hesitated to kill us if they’d had the chance?”

“Ugh, I don’t like this world.” Paige dabbed her lips with a napkin and took a swig of soda.

“I know you don’t. I’m sorry you’re in it.” He tossed his crust onto a paper plate. “You should be back in Vegas, safe with Ivy.”

“Then who’d be your wingman?” She dug her thumb into her chest. “That’s me.”

Asher leaned forward and kissed her mouth, the spicy pepperoni on his lips making their connection even hotter. “You are my wingman, but you’re much, much more, and I want to finish what we started earlier.”

She dropped her pizza and stretched her arms over her head. “I don’t know. When we were going to make love this afternoon, you were all juiced up on Preston's magic antidote. This could be a total letdown."

"That other guy today? All strength, no substance." He winked. "Do you trust the tub in this place?"

Her gaze scanned the small, plainly furnished room. "It ain't the Ritz, but it's clean. I'm down for a bath."

"Allow me." Asher pushed away the pizza box and jumped up from his chair. "I'll get things ready."

"Do you want me to save this pizza? There's no fridge in here."

"When did leftover pizza ever need to be refrigerated?" Asher pulled off his boots and socks, one foot at a time, and padded barefoot into the bathroom.

Paige tossed the used paper plates and napkins in the trash and closed the pizza box. Leaning forward, she flipped the curtains at the window.

The lights of the motel office glowed in modest comparison to the headlights of the cars passing on the highway in the distance. They couldn't have been followed or tracked this time. Asher had ditched Linc's and Peter's phones in the bay, and her own phone was turned off. Only the temp phone was active. She'd turned off Tabitha's, but this place—a motel along a string of them on a busy highway—might be the ideal location to turn it on and start entering passwords again.

As far as she knew, phones could be tracked only generally, pinging the nearest cell tower, which could be miles away.

The water stopped running in the bathroom and Asher shouted. "I'm ready. What are you doing out there, finishing off the pizza?"

"Coming." Paige twitched the curtains back in place and put the temp phone along with Tabitha's on the nightstand.

Pulling her sweater over her head, Paige started humming some striptease music as she sauntered to the bathroom. She stopped in the frame of the door and twirled her sweater around by its arm. "Are you really ready, big boy?"

Asher lowered his naked body in the tub, the steam swirling around him. "It's about time."

She dropped her sweater to the floor, yanked off her camisole and bra, and shimmied out of her jeans and panties.

"Hit the switch. I don't have candles, but at least the muted light from the other room lends a little romance to the atmosphere in here."

She tiptoed to the bathtub. "Where'd you get the bubbles?"

"Dumped half this bottle in the water." He held up a small plastic bottle of shower gel.

She dipped a toe into the water between Asher's raised knees. The tub couldn't accommodate the length of his legs stretched out, but she couldn't imagine they'd be in this little tub that long.

She sat down in the water, and the bubbles crackled around her body. Stretching her legs out as far as she could, she leaned back against Asher's chest, finally skin to skin.

Her head lolled against his chest. "I could fall asleep right here."

"You'd better not." He scooped up some bubbles in the palms of his hands and arranged them over her breasts like a mermaid bikini.

She breathed out. "Nice."

Those hands skimmed down her belly and parted her thighs.

Her head fell to the side and her tongue darted out

of her mouth and swept across the warm, soapy flesh of his arm.

His fingers stroked between her legs and she rocked with the sensations flowing through her body, creating little waves in the tub. If he kept touching her like that, they'd create a tidal wave.

She arched her back and planted her hands on his knees, digging her fingernails into his skin. The heat from their bodies seemed to bring the water temperature to boiling.

When her orgasm claimed her, she lifted her hips from the water. The pleasure clawed through her body, and her hips pumped the air with every stab.

Asher slid two fingers inside her, and she shuddered around him before falling back to the water, collapsing against his belly.

The water lapped up the side of the tub and spilled over onto the floor.

Asher nibbled her earlobe and then whispered, "You created a tidal wave."

She rolled over to face him, the water giving her buoyancy. "Now I'm going to create a volcano."

Laughing, he wrapped his arms around her. "Not in here, you're not. If I stay in this tub any longer, I'm gonna get stuck."

"Me first." She straddled him and stood up in the tub, dripping water on his head and chest.

Looking up at her, he said, "This is the best view I've had all day."

"Hope you plan to do more than admire the scenery." She stepped over the edge of the tub and grabbed both towels. "Do you need help getting out?"

He flipped the drain stopper with his toe, shifted to

his side and rose from the water like Neptune coming out of the sea.

She shook out his towel and crammed it against his chest. "Meet you in the bedroom."

Strolling to the bedroom, she dried herself and then flipped back the covers on the bed. Maybe they'd actually get to make love this time.

She heard Asher's footfall behind her, and before she could turn, he enfolded her in a hug, pressing his front against her back. "It's been too long. I'm kind of glad Peter interrupted us last time. I feel more like myself now, not hopped up on anything, not waiting for any texts or bad guys to show up on our doorstep."

As he kissed the wet tendrils of hair that clung to the back of her neck, he caressed her breasts. She shivered.

"Are you cold?" He scooped her against his body even tighter.

"A little." She wriggled out of his grasp and flung herself across the bed. "Warm me up."

He stretched out beside her on his side and kissed the bump on the side of her head. "War wounds."

He traced the outlines of her face. "I can't believe I ever forgot this face."

"The mind can do funny things. Why don't you touch the rest of my body to make sure you never forget again?"

With his fingers and tongue, he skimmed her flesh, raising goose bumps and setting fire to her nerve endings at the same time. While he reacquainted himself with her body, her fingers idly played in his hair while her other hand stroked his erection.

By the time his head was level with her toes and his feet rested on the pillow next to her head, he was fully aroused and her heart was thundering in her chest.

She rolled to her side so that Asher's erection plowed

between her legs. "I think you've proved that all the drugs are out of your system now. I need you inside me. I've waited long enough for you to remember me, remember you love me, forgive me all over again, and now I have you right where I want you."

He tickled the bottom of her foot and then his head joined hers on the pillow. "Ditto."

He kissed her mouth as he straddled her.

She wrapped her legs around his hips as he entered her, like she never wanted to let him go again.

Their lovemaking fell into the familiar pattern they'd established over their years together, but it contained another quality that she couldn't name. Deeper? More satisfying? More secure? Maybe for the first time with Asher, she didn't feel as if she had something to prove.

When they'd finally slaked their need of each other, Paige rolled to her side, snuggling into the crook of his body, a perfect fit.

He stroked her from the nape of her neck to her derriere. She stretched, curling her toes against his shins.

"Mmm, all my cares just melted away. It's going to be hard going back to the real world."

"You're like a content cat right now, a kitty cat who's lapped up all the cream."

She giggled. "Is that supposed to be some weird double entendre? Ugh, and I just flashed on Tabitha and her obsession with cats. It probably rivaled her obsession with you."

"Sorry I brought up cats."

A light bulb clicked on in Paige's head and she bolted upright. "Tabitha. Cats."

"I said I was sorry." Asher ran a hand down her arm, but she scrambled over his body to reach the nightstand and Tabitha's phone.

"I got it. I know her password."

She snatched the phone from the bedside table and powered it on. The daunting password prompt glared at her again, but this time it had met its match.

She entered the password that had come to her in a flash and yelped when the phone responded by letting her in.

"You did it." Asher gave her a high five. "What was it, genius?"

She rolled her eyes. "Tabbycat, of course."

Paige's finger trembled as she clicked through to Tabitha's email. "What's the password for the Wi-Fi in here?"

Asher reached past her and dragged a card from beneath the lamp on the nightstand. "Guest."

"That makes it easy." Paige entered the password and held her breath as Tabitha's phone loaded her emails.

Asher hovered over her shoulder, his hot breath stirring her hair. "Check her texts first to make sure nobody's looking for her yet."

Paige skimmed through the emails once to satisfy herself that no secret files jumped out at her. Tabitha had over four hundred emails downloaded to her phone. Asher was right—it could take her a while to go through those.

She flicked to the texts. "There aren't many. One from a Dr. Evans asking her where she is."

"He's a doctor at Hidden Hills. He's obviously not clued in."

"Are any of them? When Linc saw me at the boathouse, he thought I might be Tabitha."

"Linc didn't know much. Maybe they didn't bother to tell him, and maybe they didn't want to tell the doctors at Hidden Hills, either." Asher rolled from the bed and returned to the bathroom. He called out, "Do you want some clothes in here? It's hard for me to concentrate on Tabitha's texts and emails when you're sitting on the edge of the bed naked."

With a smile, Paige said, "Bring me my camisole and underwear."

"That's almost as sexy as your nudity." He returned to the bedroom and tossed the garments at her. "Anything else?"

"Doesn't look like she had many friends. Not even her parents have texted her over the past few days."

"Why would they? She's supposed to be working. They don't know she was at their cabin and maybe they didn't even see the news about that other cabin."

"Her texts haven't told me a thing. It's not like this shadowy network was sending her texts asking her to return to Hidden Hills…or to return you, if they thought she had you."

"How about the emails?" Asher sauntered to the desk in the room and flipped open the pizza box.

"What are you doing?" She peered at him over the top of Tabitha's phone.

"Sex makes me hungry. Told you this pizza wouldn't go to waste. Do you want some?"

"No, thanks." She held out the phone. "I'm busy here."

"Does she have a lot of emails?"

"Over four hundred."

"Do a search. Search for emails with attachments. That should cut down on the number. Search for Hidden Hills, although she might have a lot from her employer."

"I'll search for attachments. If she forwarded your file to herself, it probably would've been as an attachment and not a link."

Paige entered the search for emails with attachments. "That's better."

Folding her legs beneath her, she brought the phone close to her face and started scrolling through the emails. "She has several with work-related material here. Maybe that's why she was able to hijack your file without the knowledge of Hidden Hills."

"For a while, but they caught on."

"Only when they realized the depth and scope of her obsession for you spurred her on to assist you in your escape, or at least follow you."

Asher joined her on the bed, bunching a few pillows against the headboard behind him. "That escape was all you, superwoman." He pointed to the phone. "Just like accessing Tabitha's phone."

"I should've figured out that password earlier."

"Stop." He put a finger over her lips. "Don't downplay your success. I'm sure I never would've figured that out. What the hell is a tabby cat, anyway?"

"That's right. You're a dog person. A tabby cat is just a standard orange cat. Her nickname was Tabby and it was on the website. Makes sense to me."

"If you say so."

"Speaking of dogs, Ivy really wants one now."

"She's not afraid anymore?"

"We saw some puppies and now she's…" Paige caught her breath. "I think this is it."

Asher scooted closer to her on the bed. "You found the email? The file?"

"Looks like she tried to disguise the attachment by putting medication notes in the email, but this attachment popped up when I searched for your name."

"Before you even open the attachment, forward it to

your own email address, forward it to mine, forward it to your mother's. If I had Cam's personal email memorized, I'd have you forward it to him, too."

"What about someone official in Delta Force?"

"Let's see what the file has in it before we do that. What if it just confirms my accusations against Major Denver? Sending it to Delta Force could just make things worse for him."

"Okay." Paige forwarded Tabitha's email to her own email address, Asher's and Mom's. She'd warned Mom enough times about phishing emails that she just might delete it, so she added a short note indicating herself as the sender and asking her mother to save the email.

"The moment of truth." Paige clicked on the attachment, her eyes glued to the circle spinning on the display as the file downloaded. "I wish I had my laptop."

The file finally opened and Paige enlarged the text on the display. Leaning into Asher's space, she shared the phone with him. "Here it is."

They read it silently, side by side, Asher nodding each time she indicated she wanted to move on.

Asher turned and kissed the side of her head before they'd even finished the file. "You did it. That's it. Proof that the memories were implanted in my mind."

"No explanation of why or on whose orders though."

He tapped the phone. "Not yet. We haven't read it all."

Paige rubbed her eyes. "Not sure I can get through any more. It's been a crazy day. We thought we were going to get some info from Linc and head out with a car packed with food, cash…and my laptop."

"Instead we're here, and my amazing fiancée got us the info we needed to get me back on the right side of the US Army and get us home to Ivy."

She snuggled against Asher, the phone still clutched in her hand. "I can't wait."

He flicked off the light beside her and pulled her close. "Let's get some sleep and figure out where we're going to deliver this file tomorrow. Once it's in the hands of the proper authorities, I'm sure the orders for Hidden Hills will change and we'll no longer be in danger. They're the ones who are going to be in trouble now."

"I'll go to sleep once I get through this file. There's not much more."

Asher yawned. "And I don't think you're going to find anything of importance. The rest just looks like a so-called treatment schedule to me."

Blinking, Paige refocused on the display glowing in the dark and read the rest of the attachment with drooping eyelids. Nothing she read could keep her from falling asleep.

They'd succeeded—she and Asher together.

As light crept through the gap in the drapes, Paige's hand tingled. She flexed her fingers and realized Tabitha's phone was buzzing.

Maybe Tabitha finally got a meaningful text. Paige squinted at the green digits of the alarm clock and nudged Asher's shoulder. "It's eight o'clock already."

Rolling to her side, she turned on the light and pushed up against the headboard. She entered the password for the phone and tapped the incoming text message from a Dr. Evans.

She read the text once, her head tilted to one side. She read it again, the fog of sleep beginning to clear. Then it cleared all at once to devastating clarity.

She dropped the phone on the floor and doubled over, gasping to get air into her lungs.

"Paige?" Asher gripped her upper arm. "Paige, are you okay?"

She turned to face him, her lips trying to form the words that would destroy his world. She'd failed him again.

"Paige? What's wrong?"

"They took Ivy."

## *Chapter Sixteen*

Asher stared at Paige's pale face, her mouth still hanging open after delivering the nonsensical words.

"What are you talking about? Ivy's with your mom in Vegas."

"N-no, she's not. They have her. The people who are still after us have taken our daughter."

One part of Asher's mind shut down. Another part began manufacturing denials.

He snorted. "How would you know that? Your mother's not in contact with you. Nobody is."

She dipped her chin. "They contacted Tabitha, or rather they contacted me through Tabitha's phone. Ivy's gone."

Fear galloped through Asher's body and he leaped from the bed and fell to the floor on Paige's side of the bed. He grabbed the phone that had been the source of so much satisfaction only hours before.

He tapped the text and read it aloud. "'We have your daughter. Any moves from you and you'll never see her again.'"

A sob broke from Paige's throat and white-hot rage thumped through Asher's body. He sat on the edge of the bed, and she collapsed against his chest.

"We don't even know if this is true, Paige. They could be lying."

"There's one way to find out." She reached for the other phone on the nightstand, the one they'd kept powered down for fear of being tracked.

Paige tapped the display. Her body stiffened and she choked out more words he didn't want to hear. "Oh my God. I have about twenty texts from my mother—Ivy's gone."

Asher caught Paige as she began to slump forward. "It's going to be okay, Paige. I'll make it okay. I'll give them whatever they want to keep Ivy safe. What does your mother say?"

He pried the phone from Paige's stiff fingers and read through Cheryl's texts, each one more frantic than the previous one. "They've ordered your mother to keep silent, and it looks like she's complied so far. Call her."

Paige stared at the phone in his hand, her bottom lip trembling. Then she snatched it from him and made the call.

Asher reached over and put the phone on speaker as it rang.

Cheryl picked up before the first ring ended. "Oh my God, Paige. Where have you been? Somebody kidnapped Ivy and I think it has to do with whatever is going on with you and Asher."

Paige took a long shuddering breath and drew back her shoulders. "It does, Mom. What do they want you to do?"

"Me?" Her mother's voice cracked and it took her several seconds to continue. "Nothing, nothing at all—no police, no FBI, no Terrence. I haven't even told Terrence, who's off somewhere hiking. They want you and Asher. They want to make some kind of deal with him."

Asher rubbed a circle on Paige's ramrod-straight back.

"Don't worry, Cheryl. I'm going to get her back. I'll give them what they want."

"What do they want, Asher?"

"Me. They want me."

"They're not going to get you." Paige flicked back her messy hair and clenched her jaw.

"Paige." Her mother sniffled. "Let Asher handle it. This is Ivy we're talking about. Of course Asher's going to do whatever it takes to save her."

"They're not going to get Asher, and they're not going to keep Ivy. They have no idea what they walked into. They've just made a big mistake."

Asher massaged Paige's neck. He knew she'd turned into a fierce lioness when it came to Ivy, but he didn't see any other way out. He'd have to forget about his Hidden Hills file and let them use him to help bring down Major Denver. Just as long as they sent Ivy home to her mother.

Cheryl choked out, "Paige, I've done everything they've asked of me, even keeping this from Terrence. Now it's your turn. You and Asher have to follow their orders to protect Ivy."

"Don't worry about a thing, Mom. We'll rescue her. When are you expecting Terrence?"

"He'll be gone for another few days. If he were here, there's no way I could hide this from him."

"Good. Just keep doing what you're doing. I'll let you know when we have Ivy." Paige ended the call with her mother and turned to Asher, her eyes wide, her lips parted, her breath coming out in short spurts.

Asher took both of her hands. "What do you have in mind, Paige? I don't plan to make any moves until Ivy is home safe, and then I swear I'll make them all pay."

"We can find her, Asher. We can get Ivy back and you don't have to surrender yourself."

"I don't see how that's going to happen, Paige. We know nothing about these people. We don't have any idea what they've done with Ivy."

"Not yet." Paige slipped her hands from his and grabbed his shoulders. "As soon as I get my hands on a computer, we'll know exactly where they're keeping Ivy—because I had her microchipped."

He jerked back from her. "You did what?"

"I had Ivy microchipped when she was a baby—the first time you left me alone with her."

"Why would you do that? Is it even legal?"

"Elena's ex-boyfriend, the doctor, he did it for me. As to why…" She hunched her shoulders. "You know why. I was afraid, afraid I'd lose her again. I didn't want to tell you or my mom I'd done it. It wasn't going to be forever."

The enormity of Paige's confession flooded his senses all at once and he grabbed her face and planted a kiss on her mouth. "Finally your self-flagellation over your sins resulted in some good. You're amazing. You must've known this day was coming."

Paige blinked her eyes. "I-it is amazing, isn't it? We're going to be able to pinpoint Ivy's location without their knowledge—I just need a computer. I have a log-in to the website, and we'll be able to track her from that."

"If the service has a website, they must have an app for your phone. Have you ever tried that?"

"I've never even used the service, Asher. I hope it works."

He swept up her phone from the floor where she'd dropped it. "Do a search. Do you remember the name of the service?"

"Of course. KidFinder." She took the phone in her hand and froze. "Tabitha's phone is going off. It's a phone call."

"Let me." He picked up the call. "Yeah?"

"Lieutenant Knight himself. Memories all back in place, I presume?"

"Enough to know I was used to set up Major Denver. Why?"

"Tsk, tsk, Knight. Don't we have more important issues to settle? You must've verified by now that we have your daughter."

"Verified, but how do we know she's okay?"

"I'll have her…caretakers do a face-to-face session for you on the phone, this phone, and then you'll do as we say."

"You want me to go back to my original false story about what happened during that meeting with Denver and his contact."

The voice hardened. "We want you back at Hidden Hills, under our control."

Paige stiffened beside him.

"Who are you? Who are you working for? What do you have against Denver?"

"Maybe all will be revealed when you join us."

"We need our daughter back with us before I go anywhere."

"Understood. We'll do a trade."

"Where?"

"Las Vegas—she's not far from there. We weren't going to try to get her on an airplane. We'll give you a location for the trade…when you get here. You and Paige will come together. We'll send your lovely fiancée off with your daughter, and we'll take you back to Hidden Hills."

"What's to stop me from escaping again or turning on you once we have our daughter back?"

Paige punched his thigh, and he put a finger to his lips.

"You won't have that opportunity ever again, Knight."

Paige's fingers had uncurled on his leg, and now her nails dug into his flesh.

Asher understood. Once he served his usefulness to the cause, he'd commit suicide or have some other kind of accident.

"And what reassurances can you give me that my daughter and my fiancée won't be in danger from you again?"

"Why would we want to harm them? We'll get what we want from you, and once we do, your family will never hear from us again. We don't like exposing ourselves in this way—unless it's absolutely necessary."

Sounded like a pretty good deal to him—except the part where he'd have to die.

"How are we going to get to Vegas? I don't have my ID, my wallet, nothing."

"We'll get those back to you, and we'll give you the day, time and location of the meeting place."

"I'm not coming anywhere near you until my daughter is safe."

"Tell us how to get your belongings to you and we'll deliver them."

"Leave them at the front desk of the Ambassador Hotel in DC, near Dulles. I'll make sure I get them."

"It seems that we're all on the same page now, Knight. We'll have your possessions waiting for you at the Ambassador by five o'clock tonight. Be in Vegas by ten o'clock tomorrow night and we'll text you the location for the trade."

"We'll be there. If anything happens to our daughter in the meantime, I'll blow your plans sky-high."

The man on the other end of the line chuckled. "I

doubt that, Knight. You do know that Nurse Tabitha Crane is no longer around to help you."

"She wasn't much help."

"Then you won't miss her, either."

The man cut off the call before Asher could even respond. It was just as well if nobody suspected he had his file from Hidden Hills. If their rescue of Ivy didn't go as planned before the trade, Paige didn't need the specter of that file hanging over her.

Almost immediately after that call ended, another came through.

Paige tugged on his sleeve. "It might be Ivy."

It was. As soon as Asher accepted the call, his daughter's sweet face filled the display. A golf ball–sized lump formed in his throat and his eyes stung with tears.

"Hey there, Ivy."

"Daddy!"

"Mommy's here, too."

Paige leaned her head against Asher's. "How are you, little bunny? Are you having fun?"

Ivy's face slipped away, replaced by a blank wall and a hushed voice. "That's enough. She's alive, healthy and will be waiting for you tomorrow."

Asher's eyes burned after the call ended and the image disappeared. He tossed Tabitha's phone onto the bed. "They plan to kill me. You know that, right? They'll use me to bolster their story, and then I'm done."

"When did you become such a pessimist?" Paige held up her phone and tilted it back and forth. "Not only did I find the app on my phone, I successfully logged in and I located Ivy—she's at Circus Circus. They just made a big mistake."

Asher curled his hand for a fist bump and Paige touched her knuckles to his.

"Vegas, baby. That's *our* town."

## *Chapter Seventeen*

Paige grabbed Asher's hand as they stepped outside of McCarran International Airport. The high desert had a chill in the air, but the dry breeze made her feel right at home. She'd be able to shed the winter jacket if not the sweater.

They weren't going to stay with Mom or anywhere near her. They'd checked the KidFinder app as soon as they got off the red-eye from DC to verify that Ivy was still at the Circus Circus Hotel & Casino.

Paige grabbed Asher's arm as they settled into the back of a taxi. "You're sure Frankie Greco can help us?"

"Frankie the Greek and my dad go way back. Even though the Greek is retired from the mob, he still has his Vegas connections. All the hotel owners are legit now, but they still owe Frankie and Frankie owes my dad." Asher kissed the back of her hand. "Are you sure your ladies of the night can help us?"

"I've seen more hookers than all the politicians in DC have, and I've signed off on their court orders even when they missed a few sessions. They'll help us if we need it."

"We've got mobsters and hookers on our side in Vegas. How can we miss?"

Paige glanced at the rearview mirror and whispered,

"I hope they didn't harm that kid we sent into the Ambassador to pick up your stuff."

"Why would they? I don't think there's any way they could've followed him, especially not on that skateboard he took through the metro station. They just want me here in Vegas so they can do the trade and get me back on track at Hidden Hills. They're not expecting any surprises from us."

"Boy, do we have some surprises for them."

The taxi dropped them off at the hotel-casino next to Circus Circus. Paige's mom had made the reservations for them with Terrence's credit card and prepaid for the room.

By the time they checked in and got settled it was one o'clock in the morning. Asher had already made contact with the old mobster Frankie Greco, and he'd agreed to meet with them for breakfast.

Paige plucked the sweater from her midsection. "I don't know about you, but I'm getting an early start tomorrow and going shopping for an outfit. I'm sick of this sweater and these dirty jeans."

"I'll join you. We need to get a good night's sleep. It's gonna be a busy day tomorrow."

THE FOLLOWING MORNING, Paige turned on her phone just long enough to check the app. Ivy's GPS was accurate enough to pinpoint the wing of the hotel room where she was located. "They're still at Circus Circus."

"I hope they don't plan to move Ivy hours before the meeting. For all we know, they could decide to do the trade out in the desert somewhere and make a move early."

"Then the sooner we put our plan in motion, the better. I still don't understand how Frankie is going to be able to get all the guests out of Circus Circus."

"If anyone can get results in this town, it's Frankie."

An hour later, dressed in a pair of jeans with silver studs around the pockets and a top with a few too many sequins, Paige slid into a banquette across from Asher in one of the many restaurants in their hotel.

Frankie entered a few minutes after they sat down and caused a commotion as he made his way to their table—smiles, pats on the back and waves across the room.

Paige rolled her eyes at Asher. "He really is Mr. Vegas, isn't he?"

"And he's on our side." Asher nudged her out of the booth and greeted the stubby, balding man who looked more like someone's grandpa than a feared mobster. He gave the man a one-armed hug. "Thanks for meeting us, Frankie."

Frankie the Greek collapsed in the seat across from them, huffing out a breath. "When someone takes a kid, the gloves are off."

They didn't have to explain to him why these people had taken Ivy, who they were or why they hadn't involved the authorities. A guy like Frankie the Greek operated outside the boundaries of the law.

As soon as Frankie sat at their table, the waitress materialized as if by magic and took their orders. "You and your friends can order whatever you like, Frankie. The boss says it's on the house."

"Glenn may regret that, sweetheart. I'm as hungry as a bear and twice as fierce." He winked at the waitress, who blew him a kiss.

Paige slid a glance at Asher. The guy had it made in this town.

When the waitress left, Frankie hunched over the

table, blinking his bulging frog-like eyes. "So, they got her at the Circus Circus? I have my contacts there. Do you know which room?"

Asher shook his head. "We know the wing, but not the floor or the room."

"I can change that." He leveled a finger at Paige. "You got a picture of the little angel?"

Paige scrambled for her phone and pulled up a recent picture of Ivy.

"Send that to me, sweetheart. You know what the perps look like?"

Paige shoved her phone to Asher so that he could send the picture to Frankie. "We don't have the slightest idea."

Frankie peppered them with more questions, like when they would've checked in and did they know what Ivy was wearing. Unless the kidnappers had bought her additional clothes, Ivy would be wearing what she had on during their video chat yesterday.

When Frankie had exhausted all his questions, he slurped some coffee from his cup. "I'll tell ya what I'm gonna do. I'm gonna get some people to go through the security footage at the hotel and locate your little girl. We're gonna get her exact room number."

"W-we have to get her out by at least nine o'clock tonight." Paige folded her hands on the table in front of her, and her engagement ring cut into her flesh.

"Don't worry, sweetheart." Frankie patted her clenched hands. "I'll get an army of people on this. We'll find her."

Asher draped his arm around Paige. "Then what, Frankie? Storm the room? We don't want to endanger Ivy."

Frankie spread his arms. "What do I look like? An amateur?"

He laid out the plan for them, arranged to have a gun

delivered to their room for Asher and then ordered a second helping of hash browns. "The more distractions we have in that hallway, the better."

"I have some…friends I can call on." Paige crumpled her napkin next to her plate of food, which she'd hardly touched. "Thanks for breakfast, Frankie. Thanks for everything."

"You kids get lost until game time." He shoved a wad of cash toward Asher. "Treat your girl to a little spa action, Asher."

Asher held out his hand. "I can't take that, Frankie."

The old mobster puffed out his cheeks. "Do it for an old man. I owe your father."

Asher swept the cash off the table and into his pocket. "If we get Ivy back safe and sound, all debts to my father will be paid in full."

Frankie waved his hand and secured his napkin under his chin before diving into his potatoes and peppers.

When they got to the room, Paige perched on the edge of the bed, pinning her hands between her knees. "Do you think it's going to work?"

"It has to." He thumbed the stack of bills in her direction. "How about it? You want to hit up the spa?"

"You're kidding." She fell back on the bed. "I wanna throw up."

He tossed the money at her. "No time for that. You need to call your girls in and give them their marching orders."

She clapped the money to her chest. "Are you suggesting I'm going to have to pay them to help me out?"

"Well, they *are* hookers."

"They're hookers with hearts of gold, and most have kids of their own."

"Then maybe I'll get the spa treatment."

LATER THAT AFTERNOON, the call came and Asher wiped his hands on the thighs of his jeans before answering Tabitha's phone and putting it on speaker for Paige. "Yeah? Took you long enough."

The familiar, hated voice purred over the line. "You in Vegas?"

"We are. Where do you want us for the meeting?"

"We'll pick you up."

Paige poked his leg, shaking her head.

"I thought we were meeting you somewhere."

"You thought wrong, Lieutenant. We'll give you a location and we'll send a car to get you."

"I'm not getting into any car with anyone until Paige has our daughter."

"We'll be bringing your daughter with us in the car. She's very excited about riding in a limousine. We'll pick up you and Paige. You can verify the safety of your daughter, and then we'll drop off Paige and the little girl…and you're ours. And we'd better not see any information surface about our operation or the activities at Hidden Hills."

"We don't know anything."

"Right. Here's what you're going to do."

He gave them the time and location for the pickup, and Asher let out a long, silent breath. They still had plenty of time to put their own plan into action.

"We'll be there."

"Remember, no weapons, no police, no trackers, nobody following us. All those things would be very, very bad for your family, Lieutenant."

"Got it."

Asher turned off the phone and cupped it in his hands. Then he kissed Paige hard on the mouth.

"He didn't say anything about old mobsters and hookers, did he?"

Four hours after that phone call and three hours before the scheduled meeting time, Asher stashed the gun, which Frankie had sent over, in his pocket.

"Are you ready?"

Paige squared her shoulders as if heading into battle—which wasn't too far off the mark. "I'm ready. What if they see us? Recognize us?"

"How? Even if they have lookouts, which seems unlikely as there's no reason for them to suspect we know they're even at a hotel in Vegas, let alone *that* hotel, we have some pretty good disguises." Asher stroked the beard covering the lower half of his face and tugged the baseball cap over his forehead.

Paige smoothed the short, sparkly dress over her thighs and tousled her dark pixie-cut wig. "I don't think I'd even recognize you in that getup."

"And Krystal packed enough makeup on your face to practically change the shape."

"It's called contouring, and Krystal's trying to leave the life to go legit as a makeup artist."

"She could use you in her portfolio." He put his hand on the small of her back as he steered her out of the room. "Now let's go rescue our daughter."

They reached the Circus Circus Hotel & Casino just as a circus act was starting, which had brought in more people and created more activity.

Asher whispered in Paige's ear, "The more chaos, the better."

They took the elevator up to the tenth floor of the hotel, and Asher could almost feel the tugging at his heartstrings the closer he got to his daughter.

When they reached the tenth floor, they got off the

elevator and headed for the stairwell. They climbed up two flights of stairs to the twelfth floor.

Asher paused, his hand on the handle of the fire door. "Are you ready?"

"Oh, yeah."

They slipped through the door onto the twelfth floor and sidled along the wall to the vending area. Almost immediately, a swarm of hotel personnel, courtesy of Frankie the Greek, fanned out along the floor and began knocking on doors.

"Evacuation. This is an evacuation. Everyone out of the rooms and into the stairwells."

Guests began opening their doors and grumbling or shouting. Asher kept his eye on one door only.

He held his breath as a hotel employee banged on that door. "Evacuation. Everyone out."

People began streaming down the hallway, jostling each other to reach the stairwell doors. Frankie had picked the perfect time—right between daytime activities and dinner and gambling. Most people were back in their rooms getting ready for their nighttime plans.

Paige's brigade of helpful hookers further clogged the hallway and did their best to push people along and create more distractions.

Asher elbowed Paige as the door to Ivy's cell inched open. A woman poked her head into the hallway and then called back over her shoulder. A man joined her at the door, and then it slammed shut.

Asher's heart slammed with it.

Paige hissed, "They can't stay in there, right? They're going to have to come out with everyone else."

"If they don't, we'll send in one of Frankie's guys to get them."

The door swung open again, and Paige clutched his

arm as the couple appeared in the frame, the man holding Ivy in his arms.

As soon as they stepped into the hallway, Paige's friends began to march toward them, chattering and grabbing on to other guests.

As the man carrying Ivy moved down the hallway, Asher's gaze dropped to the right hand he kept in one pocket—most likely curled around the handle of a gun.

The couple passed Asher and Paige without a second look, and they stepped into the hallway behind them. Ivy looked over the man's shoulder and met Asher's eyes.

Asher looked away, his muscles coiled, but the danger passed. His daughter had never seen him with a beard before in her young life.

A clump of people shuffled to the fire door, but everyone had to wait their turn. Two of the women in Krystal's crew swooped in on the man who had Ivy.

"Ooh, is this your little family?" One of the women stationed herself in front of the man, while the other pushed up against the woman.

The man jerked back. "Who the hell are you? Get outta my way, you whore."

The woman confronting him waved a finger in his face. "That's no way to talk in front of your daughter. That's also no way to talk in front of the woman you were cuddling up to last night."

"I don't know what you're talking about. Get outta my face." The man's hand hovered at his pocket.

The other woman took Ivy's hand. "Hello, sweetie. Your daddy is a bad boy, isn't he?"

"What the hell?" The man shoved the woman against the wall, but his grip on Ivy loosened.

His companion took over and pulled Ivy from his arms.

Paige stiffened beside Asher and growled, "You take care of him. I'll get our daughter."

Asher tried to grab Paige's arm to stop her, but it was no use. He turned his attention to the man, and as soon as Ivy left his arms for the woman's, Asher charged and punched the man in the kidney.

He choked and staggered forward, reaching for his gun.

Asher had his out first and slammed the butt of his against the man's skull. Blood spurted from his scalp as he fell to the floor.

The scuffle beside him had Asher spinning around—just in time to see Paige smash her fist into the side of the woman's face.

"That's *my* daughter, bitch."

# *Epilogue*

Asher put a finger to his lips as Ivy crawled over his legs singing, "London bridges, London bridges, London bridges."

Paige swooped in and scooped up her daughter. "Shh. Daddy's on the phone."

She carried Ivy into the kitchen, where her mother and Terrence were drinking coffee.

"I don't know why you didn't call me as soon as Ivy..." Terrence glanced at Ivy's blond curls bobbing in time to the song she was singing. "You know."

"They told me not to, Terrence." Mom stirred some cream into her coffee. "You would've gone in there with guns blazing. I knew Asher...and Paige could handle it."

Asher joined them in the kitchen, pocketing his phone. "We handled the most important part, but the army still refuses to exonerate Major Denver. Said there's still too much evidence tying him to that terrorist group to clear his name."

"But your name is cleared, right?" Paige wrapped her arms around his waist. "Is that what the phone call was about?"

"Let's take this in the other room." Asher ruffled Ivy's hair.

Mom pushed back from the table. “Ivy, do you want to go to the park across the street with me and Terrence?”

Ivy curled one arm around Asher’s leg. “Is Daddy going away?”

Asher hoisted Ivy into his arms. “I’ll be here through Christmas. Are you going to stay awake so we can look at the Christmas lights tonight?”

“Daddy, can we have hot chocolate after?” She patted his face as if to make sure he didn’t have that beard that had scared her the night of her rescue.

“Of course. What are Christmas lights without hot chocolate after?”

“With marshmallows?”

“Hmm.” Asher raised his eyes to the ceiling. “I think we can find some marshmallows.”

Paige leaned over Asher’s shoulder and kissed Ivy on the tip of her turned-up nose. “As long as we can have whipped cream, too.”

“Marshmallows *and* whipped cream.” Asher set Ivy on the floor. “Now go with Grandma and Terrence. Mommy and I will be over in a minute.”

When Terrence and Mom took Ivy out the front door, Paige still felt a chill race up her spine. Would she ever feel comfortable allowing Ivy out of her sight? She still had her chip, but she and Asher had agreed to have it removed.

They didn’t have anything to fear from the conspirators at Hidden Hills anymore. Asher had turned over his Hidden Hills file to a commanding officer in Delta Force and army personnel had moved into Hidden Hills and closed it down.

Asher slumped in a chair at the dining room table. “I’m all clear, Paige. They believe my story because it’s all there in the file from Hidden Hills, but the doctors who engineered my brainwashing refused to implicate anyone else. They took the fall themselves and claimed they were conducting unauthorized experiments."

"And the kidnappers refused to talk."

"I don't see how that woman *could* talk after you clocked her in the jaw." Asher winked. "That was awesome."

Her lips twisted into a smile. "That did feel pretty good, but they haven't said anything about who gave them the orders to take Ivy or why."

"They pretended it was all a part of the Hidden Hills experiments."

"Does the army really believe that?"

"I don't think so, but nobody is talking. Nobody is cracking." Asher slammed his fist on the table. "What more do they want? Cam and Martha proved that the emails that started the whole investigation into Denver were bogus, and we just shot holes in the narrative that Denver killed an army ranger and tried to kill me while meeting with a known terrorist. What more do they want?"

"There's more to his story, isn't there? Why doesn't he come in? Why doesn't he surrender and try to prove his innocence?"

"If I know Major Denver, he'll do that on his own terms and only when he has a handle on who tried to set him up."

"He may never come in." Paige slid into Asher's lap. "But you're safe? We're safe?"

"There's no reason for anyone to come after us now. I'm out of their clutches, and the file that Tabitha stole implicates everyone at Hidden Hills. That so-called rehabilitation center is now closed and will reopen with new staff."

"Is someone going to face murder charges for Tabitha's death?"

"I guess we'll see who decides to take the fall for that. So far there's a lot of finger-pointing going on with nobody taking full responsibility."

"That's because nobody at Hidden Hills *is* fully responsible. They were following someone else's orders, and it doesn't look like we'll ever find out who's behind the conspiracy."

"Oh, we're gonna find out." He kissed the side of her head. "Why were we waiting to get married? I must've never recovered that memory."

"I just wanted to make sure…" She trailed off and rested her cheek against his hair.

"That I forgave you? Trusted you? Wanted you to be the mother of all the rest of my children?"

"The rest?"

He tucked his arm around her waist. "We both hated being only children, didn't we? I'm not putting Ivy through that. She's going to have a few siblings."

"A few?"

"Ivy's got the greatest mom in the world. It's only right she share her with some brothers and sisters."

Tears pooled in Paige's eyes and she cupped Asher's strong jaw with one hand. "And all I had to do was save you from a psychiatric prison and rescue Ivy from a couple of kidnappers to prove it."

"Paige, you never had to prove anything to me. Your love was always enough…and it always will be. Christmas wedding?"

"Are you serious?"

"Why not? We *are* in Vegas."

"Just as long as we don't have an Elvis impersonator performing the ceremony."

"You're no fun. Let's go tell Ivy—and we don't need a microchip to find her." Asher pounded a fist against his chest over his heart. "You're both always right here with me."

* * * * *

# COMING SOON!

We really hope you enjoyed reading this book. If you're looking for more romance, be sure to head to the shops when new books are available on

## Thursday 13th December

To see which titles are coming soon, please visit **millsandboon.co.uk**

MILLS & BOON